29-29
A FINANCIAL FANTASY

29-29

A FINANCIAL FANTASY

NICK BRAGGER

THE BODLEY HEAD

LONDON

For Mark

A CIP catalogue record for this book is available from the
British Library.

Copyright © Nick Bragger 1989.

ISBN 0 370 31318 6

Phototypeset by Falcon Graphic Art Ltd
Wallington, Surrey
Printed and bound in Great Britain for
The Bodley Head Ltd
31 Bedford Square
London WC1 3SG
by Mackays of Chatham PLC

First printed in Great Britain in 1989

CHAPTER 1

He re-ran the news-reel for the third time. It had cost 5000 bucks to get the original tapes, but it was worth it for the uncut footage.

This time he keyed the slow-motion button, watched the window open, and the man climb out with a terrible kind of deliberation. Locating its target, the camera zoomed up, catching the features: the waxen face with heavy, unshaven jowls, the eyes strangely out of focus, the expensive suit no longer smart after ten days of continuous wear, as the man eased slowly along the narrow ledge away from the window. If he was aware of the crowd 200 feet below he did not show it, his hands flat against the stonework, his fingers splayed wide so that every tendon cut ivory through the skin.

There were others at the window now, pleading faces with outstretched hands jostling for position, beckoning him back, yet none so eager as to chance their own fall into the canyon yawning between the towering blocks.

But not once did he glance to one side or the other.

The police were there in force – they always were – and the early evening air was alive with bells ringing and sirens wailing, the sounds of a city where life was hard, and death came cheap, every minute of every day. And with the police came the rest, the media men and paramedics, the men of the cloth, with hoards of ghoulish groupies swelling up their ranks – all there waiting for the final act in a kind of ritualised assembly. They stood there like supplicants, eyes to the heavens, waiting and willing it to happen.

They knew it would not be long, they had seen it all before. But not quite yet. Suicides had their rituals – their own curious dance of death, and Clive Feral knew that better than most. He loosened his necktie and ran his fingers round

1

the inside of his silk shirt collar as he keyed the video, moving it on one frame, then another, savouring each shot in turn as they came up on the screen.

The doomed ones never ran and jumped. They always took their time, the bleeders with two small scratches before the one big cut, the leapers teetering for many minutes on the brink before that final deadly plunge. Jack Kramer was no different. Now he was quite still, alone in his last moments of reflection and Clive Feral wondered at his thoughts. There was fear there, certainly, but was there malice or resentment? No, Clive figured, probably neither, just a resigned acceptance of the natural order of things – that he had gambled and he had lost – everything, every last dime. And Clive Feral had snatched the pot.

But there was nothing unusual in that. He always won, and the losers often chose the drop. The only difference this time was that a photo-scoop had captured it on video and sold it to the networks. That was the bonus for Clive Feral. Now he had the ultimate record of his control over the fortunes of other men, a visual display of the enormous power he wielded as owner and chairman of the Price Whitney Banking Corporation Inc.

He smiled and ran the action on a few more frames, licking the salt from his upper lip where a dew of sweat had begun to form. His shirt was damp; not from the heat but from the delicious stimulation coursing through his blood. A faint odour tainted the air, that same sour evocation which, a thousand times multiplied, rose from the frenzied crowd during the running of the bulls at Pamplona.

Kramer was a fool. He had made the classic mistake and used his own money – something you never did, least of all in a manoeuvre to outbid the master of the game, Clive Feral. Kramer had ended up with a bunch of stock worth a tenth of what he had paid, and an action for 50 million dollars by parallel investors who ran, and lost, on his advice. Fools, all of them. Clive knew his big advantage – privileged information gleaned from a mycelium of contacts throughout the boardrooms of the world. It was something they did not have, would never have, and invariably he waited for the sink to fill before he pulled the plug.

Kramer was into the second stage. His shoulder-blades were off the wall, his body leaning forward, but not yet far enough to break the balance and bring the final plunge. He seemed to linger there for ever, teetering on the brink, but then he leaned back once more, and the crowd breathed out in a solid rush that could be heard a block away. Not long now, were the unspoken words upon the jostling faces as the sound died to a new and eerie hush. They watched as Kramer began to breathe in strange gulps, his chest heaving, but this time his head was tilted back and his eyes were closed.

Then suddenly it was as if another man was standing there. His back had straightened and his head lifted, and it seemed all strain had gone from the haggard features to leave a new quiescence and tranquillity.

The sirens too had stopped and the silence was now thick with expectation. A neon hoarding on the block across the street winked its display, painting everything alternately pink, bright blue, then pink again in a frivolous carnival of colour, the canvas as strangely surreal as a bad B-Movie from the sixties. It was possible, just for a moment, to believe it was not happening at all – but it was, and with a terrible inevitability.

The man on the ledge was standing rigid, almost to attention, the soles of his shoes half on and half off the thin spline of masonry, his arms limp appendages at his side.

Even though it had happened hours ago, Clive Feral's pulse still raced as he watched. The man's eyes were open, gazing at him through the lens of the camera as though he were actually in the room – a haunting, glacial stare that seemed meant for him and him alone. More than that there was a message there, a warning. Or was it a promise? Clive Feral was not sure, but it left him with a strange, uneasy feeling that dulled the glitter of his prize.

Then the man was gone, toppling gently forward into the empty air between the blocks. He did not gyrate or flail his arms as they usually did, nor was there that terrible rending scream. It was almost as if he were already dead, accelerating and tumbling slowly over and over, his shadow passing rigored faces pressed against the glass on each of the twenty floors.

He hit the ground with barely a sound, his head exploding on the sidewalk like a rotten fruit, a rain of crimson splashing the cops and painting the window of Maybee's Drug Store the colour of an offal sluice. High above, the neon billboard flicked again from red to blue, turning the crimson to an ugly glistening black as it dripped slowly down the float-glass plate.

Clive Feral smiled again.

There were no great secrets in his method. He was a stripper. He went for the jugular of lame companies, and if a company wasn't lame, he would cripple it from the outside, then go in for the kill. The bigger he got, the easier it had become. In the early days, everything hinged on carefully planned raids on a company stock, grabbing control before the price shifted out of reach. Then it was simply a matter of firing the staff, changing the board to his nominees, splitting the company into saleable parts and banking the margin.

He remembered his first deal – the acquisition of Dando's Cabs. The business was losing money because of old man Dando's fascination with Kentucky bourbon and the girls who poured it. Unfortunately Dizzy Dando forgot Mrs Dando still owned 90 per cent of the stock, which she sold to Clive Feral for the price of a Smith and Wesson 45. Two years later, his eyes coldly scanned the few column inches that reported her execution for the murder of her husband before he turned on to the Tokyo futures.

There had been countless other deals like it. He only remembered this one because it was the first, the one that cleared the 100-dollar loan he had secured to get started. The fleet of cabs were junk and were sold to an out of town scrap merchant. The garage was another thing. Clive did not see the flaking paint or filthy, grease-soaked floor, the split hinges and the sign loose above the door that read '–ando's Cabs' with the 'D' missing, he saw a thousand square feet of prime real estate between the Chase Manhattan and City Banks.

He had wasted no time in phoning both.

"We don't buy information," Chase Manhattan's chief executive told him politely. The tone was cultured but it did not entirely disguise a Brooklyn lineage.

Clive smiled, a thin perfunctory twist of the mouth that pulled in his cheeks and somehow made his features more gaunt than before. "Just thought you'd like to know that the freehold of Dando's Cabs has just changed hands and City are planning to buy it to extend their frontage by a hundred feet," he said. "It'll make Chase Manhattan look like Hillbilly Finances."

"Now just wait a minute," the chief said, suddenly close to panic. "Sold you say? Who to?"

"That information is not for giving. It's for buying."

"We can't pay bribes," the man burst at him, his professional aplomb vanishing fast.

"Who said anything about bribes?" Clive said quietly. "What I'm talking about is a loan."

"Loan?"

"You got it. One million dollars at zero per cent."

"Well, I don't know—. I'll have to speak with the board."

"Do what you have to do. You've got twenty-four hours. But be convincing. I hate 'to think of a good man out of a job."

Five minutes later Clive was on the phone to City Bank.

"Jees! The hell it!" the man said before he could stop himself. "We've been waiting for that block to come on the market for twenty years and now you say someone's bought ahead of us?"

"Yes. It's on offer to Chase. And a very nice piece of real-estate for them to acquire." Clive spoke with the perfect English of his upbringing. "That extra hundred feet will put their frontage next to yours. You'll certainly need some bright lights now, and I don't think your shareholders will be any too happy at the eclipse."

"Who's bought the site?" the exec asked in an oddly stretched voice.

"How valuable is the information to you?"

"What d'you want? You must know very well—"

"Yes," Clive interrupted. "I know, you can't pay bribes."

"Well then?"

"I need a modest loan."

"No problem," the exec breathed in relief.

"One million dollars at zero per cent."

This time the breath came down the line like a solid wall. Clive could almost see the man go apoplectic, and it was several seconds before the voice came back with, "When can we meet?"

Clive hired two conference rooms in the New York Sheraton at the single-room rate by promising the receptionist tickets for the new musical *Mice* – unobtainable unless you were prepared to book a year up front. He also hired two secretaries from the temp agency round the corner in the basement of the Colgate Palmolive Building on 50th Street, and by sweet-talking the janitor he managed to acquire some telephones which weren't connected to anything but looked good banked up upon the table.

His only big worry was that both bankers might arrive at the same moment and recognise each other. He briefed the secretaries to identify the men immediately on arrival and steer them to their separate rooms. He had given the girls his last 20 dollars to split between them and considered it money well spent.

He lit a cigar. He was in business.

He was amazed how easy it was. The whole deal took precisely 37.5 minutes after the bidding started, but he reckoned he must have walked half a mile commuting between the two rooms before Chase eventually stuck five million short of City's final bid. And then there were the additional green-stamps – the one million bucks both banks had promised to lend him interest free.

"And I want a thousand dollars here in cash right now," he told the winning bidder.

"Of course." The man looked shaken by the speed of what had happened, his elation showing pink upon his face.

Ten minutes after the banker had gone, a messenger arrived with a sealed brown envelope. Clive opened it and sniffed the contents before pulling out the neatly layered wads of 50-dollar bills, the sight and the smell giving him the same narcosis as a junkie snorting coke. He savoured the moment for several seconds longer before calling in the girls.

"Everything all right, sir?" they asked anxiously.

"Perfectly," he told them. "You did very well, so well we have something to celebrate. Take off your clothes, honeys."

They both stood back and moved for the door. "No one said anything about that kind of deal, buster," the taller one with the full blouse told him.

He grinned at her, his gaunt face suddenly almost rakish. "There's 500 bucks on the table that says it's no bad idea."

She stalled in her stride. "Hey, honey!" she smiled at her companion. "I just reckon we might have gotten ourselves a little overtime." Her foot flew out and kicked shut the door. "How d'you like your tricks, mister? Straight A or doggy fashion?"

He looked at her unsmiling for a moment.

"Whichever you do best, honey. But make it fast and forget the chat," he told her. Already he was slipping out of his pants, his shaft gorged with dark blue veins and a sticky dew seeping from the tip. He wanted the fuck, sure as hell he wanted the fuck; but more than anything it was to help clear his mind so he could think through the new deal fast taking shape.

An ocean away it was approaching dusk. The sun had lowered to a molten ball of fading gold just above the sea, and in moments it was gone, doused to no more than a smear of pink just above the dark and brooding water.

Martin Feral had never quite got used to the sudden

arrival of the equatorial night, and he sat at his window looking out over the sea as his eyes adjusted to the gloom. Far below, beneath the towering monolith of the Holiday Inn, the streets of Casablanca sparkled as the city came awake for the night, a seething miasma of smells that mixed sweet scents with the grossest putrefaction; the noise and colour pervading everything, the living atmosphere reaching up to taint the air of his suite high up on the roof.

He did not complain. Like all Holiday Inns, this one was franchised, and he owned the franchise together with the freehold of the building and the land on which it sat. He also owned the Feral Exchange, a metal-dealing and futures complex he had built some years previously, a harsh, daunting building of almost Germanic appearance which had become the financial nub of this Afro-Arabian city. Little happened on the seaboard he did not know about, and it was generally accepted that he kept the fire burning under many of the shady pots boiling in the darker corners of the bazaar. And that was strange, for he was an Englishman.

Like his twin Clive, Martin had taken fifteen years to establish a wealth of considerable proportions. He walked out on to the roof garden from where he could see the place where it had all started those years before. Mendoza's café was exactly as it had always been. The single neon sign invited the itinerant tourist to push aside the straggle of coloured beads and come in and buy some cheap tooled leather or beaten copper, or just sip coffee on a threadbare carpet at the rear.

It was not an invitation accepted by many. The interior was dark, and there was something foreboding about the place. An Arab stood by the door, his faded robes travel-worn and dirty, his yellow face marked by a scar that started at his ear and finished at his chin. One eye seemed to point at an odd angle and Martin had never quite figured which one was glass and which was real. It didn't matter. Yassir Mendoza's emporium had been exactly what he needed all those years before, and it had taken nothing more than the offer of a reasonable financial consideration for the back room to be Martin's whenever he wanted it.

Martin Feral had left England with one idea: to get very rich very quickly. When he was only ten years old he had concluded that the only difference between honesty and dishonesty was in the spelling, and through his teens his thoughts on the subject became more profound. In moments of reflection he drew philosophical conclusions such as 'conscience is a form of mental aberration', and 'heaven is a myth to stop hell overcrowding'. Yes, conscience was definitely an impediment he could well do without, and he was supported in this view by his twin brother, Clive.

Oddly, however, neither child was ever in trouble. Not for them crass shoplifting escapades and wanton thievery. The boys shared pride in their methods. Everything they did had an element of sophistication. It was always their younger brother Paul who got caught poaching the trout, or with jam on his hands. It was Paul who was accused of stealing the 500 pounds that the twins had spirited from the school bursar's office.

They split the money equally between them. Clive took five pounds out of his bundle and used it to bribe the headmaster's daughter to drop her knickers. The remaining 245 pounds he used to buy the jewellery lifted by an opportunist fifth-former from a local country house. This he sold seven days later for 1000 pounds on the school outing to London.

Martin used his share of the 500 pounds to buy his first wholesale package of cocaine. Afterwards, when both boys had sold their purchases, they compared notes. They had each made a 400 per cent mark-up.

Paul was caned for the theft and suspended for the remainder of the term, despite the lack of proof.

Martin knew better than to establish a pattern of trading that would lead to his exposure. Until he left school he bought only the occasional consignment, sold it quickly, and then lay dormant for many months until he felt it was safe to repeat the exercise. The police knew there were sudden explosions of narcotics on the market and they were puzzled. They didn't like it, for as soon as the dope hit the streets the supply instantly dried up once more. All they were left with were several more deaths, and no trail to follow.

But Martin was learning. He was an assiduous student of human nature and could wait. He saw the pickings, he saw the mugs who got hooked, and the mugs who got caught moving the stuff. He saw the street sellers taking tiny margins at huge risk while the big boy wholesalers creamed the entire racket from the safety of the shadows.

And he knew which he would be.

The day after he left school on his seventeenth birthday he emptied his building society account of the 5,000 pounds that had accumulated, and flew to Morocco. One month later he sailed back into Chichester Harbour as deckhand on Lord

8

Ruislip's yacht. Customs clearance was a derisory affair with tea and biscuits and much haw-haw laughter.

Within seven days Martin Feral had sold his merchandise and made enough money to buy Lord Ruislip's yacht and several like it, but instead he smiled at the stupidity of such impulses. It was to be the first and last time he used that route. Customs and Excise were no fools and they were getting shrewder by the year, Nimrods from St Mawgan photographing every boat coming up from the Med so that half the consignments were intercepted before they even hit the beach.

There were better ways that did not require his personal involvement, and he gave himself three weeks to find the person he was looking for. In fact he made his decision after only two. The Mauniers Hotel in Charing Cross Road had been his home for that two weeks. He sat in his room from nine in the morning until five at night as he watched from behind the thick net curtains at his window. Even *his* resilience was depressed by the steady stream of rejected hopefuls pouring endlessly from the theatrical agency across the street – the same faces time and again, what little spark of hope that was there going in, turning to blank despair coming out. What a hell of a way to live, he mused, aloof and without compassion.

Freda and Dave Perry were astounded when the agency suddenly found them a job. At sixty-five, neither seriously expected to work again – and now out of the blue, this. It was unbelievable, like a dream, and with a cruise thrown in as well. Momentarily they had doubts when the young man told them what they had to do, but all reservations were dispelled as soon as they worked out the figures: four cruises a year at 10,000 pounds a throw, payable half in advance and half on completion, into a numbered account in any currency, in any country of their choice. And like the young man said, if the worst came to the worst, at their age it would only be probation and a stiff fine – and who said anything about being caught? They were bloody good actors, weren't they?

Over the next few years the staff of Saga Holidays increasingly welcomed the lovely retired couple who kept coming back for equatorial cruises. Even the Excise officers in the Oceanic Terminal at Southampton docks admired the game old biddys for their gritty determination and sense of fun, she with her limp and he with his electric wheelchair which seemed to weigh more than a family saloon. They were so cheerful despite their disabilities, it was a pleasure to rush them through the clearing sheds and help them on their way.

9

Even Martin found their company entertaining each time they visited him in the back of Mendoza's shop. As soon as the curtain closed and the room was in shadow Dave would spring from the wheelchair and start rubbing his legs, dancing round the room and swearing effusively in his natural Dublin brogue. Five minutes later the wheelchair would be loaded, and he would be back in it again, curled up like a paraplegic as Freda steered him back down to the waterfront where the liner was waiting.

Martin quit the drugs game when they were arrested. He had known it would only be a matter of time. There were better pickings to be made.

The night before the funeral, the storm had been the worst he could remember. It seemed that the thunder would never stop, the bursts coming every few seconds as lightning strobed the sky with jagged fingers of blue fire that annealed the heavens and earth as one.

Tessa would have enjoyed that, Paul Feral thought as he stared moist-eyed out into the blackness. She had loved everything that nature could bestow, from the simplest scented grass, to the wildness of a summer storm upon a mountain top. He could still feel her there with him now, living as she had died, in love with all about her.

Again the lightning rent the heavens. He clutched his head and stared – a woman was standing on the lawn, staring up, smiling in that familiar way. Despite the lancing rain her hair was dry, loose in a silken skein about her shoulders. Her nightdress was the pretty floral one with the lace cuffs, the one he had dressed her in as he waited for the doctor to come and pronounce her dead. Then she was gone, the blackness more intense than before. When the lightning flashed again there was nothing there, only a solitary pink ribbon in a puddle on the grass.

He turned to face the body lying in the coffin on the trestles and tried to see something of her there, but the flesh was white and lifeless. The kind, caring eyes and warm, smiling lips had relaxed into a waxen parody of the woman that she was. A tear jerked down his face as he thought of all she had done for him and all he could have done for her, but never did. He would do for their two girls what he had failed to do for her. He knew what she would want. He must do everything for the girls now – that would have been her wish.

Yes, Tessa was gone and somehow he was glad. She

deserved better than he could ever seem to give her.

As they lowered the coffin into the chalky soil of the little graveyard on the Wiltshire downs the clouds melted and the sun shone through. There were only a dozen or so mourners there, and neither Clive nor Martin had sent a wreath despite his telegrams informing them of the death. Clive and Martin, he thought bitterly of his elder twin brothers. They could have helped so much but not the merest gesture had they offered.

The girls stood by his side holding one hand each. "Don't cry, darling Daddy." Maria, the eldest, turned her little face up to meet his. "Please don't cry, Daddy. We'll look after you." He did cry, for many hours through many nights. But he did not – could not – let them see.

CHAPTER 2

The weather had broken suddenly from the great heat of a few days before. The rain was coming in slanting blinds through the gaps in the buildings as Clive Feral made his way the short distance from the Price Whitney Bank to Maybee's on 47th Street. He loathed the feel of the wet spattering the sensitive skin of his face, and the smell of the streets that lifted with the steam off the hot sidewalks. But this was one task he would never assign to another. Maybee's was the only store in Manhattan that kept its humidor at exactly the right temperature, 11.7 degrees Centigrade. He picked over a dozen Cuban Baltics before finding the exact cigar of his choice, spinning it under the hook of his nose as he savoured the delicate cure of the leaves.

The shop was not busy and the girl on the checkout studied him with a guarded sideways glance through her hair. To those who didn't know Clive Feral better, he was a curiosity, tall and lean and with a hint of a stoop. It was hard to tell how old he was, his thick hair brushed back and greying slightly at the temples, his skin pale but unsullied by the normal lines of wear. His face was gaunt and unsmiling, yet also slightly effete, its leanness emphasised by the slight hook of the nose; but it was his Arctic blue eyes that unnerved her the most: they remained constantly out of focus in a cadaverous sort of way, and it gave her the creeps.

Yes, the man had a presence of sorts but there was something unaccountably rotten about Clive Feral that could be sensed rather than seen. And others felt it too. Often she had wondered what exactly made the general run of punters steer clear of him, for even at busy times when the shop was packed with trade he stood aloof and alone, somehow managing to create his own space in the crush.

He was moving now, satisfied with his choice. He was making for the checkout and the girl unfroze her stare. "On the house," she told him, her smile wide and rapturous, only hardening to a thin contemptuous line after he had passed out into the street. He barely noticed the girl as he came and went – deferential treatment was something he had long become accustomed to, and expected as a matter of course.

He had said nothing. He never said anything. Clive Feral was never one to say 'Please', least of all 'Thank you'. Every day was the same. Once, maybe twice, he would come in, pull a 20 buck cigar, and go. The boss said he wasn't to be charged – ever. That galled. Clive Feral was currently rated the richest financier in the whole of New York State, owning 90 per cent of the stock of Price Whitney Banking Inc, and Price Whitney owned half the prime freehold in that area, including Maybee's Drug Store.

Bastard, she thought again.

There was constant speculation as to his background. It was accepted that he was a Brit of unremarkable origins, but no one could find out much more than that. At first, no one cared. The immigrant with the funny accent and the flash suits was no different than any of the Poles, Jews or Asiatics with their strange ways and ethnic peculiarities. It made New York what it was – the greatest cosmopolitan city in the world.

Four times he was mugged, and each time he swore it would never happen again, but it did – until he had enough money to hire a bodyguard. It hadn't taken long. Since then he had built a minor industry out of personal protection, the one guard quickly becoming two, the two four, then eight, then a company was formed until now the Stave Personal Security Co Inc protected most visiting diplomats, half the big names in Hollywood, and featured in the unlisted securities at a flotation of some 50 million dollars.

Yes, it was generally accepted that Clive Feral had the knack. He also left a trail of bankruptcies, suicides, and irreversible psychoses in his wake, enough to rate the obituary columns in the *New York Times* at least once a month, and he was generally considered to be the most ruthless financier east of Chicago since the days of Prohibition.

Fifteen years before Clive Feral had made his first big decision. It was made the same way he made all his decisions – with gut intuition and a ruthless, flawless logic. The time was now, he had decided, and the place was going to be New York – the

13

Big Apple – a city where the unbridled could stay that way and do their thing, a city that could give him space, and Clive Feral always needed space.

His twin brother Martin had chosen Africa, also with its freedoms, but freedoms of a very different kind, and for different reasons. Martin and Clive were twins of almost identical appearance and similar motivations, but that was where the similarity ended, for in subtleties of taste there was a divergence, if not a gulf, and throughout their childhood the two boys sparred with each other in a strange rivalry that added an edge to their parallel endeavours.

In Africa Martin was multiplying the seeds of his wealth, putting him well ahead in the stakes towards that first big million-pound mark, the first goal in their unspoken race. For Clive, that was all the spur he needed. He resolved it would be the very last time he would come second to anyone ever, a resolution that had held good since that first day he had set foot in his new, adopted land. There was of course the problem of getting there. This he resolved by posing as a travel writer for *The Times*, and he was still amazed that he had so easily persuaded Cunard out of a free luxury berth on the *QE2* on the strength of one phone call and a letter. He arrived smiling on the dockside with no more than 10 pounds in his pocket, and a tongue of liquid gold. It was all he needed.

High above, the rain came in at a steeper angle, rattling its soft drumbeat against the windows of the Garden Suite, Clive Feral's penthouse on the top of the Price Whitney Building. There Karina Darielle paused for a moment, and let her fingers rest on the terminal keyboard as she watched the droplets trace their halting lines down the glass. Like Clive Feral, success was cast within her mould too, but unlike him, her eyes were alive with a mysterious fire, one moment sparkling with a latent humour, and the next, as the mood changed, dangerously flaming with shards of light like splinters off a grinding wheel. Her lips were full and giving, and painted a lustrous pink, a colour heightened by her skin with its bronze mix of bloods from distant Indian stock.

Although relaxed comfortably in the revolving chair, there was no slump in her posture. Her legs were neatly crossed, and her back was straight, tautening the shiny fabric of her blouse. She wore fashion-suede calf-length boots and a short skirt in chamois leather with a serrated hem split to give hints of the widening softness of her thighs. She wore no stockings and a pelt of the finest golden hair softened her skin with that sheen Californian girls would only gain after hours of attrition in the sun. But that honeyed pigmentation had not always been the blessing it was now.

Karina Darielle was an orphan. After the death of her parents when she was barely eleven years old, she lived with an aunt for another year before the old lady died. Suddenly she found herself alone and penniless on the streets of New York. She was tall and gawky for a child of eleven, not quite white, yet without sufficient colour to draw the small benefits of an ethnic identity. Her skin appeared patchy with the dirty grime of a sidewalk dweller, something no one chose to question since it matched her clothes, ragged and too small for her fast-growing body. Her aunt, like her parents before her, had died leaving her nothing but love and a pile of bills that would never be paid. But the social people knew about Karina, knew she required special care and why, and that she was exactly tailored for the City Child Protection Program.

City Child Protection was to be the Santa Maria Orphanage out in Queens, a run-down institution that in theory was funded partly by the state, and partly by voluntary subscriptions. In practice the state's aid was set to a minimum contingency, and the voluntary subscriptions had dwindled back to nothing. The only beatitudes were a small trickle of legacies from grateful children of another era – these not-to-be-repeated offerings eagerly seized upon by Karl Steinman, the orphanage governor, who had numerous ingenious ways of defrauding the home of what little fat there was. And no one cared. The municipal conscience was satisfied by the very fact the place existed at all.

The day she arrived at the orphanage it was raining heavily, the single wiper on the old Ford bus barely coping with the deluge, the frayed edge of its blade sweeping hemispherical ruts through the grime to leave a greater opacity than before. Inside there were twenty or so children of mixed ages, the boys on one side, the girls on the other. Their clothes were uniformly drab, their expressions sullen, and she learned later that most were returning after a brief escape back to that wonderful world of freedom beyond the compound gates.

It was hot in the bus and it stank foul of sweat. The gag of urine was unmistakable through the lysol sluice someone had used to try and douse the stench. No one spoke. The ones with a pallor and dilated eyes were high on whatever dope they had managed to score during their short burst of

15

freedom; the others unnaturally quiet as if drowning in some deeper kind of introspection. In charge was a woman with the hardest face Karina had ever seen. The only sign of Janine Jerome's femininity was in her name. She stood blocking the exit at the bottom of the steps as the bus ground slowly through the heavy New York traffic. Her eyes were small and very black like imperfections on a tuber root, and she eyed the children with a look that seemed to throw out a challenge to try and escape again – and just let them see what would happen then. Her shape was almost square, her head oblong with a bristled crew-cut, her body heavily fleshed with middle age, but with only the barest hint of breasts beneath the floppy woollen top. Her skirt, in a blue stitch-patch denim, was long, but not long enough to hide the swelling that was already turning her ankles into the amorphous, elephantine shape of a Molingar heifer. She was, Karina thought, the ugliest woman she had ever seen.

"Don't stare," the older girl next to Karina suddenly whispered. "For Heaven's sake, don't stare at her." But it was too late.

"You!" Janine Jerome shouted in a strangely falsetto voice for a big woman. "You, girl."

"Me?" Karina quavered under her furious gaze.

"Yes, *you*. Come here," she shrilled.

Karina remembered staggering to the front of the bus, and then holding still. And then she remembered nothing. The blow hit her just beneath her ear, throwing her sideways into the sharp chrome by the steps, and the blood was already painting a riband of scarlet down her face by the time she fell to the floor. She did not regain consciousness for well over an hour by which time she had arrived within the walls of the Orphanage of Santa Maria.

At first she just lay there, huddled in a corner on the floor, unable to comprehend the images slowly forming out of the mists of her unconsciousness: vague greens and creams and institutional browns. Her eyes were darting in and out of focus, caught with the tide of nausea sweeping from her guts, and she moved her hand a little, feeling the marquetry of cracked flooring against her skin, and seeing the two-tone wall of broken tiles. She heard the echoes – the place was full of echoes, echoes of the past, echoes from the present, voices coming and going like the faces all around her. And then there was that smell again, the ammoniacal stench of excrement and other matters long decaying, and again she had to gag.

She was in some kind of assembly hall. It was dark in

16

there despite a feeble row of tungsten lamps hanging from their frayed umbilicals of wire. The ceiling was a darkened yellow, and what little daylight could be seen was heavily filtered, each window a lattice of spider's webs and hollow insect-cases. Everywhere there was a feeling of hopelessness and dereliction. Somewhere in the distance a church bell began to chime the hour of noon, a remote, woeful sound that added to her desolation.

The hall was divided by a ragged curtain hanging in great loops from the few remaining hooks that were still attached. The boys were on one side and the girls on the other and, like her, they were all quite naked, covering themselves as best they could with inadequately spreading hands. Karina tried to do the same but her limbs felt leaden and she found she could barely move.

"She's coming round," a man's voice stated simply in a deep, Louisiana drawl, any slight concern immediately turning to disinterest as the faces moved away.

"Leave the little bitch where she is," Janine Jerome said. "We'll do her last of all. Next. *Next!*"

It was some kind of medical inspection – an elderly white man in a hospital coat and a stethoscope sat at a rudimentary table in the corner opposite Karina. In front of him was an area hidden behind an old zig-zag screen on rusty castors. Janine's shrill command "*Next*" was a cue for one of the black orderlies to break ranks from where others stood in a row against the wall. Glancing first at a sheet of paper in his hand, he moved in amongst the group of boys. Instantly there was a yelp as he found his target, a young lad of no more than eight. He brought him out, tugging him roughly by the hair towards the medical man who rose from his table.

Karina couldn't see what was happening now, but Janine Jerome and Karl Steinman could, positioning themselves by the desk and staring with rapt intent into the screened area where the medical man was alone with the boy. It seemed an age before the boy reappeared, very pale and with tears upon his face. Karina was soon to find out why.

Medical examinations at the Orphanage of Santa Maria were as routine as the potage of watery fare that appeared each noonday at the table – eyes, nose, mouth, and the most loathsome part of all, an extended examination of the genitalia and anal canal, of boys and girls alike, and always with staff looking on. She remembered it happening that first time in a kind of terrible slow motion – the order to bend and spread

17

her legs, wider, then wider still, then the probing hands and glass spatula forced into places she had never known existed. All the while she felt the steady gaze of Karl Steinman and Janine Jerome lingering on her nakedness.

Despite the heat she shuddered, suddenly frightened as she had never been before. It seemed an eternity since she had lived with her aunt in her garret lodgings in the Bronx, and now she was here and she didn't know why, didn't understand. There was something evil about where she was, she was certain of it – certain there was something rank and rotten. She felt a portent of more ghastly things to come in this place they called the Orphanage of Santa Maria. And she was afraid.

Her bed that night was a cot in a dormitory with forty other girls; some who had been on the bus, and some she had not seen before. She lay there on the coarse sheets weeping silently. It was very dark and very hot, and always there was that smell.

For a full thirty minutes after Janine Jerome had locked the dormitory door there wasn't a sound. The silence as intense as a crowd waiting at a gibbet – just breathing, that gentle steady breath of listeners in the dark. Then, out of the silence came the first whisper as one of the girls spoke very softly to another. Then another followed, and another, all husky and very muted, but still it built up until a solid murmur filled the dormitory, but never once was there a laugh or a burst of giggles to lift the sombre mood.

"What's your name?"

Karina jolted in her bed. "Karina," she answered hesitantly, peering into the darkness towards the sound. "Karina Darielle."

"Karina?" the unseen voice repeated. "That's a nice name. My name's Fay Carrera. Do you remember me?"

Karina did remember, just. Fay was the older girl who had sat next to her on the bus a few hours earlier. "Yes," she said almost eagerly now into the darkness. "Yes, I think I do, although it was all so hazy. There was that accident."

"Accident," the other girl snorted. "That was no accident. Jerome slugged you for staring at her. She hates anyone staring at her which is okay by us, 'cos she's that pig ugly she hurts the eyes. How old are you?" She changed the subject abruptly.

"I'm twelve," said Karina.

"Twelve! Jees!" Fay snorted, no longer in a whisper, "I thought you were a lot more than that, you're so tall."

"People do think I'm older than I am," Karina agreed. As

18

they were talking she was trying to picture the other girl in the darkness. At a guess she was about thirteen or fourteen. Karina remembered her long blonde hair and her bright blue eyes, the same bright blue eyes of her favourite dolly the social people made her leave behind when they took her away. Tears welled again as she remembered the doll, the one last toy she had possessed.

"You should have been safe for a couple of years but I don't know now," Fay went on. "It's not how old you are, it's the way you look."

"Safe? I don't understand."

"Yeah, safe from Janine Jerome. She's a rabid dyke, queen of the dildos, screws us all eventually, but she usually goes for the older girls first. Karl Steinman is the same with the boys – he's as bent as a three-dime coin. The place is a rat hole of pervs and the only thing to do is make the best of it and do not be too pretty. Jerome loves the pretty girls. The medicals are bogus, what we call the meat rack. It's where Steinman and Jerome make their selection for the week."

Karina listened, a new numbness overwhelming her, even though she barely understood half of what she heard. Fay had stopped now, waiting for her to reply, but she couldn't. Instead she lay there as silent tears streamed down her face.

And then something began happening within her. It came slowly at first as if seeds were sown and were taking time to fruit. It was the strangest feeling – a feeling that was at once powerful and exalting; something she had felt once before and would many times again. Later she would come to terms with it and turn it to her own advantage. For the time being it was very raw, but still an awesome power her mother had once chosen to call her rage. Only once before had it flooded free and unfettered. A black man had called and pulled a knife demanding money of her mother. Karina remembered the occasion vividly, the ugliness in the man's face, the utter help-lessness and panic in her mother's eyes. Suddenly she too had a knife in her hand, stabbing upwards into the man's groin with what little strength she had, screaming, stabbing, screaming, stabbing. The knife did not plunge deeply in her tiny fingers, but deeply enough. The man's howl was the unnatural sound of a banshee wailing in the night as his mouth gaped and his eyes exploded with pain. Then he was gone, running from the street, leaving a trail of blue-black femoral blood that lasted until the rains came two days later and washed away the stains.

The fear stayed on in her mother's face as she saw the

19

expression in her own child's eyes, the smile upon her young face. It was unnatural. That same smile was there now as she lay on the rough iron bed. Already the tears had melted away, her fear a diminishing blackness against a brightening light.

"You all right?" Fay whispered urgently. "I haven't frightened you have I?"

"Oh no," Karina said, her voice very steady now.

"I'm glad," said Fay. "You'll survive. We all survive somehow," she added, without conviction. "Anyway I'm leaving here next year. They can't keep me any longer legally."

"How long will you have been here?" Karina asked.

"Five years straight, apart from the odd times when I ran away. But running away is never worth it, believe me. They'll always find you – they *always* do – and bring you back again. Then they make it even worse for you. They know nobody will ever believe you if you tell 'em what really happens here."

At that moment there was a small noise at the door, and the light came on, filling the dormitory with a sudden brilliance. Every murmur ceased – talking after lights out was a punishable offence. Janine Jerome was there, her voluminous shape filling the opening like a huge mantis hovering over its prey. Her eyes were the red of a Malawi gecko and the grey flannelette nightdress she wore was greasy round the top, the ribbon that once graced its neck dirty and hanging loose in a straggle of frayed threads.

And she was drunk, very drunk. "Som'ones talking," she slurred. "Som'ones talking. I heard you. Who was it?"

There was not a sound. The woman's mouth clenched. Her head had begun scanning slowing from side to side with a strange cocking action, as if relying more on her ears than her eyes to get a fix.

"Oh no!" Fay squeaked. "I think she's looking at me."

It was hard to tell. The woman was having difficulty getting a focus, squinting in a way that reduced her eyes to tiny coals in the halo of her face. Then she began to move forward with an odd crab-like movement, two steps forward, then an involuntary sideways kick to steady her balance between each run.

Her direction was now ghastly clear. She came to a stop at the foot of Fay's bed and tried to say something but the words sloshed incoherently from her mouth. It didn't matter. In one lumbering movement she had the covers off and the girl's struggling form bundled under her arm. Then she was

20

gone again, leaving the dormitory as dark and as silent as before.

Through the silence they could all hear the sound of a girl screaming, and then in the pauses when she took breath, a different sound like the lowing of something bovine during the crisis of a rut. All except Karina sunk a little lower, pulling up the sheets, and only a few of the girls in the dormitory heard the door swing softly open, then close again. It was only later that they realised the screams had stopped.

Janine Jerome was found at six the following morning by a black porter coming on duty. She was still alive but she never moved or spoke again, the left side of her head a pulp of broken bone. The police tried to say it was attempted murder. The city authorities said that such an event was quite impossible in an excellent institution like the Orphanage of Santa Maria and refused to sanction a full investigation. A month later the place burnt down in a mysterious fire and Karina escaped to the streets once more, and she resolved the socials would never find her again. They never did.

That same day, for two whole hours, she sat on the pavement outside the Price Whitney Bank just staring above her at the serried ranks of windows that faced up the financial centre until the police moved her on.

Now she looked down through the rain-spattered glass to the same spot in the street where she had sat fifteen years before. And she smiled. Like Clive Feral, she too had been true to herself.

It seemed as if it were only yesterday that that new zeal first burned within her like a raw sun against the blackness of the heavens. Suddenly on that fateful day she had known where she was going, where her life would lead, although she had not known how to get there, or how long the journey would take. But still she knew what she must do. She had owed herself that much, and from that day on she planned, and studied, and schemed towards the first stage of her goal: to make it into the dealing room at Price Whitney Bank.

Even before she could read she found she had a rare talent for mental arithmetic, an innate skill she first used to make a book on the mouse track races she held with the other kids in Brooklyn. It was funny now, thinking back on it. She could see herself kneeling on the sidewalk pencilling in the odds on a pack of Lucky Strikes as the little creatures made their way along a track of cardboard boxes. Usually she made two bucks in an afternoon – and that was real big riches.

Then later came the numbers game. Some bigger boys, who knew talent when they saw it, figured on a rip-off using an old Blackjack shoe they had recovered from a trash can. All she had to do was remember the cards that had been delivered against the odds of what might come next and signal the dealer when to stop and call. That was worth 10 dollars an afternoon – even bigger riches.

After leaving the Orphanage of Santa Maria the die had already been cast. Straight from the sidewalk outside the Price Whitney Bank she combed the gutters of the streets until she found enough nickels and dimes to put 11 dollars together. One dollar she spent on a fresh copy of *The Sporting News*. She then found Van Nev, a bent bookie's runner who had been a friend of her father's, and after much thought and a number of calculations, the remaining 10 dollars she put on Clouded Moon, a little known filly in the 3.30 race out at Lexinton. It came in at fifteen-to-one.

"Who you punting for, chick?" the runner asked, looking down at the little girl as he reluctantly paid her out. He was overweight for a runner, his gut hanging over his belt, his Croatian stock yielding a face that was not dissimilar to the lugubrious features of an Afghan Hound.

"My uncle," she lied.

Van Nev accepted her word. He got a lot of bets off kids running errands for relatives wanting to keep out of sight, and he wasn't going to get his head busted for scamming a kid for a mere 150 bucks.

She didn't punt again for four days, sleeping rough at night in Central Park, and keeping moving by day to avoid the Socials chasing fodder for their kiddy pounds. But now at least she could eat. She was up and walking by six each morning, first to the nearest public sluice for a wash, and then on to a paper shop to pick up *The Sporting News*. Out of her winnings she had also bought a calculator and a small book to scribble in. She kept the book but after a day tossed the calculator into a pile of trash by the sidewalk – she could figure the numbers much quicker in her head.

On the third day something shone from the rows of figures that had begun to line each page of the book, and again she found Van Nev the runner.

"Your uncle reckon he's in luck again?" he sneered through teeth clasped round a wet cigarillo.

"I reckon," she said noncommittally.

22

"Well, what d'ya want on what d'ya want?" he asked in the time-worn way.

"Hundred bucks to win on Purple Heart in the two o'clock."

"Sheesh," he grimaced, "your unc' come into money or som'n? Anyway, he won't have it for long – must be losing his marbles backing an old nag like that."

"It's not for my uncle, it's for Big Harry," she piped back at him. "And I'll tell him what you said." Despite her slender years she knew a sleaze like Van Nev would think nothing of doing a runner with her winnings and Big Harry was going to be her constant companion from now on. She wondered what Big Harry would be like if he actually existed, and guessed Van Nev was doing just about the same.

"Big Harry, eh?" he said squeezing his brow into a knit of dirty lines. The only Big Harry he knew left town a few years ago after gunning down a cop. Maybe he was back. "Only kidding," he said quickly, letting his mouth slacken into a display of yellowing teeth. "No offence meant."

Van Nev was amazed to be shelling out thousands of bucks later that afternoon when Purple Heart turned the two o'clock into a one-horse race and jetted in at twenty-to-one. "Son of a bitch," he spat. "That goddam nag must have had some dope stuffed up its ass."

"You reckon? Big Harry won't like to hear you say that," Karina told him earnestly. "Sounds like you're calling him a cheat."

Van Nev pondered on it. "No, no," he said eventually, prudence at his arm. "Sure as heck I wouldn't say that about Big Harry. But I still wouldn't have given that horse a light."

"Better take your tips from Big Harry in future," she trilled fervently. "Big Harry *knows*. You better believe it. And he doesn't like people who don't believe it."

Even from a young girl the words carried a kind of menace, and after he had paid out another few thousand bucks over two races in the same week he started taking her advice.

Karina Darielle moved out of Central Park a week later with so much money in her knickers she could barely bend when it came to sit. Her next stop was a rooming house down in Queens where money was the only thing that did the talking. "Room eleven," the janitor told her, throwing over the keys with barely a glance as he stuffed her hundred-dollar rent advance into his top pocket. "And no whoring, swearing, spitting, or drunks, d'ya hear," he

23

added in the same way he had done a thousand times before.

The following Monday, September 4, was her thirteenth birthday and she celebrated by enrolling herself at the Haytsbury Modern School for Girls, a state-run institution where the kids fought a lot and learned very little. But it had the advantage that she was now street-legal if the socials came to check.

She spent little time at school, just enough to avoid being labelled a chronic truant and transferred to a college of correction. She had better things to do.

And then suddenly things changed. In her second year Karina was put in the class of Miss Megan Grey, a diminutive, elderly woman of Scottish Presbyterian origins who, at barely 100 pounds was a mere shadow of many of her pupils. If anyone was tailor-made for nightmare treatment in the jungle of the schoolroom, it was Miss Grey. Yet hers was the only class in the whole school where there was not the constant sound of insurrection. Her hair was almost albino white and she had eyes, of the very palest blue, that seemed to reach the soul. One glance from her and a child was silent. It was almost a desecration even to think of idle talk or back-chat. There could be only one explanation of this phenomenon – that she loved children, and they loved her, without questions on either side. It was as simple as that.

From now on Karina was a model student, always there, always punctual. In return Miss Grey took her to her heart, never enquiring, yet somehow knowing that her charge was alone in life with no one else to turn to. For five years she taught her everything she knew, and that was much more than she was required to, or was dictated by the rules. Above all she taught Karina the etiquette of life, the subtle nuances and polish she would soon use to great effect. Miss Grey took her street-speak broth of dialects and put refinement there. She taught her how to dress. And always Miss Grey was rewarded by Karina giving of her best. Thus her surprise was all the greater when the time came for Karina to leave the school.

"But Karina," pleaded Megan Grey, "you really must forget this silly notion about working in a bank. You're far too bright for that. There is no university in the whole of the United States that would not be glad to have you – you know that."

"It's very kind of you to say so ma'am," she shrugged, "but it's not a question of what I'm able to do, but what I *want* to do."

24

The older woman tutted and frowned. Never before had she met such a girl. She had taught stubborn girls and stupid girls, but never such an able child as this one with absolutely no ambition beyond working in a bank. It was beyond her comprehension. "Is there nothing I can say that will make you change your mind?" she finished lamely.

"No, ma'am, I'm afraid not. But thank you, ma'am."

"Which bank do you have in mind, if you have one in mind at all?" she asked testily.

The speed of the response surprised her. "The Price Whitney Bank off Fifth Avenue," Karina said without a second's hesitation.

Megan Grey's heart sunk still further. "Oh my dear child, *not* Price Whitney, please don't say Price Whitney. They are *absolutely awful* people to work for, my dear. They treat their staff so badly."

"But they pay well," Karina argued with guileless simplicity.

Megan Grey looked startled again. "You have clearly been doing your homework, Karina, but money isn't everything."

"No," Karina agreed, smiling at her sweetly, "money isn't everything." Her features were now the fully mature features of a young woman, her eyes the softest brown with a haunting mellow look. Megan Grey's heart ached for her own daughter who had died when she was barely eight.

"Then why?"

"Perhaps it's the challenge," Karina told her.

"But university is also a challenge, and with a degree you would be able to start in Bank Management rather than just as a teller which is what you'll surely be."

"I'll be quite happy just being a teller to begin with," Karina told her honestly. "And anyhow I'll be studying for extra qualifications in the evenings."

For one dangerous instant she felt terribly sorry for this gentle-mannered woman who had looked after her so well these past few years, felt churlish for not according with her wishes after all the coaching and private tuition Miss Grey had personally given in her own time out of hours. But in the next instant these dangerous feelings passed. She would not be diverted from her course.

"I can only wish you well," Megan Grey sighed heavily, "and hope you're doing the right thing."

"I am, ma'am, I am. I can assure you of that," Karina told her fervently.

After leaving school it had been hard all the way. Later she began to hate every minute, especially staying up to the small hours studying fusty tomes on obscure financial law. But in the end she passed all the exams she needed, and quite a few she didn't, and even then the bank kept saying it wasn't a job for women and she would do far better on the counter. They were talking about her application to jump from teller to her next goal, a trainee dealer on the floor of the trading room. It was only after she had threatened Price Whitney with the Federal Equal Opportunity Board, that they relented and offered her a two-day trial at the terminals.

"But you lose the bank one buck, lady, and you're back in your booth so quick you'll think your pretty little ass never moved," the chief cashier had told her resentfully. He hated the dealers for the money they made, but never found the courage to try himself. Anyway, he knew he didn't have the talent. He would be out of a job in less than a week, exactly the same way she would be – dumb broad.

On the evening of the following day, the pit boss had come on the line and told him not to expect her back. He blanched. She had made the bank a million bucks in just five hours' dealing – a record.

"Lucky!" the chief had blurted out.

"Ain't no such thing as luck in this business, buster," the pit boss told him, and closed the line.

And that was just the beginning. She was the only woman in the dealing room and soon she was better than any of the men. She could key faster, think quicker and seemed to have a seventh sense, anticipating an index shift to the exact minute of the hour of the day, moving in and out of currencies while the men were still flicking their lighters wondering what to do.

"You ever thought of predicting quakes?" a dealer had once asked rancorously. She had smiled a quiet smile in sympathy, but had not replied. She didn't deny him his motivation – it was simple greed. Hers was far more powerful.

Then her plan changed gear. The day arrived that she had been waiting for with cold anticipation, like a panther moving one step closer to its prey.

It was 4.30 on a Friday afternoon, and the ceremony was about to begin. Unlike the men lounging with feigned unconcern, she sat upright at her console, adjusting her skirt, a very slight smile lifting the corner of her lips. The screen over the wall monitor had just cleared down and at any moment it would begin.

"Oh no, not again," someone groaned, as her name came up first upon the list.

Not a muscle twitched on her face. No one expected her to smile – that was not her style – always aloof and always alone. She was an odd one, there was no doubt of that. She was ravishingly lovely in the dark way of part-Cherokee women, but with the stature and slender elegance that came with European blood. When she adjusted her skirt, eyes followed her hands, imagining what it must be like to touch the flesh beneath the taut stretch of the material, wondering, but never finding out, for if she dated, no one knew with whom but certainly no one at the Bank, and not for want of trying. Karina Darielle was something different, that was not in dispute.

The screen was alive again and another name came up. "Geronimo," someone shouted, immediately covering his mouth in embarrassed silence. It was gross to gloat, but sometimes the relief exploded through.

The names kept coming and the breathing was easier now as the successful dealers relaxed and sucked in air. It would be a couple of minutes longer before they would know who was for the drop. Cigarettes were lit and the successful dealers began tidying up and turning off their VDUs as they waited. Some chatter had begun. It always did as the league table dropped through 5,000 dollars, moving down at what seemed a snail's pace. The spectator interest lay at the higher and the lower reaches of the scale.

The chatter tailed off. The last two names on the screen were below 2,500 dollars. It would not be long now.

There was only one this week: 1,862 dollars.

He stood up and, pulling his coat off the back of the chair, shoulders stooping, began the traditional walk to the pit boss's office. Several of his friends gathered round him, offering sympathy, but the rest were on their way to the door, when suddenly all turned round as one.

The man was not alone. Karina Darielle had joined him.

"Hey," Clive Feral shouted at her, jumping from the shadow at the back of the room. "Hey, where the hell d'you think you're going?"

No one moved. Wide-eyed, they watched things happening that had never happened before. The bank's owner and president was rushing down the aisles between the trading consoles towards the pit boss rostrum.

Karina turned. If she was surprised, it didn't show. "I'm quitting," she said simply.

"Quitting?" Clive Feral roared. "The hell you are, you stupid bitch. What d'you think you're at?"

"What do *I* think I'm at?" she repeated, almost distantly. She turned, her lip curling as she went on. "Who *do* you think you are talking to, Mr Feral? I don't like your tone and your manners are a bore. Slavery was abolished by Abraham Lincoln, and *you* may well be the son of a bitch, but I'm not your mother. I'm quitting, and that's final."

This was unbelievable. Clive Feral froze in his stride, disbelief and fury contorting his face. Almost amused, she read his thoughts: Can I afford to lose her? What's she up to? Has some scumbag offered the bitch a better deal behind my back?

Karina knew which way he'd fall. Her whole plan rested on her knowing Clive Feral even better than he knew himself.

"Wait," he said more softly now. "We've got to talk about this. And you," he turned and growled at the gaping dealers, "you all get the hell out of here, d'ya hear? *Get out!*"

They moved in a solid wave. This was not a healthy place to be. Clive Feral was not one to cross when he was in a good humour, and what could happen now was anyone's guess.

That night he had taken her to dinner at Sophie's on 29th Street off Fifth Avenue. It would have been easy to guess he owned the place, had she not already known he did. The head waiter greeted them at the door when they arrived, his smile wide, gold encrusted teeth catching the street glitter with strange mixes of colour. He strode in front of them, clearing the aisle with effusive gestures, shepherding them to their spot in a quiet alcove lit by a gallery of candles. She smiled now for the table was set with a floral composition that could have graced the best of weddings. Someone had passed the message.

"You like pretty things?" Clive asked, sensing her approval.

"Naturally," she said.

"And so do I," he answered. "It's a hobby of mine to collect the exquisite." For the first time she saw him smile. It was the polished exhibition of a man who had learned to charm, and he was studying her with rapturous intent. For an instant she thought he might have recognised her from way back – but that was impossible.

"We have one thing in common then," she returned his smile.

"Only one?" he laughed now, "Look a little deeper, my dear. You may find other things as well."

"Maybe I would. But maybe I don't want to."

"You're still cross over my rudeness today, aren't you?" he nodded. "I understand. It was quite unforgivable. Disgraceful, in fact."

"You're right. We do agree on something else. It was *bloody* disgraceful."

For a second he looked taken aback, then angry. But as quickly the feeling went and suddenly he found he was studying her with new eyes, his motives changing even as he looked at her. It was to have been a re-run of his standard routine – razzle-dazzle the lady with a little high life to begin with, then a lot of low life to follow. But this time it was going to be different. He also had to find out which bank was trying to scoop his top talent, but that would be no problem once he got into the lady's pants. They'd tell you anything once the steam began to rise.

Yes, that had been the original plan, and instinctively he had known it was going to fail.

Also he knew that even as he looked at her something was beginning to churn deep inside his guts, the way it always did when he sensed the first sniff of a challenge.

"Would you like me to apologise?" he asked, his eyes glistening strangely in the flickering light of the candles.

"A good place to start," she said.

"Okay. Please accept my complete apologies. I ask for your forgiveness."

Ask for my forgiveness? she responded silently. My forgiveness? Like hell, you bastard. A livid veil of anger flashed before her eyes, but nothing showed in her face. "Why? D'you think I'm one to bear a grudge?" she asked.

It was an odd question. "No," he told her emphatically.

She smiled. Never had a man been so wrong. Empires had crumbled because of smaller misjudgements. As her smile widened he responded, grinning at her.

She was totally lovely, her dark anthracite eyes suggesting mysterious things bubbling out of sight in the depths of her mind, her full lips moist and sensuous like clear honey freshly spun from the cone. In the dealing room she always wore demure clothes, but tonight she was moulded into a satin number that hugged every line and undulation like a shrink wrapped Barbi Doll. He could imagine the little dimples winking above the cheeks of her ass as she walked.

Yes, she was something else again. It was hard to believe that here was the shrewdest currency dealer in the whole of New York City, and he knew that he had to keep her. No, more than that, he had to have her. Suddenly the yearning was a burning, consuming thing.

"What's this nonsense about you leaving?" He broke the silence. For the first time there was a nervousness in his voice. "You can't be serious. We pay the best rates in the business."

"You *did* pay the best rates in the business."

"You mean you've had a better offer?" He was incredulous.

"Would that surprise you?"

He thought about it. Someone was bound to try and jump him sooner or later. "Maybe." He was suddenly cautious. She was giving nothing away, and for the first time he had the sneaking suspicion she might be winding him up. "Dammit, which bank is it?" he pressed, the smile gone with his patience.

"Who said anything about a bank?"

"Not a bank," he thought out loud. "Not a bank? What son-of-a-bitch organisation is there other than a bank?"

"Does it need to be any organisation?" she responded, annoyance brittle in her eyes. "There's one hell of a lot of wealthy men out there only too happy to have a pretty girl with my qualifications look after their billions. Or hadn't that occurred to you?"

He wasn't certain what she meant, but sure as hell he'd noticed how her breasts heaved out of the top of her dress when she got annoyed. It was in that instant he decided that this little cookie was no way going to leave his stable. Not now, not ever.

In that same instant the second stage of her plan blossomed into fruit.

For Karina Darielle it had been a most interesting Friday, but that was nearly two years ago now, and she pushed these thoughts aside as she prepared to serve his dinner. He would want to get that out of the way quickly, now that he knew there were treats to follow.

She had an unlimited budget to organise these *treats*, as he called them, and in that, as in everything else, she had never once disappointed.

CHAPTER 3

The one good thing to come from the years of fruitless toil and rejection was that the house was never chilly and the domestic water never cold. It was not a lot to salvage from a decade of work but it was all he had left – that, and the cottage, and their two young children. Paul Feral now knew he should never have embarked upon the project, should not have abandoned his lucrative job at the Ministry of Defence with its incremented salary and inflation-proofed pension. But a guiding star had led him forward, a siren light that had drawn him into the quicksands of poverty, hostility and, still worse, sheer ridicule. He had been a fool. He was entirely to blame for the most disastrous, yet strangely exhilarating, years of his life.

He had not expected great public acclaim. Neither had he anticipated considerable wealth from his invention. He did not consider himself a genius, although that was surely what he was. All he wanted was for the world to take advantage of what he offered, exploit his invention if they chose; but instead it had drowned him, sucking him inexorably down into oceans of cynicism, apathy and doubt. Remembering that the same had happened to greater men, to Cockroft, Barnes Wallis and Frank Whittle, did little to comfort him.

And now Tessa, the woman he had married and loved more than life itself, was dead.

They had few friends and were distanced by his preoccupation with his work. After the funeral the few there were had melted away, and he was alone with nothing but his thoughts of her, the two girls, and thoughts of what might so easily have been.

What might have been, he kept saying to himself. What might have been. He must stop thinking about it, must get on

31

with life, get a job, make some money to pay off the massive debts that loomed close at hand. That was what Tessa would want him to do now.

And then another voice would say. One more try. Give it one more try, Paul. You owe it to yourself. That's what Tessa would have *really* wanted you to do. She believed in you, she always believed in you. Don't let her down now. Don't give up.

His eyes were moist, and he went outside leaving the two girls playing on the carpet. For Maria, the seven-year-old, it would take at least a week before the shock sunk in, and for little Annie, not yet five, hopefully a great deal longer.

He went where he always went – there was no other place to go. The focus of his existence for the past ten years was out there in the converted shippen where the old stone walls had been painted an immaculate white and the inside hummed softly like a hive of contented bees. Outside the stonework was partly hidden by rows of heat-exchangers, incongruous flat black panels like auto-radiators, except instead of being hot, they were covered with a rime of condensation that dripped into little puddles on the dry flags.

This was where it had all started. It was here that he had taken two simple theories and combined them into one apocalyptic fact. And no one would believe what he had invented. The industrialists wouldn't buy it because it broke all the rules. The bankers wouldn't back it because they thought it was a fraud. His peers amongst the academics would not accept the principle without all the data, which he would not let them see. The discovery was not yet patented because he could not afford the fees.

Yet it was working and had been for the past two years. From the very first day he turned it on it had performed flawlessly, generating their power, providing their light, giving them warmth. This was their only comfort in a hostile world that seemed atrophied in mind and frozen in convention. It was madness. Here lay the philosopher's stone – a resolution of the energy needs for all mankind – and no one would believe it, no one wanted to know.

He looked across the valley to the little church on the hill where Tessa was buried. For almost half an hour he stood there, his eyes wide and out of focus, no longer seeing the tiny plot with its neat array of brightly coloured flowers. It was as if she was there beside him saying things. One more time, she was telling him. Don't give up Paul, please not now. Just one more time.

"All right, my love," he said aloud. "If that is what you want then that is what it'll be. I'll do it."

"Who are you talking to, Daddy?" Maria had suddenly appeared without a sound in the doorway behind him.

"I was talking to Mummy," he said simply, without embarrassment.

"Oh good," she sighed. "I'm ever so pleased. I dreamt about Mummy too last night. She said she wanted to speak to you. Now she has."

"I have to go out for a little while," he told her. "Just for a little while. I'll be back as soon as I can." He ruffled her golden mop of curls, and his throat tightened again, for she had her mother's hair except her curls were more tightly packed. "Won't be very long," he repeated. "Get yourself ready for bed and I'll come and kiss you goodnight when I get back."

"And tell us a story?"

"Perhaps. But only if it is not too late."

"All right, Daddy," Maria responded, snuggling in close to his hip. "I understand."

That was the trouble: she did understand, too well sometimes, and at those times he felt guilty and ashamed for not being the father he felt he really should have been. The girls would be safe with Tessa's sister Angela for an hour. In moments the car was started and he was gone. He had to get away to think.

The car meandered seemingly of its own accord through the gentle undulations of the chalk Wiltshire hills, until the spire of Salisbury Cathedral rose up as a dark pencil against the scarlet of the early evening sky. He carried on, the shadow growing quickly, expanding in its presence, an awesome sight, the finger of man pointing to the heavens to touch the hand of God. Even if it did no more it proffered a focus for the mind – eleventh century architecture by men thirteen generations dead, yet it still remained unsurpassed, quite unmatched in brilliance in a computer graphic age.

For the first time that day he smiled. Such thoughts were winsome lyricisms but they made him feel better. His spirit lifted as he passed by the ancient walls of the crenellated Close and on into the meadowed lands beyond where the five rivers met; the Nadder, Ebble, Wylye, Bourne and Avon, all drawing together in a filament of tributaries to sustain the valley in a mirror of another age unsullied by modern man. These ancient watermeadows with their soft loam underbelly, did not welcome large, wheeled diesel plant or the bespoiling swathe of huge grain-machines, so the fields stayed small and cattle still roamed the undulating dykes as they had done for centuries past.

He loved these old meadows the same way as Tessa had. They were a place of peace, time out of time, where rare plants still flowered in abundance, and butterflies dappled the air with brilliant colours like early impressionistic art. The air held a richness of its own. It was heavy with the scent of marshland herbs and fruit-tree blossoms from farm orchards near at hand. Later another sweetness would come with the drying of the hay in the pastures, but that would be after the hundred different shades of green of the first spring growths had matured into that uniform dark lushness that marked the height of summer. It was nearing that time now with the grass as thick as a horse's mane, rippling in waves across the fields in the light convecting air.

He did not need to travel much further, turning off into a narrow back-road that led down to Freeman's Mill on the River Avon, the road almost overgrown by the banks on either side, swishing grasses throwing a harvest of seeds through the window; drifts of fluff from dandelion stalks, dancing, then hanging in the air like wraiths upon a ballroom floor.

Here was a dark pool of water where salmon jostled before their final leap up the rush of the weir and where, alongside, a row of hatches hung like wooden teeth in liquid maw, holding back the waters at a higher level to drive the miller's stones and keep irrigated the pastures that flanked the upper reaches of the river.

Before the children were born, he and Tessa had had a favourite spot far upstream where the straightness of the river broke into a series of meandering curves. Here the willows formed a thick, impenetrable barrier to the casual walker, but they had persevered and found a secret place, pressing through the new growth until it suddenly gave way on to a shaded mossy knoll down by the water's edge. It was a natural oasis, quite private and untrodden by man or roving beast, a place where mosses and fine grasses padded the ground and a tapestry of shadows took the heat out of the summer sun. The bed of the river shelved from shallow gravel on the inside of the curve to a cycle of still deep water on the outside, a perfect pool clear of entangling roots, where many times they had swum naked in the balmy days of high summer. It was there, on the bank of the river, in the heat eight years ago, their bodies still wet and slippery from the river, that they made love and Maria was conceived.

After the children were born he and Tessa still went there with their secret thoughts, to walk with the children by the waters, or just sit on the bank watching the perch jostling to clean their scales on the stones downstream of the weir.

Now he sat at the same spot, but alone this time. Yet strangely he did not feel alone.

A movement caught his eye. It was a trout wriggling across the gravel bed of the river, its scales glinting a brief opalescent as it flattened over obstructions in the shallows. Then it was gone, lost in a quieter place in thick weed beneath the further bank. It was a big trout, an old trout, a many times caught and thrown back trout that was river wise enough to ignore the feathered barbs of a dozen fishermen spaced out along the bank. He smiled and watched it go, catching a final glimpse of silver as it bent around a willow stem.

He wished it well. It was alone against the odds, and so was he. There were so many things to do now he was alone with the girls, and he began reflecting on the twists of fate that saw him as he was.

His father, a joiner by trade, was bombed from London at the end of 1942 by a JU 88 shedding its load as it ran for home with two Spitfires on its tail, and with his wife he journeyed to the country like so many other refugees. In Salisbury they found a modest rented home in the old part of the city in the shadow of the spire, and he had managed to eke a living by jobbing for anyone who would give him work. It was hard during the war, and times stayed lean for a long time after that; but the old man had pride, a lot of it, and he did not start a family until he was sure of being able to keep them well clothed and, by bartering his services with other local traders, also quite well fed.

Their first born were the twins, Martin and Clive, then, four years on in the hope of a daughter they tried again, but gained another boy who had already been named Paula, and had to be renamed Paul.

Paul's memories of his elder twin brothers were distinctly mixed. For the most part they ignored his existence, always singular and secretive in a way he could never understand. His own desire to share what little he had was dampened from the start – they gave him nothing, but on occasions demanded much, and without fail he took the blame for any of their misdeeds that found their way to light.

The twins were identical in appearance and, to anyone who did not know them well, were also the same in character. But Paul was different. Although four years younger, he was already fuller in body and stronger in muscle, and with an openness of face that contrasted sharply with the twins who, despite their greater years, were lanky and more sallow in complexion. They lacked that essence of humour that bubbled through Paul's life, keeping to themselves and rarely smiling except in a secretive way, one to the other. For these reasons Paul was popular within his group but Clive and Martin were not, and were treated cautiously by the other children and with some measure of respect since they always contrived to be in funds. They always had money for all the sweets and other cherished goodies, and later they boasted the most sophisticated toys. They were also slightly feared, which was curious since neither twin was ever known to fight or get involved with the rougher side of life. It was just something about them that carried a hint of menace.

At the age of eleven, both twins managed to win a place to the Bishop Wordsworth Grammar School for Boys in Salisbury, a worthy scholastic institution within the Cathedral Close. Paul followed four years later.

He had looked forward to joining them, but his arrival went unremarked. Indeed as far as the twins were concerned, he might not have existed at all. It was not until he was older and they neared school leaving age that he began to find himself in favour, suddenly welcomed by them with warm smiles and loans of rollerskates and camera kit, and the other expensive prizes they seemed able to afford and which he could only long for. In return he was expected to perform mysterious tasks, running errands to people he did not know. It took another year before he discovered the twins' true nature – or so he thought, for like everyone else, he was not sure who had stolen the money from the bursar's office. And it was not until much later, after the twins had left the school, that Paul was able to shake off the stigma of the theft and begin to excel in all he did. Again the difference shone. The twins' school careers had been less than illustrious, unremarked on the roll of honour published every year, and after leaving school Clive and Martin moved from home to go their separate ways.

But Paul had worked on, and played hard as well, passing exams, winning games, running for his house, and later boxing for the school. And he was a popular boy, a joy to his teachers, and a buddy to his chums "An outgoing boy who should go very far", one school report had read, and at first he did go far and fast, with "A" Level passes in Chemistry, Physics and Mathematics, and a place at Cambridge. It was a wrench leaving home but he soon settled in and found new and hard decisions now needed to be taken as his range of talents ripened.

The first big question was whether to accept a place in the Boat Race crew or stick with more academic subjects. Reluctantly he turned down the cox's offer, something quite unknown for any undergrad to do, and much later wondered why, as he looked at the grey and empty space above the hearth where the prize oars would have hung.

These were joyful, exhilarating times when nothing seemed impossible and rarely proved to be so. With a First Class Honours in Physics and another in Mathematics, the Ministry of Defence snapped him up with almost indecent haste, and his final turn of luck was finding Tessa.

For the first two years before their first child was born, she lectured on Ancient History at the local polytechnic, while he worked at the MOD Airborne Weapons Research Establishment at RAF Boscombe Down. They were deliriously happy together, soul mates in every way but one: the only discordant point between them was his involvement with the technologies of war.

"Darling, please, *please*, can't you think of something else to do? I hate the thought of all your talents going into things of destruction," she had said.

He had heard her say this many times before, but never as fervently as this. "But there is not a lot of other work round here for someone with my qualifications," he responded lamely.

"Can't you work for yourself?"

"Doing what?"

"Why not develop that energy machine you have spoken of so many times?"

"But that's very speculative. The theory's okay, but it has never been made to work in practice."

"But surely," Tessa persisted, "surely *you* can make it work?"

"And what do we live on while I find out I've been wrong?" he asked.

"But you're not wrong, I'm positive of it. And we'll manage somehow."

She was right. She was always right. The TEESER machine did work, and they managed to get by, after a fashion, until she became ill.

He had first noticed the disease as a slight paling of her complexion. He had thought it was the long, dark winter evenings taking their toll, but then there came the unnatural lethargy in all her movements, and she slept a lot at times when she would normally have been filled with vigour. The leukaemia was diagnosed soon after and she died still believing in what he did and urging him on, ignoring the poverty it thrust upon them.

And now, alone on the riverbank, he was not alone somehow. But now what was he to do?

Clive and Martin, he wondered. Was it not just possible they might help? He knew they were both now very wealthy, but he had not seen them for some years, and neither had acknowledged the wedding invitation of his.

Suddenly he shivered. The raw heat of the sun had now gone from the air, and it was almost dark, the trees' skeletal shadows against the deep red of the western sky. He decided he must leave.

When he arrived home Tessa's sister Angela was preparing coffee in the kitchen. "Hi Paul," she called through. "You okay? I was a bit worried about you."

"Fine," he told her, trying to put conviction into his voice. Angela was older than Tessa, a plain, down-to-earth woman of a very giving nature. She had no children of her own and since her husband left her she frequently stayed with them and was always welcome because the children were so fond of her. Now she had become a necessity.

"Maria is still awake. She said you promised to kiss her goodnight."

"That's right, I did," he said, making for the stairs.

"You want a coffee?"

"In a minute, when I come down again."

"Okay."

He saw Maria's eyes glinting wide in the dark. She was wide awake, but he didn't turn the light on. "You should be asleep," he told her with mock severity, "or you'll be too tired for school tomorrow."

"No, I won't," she responded firmly and he heard an echo of her mother there in the little piping voice. "Anyway, you promised me a story."

"No, I didn't. I promised to come and kiss you goodnight. The story was a maybe if it wasn't too late."

"I want a story."

"And then you'll go to sleep?" he began to weaken.

"Yes, Daddy darling."

He breathed in deeply and sighed as he pulled her favourite Enid Blyton from the bookcase. "And you jolly well better!"

CHAPTER 4

The evening air coming up from the roofs of Casablanca was hot and fetid, defeating even the hotel's elaborate air-conditioning systems, everything suffused with a cloying stickiness that soiled his clothes and sapped Martin's body of its energy. Despite the fast-approaching dusk, the sun still bore down with a baleful intent, until quite suddenly it dropped behind the enormous thunderheads that had been building out at sea.

The storm had been raging off the coast for most of the afternoon, the ragged tops of the cumulo nimbus clouds like sugary confections on the far horizon, pretty and quite remote, until the sun suddenly doused, leaving them darker and more menacing, only a vestigial pink halo over the billows to remind of the brilliance of bare minutes before. Everything beneath the clouds was now totally black, the ugly black of a mamba snake, the faint blips of lightning clearer and more frequent now as if the system was sucking new energy for its assault upon the land. Martin Feral could see that it was no longer stationary, the tumult moving subtly closer, and for him it brought the first tingle of apprehension.

The feeling that all was not well had been building all day. It was not something he could put his finger on, but there was a definite pervasive aura of malevolence in the air. It's that damn storm out there, he told himself nervously. Violent electrical storms always had a bad effect on him and he dreaded their coming with unnatural fear.

"Run my bath, will you," he shouted gruffly to the two young black boys lounging on cushions strewn in contrived abandon around the room.

Boys and young men were always to be found near Martin. He liked it that way – in fact it was the only way he did like

40

it, and he never begrudged the quite astonishing cost of the presents he bought for them. It ensured that his lovers were always the very best, and more than that, clean.

"You want to make love during the ablutions, Sahib?" one boy asked quaintly, standing up.

"Not tonight," Martin waved him aside. "No, not tonight." For some reason he was not in the mood.

The boy looked at first startled, then worried. "Is everything all right, Mister Martin? We have done nothing wrong, have we? We would not want to do that." It was the truth. They could earn more here in a single night than their whole family might expect to make in a full month's trading down in the bazaar.

"No, no," he said irritably. "I'm just too exhausted. You are both dismissed for the evening."

After they had gone he went through to bathe. The bathing room was a place designed for the exquisite pleasures of the flesh, at its centre a large sunken pool carved from a single block of marble, its sides scalloped like the petals of a flower, each with its own seat just below the water so that bathers could sit back and relax between bouts of more energetic activity. Tonight he rested alone among the effusion of suds pouring from the hidden jets. He felt no exhilaration.

After a quick rub down he drew on his kaftan and returned to the summer lounge, and there he stood and stared. The whole window was crazed with a violent tapestry of lightning shards that crossed and re-crossed the sky, and the noise was immense. The storm had rushed in from the ocean with incredible speed and even as he watched a bolt hit a sub-station, blowing it in a frenzy of blue fire. All lights were instantly doused, nothing there now but a sea of empty blackness where the city had sparkled bright and alive only seconds before.

The rate of the discharges seemed to accelerate, strobing the sky like a plasma gun, some strikes dancing on the water beyond the harbour mouth, others exploding the minarettes and spires of the city into a million crumbling bits. Each time for the barest instant everything was there once more, the blue-white fire picking everything out in stark relief before it was gone again, the blackness even deeper as the eyes recoiled in outrage from the assault. It was several minutes before the hotel emergency generators took over and the lights came on again.

Then the rains began. The first fat drops were almost kindly, dispelling the heat and slanting in to mush against the glass and stir up little puddles of dust on the balcony. Then the full weight of the storm hit with a sudden tumultuous violence, the rain becoming hail, changing angle as the wind rose, beating the windows like pellets from a scatter gun, tearing the leaves off the ornamental shrubs.

Martin was superstitious. This was definitely an omen.

He held back from the window, in fear and awe of the storm as its eye moved in inexorably upon the city. Suddenly he was conscious of the great height of his apartment, sticking like a needle into the very epicentre of the cataclysm. In that moment the lightning struck the thing that pricked its heart.

Part of the discharge reached the television set, exploding it into myriad pieces on the tiger rug. However, the full weight of the strike was drawn by the railings on the balcony. With nowhere to go the arc cleaved through the stonework like a mason's shear until it reached the metal reinforcement of the building and drained safely down to earth. Martin choked. Barely half an hour before he had been standing on the pretty, terraced balcony. Now there was nothing there but a gut churning void: two hundred feet of black and empty air between him and the mess of debris at the foot of the building.

"No, no, no," he warbled incoherently, as if the emptiness would reach up and clutch him from his perch. He spun back, rushing to the bathroom where his guts gave vent. He almost did not hear the soft ring of the telephone above the roar of the storm.

"Yes?" he shouted above the noise.

"Good evening, Mister Feral," a man's voice said softly. "I am so glad to find you in."

"Who's that?" he snapped. Very few people had this private number.

The question was not answered. Instead the voice went on, "It has been too long – far too long since I've had the pleasure of your company, and I shall enjoy having a little talk with you this evening."

"You will?" Martin coughed. He now knew exactly who it was. It was Sheik Khalid Mohammed Abdul Nadir, Minister of State for the Interior. Martin's spirits sunk a little further still.

Khalid Nadir was the one person in Morocco he truly feared. As Minister for the Interior, Khalid Nadir controlled the Secret Police, which would have been an advantage had not Martin made the fundamental error of sodomising the

42

sheik's eldest son many years before. It had not mattered then, for that was before the sheik's meteoric rise into the highest strata of Moroccan politics.

Neither then, nor later, did the sheik ever raise issue over the affair. Words were never spoken. They didn't need to be. Khalid Nadir's eyes said more than any language could express, and Martin knew exactly what would happen if the sheik ever had his way. It was not a comforting thought, and now the man was coming here, on a night like this. Martin's hand slipped down to his testicles, and drew consolation from their lingering attachment.

The storm was still in full fury when the sheik stepped from the lift. Martin was there to greet him, dressed soberly now, disguising his apprehension behind a wide ingratiating smile. "My dear Khalid, how wonderful to see you. This is such a great and welcome surprise."

The sheik's smile was no less generous. "Indeed, indeed it is, dear Mister Feral. It has been too long – much too long." His hand extended briefly and they shook. Martin noticed how quickly it returned to the pummel of the short stabbing dagger he kept in the belt of his robes.

"Drink?" Martin invited. He knew that contrary to the customs of his faith, the sheik would always accept a good malt whisky on a generous bed of ice.

"Thank you."

He poured an ample measure, then one for himself, hoping Khalid Nadir would keep talking while his back was turned, but there was not a sound from behind. When he faced round again he jumped, for the sheik was right behind him, his lips curled back, the smile as warm and as generous as before. But it was the eyes that unnerved Martin: they were ice-cold eyes, sparkling with the brittle quality of flawed agate in the dim light. The man was somehow able to move without a sound, giving not even a rustle from his robes.

"And to what do I owe this great honour?" he asked, waving the sheik to a bed of cushions in the alcove.

The sheik held his glass up to the light, studying the amber liquid for a long moment before replying. "I am here to congratulate you on the remarkable performance of your companies over the past few years, dear friend. Their growth from almost nothing into institutions in the big time can only be a reflection of your personal genius."

"How very kind of you," Martin's pulse stayed fast.

"Kind? No, not kind. We are always concerned for the

financial and general well being of *visitors* to our country, as you well know from your own experience."

"Yes, indeed," Martin agreed eagerly.

"We like our *guests* to do well. It is in the nature of the Moroccan to welcome visitors to our humble country, irrespective of whether they are of our colour or creed. We are naturally a very hospitable people."

"As indeed you are. Yes indeed," agreed Martin quickly. "The most magnanimous nation in the whole of Africa." He noted how the sheik stressed the words, *guests* and *visitors*, giving them an ominous ring.

"In fact I would go as far to say that you have been more successful at generating revenue than any other single company in our state, or for that matter the government itself."

"Oh, what nonsense," Martin laughed now, but with the sneaking suspicion that it might just possibly be true. Things had been going exceedingly well, especially since he had bought a controlling interest in the country's phosphate mines, the principal earner of foreign exchange.

"I don't like my statements to be called nonsense," the sheik came back casually.

Martin looked at him hard. It was just a little too casual.

"I'm sorry, I didn't mean it like that." It was the first edge that had crept into their conversation and his nervousness increased.

"Neither do we, as a nation, like to feel that our hospitality is being exploited, Mister Feral. We don't like to think we are considered fools – the purveyors of nonsense – here to be drained of our resources and sucked dry by any international opportunist who cares to drop by thinking he is onto, as you say, a soft option." The casualness had entirely gone now, the words were spoken with an edge of venom.

"You surely don't think—"

"—that you are one of those?" the Sheik stopped him. "I surely don't think anything. I *know*, Mister Feral, because it is my business to know."

"But—"

"Yes?"

"But this is ridiculous. Sure, I make a profit, but then I employ two thousand people across the spectrum of my companies."

"Two thousand people in a nation of twenty million, Mister Feral? Hardly a riveting proportion, would you say?"

44

"Have you looked at the invisible earnings in foreign exchange my companies bring in?" Martin defended himself swiftly.

"Yes, indeed. And I have also looked at the profits you skim from your companies and re-route directly to your accounts in Geneva, Lichtenstein and Panama."

"There is not one single exchange control regulation which that infringes."

"Indeed there isn't. All we have is Article 961 of our Constitution which states that any person, or organisation, sapping or diverting the wealth of the economy to the detriment of our peoples is guilty of treason and all their property shall automatically be confiscated by the state, and the person shall be detained in His Majesty's Prison at Rabat during the course of His Majesty's Pleasure."

At another time Martin would have been amused by the curiously English syntax of the sheik's speech, the reflection of an expensive education that ran through Eton and on to Oxford. But Martin was not amused, for "His Majesty, the King of Morocco's pleasure" had been known to extend a lifetime, in the most squalid conditions imaginable. "You can't mean me!" he said softly.

"Most definitely I do, dear Mister Feral," said Khalid, the smile broadening. "You pose a very serious threat to our country and, if you will permit me, to the integrity of every boy child in the land."

The gloves were off now. There was no longer any pretence. What they both knew was now articulated, in the open. "You won't get away with it," Martin spat, for an instant fury overtaking his fear.

"Get away with what?" Khalid looked puzzled, adjusting his robes about his ankles, his other hand still on his dagger.

"Stealing all my possessions."

"Stealing all your possessions?" Khalid looked first annoyed, then contemptuous. "Moroccans never steal anything, Mister Feral, unlike some Englishmen. My country is, in fact, willing to give you a very great deal in addition to what you already have."

"Give?" Martin choked incomprehensively.

"Indeed yes."

"You're mad," spat Martin suddenly. "There is some trickery here, some trap." Subtly he was now moving towards the escritoire in which he kept his gun. "You're jealous of my success. You either want me to buy you off, or you intend taking everything I have."

Khalid laughed now. "Come now, Mister Feral. You are over-reacting. Some day I think your mind will go as soft as the young boys' bottoms you love so much. But I am afraid your choice is rather limited. You either stand trial as a traitor, or reinvest your vast wealth in a way that is more beneficial to the interests of our country."

"Oh yes?" Martin glowered at him. He had a feeling that something like this would happen one day. What he needed now was to buy a little time. "Tell me more."

"It is as simple as this. As you know, our country is almost entirely dependent for its wealth on phosphates, iron ore, fishing and tourism. We do make a little out of lead and manganese, and a very small amount out of oil. It is the underexploitation of our oil resources which is of greatest concern to us."

"What oil resources?" Martin blurted out. There was a very poor prognosis for any significant oil discovery, the whole country being dominated by the towering chain of the Atlas Mountains.

"Ah," The sheik's smile widened so his gold teeth sparkled eerily in the lightning flashes. "That is for us to guess and you to find out."

"*Me* to find out?"

"As of now you are in the oil business. You are going to liquidate your existing assets in Morocco, and with the proceeds, together with the two billion dollars you have deposited abroad, you are going to invest in developing our oil industry to its full potential. In return the Moroccan government is going to lease you, free of any charge for fifteen years, 10,000 square miles of prime virgin territory ripe for exploration."

Virgin was probably the exactly right word, Martin thought in panic. His guess was that there would be absolutely nothing there except a bottomless pit for his money. "And if I don't accept?"

"Only an enemy of the state would decline such a generous offer."

"Enemy of the state, eh?" he mused aloud, his fingers tightening round the gun.

"And I would throw that pea-shooter away," the sheik told him through a silky smile. "I can catch bullets from one of those between my teeth."

CHAPTER 5

It was good to get in off the street. Clive Feral was never completely at ease with the brash zest of the New Yorker, especially in the lower reaches of the city, where ebullience was mercurial and could change in an instant to mean, pernicious violence. A knife would flash and blood would flow, the sirens wail, and the man behind the computer terminal would update his statistics. Yes, life was ephemera – one life equalled one key-stroke with the index finger that caused barely a flicker on the screen.

Walking into the Price Whitney Bank was like returning to the womb. There was something reassuring about the austere marbled hall with its columns and balustrades, and the soft echo of voices as the tellers conducted business with mute efficiency. And it was cool in there, the air drained of the fetid August heat which could soil his shirt before the hour of noon. Yes, he considered. Buying the Price Whitney Bank was about the best thing I ever did.

No one looked up but they all knew he was back. The security guards stiffened and the tellers perked, and for an instant the video camera paused in its traverse, and he was pleased about that for it showed the duty controller was on station at his monitors.

At the end of the trading hall were three elevators. Two were public utilities operated by the usual button-paging. The third was different, slightly smaller, and only accessed by a special magnetic keying card that fitted a slot in the wall. It was also the only lift that ran all the way to the fiftieth floor where he had a private penthouse suite. Today he used the public lift, stopping at the twelfth level. His pulse quickened as it always did when he stepped out on the floor.

This was not just the heart of the building, it was his own

heart as well. This was the dealing room. Here was where his bank traded a hundred million dollars on a bad day and a billion on a good one, gambling in rates of exchange in a dozen different currencies around the world. Except that the banks never called it gambling: "strategic deployment of negotiable liquidity" was the cosmetic buzz expression.

The computer terminals were set in rows, rather like desks in a college classroom, and were manned by young men, none older than twenty-eight. But that was where the similarity ended. Their faces bore none of the carelessness of youth, no laughter lines or bright sparkle of irreverence. They were old in everything but years, tight of lip and grey in face, their hands nervously fidgeting as screens piped news from around the world. It was the only floor in the building where smoking was allowed, and the air hung heavy with a yellow fug from first call in the morning until the market closed and the cleaners threw wide the windows and withdrew again until the air had cleared. You could always tell a dealer from the yellow hands, chewed fingers and eyes that constantly flicked like a cybernetic doll.

They were also the highest paid of any bank employees in the whole of the United States – the cream of the new generation, poached with utter ruthlessness and golden hellos from wherever their talent could be found. Several of the biggest banks had suddenly discovered their dealing rooms embarrassingly and dangerously denuded of their best traders by the seductive overtures of Price Whitney. Even after the mini crash of October 1987 and the dark months that followed, Price Whitney was still in there bidding.

They lived and died for their work, pitting their wits in eerie electronic duels against silent faceless enemies in a thousand other dealing rooms across the world – from New York to London, Paris to Zurich, Hong Kong to Sydney. The Price Whitney men working the wires were the very best – they had to be. The empty chairs said so.

In every way they were different from other bank employees apart from being paid weekly, instead of once a month. This always took place on a Friday at 4.30 – and today was Friday and the time was 4.30. The ceremony was about to begin.

It was Clive's custom to be there early for the ritual. Already the adrenaline was pumping, a static charge building like the prelude to a lightning strike. In some ways he enjoyed this more than the illegal cock fights and bare-knuckle boxing matches he attended in the backwoods of New Jersey. On the

48

far wall of the dealing room the master VDU was scrolling the last of the day's prices still coming off the computer. Every eye was on it and there was a sudden silence in the room. In a moment it would clear, and the weekly roll of honour would unfold.

And that was another difference about being a dealer. They each knew what the other earned, for they were all on a basic of a thousand dollars a week and they were expected to make at least another 2,000 dollars in commission on their profits. That was the red line, and it was nicknamed the rope. And this was the hour of execution.

"Place your bets," someone laughed nervously.

The laughter didn't catch. Hands reached for cigarettes as the dealers sat back from their screens and pretended to relax. No one was fooled. You could think you'd done well, or think you'd done badly, but you could never know for sure, because you never knew how well the other guys had done. The whole thing was presented as a league table – that was the bastard.

It wouldn't be long now. Zadok Perret the floor manager, or pit boss, as he was called, had taken his seat behind his desk, the only station in the room that faced the wrong way, slightly elevated so he could watch the trading and spot the first signs of any aberrations. After last year, when a dealer went bananas and took the fast way down through the window, all the glass had been changed to polycarbonate.

"Quiet please, gentlemen," the pit boss said.

He always asked for quiet at that moment, which was pretty stupid because there was never a sound in the room. There was a flicker as the first line began to print up. The process was slow because the computer was doing the calculations in real time, analysing the week's transactions, apportioning profit and loss to each dealer, and then working out their salary plus commission.

"Wow, look at that," a roar suddenly broke the silence. "Spitz has really hit the jackpot. Ten Gs in his pocket this week. Keep that up for a year, Spitzy, and that's half a million bucks."

Spitzy didn't answer but his grin told all. He was one of the youngest in the team at only twenty-two and there was still something youthful about the way he cocked his head.

A hush fell again. A new line was painting up. "Hey that's not so bad either, Grizaffi," someone called. "Eight nice little Gs in *your* pocket. Your lady will really love you this week – if you've got the energy!"

49

There was brief laughter at the joke, pitched very high and very nervous. But they all knew what he meant. Working the markets all day left not a lot for the little lady back home at night and the divorce rate ran at nearly 80 per cent over five years – if a dealer lasted five years.

Relentlessly the computer added a new name to the screen, and the dealer gave a sigh of relief, before there was another deathly pause, almost as if the machine had been programmed with a sadistic desire to tease. Someone had once asked why the listings weren't screened later after all the calculations had been done. There was no answer, and no one had asked again.

Twenty names were now up on the display and the incomes had dropped through 5,000 dollars and were closing down to four. They were into the lower earners now and it was noticeable it was the older men still waiting for their names to appear. Those who had been drawn, were chirruping like starlings in their roost, such was their relief.

The commissions ran on, and now an awful silence descended on the room. They were into casualty time. This was the moment careers would end. Once you were below 2,000 dollars you were out of the dealing room, and you never made it back. The trick was to hang in there as long as possible.

Clive stood watching all of this, a slight sweat jewelling his brow despite the chill of the air-conditioning. If anyone had looked they would have seen the stiffness outlined in his pants. But no one turned. All eyes were on the screen.

There were two more lines to print. John Sheriton came in at 1,980 dollars and Paul Bryant at 1,720 dollars.

They were already on their feet, stony faced. They knew the routine. The pit boss would call them into his office and they would be given their papers and a 5,000 dollar goodbye – half that week's earnings for the new team leader. They would never work again, at least not in banking. Failed currency dealers were the untouchables. They had learned to live with money – a lot of it, the banks and their own – and they couldn't survive on a teller's wages – and that's where the trouble would usually begin.

High above, Karina Darielle observed the scene on the penthouse monitor. If she was moved by what she saw, it did not show, her face bland and expressionless, her flawless skin tight over high cheekbones that still showed the aloofness and arrogance of her distant Indian stock. Her hair was the blue-black of a raven's plumage, and her eyes sparkled with a dark fire even in the subdued lighting of the room.

She saw Clive Feral at the back of the dealing floor and frowned. She shared the view of the checkout girl down in Maybee's Drug Store – Clive Feral was a bastard, rotten through and through. She knew. She too had sweated out there among the men, juggling the rates until the numbers gagged her mind, and she was the best of all of them until that final Friday when she suddenly quit the floor, never to return.

She shifted her position slightly on the stool, the silk bath robe falling open. If she was aware of her near nakedness, she did not show it, her attention wholly on the computer terminal in front of her. It was identical to those in the dealing room below, and after a brief glance at the security monitor to make sure Clive was still lingering at the execution, her fingers continued to beat a rhapsody on the keys. The screen cleared and scrolled and cleared again, and for a moment she hesitated as if mulling some weighty decision. Then after a final deft stroke she sat back, and moments later the words TRANSACTION COMPLETED came up in green letters and the cursor returned to the passive position at the top of the screen. She had just increased her personal fortune by 100,000 dollars.

The timing was good. He had just left the dealing room and would be on his way on up to the suite. She turned the key in the computer's security lock and the machine instantly went dead. She withdrew the key and pushed it into a groove under the shelf and went over to the mirror to begin her composure.

The transformation was a miracle of facial engineering. By rubbing the skin and flexing the muscles she managed to soften the hard angles. She worked on her mouth, stretching her lips so the teeth bared in a wide inviting smile that would melt any man's heart. But the hardest thing of all was the eyes. They were always the problem, yet somehow she managed to moderate the brittle loathing into a kind of misty loveliness. She was ready exactly as the door opened.

"Darling, you're home!" she purred. "This is wonderful. I wasn't expecting you so soon. You must be tired. Can I get you anything?"

His hand cupped a breast, massaging a nipple between thumb and finger. "Yeah honey, a bourbon will do for starters. Then a meal. And then what you got for finishers?"

She breathed a little faster and pushed in against him and he squeezed, enjoying the slight hint of pain on her face.

51

"Darling, you do that so exquisitely," she murmured. "Do it again harder please, but later."

"Later?" he quizzed. "You got something special organised?"

"Wait and see," she teased. He was referring to his treats.

He nodded and let her go. "Going to be good, eh?"

"Uh huh. Very!" she told him, moving through to the kitchen. Oh yes, they would be good. They cost enough. The smile faded from her face as she took the dinner from the oven. Like her they gave of their very best because it suited them – them for the money, her for something else entirely.

"Hell honey, I'm hungry," she heard him call from the lounge. "What you got for me, huh?"

"Something I know you'll like," she shouted back. It was true. She went to evening classes especially to learn how to cook well to please Clive Feral. "Tonight for you it is Karina's Chicken Supreme."

"Great. Roll it in. I'm eating air."

They ate silently through the meal until coffee when she said, "Execution day today, was it?"

"Yep. A good hanging always gives me an appetite."

"How many?"

"Just two."

"Young, or old-stagers?"

"Stagers, both of them. Well over the hill. Been with us over five years, too long."

She smiled as he began to talk again, marvelling at the lack of compassion for his staff – men who had been his friends, men who had given their all for Price Whitney, but men who, at the hands of time, had committed the sufferance of growing slower and needing longer to measure the quality of their work. Men of only twenty-eight.

"I understand, my love." The bastard, she repeated to herself. She caught the keys to the terminal he had just thrown her. "Thank you, my darling," she smiled sweetly, turning the security lock. "What figures would you like first?"

"Just the bottom line for today. We can go over the full breakdown in the morning."

"Okay, honey," she said.

In an instant the display came alive again as her fingers worked, jumbles of figures scrolling up and down the screen, pi-charts and graphs coming and going, until a single figure held there steady in the soft green lettering.

"450,000 dollars," he read over her shoulder. "Hey that's not so good."

"No," she agreed with a shrug.

"Since you left the dealing room, honey, the heat's been off the guys. Our profit's down thirty million bucks on the same quarter last year – that's just how much you're costing me."

"Nonsense," she said. "D'you want to see anything else, or can I turn it off?"

"Turn the mother-fucker off," he growled, using the vernacular of his adopted tongue. "Hell, I don't know why you won't do just a few hours now and then, just to keep your hand in and keep them on their toes. You're just about the most beautiful, most crazy woman I've ever met. Sure as heck, sometimes I just don't understand you. Sure you won't change your mind?"

"About going back down there? Never. For one thing I can't stand your creepy pit boss, Zadok Perret."

"Old Zady!" he looked genuinely surprised. "I never knew you had a thing about him! I'll fire him if it'll make you any happier. You can be the new controller. Hey, that's a brilliant idea – you the new pit boss. What d'you think?"

"A lousy idea. Anyway I thought Zadok Perret was a great buddy of yours?"

"Not when he's losing the bank thirty million bucks a quarter."

"But you don't know that. How can you be so sure? Trading has been generally difficult this year for everyone."

"No," Clive dismissed. "It needs *you* down there."

"Well, I'm not going, and that's final," she told him emphatically.

He looked at her, anger kindling in him, but as quickly it subsided. She had probably gone off the boil anyway – dealers did. They needed to trade regularly to stay on top of the markets, and she had been out of the scene many months now. No, perhaps he was not losing so much after all. But at least he had stopped her working for anyone else, and she was still his, the most beautiful woman on the whole of the East Side. Maybe he'd feel differently about her eventually. He usually did.

"Here you are, stud," she locked off the machine and threw him back the keys. "Keep cool."

"I will," he said, just as the paging buzzer rang at his side. He pressed a button beneath the table edge and a wall panel slid aside, revealing the security monitor flickering with a picture of the sidewalk far below. Two women stood there.

"That them?" he asked.

"Yes," she nodded.

He keyed the remote release on the street elevator and moments later they appeared in the lobby. Karina studied them like a quality control expert on a microchip line. They were the best, or at least the best that money could buy.

Clive viewed them differently. Both girls were voluptuous, young and substantially covered – the meaty variety that he liked so much – and might have just stepped out of one of the Broadway shows. But there was a difference between them and the glossy showgirls, an underlying hardness in their faces that belied their tender years, and the shorter one with the blonde hair had a bruise below her left eye that her make-up could not hide.

"Evening, chicks," Clive addressed them. "You in good form?"

"I am," the taller of the two responded, the fire in her eyes matching the red of her hair. "But I don't know about that old scrag bag," she sneered contemptuously at her companion.

"You want to start it now," the other girl responded furiously, her eyes splintered glass as her knuckles bunched.

"Hold it, girls," Karina hastily intervened. It would take them less than twenty seconds to break the place apart. "You can go in there to change while we set up," she pointed to a bedroom.

"Where's it to be?" the first one asked eagerly.

"In here," Clive told them, his hand touching another button on the control console.

For an instant both girls stood staring in bewilderment, all animosity lost. A loud hum was coming from somewhere, and everything had begun to move, the couch, the tall lamps, the table and the chairs, the raised lounging dais, everything was sliding away towards the wall, and now they looked up and stepped back. Above them a twelve foot square of the ceiling had begun to drop, lowering slowly like an aircraft carrier deck.

"Jeez, some fancy pad you got here, buster," one girl muttered as she figured what was happening. "It'll be a pleasure to slaughter the bitch in that."

The ceiling was now well down, the wrestling ring suspended on four wires, one to each corner post. With a slight thud, it bottomed, and in that instant the main lighting of the room

54

dimmed and a stark white glare poured out of the cavity that had been left in the ceiling.

"Well, girls, what're you waiting for?" said Clive, a slight quaver in his voice. "Get yourself ready. I want to see some real action."

This time they did not need any bidding, disappearing into the bedroom with their Adidas bags.

"You sure this won't be fixed?" he asked Karina after the door had closed.

"No," she answered. "They're both from different agencies. I also found out they've got a personal grudge going over some guy, so you can expect the sparks to fly."

"Excellent," he purred. "Just excellent."

Karina noticed saliva appearing at the corner of his mouth.

"They've seen the contract," she told him, taking care to hide her disgust. "They know the deal. Ten rounds in the nude. All in rules – two submissions or a knock-out to decide the winner. The purse is set at 2,000 bucks, split 500 hundred to the loser and 1,500 to the winner."

"Fine," he said, just as the door opened, and the girls reappeared.

This time they both wore elaborate silk wrestling cloaks and no shoes, and both had freed their hair to hang lose, swishing about their shoulders, as they climbed into the ring.

"I'll keep time and referee," Clive told them, taking a small brass bell from a cupboard in the wall. "You know the rules. Make it a good fight."

"Yeah, we know the rules," the red-head sneered. "The only rule is there are no rules. I hope you're going to have fun watchin', mister, because sure as hell I'm going to bust that bitch wide open."

"The hell you are," the other wrestler sneered. "Hit that bell, fella. I'm ready for the action. And forget the rounds. When I get going on this dyke I just ain't goin' to stop."

"Okay girls, give me your gear."

Almost as if he was no longer there, they dropped their cloaks from their shoulders and threw them over the ropes. They wore nothing underneath, only a thin coating of oil applied to their skins, so that their bodies glistened like naked voo-doo dancers beneath the harsh glare of the lights.

Clive hit the bell and instantly they went into the crouch, circling each other, arms out, fingers splayed, their breasts jiggling delightfully as they crabbed, every muscle tense, mobile sculptures of coiled hatred. Clive smiled. The blonde was peroxide. Her pubes were as black as tallow soot.

The red-head moved first, kicking her oppponent in the stomach and grabbing her head as she doubled. The blonde braced and countered, screwing out of the hold and spinning the red-head on to the canvas with a neat Irish whip. In an instant the red-head was on her feet again.

"Bitch," she screamed, flying back into the attack. This time she grabbed the blonde's hair, and brought her head down as her knee came up. There was a nasty sound of fibre tearing and the blonde flew backwards before crumpling on the floor.

For a moment she lay quite still as the red-head panted over her, then with a sudden movement the blonde grabbed her leg and sprang to her feet. The red-head was caught unprepared, and hopped awkwardly on one foot as the other girl lifted the shin higher and higher, until her balance broke and she toppled over.

"Got you, you bitch," the blonde hissed through the trickle of blood running down her lip.

"No, no," the red-head squealed.

"Yes, yes," the blonde spat gleefully, as, holding the leg to her breasts, she stood on the red-head's foot and fell gently backwards on to the canvas.

The red-head's screams were awesome, rending the silence of the night far beyond the windows of the room as her legs were torn apart at an impossible angle, and in a vain attempt at modesty her hand flew to her crotch, but the blonde grabbed her fingers and snapped them back against the joint. "Don't hide your little cherry, dyke," she sneered. "That's what he's paid to see."

This was the moment Karina had been waiting for. His attention was totally absorbed with the grappling, naked women and she quietly slipped out of the room.

His briefcase was where he always left it in his study next to the suite, and she eased open the catches and began to rifle through the sheets of documentation. Mostly it was memoranda, company executives whingeing about this and that, and she quickly moved on until something finally caught her eye.

It was a single Xeroxed sheet his secretary had slipped into his pile. 'URGENT. Think you should know about this,' she had written in red felt tip on the top.

Instantly Karina pulled it out of the pile. It was a photocopy from one of the glossy brochures real-estate brokers push out

56

when they have a hot property on their hands. Diagonally across the middle had been stamped – STRICTLY CONFIDENTIAL DRAFT ONLY NOT FOR RELEASE UNTIL MONDAY 9TH SEPTEMBER'.

Karina smiled – the 9th was exactly one week from now.

Clive had generous payola arrangements with juniors in all the major real-estate offices on the East Side, an expedient which paid handsomely since it gave him first sniff at everything before it came on the market. This time the prize peddled was the Hartman Building off 32nd Street, nothing special on its own account – the usual half-billion-dollar lot, except it was between the Drivers Business Complex and the Price Whitney Futures Exchange, both of which he already owned. The Hartman Building was the only break in the continuity of his holdings, and old man Hartman's stubborn refusal to sell the lot was screwing up redevelopment of the whole site. The old boy had never liked Clive Feral. Always could smell a wrong'un, he used to say, as loudly as possible, to anyone who would listen, and Clive was delighted when he heard Hartman had only weeks to live. Now the prize would be his for the plucking. 'Okay. Go for it!' were his scribbled instructions to his secretary under her neatly written hand.

Karina was no longer smiling. Her eyes were scanning the small print like a laser reader. The screams and thumps were coming with increasing loudness from the next room and it could end at any moment now.

She slipped the photocopies back into the pile, still thinking, and was about to shut the case when something else caught her eye. It was a short telex message from England, dated several weeks earlier.

DEAR CLIVE
IT IS WITH THE DEEPEST REGRET THAT I HAVE TO TELL YOU THAT MY WIFE TESSA HAS JUST PASSED AWAY THE FUNERAL IS IN TWO DAYS TIME AND I WOULD WEL-COME IT GREATLY IF YOU COULD POSSIBLY FIND TIME TO COME
YOUR BROTHER
PAUL

Karina's eyes narrowed, the fire there again. Across the sad message had been rubber stamped in bright red the words 'Bullshit, No Action'.

Clive did not go to the funeral. In fact he did not give the matter another thought, and was all the more irritated to get a further telex from his brother:

DEAR CLIVE
ARRIVING 12 NOON YOUR TIME WEDNESDAY WILL FIND
MY WAY TO YOUR ADDRESS LOOK FORWARD TO SEEING
YOU AGAIN AFTER SO LONG PAUL.

Coming here? The hell he is. Clive had glowered at the
typed message.

Clive's attitude to his younger brother was the same as
his attitude to everything else he considered superfluous.
He hadn't seen Paul since they were at school, although a
card would arrive regularly from England each Christmas.
The gesture went unreciprocated. He felt no curiosity as to
how the years might have treated his own blood, and it was
damned inconvenient him arriving uninvited when the end of
the quarter's trading was just days away. He had to get rid of
him as quickly as possible.

Paul's memories of Clive were mixed. Both twins had
gone on to do great things in life. Paul did not know the
details, but their business deals frequently filtered through to
the press, and he read of their wealth with admiration and not
a little envy. Why had he got it so wrong, and they had got it
so right? he had often asked himself. Where was the justice
in all of this?"

But now was not the time to dwell on it. This was his last
chance to find funds to launch his invention. Up to now he
had only spoken with bank officials and fund managers, but
Clive *owned* the bank in America so at least he must give
him a decent hearing. Anyway, it would be good to keep the
invention in the family, for, despite their selfishness, Paul still
felt a strong attachment towards his twin brothers.

And it was with this forced optimism that he caught a
yellow cab from JFK and directed the driver to the Price
Whitney Building off Fifth Avenue. He had never been to
America before and he half hoped his brother might have
sent a car to greet him, but there was no one at the airport
with his name on a card, and he didn't linger in hope. Paul
guessed Clive would be preoccupied with his business interests,
and began to feel insignificant, shadowed by the hugeness of
the buildings and the awesome reputation of New York as the
melting-pot of the American dream, the financial nub of the
western world.

Suddenly his invention didn't seem like a work of genius
any more. No longer did it seem possible that the papers
neatly folded in his briefcase amounted to anything more than

a dreamer's fantasy, an eccentric's gizmo that would barely raise a smile in the patent offices of the world. Surely it must be lunacy, thinking that he could have founded a new order in man's wealth, seeded a new energy revolution that would see the demise of oil and other fossil fuels as the power that advanced man through the twentieth century.

All around him was the established order of things – vested interest, entrenched ideas. Here was where the oil and coal money came to be reinvested. Here were more people he would have to convince that they had built their castles on loose sand – that they should shift their position now and enter a different era, a time of changed values, altered horizons, and even greater prosperity if they acted soon enough. As he thought he could have wept, for he knew at once he was going to fail again.

Karina Darielle sat alone at the terminal high in her bower at the top of the Price Whitney building. It was 3.30 in the afternoon, and between bursts at the keys she glanced at the monitors which showed what was happening elsewhere in the bank. The monitors could only be activated through security locks, but unknown to Clive Feral there were few locks anywhere in the complex for which she did not possess a key. She made it her business to know exactly where he was, night and day, and for some reason right now he was seated alone in the company board room studying a bundle of papers. He only used the boardroom when he was expecting someone he wished to keep private from the gossip on the floor, and her curiosity increased when the door opened and the visitor was shown in.

He looked out of place. He wore a suit, but it was in thick utility material with no sheen, and with a hatch of creases that reflected the weariness in his face. His shoes were of the mock suede variety, cheap and comfortable but an anathema in the austere surroundings of the bank. His hands were big with a roughness that spoke of practical use in some form of trade, yet this impression was belied by his eyes – they were the large, sensitive, intelligent eyes of a thinker used to seeing past the frontiers of ordinary men. Karina's heart missed a beat for they were the eyes of a Feral, but without the ruthless gleam of a predator-in-waiting.

He was a relative, she was sure of that, a brother perhaps. But this was not the twin she knew of, the brother Martin whom Clive referred to frequently in approbative tones.

The computer VDU was flashing at her now. She barely noticed it. Petulantly it stopped flashing and printed up its message: FINAL NOTICE. ENTER INSTRUCTIONS IMMEDIATELY OR TRANSACTION WILL BE CANCELLED. She ignored it and the imprint changed to: ACCOUNT CLOSED. RE-ENTER KEYING CODES TO REACTIVATE.

She turned it off – her whole attention on the boardroom monitor flickering on the shelf. He was slightly shorter than Clive, and she guessed a few years younger, but more ruggedly built with none of the slight stoop that rounded Clive's shoulders. Although the face appeared to smile naturally it seemed to be an effort now, his whole countenance showing the kind of brooding melancholy of a man who had travelled far, and had further still to go.

For the barest moment she felt her heart soften, but in the same instant erased the feeling with a new fire of loathing. He was a Feral, genetically flawed to be a fiscal cannibal from the cradle to the grave, killing good and bad alike and gorging on the detritis. Her smile returned. She had promised herself the two brothers, Clive and Martin – now there was a third.

Her hand reached out and she turned up the volume.

"Paul," Clive was saying, "this is a surprise. How are you? It must be fifteen years." He said the words without emphasis, and the smile did not part his lips.

"Yes indeed," Paul responded eagerly, holding out his hand.

Clive took it and released it in the same movement. "What can I do for you?"

Both men were still standing and Karina noticed that Clive made no effort to proffer one of the dozen chairs spaced around the table.

"I've great news, Clive," Paul weighed straight in. "In fact I think you might even find it incredible." He saw no point in understating his case. He had heard that was not the American way.

"Really?" said Clive. "How interesting."

"Where would you like me to start?"

"Nowhere right now, Paul," Clive told him blandly. "As much as I'd like to hear about it, it's quite impossible today."

"That's okay," said Paul, his buoyancy undeterred. "How about dinner this evening?"

Clive looked sad. "Sorry, Paul. I had no notice of your arrival and my diary is totally committed for the next two weeks."

"Two weeks!" Paul's shock was evident. "Can't you find

just an hour for me somewhere. After all, I am your brother? I was going to fly out again in the morning, but I'll happily stay an extra day. It'll give me a chance to go over all the facts I have here," he patted his briefcase, enthusiasm melting the lines in his face. "And it'll be good to talk over the old times again. Papa said we should stick together after he died."

That was true. Clive remembered the old man calling the three brothers to his death bed, and he recalled listening to the long list of instructions and entreaties that preceded his demise. Both twins had sniggered as they left the room, and Clive now viewed the briefcase with the same aloof amusement as he had the old man's last wishes – junk thoughts from junk minds. Both Paul and their father lived in a world where fancies flew and little else. The old man had left the family in grinding poverty – Paul would do the same for his.

The last thing Clive wanted was Paul to open that briefcase. "Would that I could," Clive sighed deeply. "Everyone in Price Whitney is at full stretch at the moment. That's the trouble with the banking world, Paul. The responsibility of handling billions of other people's money, and making sure it's safe." Clive thought he would slip that in, just in case he was after a loan – which was out of the question.

"That I can understand."

Clive looked at his watch. "I've got five minutes, if you want to give me a brief rundown."

"Five minutes!" Paul's voice was sharp with amazement. How could he summarise a decade of research in five minutes? "Well it's like this," he started awkwardly, "I've found a way of extracting energy from the air?"

"Really?" Clive smiled.

"Yes. The concept is so revolutionary that if it was put in general use it would solve all man's energy needs for the hereinafter."

"Amazing."

"Yes, isn't it!" Suddenly Paul found his revolutionary zeal returning. "Imagine what it would be like to be without the need to pump oil, dig coal, mine uranium, dam rivers, catch the wind. The planet would be devoid for ever of pollution, rid of the unseen horrors of nuclear meltdowns and acid rain."

"And that's what you have there?" said Clive turning his attention to the briefcase with glazed eyes.

"It's all in there," Paul glowed, breathing fast. "All I need is 30,000 pounds to secure my world patents, and we are on our way, the family united again in the most important endeavour since Faraday's experiments with electricity. Would you like to see the details?" His hand was at the zip and the flap was already open before Clive could stop him.

"I don't think so," he said simply.

"No?" Paul recoiled.

"No. I'll be perfectly blunt with you. The scheme sounds lunatic. It smacks of crackpot ideas like cars that run on water, and ways of turning lead into gold."

"It's nothing like that," said Paul, suddenly angry. "Do you think I'm mad?"

Clive looked at him and wondered. "Why has no one thought of it before?" he asked.

"There has to be a first for everything," Paul defended. "One of the principal reasons is that the technique marries two separate disciplines – pneumatics and electrics, which don't normally work together."

"I can imagine why," said Clive, mistaking his meaning. "And I don't think they'll work for me either. If you are asking for a loan then I'm afraid the answer has to be, no. The Articles of Association of this Bank do not permit venture capital advances."

"Is that it, then?"

"I'm afraid so. I'm sorry, Paul. If I could help I can promise you I really would."

"But it works. I've made it work," Paul almost shouted.

"I am sure you have," Clive shrugged, looking at his watch again. "Now if you will excuse me I have to get to an important meeting with our brokers. I'll arrange a car to take you to the airport."

"Now wait a minute," Paul stood in his way. "Just you wait a minute." He hadn't travelled for ten hours to be told in as many minutes he had been wasting his time. Suddenly memories of the twins' gross arrogance came flooding back and plainly Clive still saw him as a kid brother. It was a grave mistake. Paul was no longer a foot shorter and thirty pounds lighter than the twins in weight.

Clive's face paled. "You tell me to wait! Try to detain *me*, in *my own* building!" he said very softly, his eyes narrowing with menace. "Now let me tell you something, Paul. You are a loser. You always were a loser, just like Papa was a loser. I get people in here like you all the time, their only ability in life to bring new levels of incompetence to everything they do. Failure, for them, is almost an art form, Paul, they're so good at it. And then they have the red-neck to come in here, demanding I put *my* money where *their* mouth is – in one imbecilic venture or another. No Paul, dear brother, just you get the hell out of here. Get out of here and never come back. D'ya hear, *never*."

Paul recoiled in disbelief. Then in the same instant rage possessed him. He did what he should have done years ago, and it came quite naturally now after years of amateur boxing. The blow hit Clive just below his left eye – a textbook southpaw jab. It lifted him off his feet into the air, and he did not even have time to look surprised. With the grace of a curling stone upon a frozen loch, he slid unconcious along the polished length of boardroom table and crumpled off the end into a loose-limbed heap on the floor. Paul did not give him a second look and let himself out, the veil of rage gone as soon as it had come. There was a smile upon his face now. For someone without a dime he was suddenly a happy man, and it was not until later that he discovered the broken bone in his third finger, and was almost pleased.

He would have been more so, had he been able to hear Karina's laughter high above. She had been watching the scene unfold on the penthouse monitor with amazement, and now she rocked on her stool and wiped tears from her eyes. She had not enjoyed herself so much for a very long time.

Clive normally enjoyed his lunches with Abel Satco, the firm's broker. But not today.

Satco had tenacious lines of contacts in the financial world that almost equalled his own, and over a working lunch they would usually exchange sufficient insider information to ensure each had an extra million profit on trading over the next few days. Yes, it was one of the more pleasant and civilised ways of doing business, Clive considered. But today was different and his mood was dark.

Satco looked at him with an amused curiosity as he studied the bruise. "Spot of bother, eh Clive?" he goaded gently.

Clive's face stiffened, anger there. "Not so's you'd notice. You got nothing else to say – like how the market's doing?"

"It sure as heck ain't shining like your eye," Satco grinned, refusing to let the advantage slip. Rarely was Clive's aplomb so obviously dislodged.

"Shut up," growled Clive, "or you eat alone and forget about our brokerage."

"Sorry," Satco straightened his face with difficulty. "Yes," he rallied his thoughts, "let's get down to business."

"How far d'you reckon the Dow will run up this week?" Clive asked, his voice still tight.

"I think it'll stay pretty bullish, probably good for another twelve points before the end of the account," said Satco, sinking his teeth into a mouthful of Texan rump. "Lot of heat coming on gold right now, though. The news is the Russians will be selling ten tons this month to bolster their foreign exchange reserves after buying all that grain last month."

"That's okay. We sold short on gold yesterday," said Clive.

"Good move."

"You still in oil?" Clive asked.

"Pretty heavily. Any new information?"

Clive glanced carefully round the crowded restaurant. "Yes. One of our customers, Finguard Exploration, have liquidity problems. We're going to foreclose tomorrow with a press announcement about four o'clock."

"Good," Abel smiled. He would sell shares he didn't have that afternoon – selling short, as it was called – and cover himself by buying the shares he had already sold when they had crashed after the announcement. It was highly illegal, but that was no problem, not with the retinue of nominees he used. And the profits could be enormous.

"Have fun, buddy," Clive smiled now, instantly regretting it as a shaft of agony ran upwards from the bruise to touch his brain.

"I will," said Abel. "And now here's one for you. Have you heard of the 29-29 Corporation?"

"Who?" Clive frowned. Frowning didn't hurt.

"The 29-29 Corporation."

"No. Should I have?"

"I think so. They're getting quite a reputation for being hot-shot dealers."

"Really?" said Clive, irritably. "Says who?"

Abel pulled a copy of the *Wall Street Journal* from the inside of his coat. "Look at that."

Clive read the leader half way down the page:

NEW INVESTMENT COMPANY, *the 29-29 corporation, scoop the pool.*

The first annual report from 29-29 shows remarkable profits from currency dealings and futures speculations. After a flat period where many City institutions have shown less than remarkable growth, 29-29 have astounded Wall Street pundits who are forecasting them as being a new Genesis of super trader. Profits from the year have shown 29-29 an aggregated hundred million dollars.

Clive did a swift calculation. It was a hefty slice of Price Whitney's own profits on dealings. The bastards, he thought silently. They had moved in on the talent market and culled themselves some handy dealers at a time when Price Whitney's own fortunes had ceased their meteoric rise.

His eyes narrowed. He was going to have to do something about it – and quickly. He had to get other dealers of Karina's calibre before he lost more ground. He smiled now. Where better to start recruiting than 29-29's very own stable? They wouldn't know what hit them. They would be out of business within six months. His smile broadened to a leer. There was nothing like a bit of buccaneering and corporate homicide to get the blood on the move.

"What d'you mean you can't find out where they're based," he roared down the phone an hour later. "That's the damn stupidest remark I've ever heard you make."

"That's not what I said," Victor Loeb, his attorney, answered defensively. "What I said was that 29-29's headquarters are registered at the offices of their accountants, Graf Spielburg. But that is not where they do their trading."

"Is that the sort of information I pay you two hundred grand a year for?" he shouted back. "Hell, man, they've got to have a trading floor some place. Find out where it is and who their dealers are. Buy the information if you have to, but just get it, d'you hear."

"We'll do our best, sir," Loeb said, clearing down.

Half an hour later he was back on the line.

"Victor," Clive gushed, at the sound of his attorney's voice, "I knew you'd do it. Sorry I was short with you just now. The pressures have been goddamn hot recently. You understand how things are. So tell me, who are the opposition fielding?"

"I'm afraid I haven't that answer for you yet," Loeb came back soberly. "I've been back on to Graf Spielberg, but they say they only do the books. Day-to-day accounting information is fed to them by a midtown firm of attorneys by the name of Holt & Farthingale, a subsidiary of a British company of the same name. And sure as hell they're a tight lipped outfit. When I asked for information on 29-29 they said all enquiries had to be in writing, and then hung up."

"Goddamnit," Clive shouted, his fury returning. "What the

hell's goin' on? Get a gum-shoe down there and stake 'em out. Do I need to spell out what needs to be done? What's the point of phoning me when you've nothing to tell me? You losing your grip?"

"That wasn't the reason I called," Loeb said with absolute calm. "I'm afraid I've some more bad news for you."

"*More* bad news?" Clive's eyes widened.

"We were instructed by your secretary to proceed with the purchase of the Hartman Building on 32nd Street, the one between Drivers and Price Whitney Futures."

"Yes, yes," Clive hectored. "You should have filed the papers by now."

"I'm afraid we can't proceed."

"You can't what?"

"We can't go ahead."

"But I ordered—" Clive roared, the colour rising above the pristine white of his collar.

"Quite. But it was too late."

"Too late!"

"Yes. I'm afraid it's already been sold," the lawyer said with restrained emotion.

"Sold! It can't have been. It wasn't even on the market!"

The lawyer laughed now. "Come now, Mr Feral. Someone jumped you. Your instructions came too late. We never had a chance."

"Someone jumped me?" His speech was tight and measured now. He didn't believe it. He paid enough for advance information to prevent this sort of thing happening, and it never had before. "Any idea who it was?" he asked with soft menace.

"Yes, sir," said Loeb after a pause. "I hate to tell you this Mr Feral, sir, but the freehold has been picked up by the 29-29 Corporation."

66

CHAPTER 6

The Cessna 210 lifted off from the general aviation strip at
Casablanca airport ·in a flurry of dust that curled like twin
tails in its wake, and began climbing steadily out in a wide
parabola towards the south.

The effects of the storm had been limited to some damage
to the terminal building, but there was little other evidence
of the ravages of the ·tempest apart from a few dry culverts
where the water had cut through the soft earth round the
airport perimeter. Everything in the ·coastal belt was as arid
as the bedrock of the deserts further to the east; and despite
it being barely seven in the morning, Martin was already
sweating profusely. His skin had moistened from the moment
he was out of his air-conditioned Mercedes, and now, sitting
behind the Plexiglas windshield under the raw sun, he felt his
consciousness slipping from him.

"Hey, blue!" Geoff Mace, the Australian pilot called irrev-
erently. "If you're goin' to grog on me, keep your gut off that
column."

The harsh words jolted Martin, and he straightened up.
"Sorry," he said, easing back from the control yoke.

"It'll be cooler in a minute when we're through four thousand
feet and nearer to the mountains," Mace said.

Martin didn't reply, just nodded. Flying was probably his
least favourite activity, especially with a pilot as butch as Attila
the Hun. But the pilot was right – even now it was becoming
cooler inside the machine, and the air was clearer as they lifted
above the basin of haze. Far to the north he could just make
out the Jebel Mousa Mountains, the violent rocky eminences
known to the ancients as the Pillars of Hercules, whilst to the
east and south the Atlas chain began to emerge out of the
mauve horizon like a maw of white-capped teeth.

As they moved inland the terrain beneath seemed to magnify, expanding into a vast and never-ending emptiness where it seemed nothing could ever have grown, or would ever grow again. It was here that the hugeness of the continent would hit the first time voyager, knowing that what he saw, from six or sixty thousand feet was but a tiny microcosm of Africa, the land that was God's cradle for mankind – a fearsome, frightening land – until suddenly another face would show, a place in Eden full of cool succulence and moist riches. And such a place had come beneath them now.

The ground had begun to rise, imperceptibly at first, so there was little alteration in the dun hue of the burnt out plains. Then suddenly there was a hint of green, a thin vein at first as they hit a single water-source; then another, and another, until steadily the filaments merged and closed upon themselves as one, and in a moment all had changed to a vision of a different world, a separate life, a glimpse of heaven itself.

Martin had never seen anything quite like it before and his mouth opened as his throat dried. This was a Morocco he had never known existed, a place distant from the steaming bazaars and plastic courts of business which had been his world for fifteen years. For a moment he was in awe of the wonder of what he saw. But then that fear was there again, the same fear that took him as the lightning struck.

The scene was at once verdant and desolate, perfect as far as nature had intended, but yet unruly and impossible, giving no quarter and asking nothing in return. Life was born and life died down there and no one knew, and no one cared, except perhaps the Almighty, and Martin didn't believe in him.

It would take primeval man to survive in a place like this, but that was not Martin. He couldn't. He belonged where people were, civilisation, where things were manageable, where you could hire and fire, and buy your difficulties out of the way. No, this was not for him and he closed his eyes, and lay back in the seat, loathing the turbulence that jolted his bowels and the harsh roar of the 300hp Continental engine churning up in front.

Mace glanced at him. Jeez, another spunkless city creep.

He remembered his days flying 737s out of Addis for MEA. For Geoff Mace those were golden times – all the hostesses he could manage, which, together with danger money for the Lebanese leg, made it the best job in the business. If he hadn't screwed up two medicals on the trot by getting pissed the night before, he would still be doing it instead of flying these meatballs round the African bush in a Cessna spam-can.

Yes, Mace thought, looking down at the terrain below, life could be kind and life could be cruel, and it could also be a lot worse. He had always loved the wildness of Africa, a continent with as many faces as the human race itself, and as long as you laid off the local girls who were riddled with everything from AIDS to amoebic dysentery, life wasn't so bad.

He held the height steady at 10,000 feet and the ground was rapidly coming up to meet them. Gone were the sterile plains of the eastern seaboard, instead there were now dark green valleys with high ridges and open rifts, everything covered in dense afforestation of cedar and of juniper – a place where gazelles ran free, wild boar rooted, and the panther stalked by night. Soon they would fly into the Great "V", the wide schism that divided the mountains of Dj Ighil M'Goun and Toubkal, their ice-capped peaks soaring yet another 3,000 feet above, their size reducing the tiny machine to no more than a feather wafting on the breeze.

Ahead lay another world.

The two sides of the mountain were as different as Abel was to Cain. Beyond the divide the lush verdancy fizzled into nothing, suddenly and dramatically, as if killed by some monstrous poisonous rain – except it was not rain but the hot and deadly atrophying winds that burnt from off the desert every hour of every day. Only rare creatures like the southern desert gecko fought and won life out on the barren wastelands that rolled remorselessly back towards the eastern horizon for over a thousand miles.

Even before they were out of the "V" the air had become noticeably hotter, and Mace glanced down at the gauges. The oil temperature was rising and the pressure dropping, as it always did at this stage of the flight.

Then there it was. Beyond them now was nothing but an umber carpet of primeval spoil falling away down the mountain to the desert floor 10,000 feet below where everything melted in a mobile haze of varying shades of brown. He pulled back on the power to begin the decent.

Martin heard the change in note and his eyes flicked wide. "Anything wrong?" he asked, staring with increasing dismay at the barren vastness of the lands that lay before them.

"Nope," said Mace. "Just losing some height, that's all."

With his trained eye, Geoff Mace could just make out their target through the silvery ripples in the haze. The horizon was like a line of tinsel that melted, and ran, re-forming again in images of things that had passed by, far away, many hours before.

"We nearly there?" Martin asked nervously.

"Yes," said Mace. "You can see the base camp down there about five miles at eleven o'clock. The wind is from the east so we'll be coming in on zero-eight-zero."

Martin's eyes narrowed as he tried to pierce the haze, but everything looked the same. Like his brother Clive, he hated professional technicians with their jargon that meant nothing. Eleven o'clock was a time of day as far as he was concerned. As for zero-eight-zero, well! "I can't see a thing," he grumbled.

"Just to the left, over the nose," Mace pointed.

Martin peered again without success. "If you can see through this bloody soup you're a better man than me," he muttered.

I'll grant you that, buster, Mace thought silently. He didn't reply, concerning himself with the approach. With a deft movement of his wrist he selected a gear down and ten degrees of flap. The nose lifted slightly and he pulled off more power and set the pitch in fine before re-trimming the machine to fly hands-off. They were nicely set up on the glide slope at ninety miles an hour.

"Look, there it is," Martin shouted almost like a child. "There it is, see it?"

"Sure I see it," Mace grunted.

"Is that it?" Martin's sudden jubilation evaporated as he saw the tiny huddle of huts begin to take shape out of the blanket of khaki browns.

"Yep, that is where it's all at. There's one hell of a beach down there but not a lot of sea," Mace observed sardonically.

Martin was not in the mood to be amused. What he was looking at had already eaten two million dollars of pre-exploration funding, and the drilling derricks were still not even off the lorries.

The Cessna touched down with a series of rumbles and jolts on the rough desert strip. When the Chief Survey Engineer opened the door the heat was on them like a funeral pyre.

"Get me out of here," Martin shouted, straining at the harness.

"Right away, sir," the chief responded, his massive arms plucking Martin free of the machine like a straw doll. "We've got a diesel generator running so there's air-conditioning in the site office. You'll be more comfortable there, sir."

Martin said nothing. The sun on his head was like a rivetter's torch, and he almost ran to the Portacabin at the far side of the pan. This was plainly the camp's headquarters. A mobile diesel generator fed an umbilical to the air-conditioning unit bolted on the roof, and once inside he gasped in relief for the air was sweet as the mountain altitudes through which they had flown a short while before.

He glanced about him quickly. There were several desks strewn with maps and papers, and in the corner stood boxes of equipment, and one marked DANGER – HIGH EXPLOSIVES. Already the walls displayed an array of naked pin-ups, and a clutter of empty lager cans partly filled the shelves down one wall. A group of men stood close to the air-conditioning duct, chattering and doing very little else.

Martin's face darkened. He didn't like what he saw. "Okay," he said softly, when they all were seated. "I've two million bucks already locked into this prime lump of junk real estate. What have you got to tell me?"

Rory McDermid, the Chief Survey Engineer, looked at him uncertainly. Oil bosses were usually abrasive, but they were rarely unenthusiastic. "It's pretty certain our seismic people would not have chosen this as the hottest place to start," McDermid said. "But we've made a couple of shots and surprisingly the echoes hint at possibilities."

"Possibilities?" Martin scowled. "How d'you mean, *possibilities*?"

"Well, it's going to take a lot more than your two million bucks to find out, but it could be we have more down there than anyone originally thought."

"Really?" Martin found his interest suddenly growing. "How much more?"

"I just told you, we don't know, and we won't know for quite a while."

"Can't you guess?" Martin pressed.

"I'm not in the guessing game, Mr Feral," the Scot answered frostily. "It could be anything from a couple of gushers to a new Texas or Alaska."

Martin stared at him, astounded. His original plans were now like discarded confetti after a wedding. He had intended to go through the motions of seeking oil at minimum cost and minimum risk. Then, when there wasn't any, convince Khaled Nadir of the pointlessness of the whole operation, and suggest other activities which would be mutually more beneficial.

Yes, that was the original idea. But not any more.

Texas or Alaska, he began saying to himself over and

over, Texas or Alaska. The words were becoming mesmeric, like an Eastern guru's tract. Before he knew it, he had decided he must find out for sure whether he was about to become the richest man in Africa.

"Well, what you waiting for?" he almost shouted. "What are the men doing standing around scratching their arses?"

McDermid had been expecting this. "Things aren't quite that simple, Mr Feral," he said. "Our base camp is barely established, and certainly not yet secure. The overland lorries are expected tomorrow with the barbed wire defences and the Moroccan Army have promised us a resident platoon on site – or didn't you know?"

Martin didn't know. So far all the arrangements had been handled by his agent back in Casablanca. All he had done was write the cheques. That would change now – from here-on-in this was going to be his baby and he felt the excitement growing as he thought about it. "What the hell do we need defences for?" he asked querulously.

"There are contingents of Polisario guerrillas known to be active in the area," the chief said, not elaborating.

"Oh," Martin nodded. He understood now. Living in Casablanca it was possible to forget there was a civil war simmering on the edge of the Western Sahara. "So, when can I expect your next report?"

"Depends," McDermid shrugged. "All going well we should be firing more shots within the week, and have the preliminary analyses another week after that."

"Okay," Martin nodded. "I'll wait to hear from you. Is there anything else I should know?"

"I don't think so," said McDermid. "We're getting on with the job. That's all I can tell you."

McDermid watched the Cessna climb away into the sepia haze that had thickened in the short hour the aircraft had been on the ground. He stood there alone on the primitive apron that had been ·bulldozed from the rough desert floor, unconcerned at the 120 degrees of heat that now played over the pan of smouldering sands. His eyes were narrow slits, like those of the native arab, and his skin was as black as a head hunter's trophy, the surface pitted with a myriad of tiny fissures, shot blasted by a hundred sudden storms that would whip the desert sands into a frenzy of destruction. Like Martin Feral, he loved Africa, but in an entirely different way.

Since qualifying many years before at the College of Mining, Bristol University, he had spent almost all his working

72

life on that continent – first Algeria, then Nigeria, Libya and the Cameroons, and had seen more revolutions and coups than married couples had rows. It did not diminish his love for the continent in any way. He was known and respected everywhere, for Rory McDermid was apolitical – he never took sides, only the side of his adopted land.

He smiled as the Cessna vanished from sight, and turned back towards the huts. "Okay boys," he said. "Let's get back to work. I want the perimeter line surveyed and the post holes drilled before nightfall so we can string the security fence at first light before it gets too hot."

No one said it but they all knew it was a waste of time, a cosmetic operation to satisfy the company insurers.

That night, after the sun had gone and the sands had cooled, Rory strode to the Land Rover parked on the edge of the pan, and they all heard it start, its tail lights quickly vanishing as it rumbled off into the night. There was nothing unusual in this. Wherever they were camped, Rory could disappear at odd hours. No one knew where he went or for what purpose, and he would always be back before dawn, ready to marshal the day's programme into order.

Tonight McDermid ran south, skirting the minefield, then turned slightly east towards the point of the crescent moon that had already turned the sands into a tray of silvery monochromes. He sat alone at the wheel, his eyes wide and bright. Through some innate wisdom, he had always been able to read the language of the desert as surely as the old Saharaouis arab who had taught him the native tongue those years before.

He knew there were eyes out there watching him, hostile eyes with fingers wrapped round triggers, but not a shot was fired for the rattle of the Land Rover with a slight misfire on one pot was a sound as familiar as their mothers' voices, and it was as if the desert breathed in and relaxed again as the elderly Scot trundled by in a puddle of fast fading yellow light.

The Polisario guerrillas had been fighting in the old Spanish Sahara for more than twenty years to secure the independence of their desert homelands from the Kingdom of Morocco. Their methods were the classic tactics of guerrilla fighters – hit and run, and hit again quickly somewhere else, which they did with complete ruthlessness and deadly effect at great cost to the Moroccan government.

Half an hour later Rory McDermid was sitting on a cushion on the floor of Mabilla Chiai's tent. "And now they're building a wall to keep us out," Mabilla Chiai was saying, the old warrior's leathery face creased in laughter. "A wall of barbed wire and soil! It's as if there is nothing to be learned from the lessons of history. Hadrian couldn't keep the Scots out of England, Maginot didn't stop the Germans adventuring into France, the Great Wall of China is now proving of greater value as a foreign exchange earner than it ever was strategically – and now our dear friends on the coast think they are going to wall us off from our birthright? Not a chance," he said, his laugh growing louder now, oddly in tune with the sound of gunfire echoing distantly on the still night air.

It was true. The government of King Hassan had commenced the construction of a wall of barbed wire and earthworks which, when completed, would stretch the thousand miles from Dakhla in the south to the Algerian border near Tindouf in the north.

"A proposition as sad as it is ridiculous," agreed Rory McDermid.

"We have a growing number of friends," Mabilla continued earnestly. "The Moroccan tyrant is becoming increasingly isolated. They are spending vast fortunes on artillery, tanks, aircraft, and sophisticated · electronic gadgetry in hope of defeating us, but to defeat us is impossible for we are not just a people, we are the very country itself. We don't live in towns. We live out there among the sand and the rocks – anyone wanting to raze or subjugate the people of the Sahara, need to be able to subjugate the very land itself."

This was all good rhetoric, but there was also an honesty behind the zeal, as well Rory knew. The Moroccans were bogged down in a war they could not win, and he guessed this was why the push was on to find new sources of revenue.

"And how d'you feel about our oil explorations at Zagora?" Rory asked casually. He knew that if Mabilla didn't like what they were doing, the prospecting out-station would have been destroyed in one swift assault.

"Has Mabilla ever given you any bother?" Mabilla stretched his arms expansively. "Now have I?" He didn't wait for a reply, going on, "Rory McDermid is friend of Africa, therefore he is a friend of mine. Continue in peace, dear friend, continue in peace. Perhaps later I may have to ask you to move, to another location, but you personally will always be safe. You know that."

"Yes, you old rogue, I know that," Rory grinned. He knew exactly what Mabilla was up to. Mabilla might have a sentimental streak, but he was nobody's fool. He'd wait and see what happened. If they didn't find oil, a fortune would have been wasted in the exploration. If they did find oil, his guerrillas would take over the field, and he would have a windfall of many billions of dollars in foreign exchange which would secure his people's independence unless Allah decreed otherwise. No, McDermid thought wryly, I don't think I need to worry about any sleepless nights.

Paul's eyes were unfocussed, barely seeing beyond the windows of the cab as he rode back to the airport. His brow was set in a knit of lines as black as the clouds fast-gathering out over Long Island Sound, and he cradled his right hand closely to his chest, the nerves jabbing intermittent shards of pain up his arm. A bone had been broken by the blow, but if his hand was damaged his pride was not, and a smile very briefly touched his lips. He recalled his departing memory of Clive: dear Clive, his face set frozen in disbelief as his feet left the floor under the momentum from Paul's fist. Yes, a joyous moment indeed it was, but sadly it had changed nothing.

He was now out of the cab and through the main concourse of JFK. He pulled aside from the crowds funnelling towards the moving walkway, and took his ticket from his pocket, his mind fast clearing of the kaleidoscope of feelings that had cluttered it on the journey to the airport. He had to decide quickly what to do.

The ticket was in sectors, the first pull-out leaf that had covered his flight from London to New York was already gone, and he thumbed through the remaining pages. The original plan was to have flown on to Rome, changing there to a short haul flight down to Casablanca. Yes, that had been the grand plan, New York first then on to Morocco to see Martin as a pleasurable extension of the journey, a voyage of reunion that would cement the family as their father would have wished, and bring the funding he so desperately needed.

The plan had failed, it was as simple as that. Even thinking about it broke the hard line of his mouth into a half smile of irony. How could I have been so naive? he pondered with bitterness. It was ridiculous, an act of total idiocy, travelling an ocean for nothing whatsoever. They said time was a healer. They were wrong. Clive had been exactly as he had remembered – time had not altered anything, only clarified the perception. The only question was whether to terminate the journey now and go straight back to London, or continue on to Africa as originally planned.

He considered his options.

Suddenly he was moving again, towards the Pan-Am desk. There was nothing to decide. The ticket was already paid for, the necessary funds already extracted with great difficulty from a much begrudging bank. All doubt was now eradicated from his mind. He was going on to Africa – there would be no turning back.

He returned the smile of the girl who took his baggage. "Have a nice day," she intoned, glancing at him once as the manual prescribed, before moving on to the next in line with the same smile and the same intonation.

The flight was as turbulent as his mood, arriving in the early morning after nearly seven hours' delay due to weather and the mechanical failure of the small feeder jet that plied the night skies from Rome to Morocco. After two missed approaches and a hard landing out of a dust storm, his hotel bed was like returning to the womb. He didn't wake until late in the morning when he was disturbed by a black girl coming in to check the room.

"You stay two day, sir?" she enquired quaintly, in dialect, hinting that if he was going, it had better be soon.

"No, only one," he told her blearily, levering up on an elbow. "I'll be clear of here in an hour." He could have done with an extra day in bed, but that wasn't part of the package, and he was very light on cash.

"Oh good," she said relieved, then adding brightly. "You want quick sex before you leave, sir, please?"

He grinned, and looked at her afresh. She was a big-boned girl, with black frizzy hair that had been permed straight in a simulation of European styles. She wore the hotel uniform, which was new and smart in the corporate image, but slightly too big, and he saw that despite her size there was very little flesh on her arms and legs. She was malnourished, he realised suddenly. The girl was starving in a hotel suffused with affluence.

"No thanks," he chuckled, imagining Tessa's reaction if she could see this unlikely situation. "But take this, and don't give it to your pimp." He pulled a ten-dollar bill from his wallet by the bed.

"Thank you, sir. Thank you," she snatched it from his hand, pushing it down the front of her dress. "But will not sir pleasure himself just a little?" Her fingers were on the zip of her skirt before he could reach out and knock them away.

"No!" he told her roughly, then in a more gentle tone,

"no, thank you." The scene depressed him. The hotel probably paid her nothing, letting her make what she could out of any extra services she provided for the guests. The pickings were doubtless lean because of everyone's fear of AIDs. Half of Africa was now supposed to be HIV positive.

"Okay," she shrugged in resignation. Her olive skin showed the mix of nations that was her stock, and her eyes were dark and expressive, yet oddly inscrutible as if focussed just beyond him. He looked at her hard, trying to figure out what was wrong. Then he knew. She was high. It was obvious now. But on which dope he could only guess – probably hash. Hash was more available than good drinking water round the bazaars of Morocco, and not nearly as expensive. "If there is nothing I can do, sir," she was speaking again, "I will go. Thank you, sir."

Paul acknowledged her, and she moved to the door. Suddenly he shouted, "Wait."

"Sir?"

"Sorry, just hang on a minute will you, and shut the door again."

"Sir has changed his mind?"

"No," he assured emphatically, grabbing his dressing gown from the chair and jumping out of the bed. "How well do you know Casablanca?" he asked, pulling the gown around him and adjusting the cord.

"I local girl. I know city very well."

"Good. Then perhaps you can give me some information?"

"Information? What information?" Her tone was suspicious.

"About the business community here?"

"Ah, you want to do business?" she said. Some of the glaze had gone from her eyes and there was a new look there. "You talk to me. I can arrange big business for you. Very easily. You make much money."

Paul studied her hard, and had a shrewd idea of what business she had in mind. "No, I'm not after buying dope," he told her to kill off that idea. "I'm just looking for someone I haven't seen for some time. Maybe you can help me?" It was a perversion of the truth, but it would do. She probably knew nothing about Martin or his business, and it would be imprudent to tell her more than necessary. But she was worth a try.

"Looking for someone?" There was growing apprehension in her eyes, and he could guess what she was thinking. One man seeking another in Africa usually meant there would soon

be a body lying cold in the brittle light of dawn, picked clean
to the bones if it had been there very long.

"Yes."

"What is his name?"

"Martin Feral."

"Martin Feral?" she repeated parrot-like. The apprehension
was gone, instead it was as if he had slapped her hard. There
was contempt in the curl of her lip, and he felt that under other
circumstances she might have spat upon the floor.

"You know him then?" Paul said, genuinely surprised.

"But of course. Everyone in Casablanca knows of Martin
Feral. And you say you are a friend of his?" The servility had
gone from her manner and the question was framed accusingly.

"Friend? Me? Certainly not," Paul back-pedalled. "Just
an acquaintance, you might say."

"Best you not meet him. Best you not know him at all,"
the girl stated in her broken patois, gaining bravado from the
dope.

"That a fact?" he asked. "And why would you say a
thing like that?"

"He a very bad man."

"So? The world is full of bad men."

"He also a dangerous man. He very rich with many friends
in high places." Then suddenly as if realising she was taking
grave chances, fear smothered the bravado once more. "You
sure you not a friend of his?"

"Don't worry," he grinned again to reassure her. "Who
cares if you don't like the guy? Not me, I can assure you
of that. Here, take this and tell me what else you know."
He pulled his last ten-dollar bill from his wallet and flicked
it across to her.

She caught it with dexterity, and seemed to relax again.
"Martin Feral, he like young men and little boys," she said
with scorn. "He buys or steals them from their families. He
has my brother in his Holiday Inn penthouse and we not see
him for many months. One day my brother will return to us
with much money, but it will not be my brother any more. He
will never love a woman. He will never have a family and my
father's name will die because there are no more sons."

Paul listened with silent curiosity, wondering at the dichoto-
my of morals that made it permissible for a working girl to ply
her trade, yet not a working boy. Perhaps age was important?
Anyway, who was he to judge? By excellent luck he was getting
a close-up view of his brother's affairs, even if it was costing

him his last twenty dollars for the treat. "Not a very happy situation," he volunteered. "Tell me more. The good things and the bad."

"There are no good things," she said, her vehemence undiminished.

"Okay, just the bad things then."

"He is, what you say, a bastard."

"Go on."

"He very rich. He own many things. He steal many things. He pay very little. The only thing he pay lot for is his little boys."

Paul listened to this, trying to make sense from the uneven run of syntax. As her excitement rose, the words came in stacatto bursts, her full lips tightening so she almost spat the words. But he got the gist. Brother Martin was not the hottest social property around town right now.

"So," he shrugged. The girl had a grudge, and he could see why, but it was not enough.

"So?" she questioned now. "You not believe me?"

"I believe you. But it's no big deal."

"You know nothing," she hissed darkly, fire kindling behind the fog of dope. "You not understand. You know nothing."

"I only know what you are telling me and that's not a lot," he said, a hectoring tone in his voice. It seemed he had bought twenty bucks worth of prejudices.

Her mouth closed and he could see her bridling, and for a moment he thought she would clam up and run, or perhaps something more violent than that. Then she said dramatically, "Martin Feral, he white slaver." And she judged his reaction before going on. "Martin Feral came to Africa very poor. Now he very rich through stealing from the black man and the Arab, their property and their birthright. He sells rhinoceros horn to the Saudis, little boys to the Greeks, American technology to the Russians, and Libyan arms to, what you call them, the Paddy people."

"Paddy people?" Paul frowned, then laughed. "The Irish you mean?"

"Yes, Irish. That not matter. What matter is that he exploit the Moroccan. He laugh at us. One day soon we shall laugh at him. One day his testicles will be sweetmeats on the table of Allah. One day very soon."

This was not the information Paul was seeking. He had never been interested in anything but fact – not hyperbole, however powerful. "Maybe," he said, and looked at his watch.

"You'd better go now or I'll have to pay for another day."

It was almost as if he had slammed a lid upon her mind. Her mouth relaxed, becoming full and succulent as before, her face as bland and inscrutable as the olive fruit it mirrored. "You want sex now, sir," she repeated, almost as a mantra.

"NO!"

She left without a word.

Paul had the switchboard check that Martin was in residence in his penthouse at the Holiday Inn, but decided not to make contact in advance. He needed time to think. Some kind of strategy was called for, and he had to keep reminding himself of the absurdity of it all. He was here to see his brother, not plead his case at the last judgement, yet in a way it felt just like that, the last hope for all his plans.

He spent the afternoon wandering the bazaars, losing himself among every form of life that teemed there. All about him arab traders jostled with their brass and leather baubles and brilliant bolts of cloth. Dogs scavenged for spicy pickings beneath the trays of meats and fish, disturbing flies that rose as one in a blue-black cloud to skitter fretfully before alighting once more in a quieter place, syphoning moisture from the small piles of putrifying offal always in dark corners.

It seemed as if everything was up for sale, not a step did he take without some goods or other being peddled under his nose by nimble old men and young children who ran after him, almost tripping him, some so young it was as if their first words must have been, "Buy now, sir, you buy now? Cheap, very, very cheap, but not for long."

"No thank you," he said so many times he couldn't count, until after a while he didn't bother any more.

And now and then something odd would happen that at first greatly puzzled him. One moment there would be everyone doing their business in a noisy random order, then suddenly it was as if he was in the midst of a startled flock of birds, all about him freezing still, heads cocked, before taking flight as one in a unity of purpose with billowing robes and screeches of excitement. The charge was not in any direction, but a convergence on one place in a huge and glorious scrum that did not disperse until it appeared someone had won a prize.

But what prize? he wondered, after it had happened for the third time within the hour. What the devil is going on?

He was soon to find out. It arrived out of the east where the dusk was already beginning to come as a hazy darkening pall. The sound was a soft, a kind of fluting hum, and at first he saw nothing, just joined with the rest in standing absolutely still. The sound went, and came, and went again, and the crowd swayed and craned like a mamba in a charmer's basket as they eagerly sought its source. Two dogs began to fight, sending a swarm of flies lifting in the air, and with an oath they were instantly kicked apart by their black owner. Silence reigned once more.

Then Paul saw it. At first it appeared small and almost insignificant, then as it flew closer the insect's huge proportions matched the sparrow's on the paving. The others in the bazaar had also seen it now, and their craning stopped, their hands flailing as the insect passed. The locust flew slowly on, awkward and clumsily, bouncing off the pillars and over the tarpaulins of the covered market stalls. Paul watched its progress, fascinated, the crowd following in its wake like the piper's children.

It was coming his way and he marvelled at the ugliness of the creature, a huge green grasshopper which, with its brothers could destroy a nation's agriculture in less than half a day. But this one was not going to destroy anything. It was lost, caught in an up-draft off the Ahaggar Mountains and torn many miles from its traditional feeding grounds between the twentieth and thirtieth parallels East of Tamanrasset.

Onwards it came, dodging the flailing hands with a kind of desperate intent as if it already knew its fate. Paul saw it all now. Suddenly it came back to him that in certain regions of Africa the locust was considered a delicacy, and the people of the bazaar plainly viewed such appearances as a kind of gourmet titbit arriving on the breath of Allah. It also occurred to Paul that if the thing kept coming his way, they would be both downed by a crowd that could make a football stampede look like a kindergarten break time.

Not since his training as a boxer had he moved so quickly. He ran and ran, and it was not until he heard the pounding stop and the baying start, that he slowed and turned around. He considered his situation. It was ludicrous – one large man being followed by one small insect pursued by what seemed a cast of thousands. And if amongst them there was a winner, then he must have been as flattened as his quarry. The mêlée had converged into a conical shape like an African beehive, and it seemed an age before the crush dispersed to expose one solitary soul still there upon the ground. His eyes were dazed, and blood spouted from a gash on his head, but his mouth carried the silly grin of man triumphant as a dark green ooze strained through his fingers.

Paul's stomach lurched very slightly and he looked at his watch. Three hours had passed. Now was the time to go and find Martin.

Getting directions to the Holiday Inn afforded no difficulty. A short walk and it was soon towering over him, a blandly modern building growing curiously out of the crumpled counterpane of antiquity all around.

The girl on the desk spoke English, which was helpful. Her attitude was less so. Her name was Charlene, according to her lapel badge.

"I'm here to see Martin Feral," Paul told her.

"You *do* have an appointment, I assume?" she said, checking her book.

"Not exactly."

She frowned and snapped her book closed. "No appointment, then no meeting," she said in a flat tone, and Paul guessed this was a familiar routine. The girl was briefed to stone-wall and she did a good job.

"I'm Martin Feral's brother," he said, almost casually.

"Martin Feral's brother!" she looked shocked.

"That's what I said. Now pick up that pretty little phone, Charlene, and put it against your pretty little ear and tell him I've arrived."

"Yes, sir. Right away, sir." The change was instantaneous.

Paul could only hear her side of the conversation, but it seemed things were going well. She never took her eyes off him for one moment as she talked. "He is delighted you are here," she cleared down. "If you would like to wait here and then go on up in a few minutes, he said he'll be ready for you then. The personal lift to the penthouse is over there," she pointed. "The keying code is nine-four-seven-six."

"Nine-four-seven-six," Paul repeated, and went straight over. He was in no mood to wait around.

The lift rose quickly, and the doors opened onto a spacious hall that looked out over Casablanca, a shambles of shapes and colour, so different from New York with its ordered stumps chewing unevenly at the sky. The hall itself was plainly a transit lounge for people-in-waiting, comfortably furnished with leather chairs and mature tropical plants that spread their huge leaves as if straining to catch the never-to-fall relief of rain. Set in the wall was a double door carved from a solid plank of teak so the grain each side was a perfect match of the other; the only intrusion on the plushness was a security camera, stark and obvious upon its nickle-plated mount. Paul pressed the bell and stood out of the angle of the lens.

He waited. There was not a sound, only musak from speakers hidden somewhere in the walls. Briefly his attention wavered, his gaze going way beyond the city limits, far out over the sea to where the sky was on fire, the sunset burning like hot metal over the chill mantle of the earth, welding all together in one molten union. It was an amazing sight, quite unlike anything in Northern Europe, and for an instant he was back in ancient times when pagan man searched the heavens for his personal almighty, and found him in the sun.

Then the musak stopped. "Hang on out there," a voice said from the speakers, "I'll be with you in a moment." It was Martin's voice, the familiar enunciation soft and fleshy like the brother he had known. Both doors had opened electrically without a sound, but Martin was not there.

Paul had no intention of hanging on anywhere, and strode forward, but beyond the doors he faltered in his stride. He had entered a kind of exotic auditorium, different from any apartment he had known. Velvets and drapes and chintzes mingled in sumptuous backdrop with potted vines, their foliage picked out in startling green by unseen studio lights. The same musak came from somewhere, this time mingled with the tinkle of water falling into a steaming pool that foamed like a soda fountain.

And then he saw Martin. He was stretched out quite naked, Roman style, on a skin beside the pool. His face was working in strange animated spasms and at first Paul thought he was being sick, but there was no vomit on his cheeks. The orgasm was rushing up and flooding him in a visible wave, the black boy's face gorged huge like a python on a goat as he swallowed, whole, the meat of Martin's groin. Paul just stood and stared, his face dark with revulsion. He had always suspected Martin's tendencies, but this overt exposition was something yet again.

Martin must have glimpsed Paul's arrival as a shadow out of view. The tide was receding, and his face was relaxing again, but strangely he made no effort to move, just lay there in flacid enjoyment of the afterglow. The black boy had withdrawn discreetly, and was wiping semen from his mouth, his eyes dull with dope like the girl in the hotel.

"Great to have you over Clive," Martin said, his breathing more steady now. "I was wondering when I would see you again." He made no effort to turn around, and his eyes were partly closed. "Wish you had let me know you were coming, though. There are some great girls in town right now who really do the business. I'll get something organised for you later tonight."

"I shouldn't bother," said Paul.

For an instant the silence was total. Even the musak took a breath. "Clive?" Martin queried as his eyes flew wide, trying to see round the ground-ivy.

"No, it's not Clive. It's Paul."

"Paul?" It was as if a trap had sprung. Martin was on his feet, vainly trying to cover his groin with his hands. "What the hell are you doing here?"

"The receptionist sent me up. I told her I was your brother."

"Brother? Brother?" Martin repeated stupidly, as if the word had found another meaning. "I thought you were Clive."

"So it seems."

"Well, what the hell are *you* doing here?"

"I came to see you," said Paul with control.

"Me? What for?"

"Well I *am* your brother."

"Yes, yes. I know that," Martin almost shouted, grabbing a towel.

"Well, aren't you glad to see me?" he asked, already knowing the answer.

Martin's features seemed to go into spasm as fury and decorum vied for supremacy, until eventually he regained some aplomb. "Yes, yes, of course," he said. "But I did ask the receptionist to hold you a few moments."

"Does it matter?" Paul shrugged.

Martin considered the question and didn't answer. Instead he asked again, "What brings you to Africa?"

"Two reasons, Martin," said Paul. "The first, and I'll be frank with you the lesser one, was just to keep the family patched together as Father would have wanted. But that is really by-the-by. The fact is that I have developed a unique machine that has enormous implications on the world's energy resources." He went on to explain what it was and how it worked, conscious that all the while Martin's eyes were alternating between the door and the clock. He was half way through when Martin cut in.

"Well? What is it you want from me?"

"Seed finance to get patent protection worldwide. Then we can go ahead and market it."

84

"And how much do you want?"

"About 30,000 pounds."

"You want what?" Martin almost shouted.

"30,000 pounds," Paul told him.

"30,000 pounds! Why that is absurd," Martin echoed the words of Clive an ocean away. "With respect Paul, it sounds like a scheme dreamed up by some conman who's lost his grip on the plausible."

"But it works," Paul stated simply, "it really does work."

Martin looked at his brother hard. He was of course much older than he remembered, the softness of youth having given way to the harder lines of maturity. But still the same crusader's zeal burnt bright behind the eyes; still there was the same enthusiasm for everything he did. Paul always had one idiotic scheme or another on the go and this one explored new dimensions of stupidity.

"My dear Paul," Martin tried to sound kind but could barely supress his amusement. "I do honestly wish I could help you, but 30,000 pounds is an awful lot of money to gamble – money that I simply do not have."

Paul knew this was a lie. He had often read in the press how rich Martin was. "It is not a gamble, Martin," he said coldly. "It is a certainty. The horse is already past the post."

The smile on Martin's face melted away. "Okay, Paul, let me put it to you this way. Scientific gizmos do not interest me – they never have and never will. I only get involved in things I can comprehend, and what you suggest is incomprehensible. Now if you'll excuse me I'll have to ask you to go. I have some important business associates due here this evening, I have some work to prepare. Another time maybe."

Paul could have been back in New York. The look was the same, the words were the same, the extended hand dismissing him towards the door was the same. A good right hook was already bunching in his mind, but then something happened and instead his arm relaxed and fell limp along his side. Everything was so pointless. Nothing meant anything any more. Why was he forever doing battle against the massed battalions of total apathy? Suddenly he was very tired. Without a word he turned and left.

On the plane back to London he slept a shallow, troubled sleep, visions turning to dreams and dreams turning to visions. Clive or Martin, Martin or Clive, it really didn't matter any more, a kind of doggeral ran, the jumbled sentences coming and going, running and re-running as the first snaking tendril of madness uncoiled within his reason. They were one and the same in all but name – the words kept coming – one and the same in all but name.

Suddenly he awoke. He knew what he had to do – something he should have done years ago, before he was ensnared and driven to poverty and near madness by this monster he had created.

He collected his car from the airport park and drove back down to Wiltshire. He barely noticed the two girls clamouring excitedly at his return, or the surprised face of Angela who had been looking after them. Nor did he see the strange woman sitting silently on the sofa. All he saw was the axe behind the door, and he seized it and ran outside.

"You've just gotta punt on this one, Clive," Abel Satco told him over lunch. "The syndicate have already put half a billion in the pool and they keep asking where you are."

"What d'you mean, *where I am*?" Clive rounded.

"You missed your call last week when we raided Jerico Assurance."

"My funds were deployed on another deal," Clive lied. He missed the deal for no other reason than that he was totally preoccupied with researching the 29-29 company structure – with singularly little success.

"Okay," said Abel, still looking at him hard. "You look a bit off colour, Clive. You sickening for something?"

"Not that I know of. Now what you have got lined up? I've twenty million bucks on call that needs some work to do right now. That's my stake, so what's the deal?" He was barely listening as Abel Satco explained the tactics for the killing planned on Wall Street for the following week.

Clive Feral was sick, very sick, but not in any physical sense. He was sick at heart. 29-29 had jumped him. How, he had no idea, but they had, and all he knew was that somehow he had to get control of that company to get his property back and claim his revenge. The trouble was it was a private corporation. He had no access to the shareholders and all the directors seemed to be nominees, mostly partners in the law firm of Holt and Farthingale. Who were they hiding, he wondered? Who the hell were they hiding?

"So, what d'you think?" Abel Satco prompted.

Clive jumped. "I trust your judgement completely," he parried. He hadn't heard a word, but his money would be safe with Abe.

"Thought you'd like it," Satco nodded, looking pleased. "It's right up your street. The blood'll really run on this one when the knives come out."

"Uh huh," agreed Clive noncommittally. Then quietly, "Don't suppose you have any more information on the 29-29 Corporation, do you?"

Satco looked at him hard, then laughed. "That's what's been bugging you, is it? Thought you weren't catching everything I said. Gossip has it 29-29 jumped you on the option on old man Hartman's juicy bit of real estate between Drivers and Whitney Futures."

"Yes, the bastards," Clive suddenly came alive. "But I'll pull it back once I know who I'm dealing with. You can bet your arse on that."

"I might just do that," said Satco his grin turning sly. "There is a rumour that the outfit is owned by a Greek living in London, a guy called Tuesday Nemesis. Some sort of magnet loaded with shipping and oil money they say, but no one knows much about him."

"But where and how does he do his buying?" Clive pressed.

"Don't know. The deals are usually spread round about thirty out-of-town brokers. Sure as hell wish he'd spread some my way – the volume is phenomenal, and their dealers seem to be up-front on all the latest trends. That guy sure has recruited some bright talent, no doubt of that."

"But where are his dealers?" Clive growled in frustration.

"Search me," Satco shrugged. In his opinion Clive was getting a bit too obsessed with 29-29. It could impair his judgement. "I'd wait for something to crawl out of the boards if I were you. It's bound to, sooner or later. Then you can make your move."

"*Wait*?" Clive's mouth curled round the words. "The hell I will."

CHAPTER 7

It was Saturday morning and the video lay on the table just where he had left it. There was no title, just the number forty-seven Clive had noted on the spine. Karina picked it up, balancing it in her hand, before slotting it into the player. It was unusual for him to be so careless. His private tapes were normally locked away in the safe beneath the floor of his study.

She waited for the screen to flicker into life, idly running a brush through her hair, sweeping the thick dark mane back over her shoulders as she considered her options.

He had left the night before on one of his frequent "working weekends" out of town, something for which she was ever grateful. She considered the loathsome business of living with Clive Feral as the payment for her destiny; a high price it was, but not too high to see the fulfilment of her plans. His absences came as a sweet respite, and she was looking forward to this one more than most.

Clive's away-days had, of course, nothing to do with work – Karina knew that well. When he vanished on one of his trips, the weekend could last three days or more, with no word in between. And he would never leave a number where he could be reached.

The screen was showing something now. There was no title on the run-in, just a shot of a typed sheet, with "NEW YORK POLICE DEPARTMENT. Case No 24796/90/12" stamped at the top. There was no sound, the image flickering badly as if copied from a home movie. She watched with curiosity, the picture changing to a white-tiled room, a morgue. Four men came in, carrying what looked like a door partly covered by a green canvas sheet. It was placed upon the slab and the canvas drawn back. At first she did not recognise what she saw; then her throat gagged shut and for a moment her breathing stopped. There was meat there on that door, human meat. It was a man's body, but a body completely without a skin, red-raw like an anatomical drawing, and it was nailed spreadeagled to the wood as if in crucifixion. She was drawn to the eyes, huge and lidless, popping from their sockets like puff-balls on a stump. They were unseeing now, but still reflected the terrible agony of the death, an appalling, brutal mutilation that could have lasted many hours. The man had been flayed alive.

After a ten-second dwell, the shot cut away to a new case number and a new corpse. And so the tape ran on. There were seven autopsies in all, the film ending with the restriction notice "PROPERTY OF NYPD FORENSIC LABORATORY. FOR TRAINING USE ONLY. NO COPIES PERMITTED." Karina wondered how much Clive had had to pay to break their ethical code.

She fixed herself a coffee to settle her stomach and began to make her plans. Before Clive left she had told him she was going away for a week – to her old Aunt Fay up in Maine. Whenever Clive was out of town she always headed there, but he was never happy about this and would call frequently to check. Fay dutifully passed the messages, and brought Karina to the phone. Apart from being a first rate business manager, Fay Carerra was also a damn good actress. And she valued her job – the Nemesis Corporation was the best employer she had ever had, and there had been many since she first met Karina in the orphanage of Santa Maria.

Often she had wondered how Karina had tracked her down to the bent money lender's outfit down in Queens. She was never told. All she knew was that one day Karina had appeared through the door, and ten minutes later they were walking out together. And that was the way it had been ever since. Karina took her on, had her trained, and now she juggled the balls for Nemesis Enterprises, with all its thrills and challenges. When Karina told her that the operation was to be moved from its discreet offices in Brooklyn out to Carson's Field it was at first a surprise, then a joy to leave the fume-choked city streets for the cleaner, northern air.

And that was where Karina was heading now, soaking up the miles as the car sped north, until she slewed through the gates of the airfield and stopped next to the space marked "Tuesday Nemesis, President".

"Good afternoon Miss Darielle," the pump-hop sprung from his bothy behind the lines. "Can I carry your gear?"

"Yes, it's in the trunk Jim. Take it to my apartment will you please. Is Juliette Whisky on line?"

"Gassed up and ready to go Miss Darielle."

"Good."

Karina took the path past an assortment of light planes tied down on the apron. In front of her was a long low building, in modern Spanish stucco, one end emblasoned K.D. Aviation & Flight Training, the other end unsigned with any company logo, but plainly a separate business suite. The windows were mirrored leaving the interior unseen, the only access by means of a security door with a numerical lock. Karina keyed in some numbers and it swung silently open. The interior was airy, and surprisingly bright despite the mirrored glass, and there were a number of people there behind computers set in rows. Fay was on her feet at once and the others looked up, smiled and nodded, before returning to their screens.

"Hi gang," Karina smiled back. "Any coffee on the go?"

"Hi Karina," Fay took her coat, her blue eyes bright and sparkling. "Sure thing. I'll fix it straight away."

Karina pulled a fan-fold bunch of sheets out of the wire basket marked K.D. and quickly scanned the figures. "A good month," she said, more to herself than the other listeners. "The link problem with my terminal at Price Whitney has been sorted out, thank heavens."

"Yes, and none too soon," said Fay, returning with a coffee. "The down-time last month when we couldn't contact you must have cost us a half a million bucks on the Yen transfer."

"Couldn't be helped," shrugged Karina. "It won't happen again, though. I've bought the maintenance operation and fired the manager."

Nobody looked surprised. Karina went on, "Anyway you handled the other business pretty well. You're all getting too good – I've trained you too well. But it does make me comfortable when I'm out of town. Which reminds me, I'm off to England tomorrow for a couple of days so you won't see much of me this time around."

"England?" Fay enquired. "That sounds interesting."

"Could be, but I'm not sure yet. Depends what I find when I get there. I'll keep you posted. But first things first. I need a flight – haven't been up for three weeks and I'm suffering withdrawal."

"She's ready for you," said Fay, referring to Karina's Stearman biplane gleaming on the apron. "Jim has her out and she's

90

fuelled. In fact, if he polishes it much more, he'll be down to bare metal."

"A good guy is Jim," Karina smiled, picking up her leather bomber jacket from behind the door. The jacket was the same one Chris Butler had given her the first day they met; new then, but now showing the signs of many hours of wear.

Fifteen minutes later the Stearman was taxi-ing out towards the holding point for runway 24. She waited for air traffic to give her clearance for take off, and in a moment she was climbing lazily into the late afternoon sky, the sun blazing off the engine cowl like an Olympiad's torch. At 1,000 feet she started a gentle turn to starboard, losing the sun behind her as she set course out over Moosehead Lake towards the snow-capped peak of Mount Katahdin hanging like a mauve confection against the eastern sky. Only now did she begin to relax a little, snuggle down in the seat out of the icy blast from the big 450 h.p. Pratt & Whitney engine. The stresses were unwinding slowly from her body, and for a moment she just closed her eyes and let the throb of the engine envelop her in its soft embrace. It was the nearest thing she knew to heaven on earth, and it still seemed only yesterday she formed her tryst with flying.

That weekend the summer before, Clive was also out of town, leaving her alone. Tired and jaded by three months solid in Manhattan, she decided to take a break, and without any great thought, drove north to escape the heat and the yellow fug of the exhaust fumes that lay like a shroud over the hot city streets.

She took Route 95 out of town. By Boston she was feeling better, and by Portland quite exhilarated. The air was cooler and much cleaner there. There was an openness – green fields, huge forests of climbing pines – a vast beautiful empty space. Instead of feeling more tired she had suddenly found her energy returning with every passing mile, and it was only when dusk approached that she concerned herself with her ultimate destination. For the past thirty miles there had been no hotels, no motels, nothing, so when at last she saw the lights of Carson's Field in the distance, she decided to pull in for the night.

There was only one motel, the Fly Inn Motel. It was a strange place to over-night, her first reaction being to drive past the tired-looking complex of buildings that lined up along the road, but her foot drifted off the gas and she turned in through the gate. It was plain that the Fly Inn Motel was culled out of the admin block of what was left of an old U.S. Air Force Base; tarted up a little, but still obvious for what it was. A couple of hangars still remained, and on one hung a drooping plywood board bearing the inscription "CARSON'S FIELD FLYING SCHOOL AND AERONAUTICAL ACADEMY. PROPRIETOR – CHRIS BUTLER".

She drove past the motel and on over the apron to the taxi ways. There was nothing to stop her, no gates, no barriers, only holes where they once had been. A few Cessnas and Pipers were tied down outside the hangar but there was no one else about. Cautiously she continued on, turning left to follow the perimeter track.

It was almost dusk now, and the hangars appeared to be growing taller against a pale moon just peeping through the clouds. The light breeze had died away to nothing, not a sound there now but the distant hoot of owls in the woods on higher ground.

She was not to know it then, but Carson's Field, Maine, was a wartime staging post for B17 Flying Fortresses on their way to Europe to fight the Nazi menace. Thousands of them took off from here; month after month, year after year they went, their wheels leaving American soil for another continent, many for the last time, never to return. They were proud machines flown by even prouder men, the Eighth Air Force taking very heavy losses on daylight raids over Europe until much later in the war when the first long-range P51 Mustang fighter escorts started coming off the lines.

A few bombers did make it back to America after the cessation of hostilities, tired, beat up machines that came limping in, some only to skid to their death as mangled metal in the far corner of Carson's Field. A little of the wreckage still remained, a fuselage here, some odd wings there, and a heap of Wright Cyclone engines too useless and too heavy to move.

After the war Carson's Field was abandoned by the military, and now the caulking of the taxiways had conceded to weeds that took advantage of every crack; tenacious roots spreading and lifting, thin bladed leaves edging the concrete slabs so the hangar pans looked like green-lined checker boards. There was something growing from every crack and fissure, grass dripping from the guttering of long-abandoned huts, and in late summer a floss of seeds would blow across the empty apron in lazy swirls and billows.

Karina stopped the car, her breathing shallow. It was a

haunting kind of night, rich with evocations from another age. She ran her hand along one of the old propellers, bent grotesquely now, but still hanging on its engine, and for a moment she thought she could hear aircraft in the sky, hundreds of them so very faintly. Was it her imagination, or was there the chatter of cannon fire, and the sound of voices raised, staccato orders, muttered oaths and the sound of men screaming? Then a gust blew across the field and rattled a cowling hanging loose, and the mood was gone. But to her amazement she had moisture in her eyes.

The Fly Inn Motel was clean and comfortable enough, and she slept well, awakening late to the sound of light aeroplanes already in the air. She looked at her watch – it was already half past nine, but what the hell, she thought. All inclination to travel any further had vanished with the night – she had arrived, the decision was already made.

She stood at the window staring out. It was a superb day, the sun blazing through the glass, the little planes lifting off, going round, and then touching down again like lazy whirlpools in the sky. It was almost hypnotic and suddenly she was overwhelmed with the impulse that this was something she must do – not tomorrow, nor the day after, but there and then, right now. In an instant all her lethargy was gone, and she was throwing on her casuals and a flat pair of shoes. She would think about eating later.

Chris Butler looked up when she walked into the office. Instantly he was on his feet. A good-looking girl always did something for him, but a dusky version of Monroe coming through the door on a Sunday morning, cleared his hangover more quickly than a bourbon chaser.

"Can I help you, honey?" he drawled.

"Yes. I want to learn to fly," Karina told him simply, feeling the words come to her lips more than actually speaking them.

"Sure thing, honey. We'll book you in for next weekend."

"I want a lesson now."

"Sorry. No can do. All our trainers are airborne at the moment. We haven't a plane or an instructor spare for at least a week."

"Well, what's that out there then?" She pointed to an open cockpit Stearman bi-plane outside on the pan. "What's the matter with that? And what's the matter with you? Or are you a desk jockey, or something? I want to speak to Chris Butler."

"I am Chris Butler," he looked coolly at her. "And I ain't no desk jockey. And I ain't taking any girlie student up in that ship. You'll sick your guts up and the plane'll stink for weeks."

Karina stared hard at him, her eyes suddenly brittle. "You don't know that," she said.

"I know it like I know you're standing there. Honestly." He smiled a smile that said "Believe me", and looked down at the booking forms. "Now if next Sunday at 3.00 will be okay for you, we have a Cessna with a spare slot then."

"I don't think you understand me, Mr Butler. I would like to fly now. And I would like to fly with you."

"Sorry, but *no*."

"Because you think I will be ill?"

"That and the fact that an open bi-plane is very raw and very noisy. Even if you make it through the flight without giving me a face full of breakfast, the chances are you won't come back for more instruction."

"How much is that Stearman worth?" Karina asked.

His hard gaze softened. "That example?" he smiled. "She's a beaut. About a hundred thousand bucks, I'd say. And rising."

"Okay, I'll make you an offer. If you can make me sick in it, I'll buy it and double your money. I'll pay you 200,000 dollars for that aeroplane."

He looked at her. "Two hundred thousand dollars," he said startled, and suddenly laughed, "Come on, honey, don't try to wind Chris Butler up on a Sunday morning. My head's banging and I'm not in the mood."

Karina said nothing. Instead she passed her MasterCharge Gold across the table to him. He picked up the card, the smile gone. A limit of 500,000 dollars was embossed on the bottom. He dialled the authorisation number, his face no longer the ruddy hue it had been a moment before; then he returned the phone to the hook very thoughtfully. The card was good and hadn't been stolen.

His mind was working very fast now. Crazy broads with too much dough were supposed to exist but he had never met one yet. They were all down in Florida he guessed, chasing toy-boys, not up here in Maine where the wind would scalp you in the winter. But here she was, a beautiful screwball someone had bankrolled, just asking to be parted from her readies. Well, what the hell, if she didn't need the money, he certainly did – and it was she who had thrown out the challenge, not he. "How much flying have you done in light aircraft?" he asked, suddenly suspicious.

"None."

"You haven't!" His surprise was as genuine as his pleasure. This was going to be too easy, and his pulse quickened. It was no longer time to quibble.

The Stearman had been his dream machine for several years, but the flying school wasn't doing well financially and a hundred grand injection would buy off the bank a little longer. And he would still have enough in hand to find another bird, although maybe not so good.

"You've just gotten yourself your first lesson, honey," he said, smiling broadly at her. "Just sign up the indemnities," he pushed the enrolment documents across the table, "and we'll go see what we can do for your digestion."

He waited for her to complete the formalities before he went on. "You'll need a coat. Here take this." He pulled a new leather bomber jacket out of a glass case and passed it across. "It may be hot down here, but above 5,000 feet in an open cockpit it gets mighty cold."

"Thanks," she said pleasantly. Then, "Hey, this is brand new, isn't it? How much do I owe you?"

He laughed. "Nothing, honey. Normally they're 470 bucks, but I'll throw it in with the aircraft."

"Very kind of you," she grinned herself now. "But you could be on to a loser."

"A loser? Not me, lady. You're in for the ride of your life. Just tell me when you want to stop."

"Don't count that I will."

He grunted, and said no more. She stood and waited while he raised somebody called Andy about the weather, and someone else called Max about some parts. Chris Butler was one hell of a good-looking guy, she found herself thinking, perhaps a bit too much like the World War Two stereotype with swept back hair and leather flying boots, but without the polo neck, and twiddled moustache. She tried to guess his age. He couldn't have been much under forty, although he was very lean and not running to fat.

"Okay. Let's go," he threw the phone back on the hook, and grinned at her almost boyishly. "Lesson number one coming up."

Karina felt strange. Half an hour earlier she had been listlessly wondering what to do for the rest of the day, and now here she was following a stranger towards an aeroplane that looked no more than a cat's-cradle of loose wires.

She felt awkward and ungainly in the heavy leather bomber jacket, but Chris Butler seemed to have been born in his. It was very worn, not a good fit, sloping off his shoulders as if it had finally reached the limit of its stretch, but it was in the image of the man and Karina was attracted to him, despite his bluff exterior. She smiled inwardly. He was damned sure he was going to be 100,000 bucks better off that afternoon, and she was equally sure he wasn't.

She quickly found that light planes were designed for one thing and one thing only – that was flying. They were awkward to climb into and impossibly undignified to scrabble out of. On the ground they had all the ungainly characteristics of an inveterate drunk. He strapped her into the front seat, and climbed into the rear, passing forward a headset. "Put that on," he said, and suddenly his voice was very loud in her ears. But even that was eclipsed when the engine started. At first the motor was very reluctant, slowly turning over with a course rasp of gears, quite unlike any car she knew. There were several bangs, then nothing more. He tried again. There was another huge explosion, but this time she caught, coughed, then caught again giving a mighty roar that seemed it must surely shake the little aeroplane into a thousand bits. Karina could feel it straining and bouncing against its brakes like a prize filly at the gate.

In a moment they were away, accelerating down the runway at extraordinary speed and it didn't seem a second before they were in the air, climbing at a steep angle away from the field. She lost her breath, or so it seemed. The feeling was indescribable. This was another world. Beneath them the cars and buildings were like toys on an architect's model, the sky a vast and empty cavern through which they cavorted like a foal newly on its feet.

"You okay up front?" his words came through the headset.

"Fabulous," she sung back.

"Straps still tight?"

"Killing me."

"That's the way it should be. Don't want you falling out and making a nasty mess on the ground. And that tummy – okay, is it?"

"Never better," she shouted.

She heard him chuckle, and in the next instant, the nose of the aircraft went down, then up again, the ground slowly rolling over her head in a crazy, dream-like cartwheel as they pulled through a gentle barrel roll.

"How was that?" he called, levelling off.

"Brilliant," she yelled back.

"Fancy some real aeros?"

"You betcha," she cried.

"Right," she heard him growl. "Right." His voice was lower now, and for an instant she felt a tinge of apprehension. But she had no more than a second to consider the wisdom of her response before her insides felt as if they were being drawn out by an invisible magnet.

The aircraft had bucked into the vertical where it held, climbing straight up at full power, the propeller clawing at the sky, slamming great gobs of air against the windshield. Then suddenly the wind noise was gone and she felt her hair fly forward over her face. They were falling backwards, tail-sliding towards the earth, down and down for what seemed an eternity before the Stearman flipped, falling over on its back into a vertical, gut-churning swoop. Karina swallowed, her knuckles white as she clutched the panel in front of her. The ground was rushing up towards them now, filling the windshield, and as he kicked in some rudder it began to spin like a wide-spoked wheel, one way, then the other, before he finally pulled out of the dive.

Suddenly it was no longer the world in miniature. They were at ground level skimming the tree tops at an amazing speed. The ground fell away towards a valley floor and they followed it down, turning to track the river bed as it wound round rocky promontories and outcrops growing from the sides of the rift. The valley was narrowing down and closing in and it was getting darker, and she waited for him to pull up to higher ground but they maintained their run, the walls steepening into curtains of dark jade rock that were moist and shiny from springs bleeding from the faces. Both her hands were braced against the panel, as they rolled from one wing tip to the other, skimming the sheer angles at each bend.

Then just as it seemed the ravine would close in upon them completely, it suddenly widened, and they were out over the deep, still vastness of a lake. Again the aircraft dropped lower, this time almost kissing the black water with its wheels. Her lips drew back in a wide involuntary grin, no composure in her face, just the wild look of exulta-tion.

She saw the throttle move in as he dribbled on some

more power and they were climbing once more, the rush of wind lessening as the speed bled off.

"Lesson over," Chris Butler's voice came back in her ears.

"No! So soon?"

"'Fraid so. How you feeling?"

"Fabulous," she breathed.

"Say again?"

"Absolutely great," she yelled back at him.

"Oh shit," he said. "I really thought we were on for a deal with the aircraft. So you really enjoyed that, did you?"

"Yep. Let's do it again."

There was a pause. "Not today, lady," he muttered, drawing breath. "I'm still nursing my hangover, remember."

"Shame," she said.

"Yes," he agreed. "In every way."

Ten minutes later they were back on the ground at Carson's Field, and the engine died with a wheeze and several clicks, leaving nothing but the tinkle of hot metal cooling. The silence was sudden, and almost as deafening as the roar of the flight. Her ears were singing from the assault, and she just sat there, her chest heaving, almost unwilling to believe it was over.

"Come on, honey. Out you get." He was already standing on the wing, pulling the headset jacks out of the panel. "You won your bet. Now you better come and sign up for some proper lessons so I can make some dough to pay for that jacket. You sure you still don't want to buy the ship for 200 grand?"

Karina pulled herself out and followed him down the wing. "Nope," she said. "But, you can certainly sign me up for those lessons."

"You're quite something," he nodded with a begrudging grin. "You sure you've not done some of this before?"

"You are repeating yourself," she told him flatly.

The following week she was back; and again the week after that.

Then for two weekends she couldn't make it because Clive chose to stay in town, and she felt the agony of withdrawal welling in her like a junkie snatched off dope.

"Is anything the matter, Karina?" Clive had asked over dinner one evening.

"Nothing, my love," she had responded quickly.

"I think there is," said Clive, his eyes cold and suspicious. "You have been acting strangely for several days."

"Didn't you know?" she feigned surprise.

"Know what?"

"It's the time of the month," she said with an embarrassed smile, averting her eyes.

He didn't return her smile. Clive's passion for blood did not extend to female menstruation. "I see," he said, displeased.

It was an old ploy she had used many times before. If she played it right she could engineer two periods in one month. It was an unusual way to plan her diary, but it worked.

"You will be at home this weekend, won't you?" she asked with a winsome smile to avert his suspicions.

He thought about it. "No," he said predictably. "There are some urgent matters I have to attend to out of state."

"Oh, what a shame."

"Yes," he reflected. "But I'll be back in town for a full two weeks after that."

Too true he would. "I'll look forward to that," she said.

What she really was looking forward to was her next visit to Carson's Field and Chris Butler. Flying was the escape she was seeking without previously knowing what form it would take.

She arrived at the Fly Inn Motel early that Friday evening, and took a shower. Then she fell back naked on the bed, a liquid smile moistening the fullness of her lips. The night sky was alive with the buzz of a dozen aircraft working the circuit; round and round they went, their strobes winking like fireflies in a Roman garden. Although her lesson was not until ten the following morning, tonight she had a date. She had now completed seven hours flying towards her Private Pilot's Licence and Chris had announced that tomorrow she would be going solo. Then, before she had time to take in this news, he went on, "And how about a spot of dinner with me the evening before? We can go over your pre-flight planning."

It had taken her by surprise, and it was a moment before she responded, "A nice idea, Chris, and thank you, but I'll have to let you know. It depends on how early I can get away from New York. And in any event I will insist you let me pay."

"Absolutely not," he said emphatically.

"Then I'm afraid it's no dinner. You've already bought me a jacket, or had you forgotten? If you treat all your students this way, you'll go broke, and that's for sure."

"Okay, honey," he grunted with a grin. "I know I'll never win with you."

And now it was Friday, and she imagined him out there in the sky with another student, and wondered which aircraft he was in. She could already feel the taut rein of envy mixing with a delicious anticipation of what the weekend promised. She closed her eyes, and her hand moved up and cupped her breast, squeezing the nipple and feeling it harden beneath her fingers. The feeling was quite exquisite and involuntarily she raised her hips just a little, the fine hairs on her stomach strengthening into a blossom of auburn floss that curled down between her legs. She had plans for Chris Butler that went beyond flight briefing.

He was a strange, compelling man, she had decided early on. Unlike the young, brash whizz-bang dealers whose dates she had turned down daily before moving in with Clive, Chris Butler was never keen to talk about himself. She had quickly learned that his background was with the United States Airforce, first on combat fast-jets, then later touring the world as group leader with the Angels One Display Team. Then tragically, a mountaineering accident had put paid to his professional flying career, and rather than sit behind a desk, he had taken an early discharge to start up the Flying School.

In principle, the idea was good. In practice it was not. No one had said as much, but she had found that the outfit was not doing well financially, partly because Toni Orlando, the land baron owning Carson's Field, charged an exorbitant rent, but mainly because Chris Butler was a flyer first, and an accountant second. After years under the umbrella of the USAF, he was disinclined towards and ill-prepared in skills for the more mundane aspects of commercial life. He lived for his flying, and that alone, something that had previously been plentiful and free, and he loathed with a morose intensity the mountains of paperwork that seemed to grow with the passing of each month.

What Chris Butler did not know was that Karina now owned Carson's Field. She had zeroed out Orlando's holding by the simple expedient of buying up the Five Acre Water Company which supplied Orlando's cattle ranch. Orlando was not pleased at the prospect of a drought being imposed on his thousand head of steer and in bad grace traded Carson's Field for Five Acre Water. Karina now owned an airfield, and in addition showed a book profit of 100,000 dollars on the deal – not spectacular, for she had broken all her rules. You never struck a deal on sentiment.

She planned to tell Chris that he had a new, and more reasonable, landlord but not just yet. The time wasn't right.

She looked at her watch. It was nearly eight, and their date was set for nine. She sat up on the bed and combed her hair, while deciding what to wear. He had never seen her in a dress before, only old denims or brown leather, her hair always drawn up tight with a comb. Tonight would be different. Tonight she would be out to impress Chris Butler.

He stopped in the doorway of the bar where they were to meet. The usual barflies and airfield groupies were there in their clusters, but unusually quiet, and for an instant he wondered why. Then his eyes followed to where theirs converged on a table in the corner of the lounge, and he hesitated before a grin cracked the whole width of his face. A girl sat there alone, a stunning creature in a pale blue skirt and white silk top that contrasted with the deep natural tan of her skin. Her hair seemed to reflect a dozen shades of ebony under the hidden ceiling light, pouring over her shoulders in a fluid mane that rippled as she moved. For an instant he wondered if he was not mistaken. "Karina?" he said hesitantly.

"Hi Chris," she looked up from her book.

"Karina! It is you! Honey, you look absolutely stunning," he told her in rapture.

"Thank you," she said. "You don't look so bad yourself."

It was true. There was something different about Chris Butler this evening. He had showered quickly after his last flight, and now wore a suit and tie that would not have been out of place on the dealing floor of Price Whitney. But that was where the similarity ended. His appearance was weathered and heavily chiselled, every line a cut of character, quite unlike the pale, soapstone men in front of the banks of the VDUs.

"Ready to eat?" he asked.

"I'm ravenous," she said. "I've had nothing since New York."

"Hell, you must be hungry then," he nodded. "Let's go straight through to the restaurant. The guys won't like it, though." He smiled and winked at the line-up along the bar. "They don't seem to be able to take their eyes off you. And I see their point."

Their talk over dinner was the frothy, wide-ranging chat of two people mutually attracted, yet both unwilling to admit it to each other. They could not disguise that they were easy in each other's company, leaning forward, voices low, hands close but not quite touching. She found out he was divorced, but he didn't expand. She told him there was someone in New York, and he nodded an understanding, and enquired

101

no further. It was as if between them an unspoken bond was forming, quite exclusive of their other lives. The dining room was busy but they were quite alone, his eyes crystal blue and sparkling brightly in the candle light, hers the tawny brown of smouldering peat.

"Coffee in my room?" she suggested, after they had finished.

"Sounds a great idea," he said, his eyes meeting hers.

A waiter came to the table with the bill. Karina took it without looking at it. "Put it on my number," she told him, and he withdrew. Very slowly she ran her tongue along her lips, moistening the gloss already there.

The coffee remained undrunk. In moments they were naked, falling together on the bed, the scent of fresh soap and cologne lifted from his skin in a powerful evocation. Already his manhood loomed proud from its bed of mat-black curls, glistening moist and almost threatening. She closed her eyes feeling his tongue tracing circles round her nipples, tickling the faint line of darker hairs that grew there so they crimped hard to points of exquisite pleasure. Clive was never like this, she thought in that instant before they began to move as one in a liquid frenzy. Their mewing love sounds joined in harmony with crickets calling in the grass outside, and she felt it begin to come, first as a gentle rush, then a helix of ascending bliss, tossing her from one wave to the next as heaven leant to touch the earth. "No more, no more," she whimpered at last, the blood singing loudly in her ears. "No more, my darling. Please."

He collapsed beside her, his chest heaving, his skin glistening like an otter's pelt. His lungs steadied to more shallow breathing and he turned over and smiled. "You're a young man's woman, Karina," he said, and kissed her gently.

"Uh huh," she breathed huskily. "And you're definitely a young woman's man. That was music."

The months that followed were the happiest she had known. Every hour she could escape from New York she spent at Carson's Field, loving, flying, then loving some more. She got her licence in record time and after that she and Chris would take off in the Stearman and storm the skies for hours at a time. He taught her every trick he knew, and there were plenty, and she was a perfect pupil. "I reckon you'd do well in the US Open Aerobatic Championships," he had told her more than once. "You'd fly the pants off most of the guys I know."

"Maybe one day, Chris," she parried, "but not just yet." She couldn't tell him that it was one thing flying out at Carson's

102

Field, and quite another engaging in a high-profile sport that could get her a mention in the *New York Times*. She guessed Chris half knew the truth of this, and he didn't press her again.

Then came the break in their meetings, with its terrible tragic consequence. After a particularly glorious weekend, she arrived in New York late on Sunday evening and let herself into the penthouse suite.

She stopped in the hallway. Intuitively she knew something was wrong. A faint smell was upon the air – a smell she had known and still remembered well, and for an instant she had the grossest vision of the Orphanage of Santa Maria. It was quite unmistakably the odour of vomit and urine. Her pulse raced madly as she passed from the hall into the day room. What she saw there made her gag.

The wrestling ring had been lowered from the ceiling and there was a body on the canvas. At first she thought that it was a corpse. Clive was lying there quite naked, his eyes wide open but unseeing, each limb tied to a corner post, the ropes tightened by splats of wood forced through the strands and twisted like a turnbuckle. He must have been there for many hours, perhaps a day or more. His limbs were blue, and he lay in his own excrement, diluted by blood that had seeped from numerous small cuts all over his body.

"Karina," he suddenly croaked, his eyes coming into focus at the sound of her step. "Karina! Is that you? Call a doctor. I'm dying."

Karina stood staring, disbelieving and unhearing. "Karina," he said again, his voice cracking hysterically. "Karina, help me. Please help me."

Perhaps it was his rare use of the word "please" that jolted her or maybe it was the pressure welling up inside her lungs, but this time she moved, and fled from the room. Behind the door she grabbed a cushion and leaned against the wall and shook, holding the cushion to her face to stop the laughter exploding from her throat. It was several minutes before her eyes dried sufficiently to dial the paramedics. The memory was for a lifetime. One of his 'treats' had obviously gone very badly wrong.

For the first week of his recovery Clive booked into a security suite in a top clinic out on Long Island. Then he returned to the penthouse above Price Whitney, and for six weeks after that went nowhere, hovering over the security VDUs and addressing his managers on the internal intercom. For Karina it was a period of absolute frustration. Because of his constant vigilance she was unable to progress her plans, and to move out would jeopardise the whole programme at its most critical stage. No, she had to stay and wait, and it was not until nearly two months later when Clive went into hospital for a check that she was able to return to Carson's Field. She tried to call Chris on the phone at least a dozen times, but there was no answer, so she went anyway.

It had not been a good period for Chris Butler. A series of warm fronts had come through the region, smothering the hills with low cloud which hung there for weeks on end – hopeless weather for flying when all their machines should have been up and paying the mounting bills.

It was not long before he was spending first one hour, then two or more in the clubhouse bar, taking to drink when he could not take to the air. Flying set him free. There was no clutter up there, no pervasive intrusions in his life, just a wonderful solitude in a three-dimensional heaven that soaked the centre of his brain like a strong, addictive drug. When the weather was bad, he had to have another release, and he found it in drink, leaving the unmistakable brown envelopes that carried bad news from the bank, unopened in the tray.

Karina drove for eight hours through bad weather to get to the field, and when she arrived in the late afternoon, Chris was not to be found. The staff avoided her eyes when they told her he was unwell, but said he would probably be about later. The truth was that he had gone to bed blind drunk the night before, and the night before that.

That morning he had forced himself out of bed to call the Met Service, but the outlook was bad and it would probably stay clamped for the next forty-eight hours. He fell into a chair and let oblivion return.

It was only much later that he heard the doorbell through the mists of his unconsciousness. He ignored it for many minutes but it persisted and at last he drew a gown over his nakedness and slipped the latch.

Karina could barely believe it was the same man, red-eyed in the doorway, holding himself steady against the frame. At first she said nothing, just stared at him, dismayed. His features were puffy, his complexion florid and she noticed a tiny vein that had not been there before standing out on his nose. The eyes that had sparkled with laughter eight weeks before were now dull, without life.

"Hi, Karina," he grinned wanly, after the first shock had cleared. "This is a surprise," he slurred. "I wasn't expecting you. In fact, I wasn't expecting you ever again. Where have you been?"

"I am so sorry, Chris," she apologised. "But some business matters cropped up that simply couldn't be deferred. I've called several times, and written, but you've never responded. Anyway, I'm here now."

"There's no flying today, I'm afraid," he stated, his eyes matt and lustreless.

"That doesn't matter," she said. "I'm here to see *you*."

"Oh," he absorbed the fact. "Had a few drinks last night," he said. "Not feeling too brilliant. What I need is the hair of the dog." He checked his watch. "Hell is that the time. Come on over to the bar. I'll buy you a drink. Just let me throw on some clothes."

They sat together awkward and estranged. She kept trying to catch his gaze and failing. "What's the matter, Chris?" she kept asking him, and at first he would not answer.

"It's the bloody weather, Karina," he eventually said. "We've had about a dozen good flying days since you left. No flying. No money."

"Can I help?" she asked.

"*You help*?" he almost laughed, and she would not have minded for it might have cheered him a little. "No, little lady. There is absolutely nothing you can do. It's all done now anyway."

"What do you mean?" she asked, a chill touching her spine.

He seemed not to hear. "Excuse me for a few minutes, Karina, will you please?" He swilled back his bourbon. "I've got a couple of things to do, and I'll be right back."

"Don't be long," she told him.

"Be as quick as I can," he said, and for the first time he smiled.

She sat alone at the bar, looking out across the apron to where she could see him working in his office on the corner of the hangar. He had taken some papers from the filing cabinet to his desk, and was poring over them intently. It all seemed dreadfully normal, yet something was churning in her gut. She knew she must go over to him, but with what purpose she wasn't sure.

"Chris?" she called, letting herself into his office. She glanced round, surprised. He was gone. She looked at the desk where he had been working, and her breathing stopped. There, in neat rows, were his insurance policies, exactly as he had laid them out. For an instant she just stood and stared, not believing the madness that flooded through her mind.

Then suddenly she was running. "Chris?" she cried in panic, "Chris, where are you?" There was no reply, just her own voice echoing round the inside of the hangar.

In an instant she was out and across the apron, her long legs flying, her heart a hammer in her chest. She ran towards the tower and a hundred yards to go when she heard an engine cough roughly into life. It was not the Stearman, but a Cessna trainer out of sight behind the hangar. There was none of the usual delay as checks were made and in the next instant, it was there, bucking gently as it rolled across the broken concrete pan towards the runway. Chris was at the controls – his face no longer florid but a deathly pale as he stared directly ahead without a glance to right or left. He barely slowed in the turn, all power coming on as he lined up on the runway. He was away, the machine nosing down as it accelerated rapidly into the rain.

"Stop! Stop!" she screamed, her legs wobbling, her lungs fit to burst. It was no use. She staggered to a halt as the machine sped on, throwing up a vortex of spume that drifted lazily away on the light breeze. Then it was airborne, lifting like a feather into the murky skies. The red fuselage glowed almost cheerily as it kissed the lower clouds, winking in and out of sight in the billows as it banked slowly round in a wide circle before fading to a smudge of pink, and was gone.

She stood quite still. The sky was empty but for an amorphous overcast that shrouded everything. It was the sort of fog that cocooned doomed vessels on a sullen sea and she felt an awful hopelessness, knowing there was nothing she could do. High above she could still hear the aircraft climbing, its engine note even as it laboured steadily in its upward spiral.

Then she was running again, racing for the tower with its radio transmitter.

She snatched the mike from the controller. "Tango Golf, Tango Golf, this is Carson Tower. Do you read? Over," she called, releasing the key.

There was nothing except the harsh crackle of static and the whistle of wind through the aerials. "Tango Hotel," she tried again, her voice lifting shrill. "Do you read? Over."

The ether was as dead as outer space, no hint of life beyond the mast on the tower roof. She could stand it no more. "Chris?" she cried, all procedure gone. "Chris, please answer me. Please speak to me."

The chatter in the tower died to a silence. No one was sure

of what was happening. A sudden chill had replaced the fetid warmth of the summer afternoon. Against the silence, was the faintest sound of a solitary aircraft circling high in the dense, overcast sky.

No one moved.

The tower staff knew it was him. They had seen him take off. But he had made no calls, no requests for taxi clearance and that was strange for Chris, who was a stickler for the rules.

Every eye was on the sky. Mesmerised, each person scanned the bland folds of scud blustering low across the deserted field. The cloud now obscured the higher trees on the western boundary as the base dropped closer to the ground. It was futile – they all knew it. Soon the fog would clamp the field and then nothing would get in or out.

But still they could hear the aircraft climbing high above. "The nearest place he'll get in is Stibson's Field," said Smith, the air traffic controller, scowling. "They are still ahead of the warm front and won't be clamped for another couple of hours."

"But that's forty minutes' flying from here," said Karina, her voice tight and peculiarly controlled.

"Right," nodded Smith, far from happy.

"How much fuel has he on board?" she asked.

Smith's brow puckered into furrows. "About three gallons I'd say at a guess. She was almost out when she landed last night."

The silence this time was solid as each knew what the other was thinking. Three gallons of fuel was good for twenty minutes and little more, and five minutes had already passed. There was no hope of making it to Stibson's Field.

"Jeez, what's he playing at?" Smith's voice suddenly cracked as the nervousness broke through. "He could at least try and make a run for it. He stands no chance here."

Karina spoke into the microphone again. "Chris," she called, her voice thick now. "What are you doing? Please speak to me."

As soon as she released the button the static returned, then suddenly cut, leaving not a sound as their breaths held frozen.

"I am above the clouds now." His voice came from the speaker, ethereal and strangely disembodied. There was a long pause before he went on. "It is so beautiful up here, Karina, so peaceful. Nothing but miles of snowy dunes in an empty wilderness. Here is where I belong Karina, this is my place. For me, this is closest a man can get to heaven – as close as I'll ever get, anyway."

"Chris!" she screamed into the mike. "Chris, you're almost out of fuel. For heaven's sake, mush it down somewhere flat before it's too late. Chris, speak to me." Frantically she pressed the button, realising that it was useless. He was holding his radio on transmit and jamming the frequency.

"I am sorry, Karina," he went on in a tone that had a funny kind of lightness. "You and me were really good. You know that. I know that. But it couldn't go on for ever. I've run out of money, and it's as simple as that. Orlando will be coming for his rent very soon, and that'll be the end."

"Chris!" she screamed again. "Chris, I own the field now, not bloody Orlando. It's yours for ever, for nothing. Oh Chris, please come back. Don't do anything stupid."

"It's so utterly beautiful up here," he was saying. "The sun is reflected in the engine cowl like a burnished orb and the sky is as black as a raven's plumage. I wish you could see it Karina, my love, feel the peace, the tranquillity, see the majesty and enormity of the heavens, get that feeling of being alone, yet part of an almighty union that transcends the mantras of the gurus and takes the soul to another place far beyond the reaches of the mind."

"He's boned out," Smith suddenly exploded. "He's flipped. Gone totally bananas. A basket case."

"Shut up," Karina hissed. "Shut up." She had never heard Chris speak like this before. It was like a voice from another world.

"But then," he went on, "but then you would be like me Karina, wouldn't you – a failure in all things but one, and that one thing does not pay the bills. I'm sorry, my love, I truly am. So very, very sorry. Bye bye, my love, bye bye. I love you."

"He's crazy, man," Smith almost gibbered, unable to stop. His eyes were wide and he had gone as white as marble.

"Chris, don't," Karina screamed once more, but there was nothing. He had turned the radio off. The air was filled with static.

They all heard the engine cut. "He's coming down," Smith croaked. "This is it. He's coming down. Oh shit! Shit, shit, shit!"

There was not a sound now. Even the wind that had been whistling softly rou.d the tower seemed to die at that moment as their eyes bored the sky. They heard it first as a faint rushing sound, still high above and to the south, as soft as the distant fluting of wild geese wheeling into land. Then at once the sound grew louder, increasing like a distant storm, until the air was rent by a violent shriek of wind tearing through the cowels as the aircraft hurtled to the ground.

It was in that instant Smith acted. He grabbed Karina, forcing her to face away from the window as the plane dropped out of the clouds, upside down, fully stalled in an inverted spin, the pilot hanging in his straps.

After the ambulance had taken the body away she drove back to New York, vowing never to return.

But she did return. She bought the Stearman from his estate which paid off his debts, and rented most of the buildings to another operator. She had other plans for Carson's Field now, and within two months they were in place. The Nemesis Corporation was fully installed.

Tonight she stayed up in the Stearman longer than usual, gazing into the heavens. Soon the fiery sunset sky would turn to the blue-black of chilled blood. Suddenly she shivered with the spooky feeling she was not alone. The stick felt as if there was another hand there on the controls, and for an instant she thought she could hear a chuckle. And then she smiled, knowing now for sure. Her hands were off the stick and the aircraft was flying itself, uncannily and unerringly. She just let it go, swooping, looping, rolling, and only when the fuel was getting low did she regain control and slide back the throttle.

The aircraft dipped as the power came off and she began to sink, the darkness suddenly rushing up upon her like a shroud as she dropped below the angle of the sun. The evening air was quite still with no turbulence. Everything beneath was black and featureless, until a few minutes later the first lights appeared, twinkling sporadically. In the distance now she could just make out the runway lights, dissecting the horizon like a thin line of luminous pearls. She lowered the nose and brought the aircraft round from base leg on to finals.

"Nice flight, Miss Darielle?" the pump hop called, coming over.

"Yes thanks, Jim. It was really beautiful tonight." The words hid the sadness in her heart, and she turned away to hide the tears in her eyes.

She finished her business with Fay in the Nemesis Building and drove back to New York. The following morning she was on the 09.30 Concorde to London.

"Don't!" Karina's voice was shrill. "Don't, please don't do

it!" She heard there a terrible echo of her words those bare few months before.

It was too late. The axe was already swinging through the air, smashing into the heat-exchanger panels, splicing the profusion of wires into a hundred meaningless ends, puncturing the compressor, the freon escaping with a loud hiss to leave a rime upon the pipes. There was a gasp and a flash. A pulse of blue fire flared as the machine coughed its final breath, and then nothing. For the first time in two years all motion ceased and it lay silent and quite inert.

Too late the lump of wood cracked his temple.

She stood over him, anger and frustration in her eyes. "You fool," she told the silent body. "You utter bloody fool."

Angela tore the wood from her. "You've killed him," she screamed out. "Oh my sweet Lord, you've killed him. You've killed him!"

"I don't think so," Karina scowled. "But I could have done if his skull is as soft as his brain."

"We must call an ambulance," Angela flustered.

"No," Karina caught her arm. "I really didn't hit him that hard. He'll come round in a moment. Get a cold sponge on his head."

It was true. She had back-pulled on the swing, deliberately tempering the force out of the blow, but she knew she had to stop the destruction somehow.

Paul groaned, clutching his temple. Then his eyes widened, trying to focus. "It exploded. It must have exploded."

"No, it didn't," Karina told him. "The only thing that exploded was your common sense."

Paul tried to see who was speaking but could not raise his head. It was a strange voice, a woman's voice, low and melodious with the trace of an accent that he could not place through the crashing migraine in his skull. "What happened?" he croaked. "Who the hell are you?"

"I am here on the instructions of Mr Tuesday Nemesis," she said quietly. "He is interested in your invention and wants to make you an offer."

For an instant Paul thought something had happened and his reason had departed. "Interested in my invention?" he repeated foolishly, the words echoing in his ears. "My invention? You must be mistaken. No one is interested in my invention."

She looked down at him hard. "There is no mistake," she said. "Mr Nemesis saw your preliminary application in

110

the Patent Office journal. He is prepared to gamble that your invention might just work – what d'you call it – the TEESER machine? Anyway, I have a cheque here for 250,000 dollars, which is yours to establish full worldwide patent rights, and produce a working prototype to his satisfaction, providing—" and she paused there, "—providing you will license him the production rights for an initial period of ten years. In return for these rights you will be given an equity stake of 30 per cent in the holding company and an initial salary of 80,000 dollars per annum to head up research."

Paul rolled over. Bright lights were flashing in his skull from the force of the blow, and his eyes seemed unable to converge. Now and then among the spangle of stars an angel stood above him, her hair the raven mane of a wild mare, her eyes as dark as polished cassiterite, her skin the tinted olive of an Eastern goddess, slight shadows beneath the high reaches of her bones as she stood in the backlight of the sun. His heart paused, and he blacked out again. When consciousness came back, his sight was clear and the vision had gone. Now he knew he had been dreaming.

"Come on," Angela eased him to his feet with relief. "You've had a nasty crack. Let's get the kettle on and we'll patch you up. Can't have you looking like that, can we," she dabbed a smudge of blood away from his temple.

Paul accepted her ministrations in grateful silence. Then very cautiously he asked, "Was there someone else here a moment ago?"

She looked at him surprised. "Well, of course there was. It wasn't me who hit you, although I felt like it – breaking up all your special machine like that after all those years of work!"

"There was?" Paul's heart rate jumped to double. "A beautiful dusky-coloured woman?"

"I wouldn't exactly say *beautiful*," Angela bridled a little. "Attractive perhaps, in a *dark* sort of way."

"Did she say anything before she left?"

"Yes, she left a note, and said they would be contacting you." Angela pointed diffidently to a sliver of white card on the table.

His eyes followed to where she pointed, and instantly snatched it up. It read:

HOLT & FARTHINGALE
SOLICITORS & COMMISSIONERS FOR OATHS

Underneath was written in a neat feminine hand, "*Will*

return tomorrow to discuss details." There were no initials or signature.

The following morning Paul stood at the window, red-eyed as the car drew up. He had not slept all night, working in a frenzy of molten solder and flying spanners to repair the damage he had wrought in those few moments of madness. And at last it was up and running – not as well as it should because he did not have enough Freon to properly re-gas the system, but nonetheless it was producing light and heat, and that was all that mattered.

Despite the fatigue, he was physically and mentally glowing, hardly able to believe the words of promise still echoing in his mind.

Everyone had been busy. Angela had cleaned the cottage, the girls had insisted they stay off school to give the walls some fresh white paint, and he had even found a moment to put shine on to the copper pipework that joined the compressors and the heat-exchangers. Everything seemed to have taken on new life, glowing with a burnished brilliance, and he felt suddenly exhilarated.

"Welcome to my humble abode," he smiled broadly at the two people stepping out of the gleaming Jaguar XJS3.

It was the same woman as before, this time accompanied by a thin man in his early sixties, his greying hair matching the colour of his suit. Neither of them returned his smile.

"Thank you. My name is Farthingale of Holt and Farthingale," the man announced. "We're here on the instruction of Mr Tuesday Nemesis. The initial payment has already been authorised, and I have the cheque here, together with papers for your signature."

"Excellent," beamed Paul. "Come on in. I've been looking forward to going over all the technical details with you."

"Yes, that would be fascinating," Farthingale said in a tone that inferred otherwise. "But perhaps we should sort out the paperwork first," he glanced at his companion. "We haven't a lot of time." And she nodded agreement.

Paul's smile stayed in place, but tightened a little. It seemed crazy that suddenly here were people willing to put a small fortune up-front without seeing the goods. He could be a total phoney – they had no means of knowing otherwise.

The first item on the table was the cheque for 250,000 dollars, exactly as Karina had said. His eyes feasted on it before transferring to the other bundles of papers tied with red lawyer's ribbon. "We shall leave these for you to study,"

112

Farthingale was saying. "Take them to your own solicitor if you wish, but you will find the arrangements exactly as outlined. The cheque is post-dated fourteen days from now. If we don't hear back from you in the meantime, it will be cancelled on the assumption you don't want to proceed."

"The papers will be signed, and you'll get them back without delay," Paul told him.

"Good," said the lawyer. "Some sort of energy device, is it?" he enquired casually in the same diffident tone. "How's it supposed to work?"

"How's it supposed to work," Paul repeated, at a loss, unable to define his conception in such crude terms. He took a long breath. "In technical terms it is a Thermo Electric Energy Shunt, or a TEES machine."

"A bit of a teaser," the lawyer said drily.

Paul did not miss the cynicism. "If you wish," he studied him coldly. He glanced at the woman. She was just as lovely as he remembered through the haze of the concussion, but there was not the same softness in the cold light of the morning. Her face was hard and mask-like as if cast in an exquisite mould, and she was studying him with an almost ferocious intensity. There was something manic in her stare, and he found it disconcerting.

Some of his enthusiasm waned as he continued. "There is nothing new in the TEES machine, or TEESER, if you prefer." He looked at the lawyer, who looked at the woman. "What *is* different is the application of existing technology. We all know there is nothing new under the sun."

He saw the lawyer check his watch as he continued. "The vast bulk of the world's energy resources are used to create heat which in turn is used for many things, principally making electricity and just keeping people warm. This is quite absurd when you think about it."

"Absurd?" Karina questioned.

"Yes, absurd," affirmed Paul. "Quite idiotic, because what the nuclear piles and fossil fuels are actually doing is making something hotter which is already hot."

I thought as much, the lawyer mused. He is a loony.

But Karina sat forward. "Already hot? I don't follow you," she said.

"Even water at freezing point is at 273 degrees above zero on the absolute scale. Ice is only cold to us in the relative sense. All we do when we melt ice and boil it is add another 100 degrees of heat, or a mere 37 per cent to its existing energy content."

Paul could see the lawyer fidgeting now, but he carried

on. "Exactly the same applies to air. When you warm air, all you are doing is burning something – coal, or electricity, or whatever to make it even warmer than it is already."

"Excuse me interrupting," the lawyer coughed, "but is this leading us anywhere? I really must stress the importance of time today."

Paul took his eyes off Karina and turned to him. "How much was your electricity bill last quarter?" he asked.

"About 300 pounds. But I really must protest—"

"And your heating bill?"

"I really don't see what relevance this has, Mr Feral."

"Okay. Then how much do you suppose we pay here for heating and power, all of which is electric?" Paul turned his question around.

"I'd hate to guess," the lawyer dismissed.

"Nothing," Paul told him. "Absolutely nothing."

Paul saw the look in his eyes again. The man is a fraud, they said.

"Yes, you think the scheme is fraudulent, don't you?" Paul's voice began to rise. "If you do, then you should inspect what we have here and try to find the power lines, the diesel generators, the water wheel, the wind mill, the solar panels, the hot rocks, the steam engines, the nuclear pile, the—"

"That's enough," Karina cut in. "You have our cheque." She picked it up and handed it to him. "Tell us more of your TEESER machine."

"The TEESER is a device that takes heat from air in one place and pushes it out again in another."

"Like a refrigerator," suggested Karina.

"Exactly," said Paul. "The basis of the system is in fact a back-to-front refrigerator. It takes heat from the cold air outside and makes it colder, at the same time as making the warm air inside warmer. The most important thing is that for every 3 watts of energy it moves, the motor actually consumes only 1 watt. You are therefore getting 2 watts for nothing, or a profit of 200 per cent."

"As you say, there is nothing new in that," Karina said. "All you have there is a heat pump. Lots of modern homes have those."

"Quite correct," Paul enthused. It was good that she had at least a partial understanding. "But the existing heat pumps are not self sustaining."

"Self sustaining?" she frowned. For the first time her face had shown expression.

114

"They all need an external power supply to run the motor. Mine does not."

"It doesn't?" Her surprise was genuine, and Paul wondered why, for this was what they were paying for.

"No. This whole cottage is heated and lit with nothing but the energy from the air we breathe."

"Okay, go on."

"The answer, strangely enough, comes from Russia."

"Russia?"

"Yes. Because of the vast distances involved, many of the remoter villages in the Soviet heartland still do not have electricity. Their heat is from fires, and their lighting from oil lamps. The Russians have done a lot of experimentation with thermo-electric devices to turn heat directly into electricity. Although the thermocouple effect was first discovered by Seebeck back in 1822, they have found that a new semi-conductor made from bismuth and tellurium – bismuth telluride – has remarkable abilities to generate substantial electricity when heated, and a core of this attached to a hot-oil lamp chimney provides enough electricity to run a radio. You can imagine how important that is to anyone living in the wilderness."

"How very fascinating," Karina said, and Paul suddenly realised she was sitting forward on her chair.

"Yes, isn't it? But I won't bore you with too many details," he continued, "except to say that what I have done is further improve the efficiency of the bismuth telluride thermocouple so that now—"

"—now you can use some of the excess heat from the heat pump to drive its own motor," she interrupted, her eyes suddenly bright. "I suppose all you have to do is warm it up initially and off it goes."

"Right, absolutely right," he said. "See for yourself." He suddenly took her hand. "Come see. It's not just theory, it's living, breathing fact. Turn on the lights, turn on the cooker! See for yourself!"

"What's that strange little tube sticking out the roof?" she pointed through the window.

For the first time Paul hesitated and his face coloured slightly. "I'm afraid everything was put together on a very low budget," he explained. "A proper safety valve would have cost 30 pounds so I used a child's tin whistle – it sounds when there is an excess of steam in the system."

She turned to him and smiled, and her whole face changed.

115

"What a lovely touch – a tin whistle," she laughed, a soft haunting sound that took him by surprise. Then her eyes seemed to go far away. "I do like that. Yes, I do like that. That is what we shall call it. This new venture is going to be called the Tin Whistle Company."

After they had gone he realised that he did not even know her name. He had not asked, and she had not offered.

Ten miles down the road, she turned to the lawyer and said, "We're going to have to re-think our whole strategy on this one, Farthingale."

"How do you mean, Miss Darielle?"

"Simply this. He is genuine. I've a shrewd idea his TEESER machine actually does work."

"Are you certain of that?" His scepticism was undiminished. With a degree in law and another in the social anthropology of the Maltese ape, there was no reason why he should be anything else.

"Absolutely. We've seen it work. What is more the man couldn't tell a lie if he tried. I am as amazed as you are. He is unique, quite brilliant, yet almost naive. I can hardly believe he is a Feral."

"Well, we certainly weren't expecting the damned contraption to function," said the lawyer. "What are the tactics now, ma'am?"

"We go ahead," she told him. "Mr Nemesis will want us to proceed exactly as we planned."

116

CHAPTER 8

Karina returned immediately to New York, catching a red-eye 747 from Gatwick rather than wait for the following morning's Concorde out of Heathrow.

The fleeting visit to England had been more conclusive than she had anticipated. She had expected to find a piece of the Nemesis jigsaw there, but the shape was different, and the scope much larger than she had imagined. There was a great temptation to stay longer, but she had to get back before Clive returned. Also being in the company of Paul Feral left her feeling a way she cared not to define, and for one fleeting instant she had seen Chris Butler standing there again, handsome, brilliant, charming, yet inexplicably vulnerable.

No, she told herself several times on the flight, as other thoughts came to mind. No, no, no.

But the memory of the visit lingered on, tantalising images that came in and out of focus as she slumbered fitfully on the flight. England was another land, a small country, packed with history and huge contrasts that strained the senses of those for the first time on those shores. The airport, the usual modern aseptic sprawl of buildings designed to process, not to please, opened the visitor to London and beyond. Her first impression had not been good. Cromwell Road, the main artery into the city, was divided by a ribbon of discarded cans and fractured auto mufflers that no one cared to move, or even seemed to notice. Now and then the taxi in front would brush the kerb, sending a tunnel of filth to coil like a python through the air to gag the lungs. But once in the city a sort of cleanliness returned and the tall buildings beamed proudly over the same streets they had shaded for several centuries past.

But it was not the fine architecture and domed splendour

of St Paul's Cathedral that held there in her mind. Instead her thoughts returned to the silence and tranquillity of the lush Wiltshire meadows that seemed to cleanse her like a cataract after the heat of plane and town. Without framing the words or painting views, she knew that a little of herself still lingered there, and she dared not question why. But soon she would return. That as much she knew.

It was mid-afternoon when she arrived, and the apartment was empty. Clive had recently hired a cook, but it was her night off, so Karina went to the kitchen where everything for a meal had already been neatly set in place. She was well into the preparation of dinner when she was surprised by the sound of the lobby bell. It had to be Clive, but it was strange for him to ring. "Forget your key, honey?" she called, pressing the button that allowed the lift door to open into the lobby. "Come on in, darling. I've everything nearly ready."

One eye on the boiling pots, she glanced at him coming through the door, and waited for him to come up behind her and kiss her neck as he always did. There was nothing. She didn't even feel the rush of his breath through her hair. Surprised, she turned round. "Anything the matter, honey?" she asked, reaching for his hand, but not finding it.

She stared at him hard now. He looked different somehow in a way that was hard to place. "There *is* something wrong," she stated. "Come on, honey, what's the problem?" He was staring at her as if he didn't know her, and in his hand there was a crocodile skin briefcase she hadn't seen before.

"You must be Karina Darielle," he said, extending his hand. "Clive said you would be here to let me in."

"What?" Her eyes flew open. "You're – you must be – you must be Martin – Martin Feral!" She drew back foolishly. It had never occurred to her that any twin could be quite so identical. "This *is* a surprise. I thought you were Clive."

"So I gather. Yes I'm Martin."

"Go through to the living room and make yourself comfortable," she said, her flush disappearing as her composure returned. "I am expecting Clive up very soon."

"Thank you," he said again, and she noticed how similar their voices were, but with subtleties in cadence, Martin's much more quiet and less assertive.

"You will eat with us tonight, won't you?"

"Yes, if I may. Clive said he would put me up in the guest's bedroom."

"Of course," she beckoned him to follow her, smiling as

she did so. He did not see her face freeze as she turned, or sense her fury at being wrong-footed. "You can join me in the kitchen if you like," she invited. "I'm just finishing off the trimmings. I've made more than enough so there's plenty for you."

He let her lead him but he didn't say anything, and the silence that followed was oddly strained. He accepted a drink, then remained in the kitchen with her as she worked, but she did not find his presence oppressive as she might another man so close. Unlike Clive, he emitted no powerful sexual eminence, just standing there, eyeing her with a kind of vague curiosity. Then she realised why. Martin was gay.

"When did you arrive?" she asked.

"About an hour ago."

"You live in Africa, don't you?"

"Most of the time."

"Don't you find the climate rather hostile?" She made small-talk.

"No. I wouldn't live there if I did."

She turned round, startled at his rudeness, but his face was quite bland, and she realised that he wasn't even thinking about what he was saying. She wasn't there as far as he was concerned.

"Aren't there three brothers?" she changed the subject. "Clive mentioned Paul once, and you are Martin."

"Paul!" Martin looked surprised, then grimaced with the first hint of emotion. "Yes, there is a younger brother, Paul."

"You're not that keen on him, then?" she suggested casually.

"Dear Paul," he shrugged. "I'm afraid Paul is a dreamer – the loser in the family. We used to wonder if he was quite right in the head. He gets powerful obsessions about this and that." The words were spoken without rancour, just a clinical appraisal which she found quite chilling.

"That's pretty damning," she said, trying to keep the edge from her voice.

Martin looked at her startled as if suddenly realising he was being listened to. "Form your own opinion," he shrugged. "You may meet him one day. I expect he'll be over here fairly soon looking to finance some crackpot scheme or other."

"Really? That will be nice," she said. She wasn't going to mention that Paul had already been and gone. "Perhaps he's just a bit unbusinesslike," she suggested, hoping to draw him out, but he turned inwards again, politely watching what she was doing. She found the feeling creepy and was grateful to hear footsteps in the hall.

"Martin!" Clive smiled broadly, clutching his brother to him. "This is wonderful, absolutely great. How are you? You look so well."

"Pretty good, Clive, pretty good," Martin smiled back, a warmth there Karina had not seen before. "And yourself?"

"No complaints really. The banking business is a bit slower than I'd like, but with the economic situation as it is—" he tailed off with a shrug.

"I know the feeling," Martin nodded an understanding.

"And to what do I owe this pleasure?" Clive changed the subject, steering Martin back through to the lounge.

Their voices were now no more than muffled rumbles through the wall, and Karina's lips tightened as she turned down the cooker to lessen the noise from the boiling pots. Through the gap in the door she could just see them sitting together, talking earnestly. Martin had his briefcase open, was producing a thin file of papers for Clive to look at.

Karina eased the door wider with her foot, and their voices came through clearly now. "Won't be very long now," she called, but they did not seem to notice.

"This is the big one, the one I've been waiting for," Martin was saying, his eyes glowing with sudden animation. "I'm on the verge of the mega deal of all time – at least by African standards."

"Really," said Clive with slightly less enthusiasm. "Do tell me more, old buddy."

"I've just gone into oil one hundred per cent."

"Oil?" Clive looked surprised, then worried. "But are you sure oil is the right place to be right now, Martin? It's a doldrum market, has been for months, and it could blow in any direction."

"Sure it could," agreed Martin. "And as far as I am concerned, it can."

"Don't follow you."

"Perhaps I should qualify that by saying that as long as it doesn't drop below three dollars a barrel, we are into profit."

"Three dollars a barrel!" Clive whistled. "That must be some kind of record! The bottom line hasn't been down there for twenty years. How the hell are the production costs kept so low – and who is the production company?"

A smug expression came on Martin's face, his lips pouting in a sybaritic imitation of a rather pleased cherub. "The MECA

120

Corporation are the holding company, to answer your second question first. And in answer to your first question, MECA have a twenty-year lease on 10,000 square miles of prime oil-bearing territory – at zero cost."

"Zero cost? Why man, that's just amazing, absolutely amazing!" Clive's eyes widened. "Sure as hell that is some deal."

"Yes indeed," agreed Martin.

Then Clive frowned. "But who are MECA? I've never heard of them. They're not among the listed securities, I'm sure of it."

"Right again," said Martin. "And the reason why?"

Clive recognised the sly look on his brother's face. He had seen it many times before. He grinned back, his expression suddenly boyish in the conspiratorial way of their youth. "You're telling me MECA is your personal little baby, is that it?"

"On the button, my dear Clive."

Clive breathed in and gave a low whistle. "You sure haven't lost your canny nose for a deal, have you, Martin?" he said wryly. "Where is this tract located?"

"The Moroccan Western Sahara."

"How far west?"

"The foothills of the Atlas Mountains."

"You're kidding, aren't you? No one has found any oil there before. Are you sure of your facts?"

"Absolutely certain. It started off as a low budget exploration – a couple of million bucks. Like you say, that region was thought to be as barren as the dunes of Nevada, but then my seismic team came up with this."

His hand reached out to the bundle of papers, and Karina saw that they were not a single sheet, but continuous printout off a computer. "Look at this," Martin pointed at the run of peaks and troughs on the chart. "I'm not an expert, but I've got the best expert in the business. A guy called Rory McDermid and his team tell me this is the most portentous exploration data he has ever seen. He said we would find oil, and he was right. We have already run one well down and hit a gusher."

"The devil you have," Clive shook him by the hand. "Dammit, man, this is unbelievable! I knew you'd made it good, but this is mega bucks. The stuff that dreams are made of. But what sees you here in New York?"

"You're right, Clive. It is big, almost too big. I've got two choices. Either I let it build within the limits of my own resources and the income it generates as we go – in which case the wells will be running at their fullest capacity when the twenty-year moratorium runs out, or—" and he paused as if almost afraid to float his next suggestion, "or I pull in some extra funding and go for the big kill."

"That would pull the plug on the price of oil."

"Who cares? At our prices we can take on all comers."

Clive moved back slightly. "You really think so?" he said, with the first hint of scepticism. "Maybe you're right. I'm not too sure. Where are you thinking of raising this extra funding?"

"We've always worked well together in the past, haven't we Clive?" Martin evaded the question.

"Well, yes, sure we have."

"As a team we are unbeatable, Clive," he enthused. "You can't deny that."

"Of course not."

"What we've done together in the past is peanuts compared with this. This deal could give us the chance to motor as a team like never before. The Feral twins could be unstoppable. We could control markets, force trends, orchestrate the financial infrastructure of the whole oil business across three continents. OPEC could be forced into our camp, or disband."

"An entrancing proposition, Martin. But what exactly are you getting round to?"

"That we run together on this one. That you come in with me, Clive. Together we would form the biggest banking and oil consortium in the world."

"And how much is this likely to cost Price Whitney to buy in on this act?" He remembered Nelson Bunker Hunt and how he had tried to do the same with silver futures, and failed spectacularly.

"About one billion will see us as partners in the African Venture, some of which can be Price Whitney stock which would be collateral for external borrowing."

Clive did not recoil. His gaze was out of focus on the security video, its camera monitoring the departure of the dealers from the trading room, as he considered the proposition. Martin's judgement had never been flawed before – but neither had his own to any significant degree. Yet something about this gnawed at his mind, something did not feel entirely right. He could see the reason for Martin's dazzling enthusiasm, and the broad foundation of the logic, and he could think of no reason for the bells of intuitive caution to ring so loudly in his mind.

It was natural prudence, he surmised, before he spoke

again, saying quietly, "There's a lot to think about here, Martin. There's nothing wrong in what you say in principle, and we can go into greater detail tomorrow, when we are both a little fresher, but for the moment I'd like to sleep on it. Right now I'm sure as hell pretty damn hungry. Hey Karina," he shouted through the open door, "any news from your department?"

"There soon will be," she called back, smiling sweetly to the cooker as she turned up the burners. "That sure is something you can count on."

"What's that?"

"I said it won't be long."

Clive did not sleep at all well that night, and Karina's voluptuous shape curled close did not arouse him as it usually did. He awoke in an irritable frame of mind and stared out of the window at a sky that seemed grey and sullen after the heat of the previous day. Karina served the two men breakfast at half past seven, the time Clive always chose since it allowed him to be on the dealing floor for eight when the first prices would be coming in. The two brothers sat huddled close, murmuring now and then, but little more was said. Both fell silent after she joined them at the table.

"Busy day coming up?" she enquired brightly.

"Uh huh," Clive grunted. Then, "You going to be here this evening when we come up?"

"I've no plans to go anywhere."

"Good," he said.

"Shall I tell cook to expect to feed you both this evening?" she asked.

"No, honey, I think we'll be going out instead. There's just a chance we may have something to celebrate."

"Wonderful," she said. "But who's *we*?"

"Martin and I," Clive told her.

"Not me? Am I not included?"

"Sorry, honey, but no. It's a business dinner. It would be very dry for you. Lots of stuff you wouldn't understand."

"Oh," she smiled. "Never mind then."

Clive remained unsure throughout that morning as he sat in his private office next to the dealing room floor. Through the one-way window he could see the hurly burly of normal trading unfold in its hectic progressions, the excitements and the gloom showing in the dealers' faces as the results of their judgements came through on the screens. But he wasn't watching with his usual relish and concentration. He still wasn't sure. Martin had gone out to do other business in Manhattan, for which Clive was grateful. He needed time to think.

Eventually he picked up the phone. "That you, Abe?" he said at the sound of his broker's voice.

"Sure is." Abel Satco came back, instantly recognising the caller. "Good to hear from you, Clive. Thought things had gone rather quiet at your end. That deal is all set up to scoop the pool for early next week now. That *is* why you called, I suppose?"

"Not entirely," said Clive. He had almost forgotten about his stake in the syndicate raid. "I'd just like to know your feelings on another deal I have in the offing."

"A new deal? That sounds interesting. I could make time this morning, but I'd prefer to chat over lunch."

"That'll do me better too," said Clive. He needed that extra time to think.

Deep in contemplation, he wandered down to Maybee's and chose himself a cigar.

"Have a nice day," the girl at the cash desk smiled, waving him round the queue.

His face didn't flinch. It was as if he hadn't heard and when he was out of earshot she said to the next customer. "Pig-ignorant bastard. All the money in the world and he comes down here thieving cigars off my boss!"

"Uh huh. Sure is typical of them rich guys," the large black woman responded bitterly.

Clive Feral smoked the cigar, and another like it before one o'clock when he called for his chauffeur to run him down to Chantilly's Gastronome on 2nd Street. Abel Satco was already there waiting, and he stood up when Clive came in.

"Good to see you, Clive," Satco greeted warmly. "If you hadn't called me, I was about to call you."

"Oh?" said Clive. "Something important?"

"Not directly. You tell me your news first."

"My brother has offered me an oil deal in Morocco on very attractive terms, and it seems pretty watertight. It's just that I've never done much with oil because it's too unstable on the commodity markets. Just wondered what your current attitude is."

"Now there's a coincidence," Satco looked surprised and pleased at the same time. "Let me tell you my bit of news and maybe it'll answer your question at the same time."

"Oh yeah?"

"You know I mentioned a while ago, jokingly, that I

124

wouldn't mind a bit of the 29-29 Corporation's dealing business because it is so vast."

"Yeah, I remember."

"Well, today, for the first time ever, they've routed some heavy buying through my office."

"The hell they have," Clive glowered.

"Don't worry about it," Satco rushed in, seeing what he was thinking. "Our relationship is as firm as it ever was, Clive, you know that. But I just thought you'd be interested – especially in what they're buying right now."

Clive looked at him sideways. "I may be," he said.

"You will be," Satco assured him.

"Spill."

"29-29 are getting very heavily into oil right now," Satco grinned, his expression like a boy who had found a hole in the orchard wall. "How does that grab you?"

"Oil," Clive was startled. "That a fact?"

"Sure is. And on their record there has to be something there. This time it's not too hard to see their reasoning. After Three Mile Island, the Chernobyl melt out, and the latest French disaster in Brittany, they are saying that there'll be a nuclear catastrophe on average every five years at the current rate. Can't be bad for oil, can it? And 29-29 have never made a bum deal yet."

"Not yet," Clive agreed reluctantly. "No, not yet they haven't, but there can always be a first time."

"Maybe so," said Satco, disappointment edging his voice. "But I'd certainly rather punt on them winning than losing."

"Me too," said Clive suddenly smiling and patting him on the back. "Sorry to sound ungrateful, Abe. It's just that these damn people really screw me up. Don't suppose you have any more information on them, do you?"

"Not a squeak," said Satco. "All their buying orders are routed through the accountants, Graf Spielburg, using their settlement number. I've checked with a couple of other brokers who tell me that this is how 29-29 always trade. So who makes up their dealing team is still a mystery."

"Shit," muttered Clive, resolving to get on to his attorney as soon as he was back in the office. Vic Loeb should have something from the hired gum-shoe by now, he thought.

But apart from that, Clive was feeling decidedly better. One hour later he beamed at Martin as he walked back into his office. "Have a good morning, did you?" Clive enquired of his brother.

125

"Certainly did," Martin smiled in return. He indeed had passed the morning most pleasantly in the gay bars off 49th Street. Unfortunately it was a look-no-touch situation because of the risks – New York was as rife as Africa with every imaginable disease – but he still had a good time and made a few contacts who might prove to be clean. "You made your mind up yet?" he asked.

"Of course. Was there any doubt?" Clive threw his arms wide expansively. "I'm with you all the way."

"Splendid," Martin took the hand that was offered. "Just like the old days, eh?"

"Better than the old days," Clive told him.

"Yep, better than the old days. That's the way it's going to be."

CHAPTER 9

Getting a flight to Morocco was not difficult. Getting a flight out into the wilderness beyond the airport was. The Polisario guerrillas were active east of the Atlas Mountains and had already shot down two American relief planes and a Live Aid helicopter in recent months. No air taxi would touch the journey and Karina estimated she had walked two miles round the clutter of airport buildings before she spotted the Cessna 210 light single with MECA EXPLORATION in new paint on its side. Well, if I can't get a regular flight, I'll use the firm's transport, she decided.

She walked into the hut behind it. "Can you tell me who the pilot of that aircraft is?" she said to the man sitting with his feet up on the desk.

"Me," said Geoff Mace without looking up from the calendar he had just pulled out of a girlie magazine. "Jeez, there's a Sheila for you. Just look at those tits."

"I want to hire the Cessna."

"That aircraft is not for hiring," Mace said, rummaging in the drawer, and finding a lump of BluTac. "Sorry."

He turned his back on Karina, and stuck the pin-up to the wall with an eighteen-carat leer, caressing it flat with his hand.

"Magnificent," she said.

"Yes, ain't she," said Mace.

"You like them big, do you?"

"The only sort."

"My guess is she has more silicone than you've got brains," Karina told him softly.

Mace stopped stroking the paper as if he had been slapped. He turned round scowling. "You reckon you could do any better?" he said, looking at her for the first time. Instantly his expression changed, and he grinned, realising she probably could. "What can I do for you?" He dug for his charm, holding the grin in place.

"I've just told you. I want to hire that ship on the pan outside."

"I'm sorry," he repeated, genuinely this time. "It's a private company aircraft. It's not for rental."

"No?" She dropped a 500-dollar bill on his desk.

He looked at it, his grin slipping. "Well, maybe."

She put another 500 dollars with it. "That should make the *maybe* a *will be*," she said.

He picked them up, his grin back. "Where do you want to go? We'll have to be back by dusk."

"Out to the desert. There'll be ample time."

"Oh yeah? Why? It's pretty bloody heathen out there at this time of the year. That's forgetting the guerrillas who lob up SAM 7s at anything that moves. What's your interest?"

"I'm a journalist for the *Washington Post*. We're doing a feature on North African mineral resources."

"Really?" He didn't know whether to believe her or not, but it didn't matter. A thousand bucks for an afternoon's jolly, and nothing mattered. "We'll have to stay low, and it'll be rough."

"Let's go," she said.

"Okay," he shrugged.

She followed him out to the aircraft. The man was an animal in a transparently charming sort of way. She would have to watch him, she knew, but how good it was to be away from the mish-mash guys with their designer brains that teemed through the yuppie stratas of New York. Here was an irascible old lecher not pretending to be anything else. Wonderful, just wonderful, she thought. I can handle that.

"Hop in lady," he ordered, "—before I change my mind."

She could only guess the risks he must be taking. He was probably breaking every rule in the company book.

She sat close beside him in the narrow seat of the Cessna single as he fired up the engine, the machine shaking and jerking as each pot came in, one by one, until it was running evenly when he released the brakes and they were taxi-ing out towards the holding point for the active runway. After terse exchange with air traffic, they were airborne, climbing steeply out towards the east.

Only then did he turn to her again. "And what's a nice girl like you doing on a lone assignment like this? Beyond the city limits Africa is a pretty damn heathen place. How's your stomach for heat, dust, flies and disease? Because if one doesn't get you the others will."

"That's many questions in one," Karina answered. "First, you don't know that I am a nice girl – and I'm not inviting you to find out. Secondly I doubt if Africa can be any worse than some of the other places I've been."

Jeez, he thought silently, we've a real one here, and he began to hope for some turbulence that might shake up her composure. "What exactly is the angle of the piece you're writing?" he ventured again.

"It's about the new Atlas oilfields," she told him.

"Is it indeed!" he nodded, his eyes narrow slits as they peered into the haze. "That's very interesting. I understood no one was supposed to know about those new fields yet – and why has your rag sent a woman on what could be a dangerous assignment?"

"Probably because they didn't think it was particularly dangerous. And neither do I."

For every question she had an answer, or avoided giving one, and he drifted into silence now as he looked for a gap between the thunderheads fast building as they moved in towards the eastern ranges. Get caught in one of those anvil clouds and it would either pluck you high at terrible speeds and tear your wings off, or throw you down into the foothills of the mountains with no chance of regaining height before you hit the rocks. They were best avoided.

Out of the lowland haze the air was clearer: one moment the tiny aircraft was forging through the raw heat of the sun, the next lost in semi-darkness as they skirted the vast contusions that writhed and spread upwards in bloated columns of black and angry air. Now and then a spear of lightning rent the gloom, darting like a reptile's tongue at some unsuspecting thing far below. Just as quickly it was gone again, leaving the sound of thunder as its only footprint in the sky.

In that moment he made one of his rare mistakes. Her skirt had wriggled up her thighs, inching a fraction more with each jolt from the peripheral turbulence of the storms. One more lurch and he would know the colour of her knickers. He glanced down to check the state of play. In that instant a crosswind took the aircraft, sucking it sideways with a sudden lurch, and before he saw the compass move, they were into cloud, nothing there now but an amorphous swirling fog.

"Shit," he muttered as the aircraft bucked like a stuck mule. "Shit and damnation."

This was going to be a rough ride, he knew that for sure, and very dodgy as they were well into the Great "V" with mountains he couldn't see soaring high on either side.

Suddenly the aircraft broke into a vast cavern of clear and empty air. There was no sky above or ground beneath, just billows of cloud hanging suspended like the glacial walls of an arctic grotto. Subtle shades of vermilion and purple-blues tinted the blanket grey, giving a hint of solidity and substance that could deceive the untrained eye. Here and there uncannily symmetrical formations ran in line like the vaulted arches of a phantom cathedral, before the tunnel began to dwindle down to a tube of clear air that twisted like gut through the sky. Haloes of colour danced where the rain was falling, rain that would turn to steam and evaporate again before it hit the ground. Pale pinks mixed with crystal green that grew bold, only to fade once more into darkening shades of grey.

The aircraft sped on, kissing the scrolls and folds until the floor of the cavern suddenly dropped into a chasm of emptiness where thin shafts of sunlight slanted like rays through a stained-glass window.

Momentarily they hung suspended, before he thrust the yoke forward, plunging them downward into the base of the void, following a dark gulley flanked by translucent pillars of cool green marble, until without warning the gulley took a sudden left and there in front of them soared a wall of dripping jade green rock.

"Oh shit," he muttered again, banking steeply, trying to steer the machine through a small archway in its face.

The angle was too tight and the aircraft slewed into a tranquil sea of swirling mists. He heaved back on the column, searching for height. The prop clawed the air as the speed bled away, and he sat there waiting as the stall warner blared, his eyes boring the murk, waiting for the mountain to appear, and then the crash. At least when they hit, it would not be at full kilter. Yes, slow enough to be survivable, he thought, cursing his stupidity in contriving this situation.

Steadily the altimeter was clawing up until just as suddenly the dark grey had become a fluffy meringue of light mists, and moments later sharp filaments of sunlight darted through to scatter like wintry tinsel on the engine cowl. They burst free into an arctic landscape of snowy dunes that bubbled into the distance as far as the eye could see, the sky a deep blue-black,

130

the sun glaring down with an intensity that scalded the eye. He reached for his dark glasses and levelled off with relief, only then remembering he had a passenger.

"One thing I hate is nervous pilots," Karina said, a smile on her face. She had been watching him. She knew exactly what had happened. She also saw how his hand was shaking slightly as he pulled a cigarette from the Rothman's twenty pack sticking out of his shirt pocket.

You cheeky little bitch, he thought in fury before his composure returned. "Pull your skirt down, lady," he ordered tersely. "You're fucking up my judgement."

They said nothing as the scene changed yet again. The ground was running away from the high wilderness, the melting desert heat burning into the fluffy clouds that first thinned to tiny wisps, then at once were gone. It was hard to believe that behind them giant storms still crashed about the mountain peaks, splitting rocks with bolts of electric fire, pouring solid blinds of water over the succulent afforestation that covered the western face, hard to believe that any mountain could have such a schism through its axis. Two worlds together, yet so totally different. Below them now was nothing but simmering, dun-brown haze.

The pilot picked up the mike and keyed the transmitter, "Flyer to Digger, do you read? Over."

"Roger Flyer," the word came back after a moment's pause. "This is Digger. Reading you strength five. What you want? We weren't expecting you until tomorrow with Farty Marty."

Karina's composure melted at this reference to the great Martin Feral, and she chuckled loudly, nearly missing Mace's come-back.

"Got a journalist in tow, Rory. Strictly non reg. She wants to have a chat with you."

The radio fizzed, showing it was alive, but for a moment all that came over was a heavy silence. "Woman?" Rory McDermid eventually coughed, as if he had invented the word. "You're bringing a *woman* out *here*!"

"That's the idea. Thought you wouldn't mind giving her five minutes of your time. Wants to do a piece on the current state of oil exploration in the western Sahara."

Again there was a pause.

"If I hadn't known you for ten years I'd say your brain has just had a melt-down."

"A thousand bucks *does* tend to have that effect on me."

131

"A thousand bucks," McDermid chuckled now. "Okay. Bring her in but tell her she ain't going to like it here. Tell her she ain't going to like *me*. Tell her she's got ten minutes of my time, no more. Tell her that I don't like women on site, least of all women journalists who turn up uninvited. Tell her that any wobblies, sulks, or pre-menstrual paddys and she's back on that plane before the first flea jumps out the sand to bite her pretty little arse."

Karina snatched the mike from Mace's hand. "And tell Rory McDermid," she shrieked, "that if he knows as much about oil as he knows about women then he's wasting my time, and that is something I do not like."

The pilot retrieved the mike. "Just won yourself a friend," he said with a grin.

"I hope not," she spat furiously. "I can't stand men like that."

The pilot looked at his watch, eyeing the door to the sectioned-off part of the Portacabin that McDermid kept as his own private office.

He had seen women bristle before, and he had seen Rory McDermid bridle before, but he had never seen two fighting cocks square up for a scrap so obviously as these two as they walked towards each other over the silvery, burning sand.

"You can come into my office," Rory McDermid glowered at her, and Mace grinned inwardly. He had seen this routine before. The air-conditioning had been turned off some time before they arrived and the Portacabin was already like the inside of a marinating oven, stinking of sweat, spilled beer and other things.

But the girl seemed not to notice. She really was quite extraordinary, he considered. Beautiful in that haughty sort of way he found so tantalising in the few women he had loved for anything more than their bodies. She wore no make-up – she didn't need to, there were lustrous depths of natural colour in the tones of her skin, and she moved with a powerful elegance in nothing more than flat shoes and cotton skirt and top. He studied her face, trying to figure out her nationality, but there was too much of a mixture there. All he knew was that her shining black eyes carried a heat far greater than the desert sands. And she wasn't even sweating.

Mace let the sleeve of his shirt drop back over the watch. Ten minutes, McDermid had said, and ten minutes it would be, and he settled back to wait as the heat continued steadily to rise inside the metal cabin.

After five minutes he looked at his watch again, wiping a dribble of sweat away from his eyes. For the first few minutes there had been the sound of voices raised, then curiously all went quiet, and he found himself straining to hear anything behind the crude wood door.

Ten minutes came and went, as did twenty and thirty. By this time, Mace was not the only one looking at his watch. The other men in the Portacabin trying to work on survey reports were dripping sweat on the sheets, eyeing the time as the minutes ticked by and the temperature soared.

"I can't take any more of this without the freezer on," one of the surveyors spat at last into the ashtray, rolling up his papers. "Let me know when he's ditched the bitch. You'll find me in my quarters."

"Me too," another joined him on his feet. "She's either passed out, or she has the constitution of an armadillo."

In that instant the door opened and McDermid stood there. His face was the mottled red of a Sumatra turtle, but strangely all the animosity had gone, and his eyes held a far-away, pensive look. "Get that air-conditioning back on, Jerry," he called down the cabin. "This could take a little longer than I'd thought." And he shut the door.

"And now I've seen a flying pig," someone muttered in amazement. "Did you see his face? He's listening to her! In all the years I've worked with Rory McDermid I've never known him listen to a woman yet."

Only Mace wasn't surprised. That lady was more than a lady. She was something else – what else, he wasn't sure, but he had a shrewd idea if he troubled to make a call to the *Washington Post*, they'd tell him they'd never heard of this little Sheila. "What worries me is whether they'll finish before sundown, because my ship won't fly over the peaks without oxygen, and I'm damned if I'm flying through those valleys in the dark."

He needn't have worried. The door opened again, and this time they both came out. She looked cool and as unflustered as when he met her at the airport earlier. It was McDermid who looked as though he needed a good sluice and a long night's sleep.

"You all right, boss?" one of the assistants asked him after they had gone.

It took a moment before he said absently, "Certainly I

133

am," and he faltered again before continuing. "That gal told me something that I've been thinking for quite a while – that the oil business is going to dwindle to a fraction of its present volume long before supplies run out."

"That sound's like crazy talk to me," the assistant said.

"No, it's not. Not when you think about it. Reserves are far greater than were ever perceived, the techniques for locating it are getting to be almost infallible, and we have another set of technologies designed to minimise its consumption – super efficient engines, total thermal insulation, alternative sources of energy."

"Nothing will ever replace oil," the assistant asserted.

"You're right there. But would you like to place bets that in time some things might not come pretty close?"

The assistant stayed silent, studying the old oil dog of the desert with respect, until eventually he said, "Is there something you know that I don't?"

"Maybe there is, and maybe there isn't," Rory McDermid grinned at him through tobacco-yellowed teeth. "How long have you worked for me?"

"Coming up five years."

"Five years, eh? I guarantee that if you're still with me in five years' time we'll be sailing on a different ship."

"You reckon, do you? Anyway I hope I'm still with you, boss," the younger man assured him sincerely. "But I'm not exactly reading your drift too good."

"I'll put it to you this way. Jerry. As of now I'm leaving the oil business for a while and backing a hunch. You can come with me if you want. If you do, in the beginning it's going to be just a small show, and it could be hard going."

"Phew," Jerry slumped down in his chair. "Just like that. Don't tell me that girl had something to do with it, that journalist woman."

"Journalist?" Rory laughed now. "She's no more a journalist than I am. She's a head hunter. See this," Rory pushed a single piece of paper under Jerry's nose. "That's my hello. And there is an unlimited budget for equipment and bloody good wages to follow."

"150,000 dollars," Jerry whistled. "How the devil did she find out about you. And what exactly are you – we – looking for?"

"Completely new deposits of certain minerals."

"Such as?"

"Bismuth, tellurium and lead."

"Bismuth and tellurium," Jerry almost spluttered. "Who the hell wants those obscure metals in any quantity?"

"Right now, *we* do. And I know exactly where to start looking."

"And who is the outfit behind the operation?"

"The Tin Whistle Company."

"The Tin Whistle Company," Jerry repeated foolishly, before he began to choke on a burst of slightly hysterical laughter. "Now I know you're joking."

They moved steadily on, the tiny machine cleaving fast through the upper air, sucked by the tailwind rushing in to fill beneath the thunderheads boiling upwards into the evening sky. It was cooler now with the lowering of the sun, and soon the vast voluminous contusions would melt away to nothing and the heavens would fill from east to west with a vast carapace of stars.

But that hour was yet to come, and the air was still petulent with sudden lumps of convection that jarred the spine, and split the bubble in the compass as it turned within its mount. Here and there squalls of rain blustered from the clouds to rattle on the Plexiglas and wash away the sheen of dust that had painted the fuselage the colour of a dirt road dragster.

They were past the high point in the Great "V" divide. The mountain had changed from a morbid sepia to an exquisite vision of its other self, dark conifers and rare succulents throwing forth greens in every shade; and far beneath, in a shadow out of the angle of the sun, the thin vein of a waterfall began its hesitant drop, tumbling gently at first, then at once a solid cascade falling for hundreds of feet into a pool of the palest emerald that glinted like fresh-cleaved ice from off an arctic glacier. A ring of mists was rising from the pool, bubbling and boiling like hot springs from deep volcanic rocks, before dispersing in running waves over a wide plateau covered in lush grasses, all that could thrive on the bare inch or so of soil that cloaked the naked rock, until, just as abruptly, the flat pasture ended, breaking into another drop where only the gazelle and mountain goat could hope to find a hold. After the attritions of the desert it was the most beautiful thing Karina could have imagined. Something stirred within her.

"How good a pilot are you?" she broke the silence.

"The best," he turned and grinned at her.

"See that pool at the bottom of the waterfall?" she pointed.

"Yeah. What about it?"

"I want you to put down on the plateau next to it."

"*Put down*?"

"That's what I said."

"You mean *land*?"

"Yes."

"You're kidding," he said, his grin gone as he realised just as certainly that she wasn't.

"I can think of no other words to describe putting an aeroplane on the ground other than perhaps, crash, which I hope you won't."

"You're crazy. It's impossible," he said irritably.

"I thought you said you were the best," she goaded, her eyes smouldering wickedly. "Any bush pilot still wet behind the wings could land on that pea patch and get off again without turning round."

"So you're an aviation expert all of a sudden as well, are you?" he scowled back at her. "It's too dangerous, I tell you. The wind could throw us into the rocks. Unless madam thinks better and would like to have a go and find out for herself?"

"What are you suggesting?"

"That you fly it if you're so damn clever."

"If you like," she answered, not moving.

He noted that she was sitting on her hands. "Okay. You can have her," he blustered. "Get your pretty little dabs on the yoke and let's see what you can really do."

Still she did not move. "Are you transferring control to me?" she asked evenly.

"That about sums it up," his grin came back as he dropped his hands off the controls and leisurely folded his arms. "She's all yours, baby. Have a ball."

It was quite safe. The ship was fully trimmed out to fly hands off, and he could steer it anywhere he liked with his feet on the rudder bar – but she didn't know that. He hadn't pulled this routine for quite a while – it was not something you did if you wanted to stay employed. But this lady was a one-time customer with a paid-up account.

He was still thinking these agreeable thoughts when the roof slammed down to crack his skull.

"I have control," she called, as with one continuous motion her hands swept up and pushed the yoke forward, leaving him suspended in his straps. All lift had gone from the wings and they were falling like a stone towards the valley floor, following

136

the rain down, the droplets hanging still like jewelled baubles outside the aircraft windows.

"What the shit," he spluttered uselessly, trying to reach the controls, but she was holding the "g" on negative so everything stayed tantalisingly beyond his grasp.

"Good pilots keep their harness tight," she told him, locking the yoke with her knee so she had a hand free to brush a straggle of hair from her face. "It is not very good for the machine if someone tries to push their head up through the main spar."

Suddenly the "g" came back on again and he dropped back in his seat. "That better?" she enquired, pulling out of the dive.

"Give it back to me," he roared, grabbing for the controls.

"Uh huh." She smacked his hand away. "I still have control and that's a fact, and that's legal. You can fly it out, I'll fly it in."

He saw that her hands were already working at the trim control, and the speed was coming back fast. Her hand reached for the flap lever and she selected 15 degrees before she settled in to a comfortable glide that sliced down the face of the rock towards the bright oasis of water that glinted like liquid jade in the lowering sun. Moments later they greased to a halt on the very edge of the plateau, a bare ten feet from a void that fell for another 5,000 feet.

"I don't think you'll have any trouble getting airborne on the way out," she grinned, pulling the mixture to fully lean to kill the engine. Moments later there was nothing but the brittle tinkle that hot metal makes when it cools, and the hammer of the rain on the aircraft skin.

"You never said you had a licence," he growled furiously. "A stunt like that could have killed both of us."

"It could have but it didn't," she said in a bland tone. "It's all a matter of judgement. I expect I have more hours in light singles than you have. You're a big jet man – I've already checked you out – 20,000 hours driving stove pipes through the skies, which is a fat lot of good when it comes to this type of operation."

"Oh yeah?" he spat, realising she might just be right. "And where did you learn to fly like that?"

"The best place – in the sky," she jumped out laughing. "Where did you?"

"Bitch," he swore after her, but she did not hear.

The rain was as warm and blissful as a shower in a tropical garden, and she lifted her face and raised her hands in primitive supplication. The drops were fat, silky smooth and soft like ass's milk, and she let them oil her skin, cleansing it, balming away the tired cracks and dryness of the desert, as for the first time in many months she came close to feeling good. She breathed in deeply, her eyes closed. The air was alive. All about her were the mysterious scents from the primeval past, the oils, the nectars, the juices that linked hands through the millennia of time to bare the image of life itself in the most uncorrupt of all its forms.

Something was living in the scented mists that cascaded from the fall. The rain caught the evening sunlight slanting through the mountains, taking it and splitting it into a thousand brilliant shades, colours that danced and ran in gossamer clouds, dissolving and re-forming and dissolving again, at last to settle as a dew upon the soft green velvet loam of the plateau.

She was running now, barefoot on the turf, the moss and fat leaved lichens a down beneath her feet – a lone figure like a dark angel flying through the mists towards the pool, until suddenly she was gone, hidden behind a spoil of rocks piled loose upon the water's edge.

"Hey, wait for me," Mace shouted, but his voice was lost in the roar of the waterfall, the sound beating back and forth between the cliffs like a salutation to the thunder still raging high above.

Cursing gently he was out of the machine before he could judge his motives, running after her, then faltering and feeling foolish, but moving on again driven by some strange compulsion that seemed to come from the eminence of the place itself. His older bones did not match the speed at which she moved, but he was soon across the gap and almost at the rocks when he faltered in his stride.

For an instant she was there, standing still and quite naked, her face to the sky, before her back arched and she was gone, ephemeral like a nymph on a lily flower as she dived deep into the soft green waters of the lagoon.

"Jees," he muttered to himself in awe, "This sheila is certainly a bundle of surprises."

Suddenly her head reappeared. "Come on," she called. "What are you waiting for? You don't know what you're missing."

"He *did* know what he was missing. He could *see* what

138

he was missing. Her limbs moved fluid like a poem within the womb of clear water, strong powerful limbs that kicked and writhed, and melted from one movement to the next, her breasts like full fruits ripe enough to fall. His eyes could not mistake the dark shadow that winked briefly as she rolled, teasing and insinuating things he could not see.

She was stroking away from him quickly now, moving towards lime green foam where the torrent cascaded into the pool beneath.

"Come back," he shouted after her. "Not so far. You'll drown yourself, you fool. Come back!"

If she heard, she did not falter, almost lost now in the boiling waters beneath the fall.

"Shit and damnation," he cursed, throwing off his own clothes. He was in. The water was colder than he'd thought, clearing his mind as he reached into an overarm crawl. He was guessing as he swam, for he could no longer see her, and he again felt the tinge of fear tread lightly on his spine. A current was working at his legs and already there were bubbles bursting like a soda fountain round his face as air boiled up from the deep.

"Where are you going?" she called, her voice suddenly behind him now.

He stopped, treading water, spinning round, seeking where she was, and his mouth opened, choking on a mouthful of water before he coughed it clear. She was already out, laughter in her face as she stood there dripping on the rim of the pool, her hands on her hips, her breasts heaving majestically as she regained her breath.

"Bitch," he bubbled once more, clawing back towards the water's edge.

She stood watching him, smiling, as her breathing subsided. With a sweep of her head, she swung her hair back over her shoulder so it fell long and flat down her back like the mane of a fiery mare. She stood and waited.

It seemed as natural as night must surely follow day. They made love to the sound of the torrent raging from above. They laughed and rolled as the lightning cut ribands in the sky. She bit and clawed, and he thrust and she thrust back, and he groaned with the magic that came and went and came again before at last both were spent and they lay there washed by the warm, healing, cleansing rain.

They both knew it was a madness, the rage of the wilderness, the heat of the rut. But to deny the need was to live a lie, was more perverse than the passion itself. She looked at the face of the man by her side. That was when her sadness came; for the face she saw was not the face she had seen within her mind.

CHAPTER 10

"Wednesday October 23rd," Paul repeated uncertainly down the line. It was barely six weeks away. "And at the Lincoln Institute in Washington?" he questioned. That was the difficult part to believe. The recently formed Lincoln Institute of Innovation, a branch of the Smithsonian, was the most prestigious place any individual could hope to launch an invention, and Paul half expected to hear in the next breath that the date was cancelled, the whole thing a terrible misunderstanding.

"That's right," Farthingale reaffirmed.

"Unbelievable," Paul breathed.

"It's all been set up with the institute director, Professor Zachary Weinberger, who is as keen about it as we are. But Tuesday Nemesis is insisting on absolute secrecy before the launch, so apart from the patent applications which have now been completed and filed, the world is not to know anything of what you are doing until October 23rd."

"That suits me well," said Paul. He also noticed how different Farthingale had been in their recent conversations – respectful, deferential almost, and for the first time in months Paul began to feel his self-assurance returning just a little.

"Good," said Farthingale. "Everything else going well, is it?"

"Very," said Paul. "Excellent, in fact. I have a second prototype up and running, and I'll now start preparing the pre-production model immediately. That is the version we'll have on show at the inauguration – it'll have the full paint job with screen-print labelling and all the other trimmings."

"Sounds exciting," said Farthingale with genuine enthusiasm this time.

"That's the way I feel."

"Mr Nemesis's assistant may be over again fairly soon.

She said she'd like to spend a little more time with you than before."

"Really?" said Paul, becoming cautious again. "Does she need more information than I have provided?" He had prepared a report that had run to fifty sides of closely written A4 sheets, and he wondered what he might have missed.

"No, I don't think it's anything like that. I just think she just wants to feel more involved with what you are doing."

"Oh," nodded Paul. With the sort of investment they were putting in, it did not seem unreasonable. "But please give me a little more notice than last time."

"Most certainly." The lawyer laughed briefly. Paul had never heard him laugh before, and it sounded like old dry bones being crushed down to chalk.

The lawyer's office did phone him, two days later. It was not Farthingale but his receptionist, and she seemed barely in control. "She's on her way," the woman twittered, high pitched and very nervous. "Mr Nemesis's assistant has just arrived out of the blue from the States, dropped into the office, phoned Avis for a car, and left again."

"Are you sure she's coming here?" Paul ran a greasy hand through his hair.

"That's what she said," the receptionist replied.

"Damn, damn, damn," he muttered. This was all he needed. If she had already left, she could be there within the hour and he was covered in oil and the whole damn assembly was in a hundred bits. He could imagine her taking one look, and cancelling the whole deal.

He heard a car come up the lane, and he glanced through the window, and relaxed again. It was a small Ford – probably one of the young women from the village who had been delegated to keep an eye on him by the vicar's wife, a lady who considered him in the mould of her husband, benign but charmingly eccentric and, like all men, quite useless when it came to looking after their own well being.

Paul climbed back under the compressor – he would dismiss her as politely as possible when she put her head round the door.

"My, what a mess," the woman said in a soft lilting voice he could barely hear.

"Not now," he shouted above the noise of the compressor.

"I beg your pardon?"

"I can't speak to you now, I've got to get this finished. I've got someone coming."

"Okay, I'll wait."

"I'd rather you didn't," he bellowed, for a moment taking his eye off the nut he was spannering. All he could see was the woman's feet and lower calves. "I haven't time to stop, chat, eat or even think today. Damn," he cursed as the spanner flew off the nut and out into the open. "That's what happens when you get distracted."

"Sorry," she apologised, picking it up and pushing it back under the machinery to where he could reach. "Is there anything else I can pass you."

"No," he grunted.

"Oh," she said, sounding almost disappointed.

He fitted the spanner back on the nut and tried again, and again it twisted off. The angles of the nut had burred over to a semi oval and no longer offered grip. "Damn the bloody thing," he growled, catching a drip of oil on his face.

"Are you sure there is nothing I can do?" she ventured cautiously.

He turned his head. "You still here? I thought I asked you to go away."

"Would you like a coffee?" she ignored the riposte. There was a kettle and some Nescafé on the bench among the tools.

"Anything, anything," he muttered in exasperation. "Just stop talking to me, for heaven's sake."

"Certainly Mr Feral," she said, filling up the kettle.

"Yes, there is something. Push my socket set over to me. It's on the floor over there." If the spanner wouldn't touch it a socket would.

"What size do you want?"

"$^{11}/_{16}$ AF and the ratchet," he said without thinking.

"$^{11}/_{16}$ socket and ratchet coming up," he heard her say, and in an instant it appeared ready for his hand.

"Thanks."

"Anything else?"

"Yes, you can tell me what the gauges are reading."

"Gauges? Ah, yes. The one on the top of the heat exchanger is steady at 45 psi, and the one at the back of the compressor is a little hard to read – it's hunting roughly between 20 and 30 psi."

"That's normal," he found himself saying. "Hey," he shouted, surprised, "you seem at home with machinery. Have you done some engineering before?"

"Not as such. My dad used to have a taxi business, and I used to help him when my mum would let me in the garage.

I used to love it – the smell of the cars, the oil and the grease."

Paul stared hard at that length of calf he could see. It did not seem to belong to the comely ladies of the WI who came to cluck with eager relish over their new waif – kind women of enormous heart but insensitive to his truer needs.

"That a fact," he said, understanding now. She was young and keen, and she sounded nice. Probably the daughter of one of the village women. Funny accent though – but it was hard to tell with all that racket going on above. "Then perhaps I *will* make use of you. Find yourself a brush and get some of that swarf cleaned off the floor. And where's that coffee? You've got to be quick if you want a job with me."

"Right away, sir," he heard her laugh, a delightful tinkling sound that lifted his spirits as he worked.

Now and then he glimpsed trim ankles floating past his eyes, the length of calf tantalisingly obscured just below the knee, and he tried to imagine how she might look. He was tempted to slide out and take a break, but Nemesis's assistant could be there any time now.

"What's all this panic for?" the girl eventually interrupted as spanners flew and oaths came from beneath the pulsing machine.

"This device has been commissioned by some financiers and their representative is arriving any moment now. Nice people, but damned inconsiderate not giving a bit more warning. Can you tidy up that bench, please? Get all the tools laid out in some sort of order so it doesn't look too Heath-Robinson."

"I've already done that. What's next?"

"Go outside and tell me if you hear anyone coming down the lane. It'll probably be a big Jag."

"I can see through the window down the lane. I'd rather stay in here with you. What sort of people am I looking for?"

"I've only met one of them. A woman."

"What's she like?"

"American. Quite young and pretty in a filmstar sort of way. Very high powered, and probably utterly useless at anything that doesn't involve managing money, or men."

"You a good judge of women then?" she shouted huskily.

"Was once," he called back. "I was married to the very best until she died a few months ago."

"I am so sorry," the girl sympathised.

"She would be happy to know I've got a backer for my scheme though, very happy."

"Perhaps she does know."

144

"I like to think so. I somehow know she's still around. But anyway, enough of that, I reckon I've got it fixed. We're back in business. You can turn it off and let it cool down. The master switch is on the main casing. And then I shall inspect your work!" he joked, relieved.

He pulled himself out from under the machine, and for a moment was dazzled by the strong sunlight pouring through the window. Then he froze. "It's you!" he said, in disbelief.

"Indeed it is," she grinned at him, her voice all too familiar now, no longer masked by the noise.

"And you let me go on thinking—" he stumbled.

"It was fun," she said. "I haven't enjoyed myself so much in a long while."

"But your dress," he pointed at the black smudges of grease. "It'll never come out."

"So what?" she shrugged. "Clothes are only clothes."

"And what are you going to say to Mr Nemesis?" he asked, his earlier concern returning. "Are you going to tell him that everything is in a state of chaos, and as soon as you turned up you were given a broom to clean up the mess?"

"It's working, isn't it?"

"Perfectly." he said.

"And it's all nice and clean and tidy."

"You cleaned and tidied it."

"So, where's the beef?" she laughed again now. "I'm happy if you are."

"I am sorry about the way I described you," he apologised. "That really was rather unfortunate."

"High powered and useless, wasn't it?"

"I didn't mean it quite like that. In any event it seems you're not."

"I didn't mind anyway. It's always fun listening to someone talking about you when they don't know you're there. Also, I misjudged *you* to begin with as well."

"You did? How?"

"In several ways. Maybe I'll tell you later. In the meantime, d'you think we could both get cleaned up. To celebrate how well the programme is going, I'm taking you out for a meal this evening – unless you're doing something else?"

"Not a thing," he said quickly. It was true. He hadn't been out in the evening since before Tessa was ill.

"That's settled, then. D'you know anywhere special we can go?"

He thought about it. "Could be a problem," he said. "All we have in this neighbourhood is a couple of rustic pubs that do good food. They've got plenty of atmosphere, but not a lot of class."

"So I strike you as a classy lady?"

"Yes," he said, frankly.

"Covered in grease?"

"Well—"

"Well nothing. I'll take the pub. It sounds just great."

"Fine," he grinned at her now. "If it's okay with you, it's okay with me. But just one thing."

"Yes?"

"Shouldn't we be introduced at some stage. I don't even know your name."

"I'm Karina Darielle," she said, "but I'd like you to call me Karina." She returned his grin with a wide smile, showing flawless teeth, brilliant white against the ruby of her lips. But more than that he saw her eyes smile with her mouth, twinkling merrily with a language of their own.

He stared at her almost startled – there was a warmth there he had not expected – certainly it was not there at their last meeting. "Come on in and let me show you around," he invited.

At first he was conscious of the cottage, a shrew of a place with a thatched roof and tiny rooms, but Angela had seen to it that all was clean and neat, and Karina's smile did not waver and she stepped in. "Hey, this is amazing – it's really great," she said delightedly. "It sort of wraps itself round you and loves you, doesn't it?"

"Exactly the way I feel about it," agreed Paul.

Angela and the girls looked up, surprised at the sudden interruption. They were sitting in a huddle on the couch and the girls' animated chatter stopped abruptly as they turned to stare wide-eyed at their visitor. Paul turned to Angela first. "Karina, this is Angela, my sister-in-law, whom I believe you've met before."

"Hello again," said Angela, extending her hand for the briefest time and withdrawing it as quickly.

"Hi," said Karina, nodding, but no more.

Paul hesitated. The two women did not like each other, he sensed it instantly. "And my two daughters," he went on, pride in his voice. "Maria is seven, and Annie is five."

"Seven and a half," Maria cut in haughtily. "I'm seven and a half now, Daddy."

146

"Yes, yes, I know," Paul ruffled her hair. "You don't have to keep reminding me."

"Hi girls," Karina smiled.

"Hello," said little Annie in her guileless way, but Maria just pouted, and studied the new female in their midst with the same proprietorial air of disdain as had her aunt Angela.

"We'll chat some more in a minute or two," said Paul. "First Karina needs to clean up. The shower is through the kitchen in an annex at the back," he told her. "And mind your head. Not for nothing do we call this the Nutcracker Suite."

"Yes," she laughed. "The ceiling is a bit low. You Englishmen must have been pretty small a couple of centuries back."

He noted how she referred to *"you Englishmen"*, and wondered what her own origins were. Her skin had a tan that did not come from the sun or artificial lotion, and the bones of her face seemed to mirror the aloofness he had seen the first time they met. But today she seemed so different, unworldly almost, soft in a gentle kind of way and it was hard to believe it was the same woman. "If you'll pass me out your dress while you're showering, I'll get some solution working on it which will remove the worst of the stains."

"Great," she purred, and disappeared.

They decided on her car. Her hired Escort GTI was new and clean, unlike his old battered Triumph which he kept hidden when not in use. One hour later he was showing her through the back roads of the chalk Wiltshire Downs on their way to the Henry VIII, a Tudor pub hidden in a valley down on the banks of the Avon. Their table was booked and waiting for them.

"Hey, I like this," she called, and he noticed how her accent grew stronger when she was excited.

"I just thought you might," he said, pleased. It was exactly as he remembered the last time, that last time he brought Tessa there before her disease was diagnosed.

"This is really something else," she stated, looking around at the old copper bits and pieces and china bric-a-brac. "In the States we don't have any genuine antiquity, just imported gear and loads of repro."

"Yes, we are lucky that way," he agreed. Then, "What wine do you like?" he pushed the list across the table.

"You choose," she said. "If I had to live off my knowledge of wine, I'd starve."

"I'm a bit that way as well. I think we'll settle for a German hock, it's cheap and pretty good as a rule."

"Cheap!" she laughed. "Don't worry about the expense. This is on Mr Nemesis."

"I always worry about expense. It's a habit. I doubt I'll ever lose it. Have you worked for Mr Nemesis very long?"

"A while," she said.

"He seems to be something of a mystery man. Where does he live? What does he do?"

"Tuesday Nemesis is an intensely private person," her tone stiffened slightly. "He's a financier, but there is not a lot I can tell you beyond that."

Paul saw that this was not an invitation to be curious, indeed at that moment he found the faceless Mr Nemesis considerably less beguiling than the lady in his employ sitting directly opposite.

She really was quite stunning in a Latin sort of way. There was something unfathomable there as well, something that ran much deeper than the mischief that sparkled in her eyes and bubbled when she talked. He tried hard to figure it, to glimpse behind the liquid smile, but all he saw was a delightful effervescence that lifted his mood in a way he would not have thought possible a few days before.

"Have you to go back to London tonight?" he asked, trying to sound casual.

"Afraid so," she said.

"That's a pity. I could have got you fixed up overnight in the pub, and we could have had a longer chat in the morning."

"Yes, that would have been nice," she agreed. "Perhaps next time."

"Next time I shall insist," he said.

"Will you?" she laughed, her eyes twinkling wickedly in the candle light. "Will you, indeed."

"Sorry—" he hesitated, "perhaps I shouldn't have put it quite like that."

"Why not? I like men who insist."

"And dinner will be on me?"

"If you say so. But beware. You are courting problems."

"Problems? What problems?" Paul sat back.

"You already have two ladies in your life who are exceedingly jealous, and they don't like me one little bit."

"I'm not with you," he frowned.

"Typical male," she chuckled, "seeing nothing until it's mounted billboard size. I don't know what plans Angela has for her life, but my bet is they include you. And as for little

Maria. That young madam shows the makings of being more protective of her daddy than a mother tiger. Both those ladies see you as being exclusively theirs, and I wouldn't like to cross either of them."

"Oh come on," it was Paul's turn to laugh. "You're imagining things."

"Am I?" said Karina. "Am I?" and suddenly Paul found he was looking into eyes that melted and swam like liquid honey, picking up the lights from the candles and sparkling with messages he was almost afraid to read.

"No. I'm sure you're wrong," he coughed to clear his throat.

She leaned across the table and took his hand in hers, her expression unchanging. "Mr Nemesis does not pay me to be wrong," she said. "Not about anything." Her voice was so soft he could barely hear it, and his flesh tingled. This time he believed her.

CHAPTER 11

"You what?" Martin Feral roared.

She stared back at him apprehensively across her desk. She had never heard him shout before. "That's what the radio operator said, sir," she confirmed.

He glowered at her through narrow eyes. For an Arab, she was a passable secretary and wasn't given to making mistakes. "Get the radio shack on my private line immediately," he ordered.

"Right away, sir."

That was the trouble with the oilfields on the Eastern slopes – bloody awful communications. The mail had to be flown in and out, and the radio only worked properly when there wasn't a storm raging in the mountains – which was just about never. He hoped there was some kind of mistake. To lose McDermid now could create serious problems, and he stared again at the paper on his desk as if he could somehow change the words.

INTERNAL TELEGRAPH

from: rory mcdermid.

to: meca chief personnel officer.

please accept resignation as of next monday, 1st September. will forego one months salary in lieu of notice.

But the words did not change, and moments later the operator came back confirming there was no mistake.

"Get a radio link hooked up to my phone immediately," Martin ordered.

"Okay, sir, if that's what you want," the man said. "But I'm afraid all you'll get is a bundle of static until the weather improves in the mountains."

150

"Okay, forget it – forget it," he spat angrily.

Apart from McDermid leaving, which was bad enough, there was the question of where he was going to – and why the hurry? Something was happening, something was wrong. Intuitively he knew it. On his desk was another piece of paper confirming the transfer of one billion dollars from Price Whitney to the MECA account in the Royal Bank of Morocco – exactly as Clive had promised. Only moments ago it would have given him a high of jubilation but now, for some unaccountable reason, there was a queazy feeling in his stomach. He picked up the phone and had the switchboard put him through to personnel.

"That you, Maynard?"

"Yes Mr Feral, sir," Maynard recognised the voice instantly.

"What d'you know of McDermid's resignation?" Martin said.

"Ah, you've got the telegraph," said Maynard full of apprehension. "I did speak with him on the radio briefly between the storms. Couldn't persuade him to change his mind though, sir."

"Why the hell not? You know his importance to the exploration programme."

"I did my best."

"Well, your best isn't good enough," shouted Martin. "Personnel controllers are dispensable but the best seismic expert and geologist in Africa is not."

"Sorry, sir."

"Sorry? Sorry?" Martin spat. "What were his motives? What were his reasons? Where is he going? What did you find out?"

"Not a lot," Maynard admitted. "All he said was that his services have been acquired by the Tin Whistle Company."

"The Tin Whistle Company!" Martin exploded. "What kind of crap outfit is that. I've never heard of them?"

"Neither has anyone else," said Maynard with more confidence now. He had done his research. "They are not a listed company anywhere, sir. But of course they could be very new."

Martin killed the line, and tapped the key to get the switchboard back. "Get me my brother in New York," he ordered.

It was the sort of job every private eye dreamed of, and worked all his life to get. Up to now Ephraim Krebs had made a steady, if not spectacular, living haunting the lives of matrimonial defectors and he was damn good at it. He had to be – a guy with his pants down and the rest up could get a mite .angry when confronted with a motor drive Olympus firing two frames a second round the bedroom door. You had to be fleet of foot and have an unmemorable face to stay alive. Even so Ephraim Krebs had been shot at more than once.

He checked his watch. He had been told to be there sharp at eleven and he straightened his tie, then spat on his hands to slick his hair. Old habits die hard.

There was time to spare, and he reflected on his luck. He wasn't sure how the Price Whitney assignment had come his way, but it had, and this was the one he had been waiting for – the foot in the door to a different league. Yes, Krebs thought, as he gazed reflectively out over the grey sprawl of downtown Brooklyn, it sure is time I took a hike, and when I do there ain't going to be no looking back.

Round the corner further up the East River, Clive Feral and Victor Loeb were looking out over a different view. "You sure this Ephraim Krebs is the right man for the job, Vic?" Clive asked his attorney as they sat together in the board room.

"Given your criteria I reckon he's about the best to be had unless you want one of the big-shot investigation bureaux."

"No. Most of their operatives are too well known. Once they show their face, more doors close than open."

"You won't find that with Ephraim Krebs. He's got a face you'd forget in a room of two. Also he's hungry to get out of the matrimonial treadmill. Too many bad bills, too little dough, too many risks."

"Hungry, eh?" nodded Clive. "That's the way I like 'em."

"Shall we call him in?" said Loeb.

"No point in waiting. You should know what you're talking about, Vic." He pressed the buzzer on the intercom. "Send Mr Krebs in, will you, please Gudrun?"

Vic was right. The man was totally nondescript, almost faceless in fact. He came through the door as if he didn't need to open it, and stood close to the wall until Clive waved him to a seat.

"Mr Ephraim Krebs, Mr Clive Feral," Loeb introduced.

Clive reached out and took the investigator's hand. It was damp and warm, like fresh excrement.

"Pleased to meet you, Mr Feral," Krebs said softly. "And I look forward to doing business with you."

"That's as maybe," Clive came back, "You're not on the job yet. Not until you can convince me you're up to it."

"Convince you?" Krebs looked mildly amused. "How do I do that? Mr Loeb will tell you that I turn in the goods."

"He already has," said Clive. "But I like to be impressed first hand. Impress me."

Krebs shrugged. This was not quite the opening he had been expecting, but if the high-roller wanted some theatricals, he'd go along with that. He had no intention of losing the account, no sir. "They say I'm pretty hot on intuition, Mr Feral," he said. "Right now my intuition tells me that you are concerned about losing the Hartman Building to the 29-29 Corporation which makes your holding on 32nd Street kinda like an oyster without the pearl. That, and a few other things besides."

"How d'you know about that?" Clive jumped to his feet, colouring brightly. He tried to catch the detective's eye, but his gaze was somehow elusive.

"My business is knowing," said Krebs. "But if I was in the guessing game, I'd guess that the brief for this assignment is to plug a hole in your operation, and make a hole in someone else's. But, like you say, I'm not on your payroll yet—" He stopped there, a thin smile bending his lips.

"Where did he get this information?" Clive suddenly turned on Loeb, glaring at him accusingly. "Have you already filled him in?"

"No," said Loeb hurriedly. "But like I said, he knows his stuff."

"Almost too well," said Clive, his eyes narrowing to pensive slits. He hadn't liked Ephraim Krebs from the moment he came through the door. He was smart, too smart, and verging on the insubordinate. But Clive knew he didn't have to like him – personal likes and dislikes did not come into the game he played. In this game you stabbed your friends and honoured your enemies if it closed a deal with the right margins. "Okay Krebs," he went on. "You've got a month to come up with some hard information, or you're fired."

"A month's a long time in this business," said Krebs, a sanguine expression on his sallow features. "You better tell me what you want to know, and provide me with as much background as you can. There may be information you don't want me to have – but weigh carefully the risks of holding back on stuff that could give me a quick lead."

Clive's face was stony. "Thank you for your advice, Mr Krebs. I am sure you can rely on me to take the appropriate executive decisions. Mr Loeb, my attorney, will fill you in on the fine details, but in broad terms your speculations are quite accurate. I need to know how I came to lose the Hartman Building to 29-29. You are also to find out everything there is to know about 29-29 for I believe they may be acting on insider information. There may be a mole in my camp, Mr Krebs. If there is, I want him identified and quickly."

"Is that all?" asked Krebs.

"For the moment, yes."

"Then there are two things which need to be done with no delay," said Krebs.

"What?"

"The first is that you arrange to ensure that my application to join Price Whitney as an assistant in the mail department receives an easy passage. It will be a good cover for my initial investigation. The mail department always knows what is going on in any organisation – the scandal, gossip, who's screwing who – the usual things."

"And the second?"

"Ah, the second and most important," said Krebs, his face suddenly losing the ethereal look as his eyes came sharply into focus. "I want to know who's on the other end of that security camera, because it's been monitoring every word we've said."

"It can't be, it's—" He was about to say it's switched off, but the words cloyed in his throat. He stared in astonishment at the tiny neon "active" lamp blinking almost invisibly near the ceiling. He would never have noticed it, but sure enough, the camera was live and working. Someone was listening in.

There were only two monitors wired to that camera. One was in the main security control room, and standing orders said it was never to be live during normal trading hours, and the other was in his own private apartment.

The next week was good for Clive Feral. On his orders the rope had been raised from 2,000 to 3,000 dollars and a dozen dealers had gone that Friday. Two had wept, and another made for the window, but security had grabbed him before he jumped, and held him down while the medic gave him a shot of 50 mg Diazepam i.v., and he was shipped out on a stretcher.

Word was out that Price Whitney were offering the biggest hello in the business, and there was not a dealer between East River and the Hudson who hadn't toyed with the idea of moving. But it was risky. Price Whitney might be the best payers, but they were the toughest employers in the whole downtown business sector – the slowest to hire and

154

the quickest to fire. And if your own bank discovered you were hungry for a change, but failed to make the break, you were out anyway.

But still they came, and it had paid off. Price Whitney's trading profit had jumped 20 per cent on the previous week, and was set to go higher still with the new faces in the dealing room. Some of them Clive barely recognised, and even the long stayers seemed almost strangers now, their faces drawn, their eyes sunken, young men old before their time.

The air was alive in there. He could smell the adrenaline, sense the fear, see the deals come bad or good on the dealers' faces, and he loved it, loved every trauma, every drama, every single minute of it. He saw men have a good run, and trip out on the narcosis of their high, and other men have a bad run and wilt before their screens – that was the best part, the losers losing, – it was what pulled him to the illegal cock fights up in Maine, and the bare-knuckle fights down in Georgia. It was what might have pulled him, in other times, to see the lions eating Christians.

Abel Satco, his broker, watched him as they sat together in the observation gallery above the dealing floor. Clive's face was strangely alive as his gaze bored through the one way glass, and Satco saw there things he considered primitive and potentially dangerous. He often thought it just as well he didn't have to like his clients for he would have been a poorer man for that – especially in the case of the Price Whitney account. Clive Feral's aberrant sexual preferences did not diminish his value as a customer – at least not to the tune of a million bucks a quarter, it didn't.

"So things are looking up," Satco observed.

"Most definitely, Abe," said Clive. "We've made a few changes in our dealing room."

"So I've heard," Satco nodded. "Quite a shake up, by all accounts."

"The only way," Clive told him. "Dead wood leads to dead companies."

"Sure does," Satco agreed. He paused, waiting for Clive to come round to his favourite topic. He didn't have to wait long.

"What's the latest on 29-29? I heard they've gone rather quiet in the market."

"You heard right. On the futures side they appear to be going for consolidation. They're liquidating a whole bundle of stock right now – in fact they appear to be getting out of everything but oil."

155

"That's good news anyway," said Clive. He hadn't liked the late night call from Martin saying that some strange company called Tin Whistle had just recruited their top seismologist. Yes, he wanted nothing else to rock his confidence in that boat right now.

"I thought you'd say that," nodded Satco. "My feeling is that 29-29 are preparing for a big push in some direction, but where, I've no idea at the moment. Of course I'll keep you posted."

"But that's just the securities market. What about their currency dealings?"

"That's more difficult to keep tabs on. They spread their buying and selling through at least twenty major banks. But my contact in the Federal Exchange Bureau tells me they're busier there than ever, hinted they could be making a million bucks a week on straight dealing. That's a lot of dough."

"Tuesday Nemesis," Clive growled almost to himself.

"That's the guy you're after," agreed Satco.

"I've got an investigator working on it," Clive confided. "Our latest drive has produced some good talent, but there has not been a single defector from 29-29. That's goddam amazing. I just don't understand it."

"Perhaps they offer their people a better deal?" said Satco.

"That's impossible," Clive glowered. "Everyone knows Price Whitney are the best payers in the business."

"Best payers, maybe Clive, but not too much security comes with the package."

"What are you saying? You suggesting 29-29 have some loyalty kick working for them? That's impossible. You can't live in business once you get sentimental."

"I'm not offering answers," Satco hurriedly defended. "Just suggesting possibilities. All I know is that 29-29 run a tight ship that makes plenty of dough, and there's no one going around the Street slagging 'em off."

"We'll see," Clive muttered darkly. "Sure as hell, we'll see."

For the first time in many months Ephraim Krebs opened his mail with total confidence, knowing all the bills would be paid. It was a glorious and unusual feeling, and he attacked the envelopes with a zestful plunge of the knife, stabbing each invoice on the spike with an almost personal hatred. The attritions of penury had been for him like toothache; continuously there, an abiding cross to be borne as the price of his chosen profession. Sometimes he wondered whether to quit and go

156

into something steady, like the security business, or personnel vetting. But he never did. He knew he never could. Being an eye was the life he loved, and his wife had walked out all those years ago because, in her words, "You're a junkie, Ephraim, just another goddamn junkie. The only difference between you and them suckers snorting coke is you're hooked on your own adrenaline."

She was right. He never denied it. He lived for the thrills and spills that went with the business and now that he was getting paid as well, things were really looking up. In fact Ephraim Krebs had not felt so good in quite a while – even the drab view out over downtown Brooklyn seemed suddenly alive and vibrant with expectation. The only trouble was making the job last. His guts told him he could bust the case in ten days flat, but he needed two months at a steady five grand a week to clear all his debts, so he was going to have to do some spinning.

The last envelope emptied and tossed in the bin, he stood gazing out of the window, watching the heat rise in waves out of the ghettos far below. The case had classical overtones. A mega roller with paranoia, a piece of ass stashed in his apartment who was too bright for her looks, a couple of thousand crew who, to the last man, thought their chief a bastard, a new company threatening the old. And there was treachery, the treachery Clive Feral was planning on his own account, and the treachery he suspected planned against him. Yes, Ephraim Krebs considered as he gazed narrow eyed into the haze, there sure could be some meat on this little ol' bone.

He considered what he knew already. There were two monitors hooked up to the camera in the boardroom – one in the security control and the other in Feral's own apartment. The one in security was off and dead cold. The monitor in Feral's apartment was also off, but he thought he detected some residual warmth there. It wasn't possible to be sure because for some reason the damn lift had quit and they lost ten minutes walking up – time enough for someone to turn it off and let it cool. The apartment was empty when they arrived, but there was still the subtle fragrance of a woman's scent upon the air. She hadn't been long gone. "Your lady about?" Krebs had asked casually, trying to imagine the woman who went with the scent.

Clive picked up the piece of paper folded in front of the ormolu clock. "Gone shopping," he selected from the smoochy little note.

"Okay," nodded Krebs, with no inflection in his voice.

157

That was three hours ago. The girl was called Karina Darielle, a chick Feral had pulled out of the dealing room pool and installed in his upstairs suite. She was going to be one interesting lady, Krebs decided, for when he called his buddy in the Federal Bureau of Records the only ID they came up with was for a woman of sixty-eight who had died ten years ago. Miss Karina Darielle was 100 per cent phony.

Delving into 29-29 was also an interesting programme. Ephraim Krebs had never had to probe a ghost company before, for that was what it appeared to be. 29-29 had only two public faces that came to the surface as far as he could tell. They were a firm of downtown accountants called Graff Spielberg, and some obscure English law firm called Holt and Farthingale. The word on the Street was that 29-29 was owned by a Greek guy called Tuesday Nemesis, but Krebs' search of company records showed 29-29 was in fact owned by an outfit based in Panama, which in turn was owned by another in the Cayman Islands. There the trail went cold, or as cold as any trail could get on the end of a dead telephone.

Krebs dropped the receiver in its cradle, and wondered what expenses they allowed. He had a gut feeling that if the marionette was in the Big Apple, he was equally sure the guy pulling the strings was someplace else. There was some leg-work to be done – and this he was going to enjoy.

He propped a photograph of a woman on his desk – a studio shot of a glamour girl, or so she looked. He grinned and poured himself a bourbon. Chase the Lady was his favourite game of cards. "To Karina Darielle. The Lucky Lady," he toasted, raising his glass to the photograph. "Keep smiling, doll, cos you sure ain't gonna stay that way much time longer. Old Ephraim 'ere is about to turn your card face side up."

CHAPTER 12

"You fly Concorde all the time?" Paul's surprise was genuine.

"How else could I afford the time to flit back and forth from the States to check how you were getting on?" Karina answered with a smile.

Each time she came to England she seemed warmer and more relaxed than before, and he noticed how the smile changed her face. "Everything is going extremely well," he told her, the pride bright in his eyes. "Come see." He led her out to the workshop. "And this time I promise you there's no cleaning to be done."

"But does it still work?" she joked, looking at it with eyes anew. The TEESER machine was painted and cowled like a factory exhibit, the stovework pristine, the piping burnished.

"Certainly does. Even better," he said.

"Only a month now, and you're on at the Lincoln. It's all organised. Everything has been taken care of."

"It's hard to believe," he said truthfully. "I never thought the day would come."

"So all the work is almost completed?"

"Yes."

"In which case, let's take the day off," she announced quite suddenly. "Don't you Brits have a saying: All work and no play makes Jack dull, or something?"

He thought about it. "An excellent idea," he suddenly beamed. "I can show you round the area. How much do you know of Southern England?"

"Very little. But I sure am getting pretty handy on your M3 Freeway though."

"M3 Motorway," he corrected, laughing. "But that shouldn't be your lasting memory of the country. And neither shall it be." He began to take off his overalls. "Today we will enjoy ourselves, Karina. Today you will be my guest."

"Great," she said. "I'll go along with that."

They walked round the mysterious circle of Stonehenge in the heart of the Wiltshire plains. They saw Magna Carta in the majestic splendour of Salisbury Cathedral. In the evening they sat quietly exhausted in a nook in the Old Mill pub on the Avon near Downton. It was here fishermen had come for a hundred years to catch the fine trout that thrived in the chalk streams that flowed off the crumpled blanket of hills rolling for mile upon mile across the southern plains. Round the walls prize fish were cased in glass displays, tributes to the taxidermist's art, and the place hummed to the buzz and twitter of young folk enjoying the leisure of a warm summer's evening.

"How I love it here," she murmured moving closer, and he smelt the musk of her perfume on the air. "It's so quiet and peaceful."

"I'm glad," he said, taking her hand, and only realising afterwards what he had done. But she did not pull away.

"Shall I tell you something?" she said softly.

"Please do."

"This trip to England wasn't strictly necessary. I came because I wanted to. I needed the break."

"I'm very pleased you did. You've arrived in my life like manna from somewhere. And you're great company. I'm enjoying myself more than I have in a long time. If you weren't the boss's envoy I'd—"

"Yes?"

"Probably invite you home," he grinned. "Angela has taken the kids off to their Granny for a couple of days."

"Are you trying for an answer without risking putting the question?" she looked at him sideways through her hair.

"Sounds that way, doesn't it," he laughed. "Okay. But why not? There's no need for you to rush back to your hotel, unless you want to. There's a bed made up in the spare room."

"You Englishmen," she sighed. "Always so *proper*."

Paul gazed at her silently for a moment. "You told me Nemesis paid you to get things right," he said .

"Yes?"

"Well, you could be wrong this time," he grinned.

They made love in the light of a full moon slanting brightly through the window, a zephyr wind coming hot off the meadows where cattle lowed softly in the night. The air was rich, heavy with scents that perfumed the darkness and gave it life, and there was a mystery and magic in it all. She flowed in a symphony of motion, and he flew with her, sometimes leading, sometimes following, like a pair of doves upon the wing, so it seemed they were moulded in a unity he never thought possible ever again. When all was spent he held her close, and she melted in his arms.

"Oh Paul," she sighed. "If only life could always be as good as this."

"It could be, couldn't it?" he said softly. There was now something he wanted even more than the success of his machine. "Tell me why it should be any different?"

"Many reasons," she said quietly, "Too many reasons Paul.

"But you will keep coming back?" he felt foolish asking.

"We've a job to complete, haven't we," she murmured, "And now, my love, shall we get some sleep?"

But she did not sleep immediately. Perhaps it was the lag in time or perhaps it was something else. An hour later she was still lying there, wide awake, smiling in the darkness, listening to his steady breathing at her side. This time her lover's face was exactly as she imagined.

The flight from La Guardia to Panama had been pleasant enough and he didn't make the mistake of accepting the free Tequila proffered by a dissolute stewardess who looked more in need of its invigoration than he did. The pleasantness ended with the departure from the airport building. The best hire car he could get had not been cleaned since the beginning of the drought a month before. The volcanic clays in the Panama isthmus had turned into a pan of dust that followed the wheels like two pythons writhing in his wake.

After half a day of driving down unspeakable roads, Ephraim Krebs eventually arrived at the small fishing village of Puerto Piton, wondering whether it was all worthwhile. He had already established that 29-29 was a subsidiary of a holding company in Panama, which in turn was held by another in the Cayman Islands. But it was not his way to accept the easy supposition – especially when he was in no hurry to file his report – and especially not when the full tab was being picked up by the client.

He checked into the only presentable rooming house he could find, and then went looking for his target. It was much as he had expected. On one side of the door high up, and almost inconspicuous, was the announcement, CHEY SANTOS, ATTORNEY AT LAW, while beneath it ran, REGISTERED OFFICE OF THE FOLLOWING COMPANIES.

The list was huge, some 500 names in all, each neatly tiered one upon the next like columns of print on a broadsheet title. The 29-29 Corporation was at the very end, presumably because it was a number, and satisfied he was in the right place, he pushed the door and entered. The building was in the early Spanish colonial mould with red pipe-tile roof and whitewashed walls. Very little had been done, or indeed needed to be done, to convert it to its new purpose. Hosting the shells of off-shore corporations demanded for each a single manila folder and very little else.

The reception hall was dressed out in the traditional style, the ceiling holding an ornate chandelier at each end, while in the middle a hanging fan lethargically swept the air with its three brass blades, disturbing the flies but making no mark on the damp heat that came in waves off the inland sea not a hundred yards away.

The girl behind the mahogany desk in the corner looked up as he came in. "Can I help you, signor?" she asked.

"Sure can, honey," Krebs said, wiping a line of sweat from his brow and applying his most winsome look. "I'm after some information."

"Ah, information," she seemed sad. "That could be very difficult. We only keep a register of companies here, signor. I can only help you if you want to register a company with us."

"Then let me speak with Signor Santos."

"I'm afraid Mr Santos is away on business at the moment."

"Really?" His doubt was evident. "I am interested in the 29-29 Corporation," he continued, sliding two one hundred dollar bills out of his pocket and fanning them flat upon the desk. "They are registered with you, aren't they?"

"Si, signor. The name is on the wall outside."

He noted that her eyes had dropped down to the notes, big brown hungry eyes. He guessed she hadn't seen as much money as that in quite a while. "I'd like to know who owns 29-29."

"Well I don't know, signor—" She hesitated, still looking at the notes.

He made as if to pick them up, and she instantly went on, "But maybe I could look."

"Good. You go look," he told her.

162

She stood up and went to a row of filing cabinets against the wall and rifled quickly through. "29-29 are owned by a company registered in the Cayman Islands," she said softly, not looking into his eyes.

"Sure, I already know that, honey. What's the holding company called?"

"It says here they are listed as 29-29 Ltd, but you'd need to go to Grand Cayman to find out more."

"I haven't finished here yet," he told her. "You recognise this dame by any chance?" He pulled a photograph from his pocket.

She looked at it hard. "Yes. That is the representative of 29-29 who came here to register the company and attend to the paperwork."

"I just thought it might be," a smile lit Ephraim Kreb's sallow features. "All I need to know now is who 29-29 are registered with on Cayman."

"That's easy, signor," she said, consulting her files again. "They are registered with a subsidary of a British law firm called Holt and Farthingale."

"Holt and Farthingale," he whistled. Now there was a surprise. That name was cropping up every time he turned a stone.

"Thanks, honey," he pushed the notes across the table to her waiting hand. "See you again maybe."

"Thank you, signor. I hope so, signor."

She waited for him to leave before she picked up the phone and dialled a long string of numbers. "He's on his way," she said softly down the line.

Ephraim Krebs was glad to be climbing into the Eastern Airlines 737 waiting on the apron. A hooker had rented the room next to his and all night there had been a cycle of disturbance that continued even as he was checking out at five that morning. He figured if he wasn't going to sleep he might as well be on the road, and anyway it was sensible to cover the major part of the journey before the sun began blistering through the thin metal of the car.

But apart from the attritions of coming to a goddamn place such as this, he was feeling quietly jubilant. It was a short-haul of a bare 700 miles north to George Town on Grand Cayman Island, and he lay back and closed his eyes. One hour and twenty minutes later he opened them again as they slid in over the rocky promontories that sheltered the islands from the sudden raging storms that blew in from off the sea.

He stared down with a curiosity that was only mild. The Caymans were known for very few things. Those who read the guides would learn the islands were bedded on coral and almost entirely flat with no rivers, offering little to the itinerant tourist other than good shark fishing and the island's speciality, real turtle soup. What the guides did not mention was that the Caymans were also considered one of the coolest places for hot money in the western hemisphere, and sympathetic legislation ensured that anonymous holding corporations stayed exactly that. Ephraim Krebs knew this was not going to be quite as easy as Panama.

Holt and Farthingale were located in a new high rise block on the edge of the commercial district. As was normal, the name of the firm was printed small, allowing room to list the hundred or so other companies to which its offices played host.

"You have an appointment?" the black secretary asked. Her manner was neither welcoming nor abrupt.

"No," he told her, winding up his smile. "I was hoping you might help me."

"I'm afraid you'll need an appointment if you want to register a company," she told him.

"I'm not here to register a company," he said. "I'm here to get information on a company."

"Sure, sure," she said with a yawn. "We get someone from the IRS here every day. There's the door, buddy. Do us both a favour and use it before I call security."

"I'm not from the IRS," he hurried.

"I sure don't care where you're from," the girl said as her anger mounted. "If you're not registering, just get your ass out of here, d'you hear. *Out!*"

This was not a moment to finesse. Her hand was already on the phone as he reached into his pocket and in a second he was counting fifty dollar bills on to the table. Her hand froze and he watched her lips move as she counted with him until he stopped at two hundred dollars.

"Okay, so you're not from the IRS," she said, her eyes narrowing as she looked at him anew. "What are you after?"

"The 29-29 Corporation is registered with you here. I want to know who the holding company are, or, if there is no holding company, to see the list of shareholders."

"The 29-29 Corporation?" she repeated as if it meant something to her.

"Yes," he said eagerly.

164

"That's a lousy 200 bucks on that table," she looked down with a sneer on her lips to where the money lay. "Pick it up, buster. If you want any information, you'll get nothing for less than a grand. Meet me with the money tonight at eight in Nino's Café on the Broadwallk. Then maybe we'll have a deal. I only say, *maybe*. Now blow."

He left. He had no choice. But 1,000 dollars? He shook his head, that chick certainly knew how to negotiate like she'd seen it all before. He made his way towards the cable office. He needed to wire for more money very quickly.

They met exactly as she said. He was already there when she came through the door as the clock on the municipal building struck eight. "Got the dough?" she asked, her ebony face glossy and quite expressionless.

"You got the information?" he threw back. He didn't like hustlers – they made him feel dirty, and despite everything he didn't consider himself in a dirty business.

"You betcha," she nodded.

"Well, where is it?" She wasn't carrying anything but a small bag.

"In my head," she told him. Then, "We eating?" She pointed to an empty table.

"Yeah, we'll eat," he growled. "But if this deal goes through you pick up the tab."

"Sure, sure," she shrugged.

"Waiter," she called with some authority. "A quiet table please."

"You know this place pretty well," he observed when they were seated.

"Should do," she said. "It's a small island."

He looked at her narrowly. "Okay. Give," he said. He was not prepared to fool around any longer.

"Pass the dough first," she ordered.

"How do I know you've got the goods?"

"You don't," she said. "But since you're sitting between me and the door, and the Chief of Police is at the next table there's a fair chance I won't do a runner."

His eyes narrowed. This was developing into a stand-off, but what she said was at least in part true – she wasn't getting out the door with his money if the cupboard was bare. "Okay," he said begrudgingly, passing the envelope across the table. "There's a big G in there. Check it if you want."

She did, very quickly, with a practised thumbnail without

removing the notes from the envelope. Then she said, "There is no list of shareholders for 29-29. 29-29 is one of two wholly owned subsidiaries of the Tuesday Nemesis Corporation which has its registered office at Holt & Farthingale's subsidiary in Liechtenstein."

"Liechtenstein?" Ephraim Krebs' spirits sank.

"Afraid so," she said, smiling for the first time. "Looks like you still have some travelling to do, buster."

"You said there are two wholly owned subsidiaries. What's the other one called?"

"It's only just been formed. It's called the Tin Whistle Company."

"The Tin Whistle Company?" he murmured almost to himself. That name rang a bell. Didn't he remember Clive Feral muttering something about an outfit of that name pirating one of their employees out in Africa? Krebs racked his brains but could remember no more. It hadn't seemed relevant or important at the time, but now it definitely was. "And what d'you know of this Tuesday Nemesis guy?" he changed tack.

"Never met him. He's supposed to be a Greek magnate, or so they say. It's the Tuesday Nemesis Corporation that heads the whole thing up as far as we can tell."

"That a fact," he said. "But who d'you normally deal with?"

"Most of our instructions for both Tin Whistle and 29-29 come from Liechtenstein. Occasionally a representative of the Tuesday Nemesis Corporation comes round to sign papers and keep the documentation straight."

"What's this person like?" Krebs was suddenly eager again.

"It's a woman. A white woman," the girl shrugged.

"Does she look as though she has some Indian blood in her?"

"Now you mention it, yes."

"Does she look like this?" Krebs produced the photograph again.

"The one and the same."

"You can keep that grand," Kreb's told her, standing up. "Good night, lady."

"Hey, ain't you staying for a meal?" the woman looked surprised.

"No. But you can. You're picking up the tab, remember."

She smiled again as he went out the door, and beckoned the waiter over.

"All go well, honey?" the waiter grinned at her.

"You betcha," she called back softly. "We can eat well

again this week. Get the phone to my table, will you? I have to make that call."

The waiter watched as his wife seemed to dial for ever before she eventually connected. "He's on his way, but he may be delayed. There's a hurricane coming through," was all she said and hung up.

Krebs looked out of his hotel window into the mounting storm with awe and trepidation. Barely an hour before, the air had been viscous still and treacly hot, the sky a solid carapace of blue tranquillity from east to west as the sun bore down with its relentless intent. It seemed impossible all could change in so little time. All he had done was grab a shower, and now the sun had gone like it had never been, and the heavens had darkened to the colour of an angry bruise, raging blisters of cloud chasing across the sky like the devil's horsemen in grey montage. Even as he watched the palm trees leaned a little more as the tumult grew, and he suddenly had an awfully queasy feeling as he stood there on the twentieth floor of the Grand Prima Hotel. The building had begun to sway just a little.

Ephraim Krebs was no longer a happy man.

It was two days before Hurricane Angel eventually blew herself out over the Florida mainland, and those two days were the longest in his life. It had seemed that he was sitting in the centre of Dante's catastrophe as trees were snapped off at the ground, and the waves lifted up, darting at the shore like the foaming mouths of a thousand vipers. Countless small craft simply vanished in the tumult to become a scum of dross fetching up along the coast, and several large steam-tramps had been blown inland, and now sat high and dry above the sea where they would stay until they rusted back to dust.

But the worst part was the frustration – knowing what he had to do, yet not being able to do it. The investigation had been going well up to that point, and he had been set to leave for Europe when everything was closed down by the hurricane. The lights went out, the staff ran out, the catering failed, and of course the lifts quit working within an hour of the first breath of wind, leaving him captive in a gilded cage that became less gilded by the hour.

He arrived in the Principality of Liechtenstein unhappy and unshaven, and was less than civil to the taxi driver who refused to speak anything but German.

This time Holt & Farthingale had chosen space in a Medieval fortress on a high bluff overlooking the town of Vaduz to host their clutch of companies. The office was of modest appointment, just one room in what was once the keep, but it was nonetheless impressive for all that, enjoying magnificent views across the valley to the blue-mauve splendour of the Swiss Alps far beyond.

But Ephraim Krebs was in no mood to appreciate the aesthetic. He listened to the mechanical bell sounding somewhere deep within the walls as quickly he scanned the lists of names. Tin Whistle and 29-29 were both there, but there was still no mention of Tuesday Nemesis or any corporate body of similar name. He almost fell inwards when the stout oak door opened beneath his hand.

"Sorry," the girl said, looking surprised to see him. "Have you been waiting long?"

"No," he responded quickly. "Just arrived."

"From America are you, sir?"

"Right on, honey." He was relieved she spoke English, even if in rather a Mary Poppin's voice.

"How nice," she said. "And what can Holt & Farthingale do for you today, sir?"

"I believe the owner of the Tin Whistle Company and the 29-29 Corporation is Tuesday Nemesis. I am trying to track down their head office on behalf of my client who may be interested in making an offer to buy them out." It was a grand gesture, but he was beginning to feel grand gestures were needed.

"Indeed, sir. How most interesting," she said, as if genuinely thrilled with the news. "What a shame I can't help you beyond referring you to our London office. They handle the main Nemesis account, I believe. I am sure they will be delighted to assist you as far as they are able."

"That a fact?" he said in a jaded tone. "I really hope you're right, honey." He didn't bother to produce the photograph. He didn't need to – the answer would be the same. He was just grateful it was only a short haul across France to London. Time suddenly seemed no longer on his side. With Saturday tomorrow, he would have to make England that same afternoon to avoid a two day break.

"Goodbye, sir," she called as he swept out the door. She waited for the solid oak portal to latch firmly into place before she began keying her desk-top FAX. One minute later a similar machine in London was spewing a sheet of paper into the waiting hand of John Priestley Farthingale. Farthingale came out of his office and gave it to Karina who read it silently.

URGENT TARGET DEPARTED VADUZ OFFICE TEN HUNDRED
HOURS. ANTICIPATE HE WILL CATCH ELEVEN HUNDRED OR
THIRTEEN THIRTY FLIGHT TO HEATHROW. LYNDA.

"That should fit your schedule almost exactly," said
Farthingale, after she had read it.

"Yes, the timing is very convenient," she agreed.

For Paul, the ten days since Karina had last appeared
had dragged interminably. The TEESER machine was
working near to perfection, and he was frustrated by the
odd feeling of having his project to launch, a new lady
in his life, but both, it seemed, were an eternity away.
When a call did come from London to say she was on
her way, his spirits lifted, and he was not surprised to
feel his pulse stepping up its beat.

Half an hour later he was out standing at the gate,
listening to the approach of an engine in the distance. At
first he thought it was just the one, but then he thought he
detected two sets of tyres squealing round the corners, and
when she finally spun through the gate, the second car,
a powder-blue Palermo was late on its brakes, bouncing
off the hedge, before continuing out of sight.

"Hi," she called with an enormous beam, appearing
not to notice.

"That was a close shave," Paul laughed, relieved.
"Am I glad to see you."

"And me you," she jumped out, her face radiant as
she gave him a hug with the strength of a man. "There.
That's for being patient."

"Doesn't Nemesis mind you sloping off like this?" he
took her hand and led her into the cottage. "The whole
thing is costing him a fortune, and we don't want him
questioning the wisdom of the venture."

"Mr Nemesis takes his advice from me," she said
firmly. "Now enough of him. It's Friday afternoon and
we have one lovely long weekend in front of us. And after
ten days in the States I can tell you that the green fields of
little ol' England are truly the most beautiful sight in the
whole wide world. Second only to my magnificent man
with his super machine."

"That could be misconstrued," he said, his eyes laughing.

"Whoops. Sorry." Her hand flew to her mouth, as

she realised what she'd said. "I didn't mean it quite like that."

He could have swore she blushed, and she seemed impossibly more lovely for that. This time her hair was loose and she wore no make-up. She wore a simple cotton frock and flat shoes. She carried a freshness that did not hint of city life, there was a litheness in her movements that spoke of a young deer in a forest glade, her arms covered with a soft pelt of gossamer hairs that shone gold in the early evening sun.

"You can do or say just anything you like and it's wonderful by me," he told her, kissing her lightly on the lips.

"I'll do a lot better at everything if I take a shower first," she said.

Whilst she showered, Paul phoned and booked a table at the Henry VIII. She wouldn't hear of going anywhere else. "The pub's good. The food's good. What else do I need but you?" she had said.

She seemed totally relaxed, and an hour later she drove with great slowness now through the country lanes, until he joked, "We've a queue of cars backing up behind us Karina. Where's all your verve and zest?"

"Verved and zested off," she told him, making no effort to increase her speed. The powder blue Palermo was lying four cars behind.

They sat at their favourite table by the window overlooking the Avon. There had been little rain in recent weeks and the river ambled quietly through the summer meadows, its surface a glossy calm over which myriad flies played dangerous games of tag. Without warning a fish would rise and there would be an explosive flash of jaws, for an instant putting frenzy in the clouds of insects, before the memory quickly faded and they returned to their lethargic, triangular swim.

After Paul and Karina had eaten, they just sat and talked, hands clasped, enjoying a second bottle of wine.

"Okay, so you're on the verge of a great success, I'm absolutely sure of that," she said earnestly. "But then what are you going to do? People like you can never sit still for very long."

"I don't know yet," said Paul, regretting the serious turn. "I'm not used to looking that far ahead. Up to now each day has held enough problems."

"Not any more for you. My bet is soon you are going to be very wealthy."

"Maybe. Money has never bothered me that much. My abiding problem has always been the lack of it."

"Something soon to be in the past. Have you another project to follow this one?"

"Most certainly," he surprised her by saying. "And in its way, almost equally as exciting."

"And what is it?"

"A new type of small but very powerful internal combustion engine which is not a gas turbine, nor is it rotary- or piston-driven."

"Stop there," she held up her hand with mock severity. "I can't cope with all this technical stuff. The TEESER machine is enough for me for the moment. Let's just talk about you for a change. You've never mentioned your family."

"No? Maybe it's because there's not a lot to talk about. You've met most of them."

"You've no brothers or sisters?"

"No sisters," and then Paul's expression darkened. "But I do have twin older brothers."

"Really? How interesting. Tell me about them."

"I'd rather not."

"No? Why not?"

"Because they're both absolute bastards, that's why," he said with a vehemence she had never seen before. "They are rank rotten in every way you can imagine. More than that, everything they touch begins to stink the same way they do."

"Wow, wow, this is heavy," she tried to stop him now, but he went on.

"I met them both very recently, and they have not improved with age. I cannot imagine them as family any more. I am having nothing further to do with them – their company, their money, anything, or anyone who has dealings with them. I would never want you to meet either of them, for something about you would surely be irrevocably spoiled."

Suddenly the atmosphere had become very cold, and his hand had gone from hers. It was a different person sitting opposite – powerful, resolute, yet lost in an awful desolation. "And the bastards never even bothered to respond to Tessa's death," he finished.

The chill reached deep within her. She could feel its icy hold. Something was slipping away. The man was strengthening as she watched, but drifting into a private isolation from which she was excluded. Things were happening she was not used to. Something within her grasp was being prised away, her hand opening, her fingers forced apart, and in moments it would be gone. She then knew it must not happen, for this something was the thing she now wanted more than any other.

"Forget your brothers," she tried lightly, finding his hand again. "You have the children. Little Annie and not so little Maria. They must be worth their weight in pleasure." And she nearly added, and you also have me, but now she was uncertain of herself in a way she had not been for many years.

"Ah yes, the girls." His face softened. "They indeed are bright side of the moon."

"And Angela?"

"Yes, and Angela," he agreed, and she looked for an inflection in his voice, but there was none.

"Some people would say you were quite lucky, really."

He seemed to think about it long and hard. Then he finally grinned, his face changing completely, and it was the Paul she knew once more. "And they could be right," he nodded. "Sorry about the outburst, Karina, but when I feel strongly about something, that's the way it is, and that's the way it stays."

"So I see," she said. "Perhaps we should change the subject. D'you want to know about what's been happening?"

"Of course. Yes, please."

"Mr Nemesis has bought some exploration rights in Africa under the name of the Tin Whistle Mining Corporation and has hired Rory McDermid, the top seismologist and geologist in Africa, to head up the team. McDermid has just cabled us to say he's already on to some interesting prospects. Reckons if what he has found comes good, it could throw the world's commodity markets into considerable disarray."

"Really?" said Paul. "So quickly. Fortunes can be won or lost in this kind of situation."

"Indeed so," she agreed.

"What are these minerals?"

"Even I'm not sure yet. There are terrible problems

getting radio signals through the Atlas Mountains due to atmospherics. I've got to go there and get McDermid's report first hand."

"It sounds very remote. How the hell do you get into a place like that."

"Actually it's quite fun really. I catch a scheduled flight down to Casablanca, then hitch a lift with a bush pilot called Mace who flies for the MECA Corporation. They run a Cessna 210 and he bolsters his income by doing a little freelance air taxi work on the quiet, if the price is right. We're getting our own aircraft soon, but this arrangement is handy in the mean time."

"I can imagine," Paul nodded almost absently, and suddenly she realised he was no longer looking at her.

"Anything the matter?" she asked.

"I don't know," he said in a quiet voice, gazing over her shoulder. "But I could swear that fellow behind has been listening to every word you've said."

"What fellow?" she swivelled round.

"Him – that man just going out the door," Paul pointed now, a new energy in his manner. "Look, he's barely touched his meal."

She glanced briefly at the table and then the empty door, and shrugged. "Silly," she said with a smile. "You're just imagining things."

CHAPTER 13

Geoff Mace pushed the control column of the Cessna forward to let the speed build up before he hauled back on the throttle and re-trimmed for cruise. His face wore the slightly whimsical expression of a man who had just made love, or was just about to. Neither was the case. He was thinking wistfully of Karina Darielle. That one time would be the one and only time, he knew that – a delicious and lingering memory never to be repeated. She had of course been in touch several times since then, charming and quietly aloof, as if he was her iocal Avis rep, not a recent lover. It was not the most satisfying of relationships, but it had its compensations – this latest assignment, 10,000 dollars in compensation. His right hand free, he let his fingers massage the solid wad of 500-dollar bills in the top pocket of his safari jacket, and smiled to himself. The job seemed to have never-ending possibilities, and had cured his alimony problems – at least for the time being.

Beside him his passenger was thinking parallel thoughts that were no less pleasurable.

Ephraim Krebs never relied heavily on luck, but accepted its generosity when offered, and there was certainly a lot of that right now. It was remarkably good fortune finding the girl coming out of Holt and Farthingale's London Office. That was the big break – that, and tailing her all the way out to her rendezvous with the weird researcher down in the boon-docks. Everything was opening up like a busted can of pilchards, and he could almost admit he was a damn sight better at the job than even he ever thought he was.

The trip into the desert was going to be the clincher. Once he'd found out what was going on out there, there would be enough meat on the bone for a substantial preliminary report, and a possible hike in his fees from Price Whitney – an altogether attractive proposition. The question was, could he get Rory McDermid talking? Ephraim Krebs had two bottles of best Highland malt in his briefcase that from experience said he could.

The woman raised other questions, though, questions for which he had not the answer yet – but they would come. It was simply a matter of establishing her motivations and her paymaster – and right now that pointed to Tuesday Nemesis. Overhearing her at that dinner was the sort of good fortune that rarely came twice on an assignment. What she said could be true, the real pickings lying out here in the Sahara, and he had to get in, pull the facts, and get out again before she turned up. In the meantime the rest could wait.

Such thoughts were meandering pleasantly through his mind when the first hint of trouble came. At first he thought he might have imagined it. The motor pecked once, then ran on as sweetly as before, its rumble as monotonous and soporific as distant surf in the heat of the noonday sun.

"What was that?" he enquired casually of the pilot.

"What was what?" Geoff Mace frowned at him.

"I thought the engine missed," said Krebs.

Mace cocked an ear. "Don't hear anything," he said.

"Listen, there it is again," said Krebs, his back suddenly straightening. The engine had coughed twice this time, before returning to its stable drone. "You must have heard it that time."

The pilot didn't answer. Instead his hands began to flash over the instruments, checking this and adjusting that. The engine had begun to misfire regularly now and the speed was steadily bleeding back so their ears were no longer buffeted by the roar of the wind.

"What's happening?" Krebs pressed. "What the hell's going on?" Despite the heat an icy chill seemed to be freezing the sweat in a line down his back.

"We have an engine malfunction," said Mace quite calmly.

"We're going down!" Kreb's voice raised to a shout. "We're falling. We're going to hit!"

"We will, if we carry on. I'm going to do a precautionary landing and check out what's wrong."

"Precautionary landing?" Kreb stared aghast at the vertical mountains rising all about them. "Are you completely mad?"

"Uh huh," Geoff Mace shook his head in the negative.

"Look down there, buddy. See that waterfall? That's where we're going."

"Where?" Krebs choked, trying to swallow.

"Half way down the drop, the fall is broken by a ledge. You'll see a pool there. You'll also see a narrow plateau of green. We'll put down on that."

"But, but it looks no bigger than a pea patch."

"Accept my judgement," Mace snapped back. "Listen to that motor. She's only firing on two pots now. You can jump if you want. It'll be just the same as flying into the rocks, which is what we'll do if we try to keep going. Or you can stay with me and shut up."

Ephraim Krebs shut up. They were slicing vertically between the mountains like a wire through new-pressed cheese, and suddenly the tiny patch of green was no longer tiny, growing by the second from a minute blade of green to almost fill the perspex in front of his eyes. There was nothing from the engine now – all hint of life had died, and in the next instant the air too was silent but for the sound of rushing water as they slithered to a halt on the narrow mossy spline.

"Jees," Krebs gulped. "I never thought I'd see another day."

"We can all be wrong," Geoff Mace told him with a thin downturned smile, as he unlatched the door and jumped out. "Come on, blue," he called from the outside. "I need your help. I've got to unship our cargo to get at my tools."

Krebs eased unsteadily out on to his feet, and in the next instant found himself fielding box upon box as they were thrown out by the pilot. It all seemed to be camping provisions of one sort or another, the type of gear a well-equipped backwoodsman would stow for a month away. Amongst what he could identify was food, a tent, batteries, a powerful radio receiver, a torch, and fire lighters. There was also a revolver and some ammunition and a hunting rifle. It was expeditionary stuff and he wondered at the nature of the man for whom it was intended.

"No time for idling." Geoff Mace's head was back out of the cargo compartment. "Can you go up to the lagoon and get me some water?" He handed Krebs a canvas bucket and pointed to where the waterfall creamed into a mist out of sight behind a scree of rocks.

"Water?"

"Under that cowl there is a furnace cooking, fella," Mace told him. "I can either work on it in the cool of the evening, in which case if I get it fixed, we'll fly out tomorrow earliest.

Or you can keep me sluiced down with cold water and I'll try and fix it now. It's up to you."

Krebs said nothing. There was nothing to say. He turned and began to make his way across the spongy surface of the plateau to where the waterfall crashed into a lagoon of the palest emerald. It was further than he thought, and he was perspiring heavily by the time he got there. He dropped down and sat with his back against the rocks as he waited for his breath to return, watching the spray paint myriad tiny rainbows that wafted slowly away on the light air.

He was just thinking how idyllic this spot could be under other circumstances when he heard the aircraft engine begin to turn slowly over. There was nothing there, just the rasp of dry metal on dry metal as the starter gears engaged. He listened to the big motor labouring through each compression for what seemed an age, wondering why the pilot was draining the battery when the machine was plainly as dead as the Texan buffalo.

Then suddenly it backfired.

The sound was like a cannon round bouncing between the mountains, silencing the braying of strange creatures far below. He heard the started motor re-engage. There was another backfire, and another. This time, after the echoes had ceased battering his ears, he detected a continuous rumble, and his spirits soared: the engine was idling quite sweetly with not a hint of any roughness. He was on his feet in an instant – in time to hear the soft idle change to a detonation of the rawest power as Mace pushed the throttle home.

Krebs just stood there staring, his jaw agape as if it must surely be adrift from its hinges. The aircraft was already airborne, lifting lazily off over the edge of the plateau, diving at first to gain speed, then beginning a slow ascent towards the West. It neither faltered in its climb or its direction, and within a minute it had become the merest dot in the sky, the hammer of its engine weakening from a buffet to a faint throb, then nothing at all. All he could hear now was the cascade of water behind him and the bellow of some unseen animal echoing up from the valley floor four thousand feet beneath.

Ephraim Krebs was in a daze as he walked slowly back towards the litter of boxes that still remained where the aircraft had stood. On the top of the first box a letter had been pinned.

He lifted it off and pulled the contents free, trying to believe this sudden turn of events was not one of the ghastly nightmares he suffered after heavy bouts of drinking. In his soul he knew it wasn't.

He started to read.

FOR THE ATTENTION OF MR E KREBS

Dear Mr Krebs,

I must first apologise to you for arranging your arrival at this rather desolate spot. I am sure you will understand it is not a practical joke, rather a necessary expedient to prevent you jeopardising important plans that have been in the making for some time. You may find it consoling to know this action would not have been necessary had you not been so obviously good at your job.

As it is I hope you will accept your enforced sabbatical with good grace. An aircraft will be returning for you in a little over three weeks and in the meantime I think you will find you have been adequately provisioned. I personally picked the hamper from Fortnum & Masons.

At some stage Mr Clive Feral can be expected to remove you from his payroll. So that you are not financially disadvantaged, the shortfall on your earnings will be made up by myself.

Listen to the BBC World Service on 15.070 MHz short wave – I believe you will find events at the end of October quite interesting. Similarly I hope you manage to enjoy something of a holiday – you are in probably one of the most idyllic settings in the world – but I must council against trying to escape. There is no way off that ledge without wings.

With best wishes,
K.D.

Ephraim Kreb's eyes lifted from the thin sheet of paper. There was no signature, just the typed letters K.D. and they seemed to linger indelibly on his retina as he stared out of focus into the blue haze that painted the ice on the distant peaks. Then with a sudden rush of breath his lungs expanded and his fists clenched and he roared like a wounded bull.

"You bitch," the word exploded back and forth between the rockface of the cliffs. "Bitch, bitch, bitch," he said again, softer this time as he sank down slowly on his knees and his fists began pounding the lush green loam. "You bloody little bitch."

CHAPTER 14

The word had come through on the grapevine the way it usually did. Sabine Banking Inc, a small finance house out in the Midwest was on the verge of going bust because of the depression in the farming business. It was one of the little gems that came up now and then: a bank with no more than a dozen branches with low issued capital and plenty of collateral, a nice little bauble to pick up for Price Whitney's portfolio without interfering too much with the main cash flow. There was also the rumour that Sabine were holding security on some oil-bearing shale. If that came up trumps he would have one to throw back at Martin.

To Clive it was also an excuse to get out of town. A lot of farmers were now staging illegal dog fights to stave off the recession. Like the cattle girls, they were doing a lot of things they wouldn't normally do to make up the extra dough, and if anyone knew how to exploit a situation, he prided himself that he did. Yes, he considered, things were looking pretty good right now, and the bank's profits were continuing their hectic rise.

After the feeder plane landed at Belle Canyon's local field, he got a taxi round to the head office of Sabine Banking, and walked in unannounced. He always arrived unannounced – it caught people showing a face they might later try to hide.

"Mr Sabine about?" he enquired casually at desk four.

"Mr Sabine is in conference at the moment," the girl said, looking at him sharply, trying to get a fix, knowing the face but not knowing the name.

"Well, get him out of conference and tell him someone is here to see him."

"Can't do that, sir," the girl was emphatic. "It would be more than my job's worth."

"It's more than your job's worth if you don't," he smiled at her now. She was a pretty little thing, neatly proportioned with red hair and a freckly nose, and she looked a lot younger than she was. That was the one for tonight, he told himself.

"Let me take your name, sir," she looked worried now. "I'll have a word with his secretary."

"I'm Clive Feral of the Price Whitney Banking Corporation."

"Not *the* Mr Clive Feral," she spoke on an intake of breath.

"Yes," he said, the smile unmoving on his face. "Now shift your pretty little ass, honey. I haven't got all day."

She was gone in an instant, and moments later another older woman appeared. "Sorry to keep you, sir," the woman said anxiously. "Mr Sabine will be with you in a minute or so."

"Good," said Clive letting himself in through the security gate. He saw the guard's hand go for his gun, but in an instant the woman waved at him to put it away.

"Come this way please, sir. He's just coming to the end of his meeting, if you care to take a seat."

Clive ignored the chair she offered. "Which room is he in?" he asked.

"That one, sir," she pointed, "but I don't think you should—"

It was too late. He did not pause in his stride, opening the door on to a room of grey faced men in earnest discussion.

"—that is why you see we have no choice—" Sabine tailed off, shocked at the interruption.

"Carry on," Clive told him. "Maybe I can add something when you gentlemen have finished talking."

For a moment the silence was so total you could hear the birds singing in the park across the block. None had met Clive Feral before, but all knew his face from its almost daily appearances in the financial press. "Ah, er, Mr Feral, this is a surprise." Sabine gathered himself, "Let me, ah, introduce you to the other directors. We were just discussing your offer."

"Don't bother with the intros," said Clive coldly. "I've a bad memory for names, but I never forget a face or a fact. I assume you have reached a decision."

"Not yet, but we are close."

"Okay. Don't let me stop you."

"We had almost finished in fact."

"Okay. Finish."

"It was a *private* meeting, Mr Feral," said Sabine, his face reddening now. "If you don't mind leaving us alone."

180

"I *do* mind," said Clive blandly, perching on a side table. "Consider me one of the family. I already own 20 per cent of your stock. In 30 days it will be 50-plus. Looks like I have better reason to be here than most of you."

The grey-faced men shrank still further in their chairs. A year ago their shares in Sabine Banking had stood at 527 dollars a unit. Today the figure was 195 dollars and falling, and they all had a substantial personal equity in the business. Feral's offer had come in at 175 dollars and held good for one month. On the face of it, it looked better to deal on the open market, but a massive unloading would depress the shares way below Feral's offer, so it was one choice or none. It was going to break many of them in the process and the whole exercise had become one of damage limitation.

"Well, what's your answer to my offer?" Clive went on. "Are you going to recommend acceptance to your shareholders, or are you going for broke?"

There was a look of anger on some of the faces, frustration on others. Hatred was on all of them. "Okay," said Clive. "Take your time. While you're mulling it over I want to have a word in private with Mr Sabine, if he doesn't mind." He lifted a finger and beckoned the banker out of the room.

Sabine moved instantly to follow. "Of course, Mr Feral. I am sure they can manage without me for a moment. What can I do for you, sir?"

"That red-headed girl in booth four. I want you to arrange for her to be at my motel tonight at eight."

"Red-headed girl," Sabine repeated as if mesmerised, his face paler than the magnolia blossom on the table.

"You got it," Clive smiled.

"That girl you refer to, Mister Feral, is my daughter," Sabine said very quietly, his dark eyes pockets of fire. "If you were anyone else, anywhere else, you wouldn't be still standing now."

"Your daughter, eh, Sabine? Even better," Clive grinned. "Make it seven thirty – I'll have longer with her, then."

"You're the bastard they all say you are, except worse," Sabine spat. "You just take a hike, Mister Feral." He turned his back and made for the board room.

"Just one thing," said Clive. "If she's not there, the deal's off."

Sabine sat alone at the head of the director's table. All about him faces jostled and arguments raged and fists were shaken, but he heard none of it. Several times he was spoken

181

to, but he did not respond, and soon he was ignored as if he wasn't there.

He sat with his eyes closed, going over the good days that had been not so long ago when the bank was thriving and he was the most popular man in the neighbourhood, a time when people doffed their hats and smiled, and gave him flowers for his coat. The Sabine Bank was an institution in itself, and he was, as its president and principal shareholder, financing the local farmers and much of the town's business, always offering a kindly word and more often a helping hand after a few stern words of caution on the evils of profligacy. Twice he had been put up for town mayor, but each time he had gracefully demurred, saying it was for a younger man better qualified than he. They accepted his answer with regret and half knowing it was not true – knowing that any spare time he had, he took with his family up in the mountains where they had a weekend lodge. They accepted that. After God, in that neighbourhood, the family was almighty.

That was then. Now he was spat at in the streets, and women screamed with vehemence. Now he was the man that closed out farms, threw families on the streets, auctioned men's last possessions on the steps of the bank, taking everything and giving nothing in return. If the devil had an incarnation it was he, and it mattered not a jot to talk of legal obligations or the little men whose share or two were becoming more worthless by the day.

And his own fortune, everything he possessed, had vanished like an ephemeral puff of smoke. But worse than that, he had also borrowed double what he owned to recapitalise the bank when the shares were standing at 400 dollars and climbing. That too was gone – every single penny of it.

And now this man had come, demanding his daughter.

Very slowly Sabine rose from his chair and suddenly all noise around him ceased. There was something awful in the way he just stood there, swaying slightly, looking past them with misty eyes through the window before he turned and walked like a ghost from the room.

None of them jumped when the shot came. To a man they had sensed the moment he pulled the trigger and the copper nosed bullet entered his temple and took from the planet one of the finest people they had known, or were ever likely to.

Clive received the news in his motel room. He scowled momentarily as he adjusted his silk bath robe, then slung the receiver back on the hook. He had gone off the idea of the girl anyway. He had had word there was a champion dog fight going on out of town that night, and that was something really special.

"A hundred million bucks – but that is excellent," Clive beamed over his lunch in New York the following day. "Split six ways that leaves us sixteen and a half big ones each. Not bad for a week's work. You've done very well as usual, Abe."

"Less my commission, of course," Abel Satco said, basking behind a wide smile.

"But naturally. And you've earned every penny of it."

Abel Satco reckoned he had. It was a very risky business putting together raids on company stock using insider information. Every state penitentiary had inmates who had tried for the mark, and failed. But the rewards were equally great. He charged 10 per cent on profits to put the deals together – that was ten million bucks this week alone, with not a penny of his own money at risk up front.

"How's things with you, Clive?" Satco changed the subject. "Heard you've bought out Sabine Banking out in Belle Canyon. Is that right?"

"Sure. Picked it up clean and cheap. I wanted to talk to you about that, Abe. Sabine holds security on a bundle of tract that's reputed to be oil bearing shale. What d'you reckon I should do?"

"Tie it up immediately," said Satco. "Oil seems generally set to do things again. You got full title to the land?"

"Nope, not yet. But the farmers who own it are in a pretty shaky state. And there's never been a proper valuation done."

"That's easy then," said Satco. "I suggest you foreclose on the farms at once."

"Exactly what I thought," said Clive. "I'll set it up straight away." Then, "So what's the latest on oil?"

"I can see the market turning very bullish," Satco mused. "What goes round, comes round, as they say, and we are getting a bundle of buying orders – and a lot coming in from 29-29. Is your man still working on them?"

"You betcha," said Clive, frowning at the same time. He remembered that he had heard nothing from Ephraim Krebs for over a week. It was already October 7th, and he'd give Krebs until the end of the month and not a day longer. "I must admit he hasn't gotten too far yet though."

"I'm not really surprised," said Satco. "29-29 are the talk

of the Street. I tried to get my buddy in the Federal Reserve Board interested, but he wouldn't touch it – said that unless and until there were any irregularities, he'd be putting his job on the line. Said it would be less risky if he knew who was heading up 29-29 – could be a friend of the Senator, or the Senator himself. That could be a fizzer."

"Yes, pity," said Clive, disapppointed.

"Excuse me, sir." A waitress arrived at the table with a phone in her hand. "I have a call for you sir."

"The hell you have," Clive grumbled. It was a standing order he was never to be interrupted over lunch. "Who the hell is it? Why didn't you tell them to call my office?"

"Sorry, sir. He didn't give his name. Just said it was extremely urgent." The waitress backed away from the table, sensing trouble.

Clive snatched the phone from her. "Yeah, what you want?"

"Clive, it's Vic Loeb," his attorney responded softly. "Can you get round to my office right away?"

"I'm with Satco right now," Clive mellowed slightly. "How about tomorrow morning first thing?"

"That's up to you, but tomorrow may be too late."

"That important, huh. What's it about?"

"I've gotten wind that a certain company you might be interested in could be coming up for private sale very soon."

"That a fact?" said Clive with only mild enthusiasm. "Which outfit is that?"

"I don't think it would be wise to tell you any more on the phone," Loeb continued in a low voice. "In fact, very unwise."

"Really?" Clive's eyes lifted a fraction. "Why?"

There was a long pause before Loeb said, "That's probably a radio phone you're hooked up to, so someone's almost certainly listening in. All I say to you is, think in numbers, not in names."

"What the hell is that supposed to mean?" Clive glowered at the instrument after he hung up. Why did these expensive goddamn lawyers always talk in riddles?

"What was that?" Satco asked him curiously.

"Vic Loeb. Said he'd heard a company I would be interested in was coming up for sale. Wouldn't give the name – simply said to think in numbers, not names."

"Really?" Satco puzzled. "Not the 29-29 Corporation, surely?"

Satco had a pleasant, if solitary, lunch on Clive's account.

184

His client had spat out the bread he was chewing and run for the door, his face like Moses at the first sight of the tablets. Satco had never seen him move so fast, indeed never known him move quicker than the elegant walking pace he adopted to keep his suits in good line. Satco's face carried a trace of mild amusement, as he wiped his mouth and left.

"Where did you get this from?" Clive strode into Loeb's office.

Loeb waved him to a seat. "Cigar?" he offered.

"Cigar nothing," Clive remained standing, towering over his attorney. "Is it 29-29, or isn't it?"

"That's the information I have," Loeb confirmed.

"Well? What's the story?"

"I had a call from Ephraim Krebs' secretary this morning because she couldn't get through to you. Apparently Krebs is in London tracking down the origins of 29-29 and its connections with this Tuesday Nemesis."

"Go on."

"Seems the whole thing is held together by a firm of lawyers in London called Holt and Farthingale. As you know they've also got an office in New York, but that's by-the-by. Krebs had been doing a bit of clever digging and found this guy Nemesis is thinking of quitting the currency and commodity business for a sojourn in real estate."

"The devil he is!"

"Yeah. Apparently the word is out among the Greek shipping magnates that 29-29 is open to offers – lock stock and barrel. But that's all very hush-hush."

Clive took a deep breath and sat down. He knew the next question, but almost dare not ask it. "How much?" he enquired at length.

"Don't know yet. D'you want me to set to work on it?"

"You betcha. I want every fact, figure, and detail. This could be the biggest thing Price Whitney has ever done. 29-29 have some extraordinary talent apart from the collateral they own. Could give enormous strength to our bank – double its volume, double its profits."

"Sounds good," nodded Loeb blandly, and Clive wondered why it was in the nature of attorneys to never enthuse about anything. Still, he was about the best attorney that money could buy, which was just as well because his charges were astronomical.

"Get to it Vic," Clive told him. "When can I expect your report?"

"I'll have something first thing tomorrow. Join me at my office for a working breakfast at eight. We'll be near to my Fax machine, ready for any data transmissions."

"Sure thing, buddy." Clive beamed at him now, and Victor Loeb smiled in return with a rare show of teeth.

Victor Loeb's day started at five, and a working breakfast was quite normal – it enabled him to be at the golf club no later than two in the afternoon after a full working spread. The following morning he watched the chauffeured limo arrive prompt at eight. The anteroom was already set for breakfast by staff specially retained for early morning catering, and the hash browns were cooking in the pan giving the air a deliciously appetising aroma.

"Well?" questioned Clive, throwing his coat on the stand. "What you got for me?" He didn't look at the girl who took his hat.

"Some things you'll like, and some things you won't," said Loeb. "Take a seat and relax. What you having?"

"Anything. Fill the plate," he said impatiently. "I'm not in a relaxed frame of mind, Vic."

"Okay. Understood." Loeb poured them both a coffee from the side-server. "The situation appears to be this. We haven't been able to raise Ephraim Krebs again – he seems to have gone to ground. But I've been on to another agency we use in London who are pretty good, and they've come up with some interesting stuff. They've confirmed that Nemesis is selling 29-29 and is open to offers, but not on the open market. It caused something of a flap when our man approached Holt & Farthingale directly – they wanted to know how he got on to the deal. Our guy earned his money by bluffing that he was connected to a Greek shipping consortium. Seemed to do the trick, and they began to open up."

"Good, good," said Clive.

"Apparently the terms of sale are very stringent – and you haven't got much time."

"Oh?"

"The sale of 29-29 is set to take place with an exchange of contracts on the morning of Wednesday 23rd October. That's fifteen days from now."

"That is short," Clive frowned.

"Yeah, and that's not all. It is stipulated that the sale has to be to a consortium, not a private individual."

"That's strange. Why should Nemesis care?"

"I don't know," said Loeb. "But that's the deal."

186

"What else do you have? Like price?"

"There is no price fixed as yet. The deal is open to offers, but it was hinted that the starting point would be around one billion bucks."

"The big one," nodded Clive. "More or less as I thought. What comes in the package? You got the details?"

"Only roughly, and there will be no official confirmation until a firm offer is on the table. But I can tell you this, which will please you, the Hartman Building is currently included in their portfolio of real estate, as are one or two other nice properties around the business quarter."

"The Hartman Building," Clive almost glowed as his eyes narrowed to thin vengeful slits. "That's the baby I'm after. That's the one, along with the dealing operation. You got any more information on where the dealing room is, and how it works?"

"No. But let me finish. The package is almost equally divided between their property holdings at fixed valuation, and a float of 500 million dollars constantly in cycle on their dealing floor. My man tells me it will be in the contract that the buyer takes over the entire trading account – that is all cash, stock, and assets, property and profits – at the precise moment of signature at 9 a.m. on 23rd, and no trading will take place on that day until all formalities have been completed."

"Hey, I don't like the sound of that," Clive frowned. "The cupboard could be bare."

"They seem to have thought of that," said Loeb. "A business indemnity is being offered on Lloyds guaranteeing a valuation of the company at no less than one billion dollars in stock and assets at close on Wall Street the previous day."

"That sounds better," Clive nodded.

"It might be about as good as you're going to get," continued Loeb. "There appears to be no question of them divulging any trading practices before the sale. Presumably they feel it would leave them vulnerable to a dawn raid – not without some reason," Loeb allowed himself a smile. He knew Clive's business methods very well.

Clive glowered at him. "They think they're so goddam clever," he hissed furiously. "But if Krebs keeps at it he may come up with another angle."

"He may do – but I shouldn't count on it. Hey, why don't you have some more hash browns?"

CHAPTER 15

Thought you would be interested in these, honey, she had scribbled hurriedly on the outside cover of October's *National Geographic*, which had arrived in the same parcel as the latest copy of *New Scientist*.

Paul wished she had added more, but that was it, and he began to thumb with eagerness through the glossy pages. He almost missed it. It was a scant few lines at the bottom of page 47 beneath a piece on the Polisario guerrillas in the Western Sahara. *New push for rare minerals in Shadow of Atlas Mountains, it read. Renowned mineral expert Rory McDermid is reported to have discovered important deposits of bismuth on edge of desert. The exploration and development company, Tin Whistle Ltd, have refused to confirm or deny these reports, or give any reason for their push in this direction. It is hoped to have more information in next month's issue.*

He found the article in *New Scientist* more easily. She had circled it in red felt-tip:

UNUSUAL SECRECY AT LINCOLN UNVEILING

Professor Zachary Weinberger, resident director, has confirmed a news blackout has been ordered on the unveiling later this month of a revolutionary energy-creating device. He will only say that the TEESER machine, as it is called, could cause a dramatic shift away from conventional thinking on the whole question of power generation. He confirmed a further press announcement would be made shortly and apologised for not being more forthcoming. Our energy editor says this is a most extraordinary departure as such unveilings are normally the subject of considerable, and mostly unjustified hyperbole, well in advance of the event.

Paul read the pieces and the tingle was like a mild electric shock. It was hard to believe that on this dewy morning in autumn, here was he, remote in the isolation of his own anonymity with only the rooks for company, setting in motion a growing panjandrum which could lead the world into a new era. A month ago waves of self-doubt had flooded over him, but no longer. His eyes were bright and his breathing deep for it felt now as if every burden had been lifted, and his life had shifted into another gear, blowing forward on a wind of destiny. It was a heady feeling and he rocked just a little.

But the work had not yet finished. Now came the strangest task of all, or so it felt, for this moment of reflection was taken at the expense of the task in hand – pulling the whole thing apart. Already his workshop floor was littered, ankle deep, with a scree of nuts and bolts, bits of pipe, coloured wire and ambiguous lumps of machinery, each neatly labelled with a coded tag ready for reassembly, an ocean away in what was now a few days' time. Tomorrow was Thursday 10th October, the day Pickfords had been booked to come with their special crates to pack the TEESER ready for airfreighting the following Monday. It was a strangely emotional moment. He felt like the mother of a bride, torn between the happiness of the betrothal and the sadness of the loss. He knew it was going to be a long weekend – made all the worse because he would not be seeing Karina until he arrived in the States.

It had been an emotional parting. "I am sorry, my darling," she had said. "But I shan't be able to get away much over the next few weeks. I have a full diary every day. Everything is taken care of, though, and I shall be with you for the grand opening. I'm looking forward to that. And I know I shall miss you terribly."

"You'd better be there," he had ordered. "It has become almost as much your baby as mine."

"It'll never be that," she had laughed. "But I may borrow it for just a bit."

The remark had not registered at the time – only later did he think about it, and find it odd. It was in moments like that he wondered about Karina Darielle, wondered and worried for he knew almost nothing about her. The lady was something different in more ways than he had first imagined, sometimes hard, sometimes as warm and as soft as the duck-down cover of the bed they shared, but never vulnerable – and that worried him. In that one thing she was unnatural in a quite chilling sort of way.

A few days later Paul Feral stood for the first time on the steps of the Lincoln Institute in Washington, staring upwards at the massive edifice, honoured and in awe of the august body of his peers who had invited him there to demonstrate his discoveries. The correspondence with the institute had a sincerity and depth of warmth he found both surprising and enormously encouraging.

It was still only Wednesday 16th October – a full week before the grand unveiling, but there was much to be done in the setting up and he had the horror of some sudden problem manifesting itself and the whole demonstration turning into a terrible fiasco. The nightmare was as impossible as it was ghastly, for every system had been checked and double checked time and again, but he still worried.

"Paul Feral," Professor Weinberger almost ran across the marble floor, a broad smile on his face. "How wonderful to meet you at long last."

"The pleasure is entirely mine, sir," said Paul, accepting the extended hand. "I've heard so much of you."

He felt dwarfed by the professor's tall lean frame towering over him, and the professor's grip, like the person, was firm yet sensitive. Paul guessed him to be in his early fifties – a man of impressive stature, and Paul noticed the half frame silver spectacles failed to disguise a latent wildness still in his eyes from a youth that was as colourful as it was academic.

Professor Zachary Weinberger was not only a distinguished mathematical theoretician, he was also a founder member of the American Chapter of the Dangerous Sports Society. Outside the esoteric circles of quantum physics, Zachary Weinberger was remembered more for jumping off the Golden Gate Bridge on a bungee rope, than for discovering the sub-atomic Pesar particle held as the key to electro-magnetic radiation.

"What you've heard is not all bad, I hope?" the professor laughed.

"No, sir," Paul grinned back, still uncertain how to take this giant of a man.

"Good. And I think we'll be hearing considerably more of

you too," said the professor. "I've been reading your papers, and I must say I'm absolutely amazed. I can't wait to see your TEESER machine up and running."

"Yes, I'm looking forward to getting it re-commissioned," confirmed Paul, disguising how keen he was to do just that. "When can I start work on it?"

"As soon as you like. We've given you space in the Arnot Gallery and the packing cases are already sitting on the floor. We can provide as much labour as you'll need, and if you're short of anything all you have to do is ask."

"That really is excellent of you, Professor. I can't thank you enough."

"No thanks are needed, Paul. This is just another case of little ol' England handing the world their best ideas and brains on a plate. Why you Brits don't do more with your bright ideas I really don't know."

"Neither do I," said Paul, ruefully. "The trouble with British bankers is they always see the tunnel at the end of the light."

"Must be something like that," Weinberger nodded. "And please stop calling me Professor. It gives me delusions of grandeur. You call me Zak, same way everyone else does."

"Okay, Zak, if that's the way you want it."

That night in his room after a swim in the motel pool, Paul was as content as he had been for many months, the contentment only marred by not having heard from Karina for nearly two weeks. She had told him she was going to be busy, but that she would be there for the grand debut. But that wasn't enough. He was missing her more, and wanting her more, with every day that passed. Yet at the same time something cold was lurking deep within his guts – an elusive feeling that was a mixture of imagination and a fear he could not define. It was this that kept him awake, and when he finally dropped off it was into a fitful sleep, only to be awakened a few hours later by the sudden peal of the phone by the side of his bed. He checked his watch – it was still only six in the morning. "Yes, what do you want," he muttered irritably.

"Your car is here for you, sir," the receptionist said.

"What car?" he barked back. "I didn't order any car. You've got the wrong room," and tossed back the receiver.

Instantly the phone jangled again. "You are Mr Paul Feral?" the woman asked.

"Yes," he said wearily.

"There's no mistake then. The Lincoln have a car here ready for you, sir. And there is a message as well – the messenger says it's urgent. Shall I send him up?"

"If you have to," said Paul, climbing unsteadily out of bed.

It seemed the next instant someone was knocking on his door and he opened it to a man wearing uniform. An ID wallet was flipped open and closed again under his nose before he had a chance to see more than some embossed gold lettering. "Mr Feral, sir?" the man asked.

"Yes."

"Sorry to disturb you, sir, but I have an urgent message," he passed Paul a sealed manilla envelope. "You'll find me in reception when you're ready." He turned and left.

The letter was worded like a telegram.

STATE SECURITY CLASSIFICATION I

TO: MR PAUL FERAL.

FROM: ZACHARY WEINBERGER.

ON INSTRUCTION OF THE PRESIDENT, IMPERATIVE YOU COMMISSION TEESER MACHINE IMMEDIATELY READY FOR PRIVATE DEMO TO SELECT MEMBERS OF LEGISLATURE NO LATER THAN FRI 18TH PM. PROJECT NOW HAS A PRIORITY SECURITY CLASSIFICATION – ESSENTIAL NO INFORMATION IS DISCLOSED TO UNAUTHORISED PERSONNEL WITHOUT PRIOR CLEARANCE.

Clive Feral loathed Saturdays the same way he loathed Sundays. For no reason that could be defined in logic, every goddamn thing ground to a halt for two whole days a week, two days when he had to find other diversions to replace the excitement and thrills of the dealing-room floor. But first he would read the Saturday papers after a substantial breakfast of egg and hash browns which Karina would deliver to his bed.

He skirted over the main headlines – a report of a mud slide in Paraguay with 200 dead, a bomb outrage in Bogota, the Supreme Court's ruling on a constitutional issue affecting Hispanic rights, and the latest rumours rife in Washington about some new device for creating energy. All these pieces were for Clive mere stepping stones to the page on which the first of the financial reports began. His eyes alighted on the article he had been looking for:

After a disappointing start to the year, Price Whitney have shown a remarkable recovery and seem set for record growth. Once again the controversial management of Clive Feral has confounded the pundits who saw conventional banking operations declining in the face of stiff competition for talent from entrepreneurial specialist dealing houses like the 29-29 Corporation. 29-29 are still reckoned to be tops in the speculative dealing business, but to quote Feral, "Not by far and not for long."

And they've sure got that right, thought Clive, as his eyes swam with misty self-esteem and a half smile twisted his lips. Price Whitney with 29-29 would be an invincible combination and it was just a matter of time before they accepted his offer. Loeb held the satellite link open, but it was still taking one hell of a time to get the answers back. The word coming out of Holt & Farthingale was that Tuesday Nemesis was holed up in London somewhere and difficult to reach. However they had confirmed that Price Whitney's nominee would be given final refusal, so the deal was safe in that quarter.

"Everything all right, darling?" Karina called through.

"No complaints, honey," he responded. "Trade never looked better. Reckon I've now gotten some boys down there who are almost as good as you – might even be better in time."

"That *is* good news," she purred. "I am so glad everything is going so well for you."

"Just shows you're not indispensable." He re-emphasised the point.

"Isn't that just what I've always told you?" she glanced round the door, her smile wide and generous. "Anything special you fancy when you get up, honey? I'm sorry I've been away these last few days, but I'll make it up to you, I promise."

He had barely noticed her absence, and was beginning not to care. With the thrust of Price Whitney into ever higher profits, the shine of Karina Darielle was losing much of its burnish and she seemed less able to please than before. "I'm going up-state for the weekend," he said without looking up. "Pack my bags, honey, will you?"

He didn't mention that up-state was a new mansion he had just purchased, and in which resided two ladies whose fascination with bizarre sexual practices all but exceeded his own.

After he had gone she recovered the newspaper from where it had been discarded as a mess of single sheets beside the bed, and began to rearrange the pages neatly one by one. Then with care she began to read from the front page through to the end, missing nothing, dwelling for some time on the piece about rumours in Washington, before moving on to the minutiae of the financial world. Only then did she fold it tidily in quarters and throw it in the bin. For a moment she stared reflectively across the jagged expanse of the New York skyline. Then, a smile upon her face, she took the secret key from beneath the shelf and turned on the trading terminal.

Yes, she too was delighted Clive Feral was doing so well, but for entirely different reasons.

CHAPTER 16

Ephraim Krebs' moments of reflection were considerably longer than Karina's had been. For hours at a time he just sat in front of his tent on the edge of the plateau, staring pensively into the primeval wilderness that lifted above into the ragged, snow-capped peaks, and fell away in steps into the abyss thousands of feet below. He never ceased to marvel at the shades of colour that seemed to melt one within the next until at the farthest reaches of the eye all became one in the uniform mauve of a cleric's vestment. It had taken two whole days before his fury at being tricked had finally subsided. Now he was almost finding enjoyment in his predicament, if not a little humour.

She was a bitch, a witch even. He would never retract that – at least not yet he wouldn't. But he was beginning to admit that she might have some mitigating features, just *might*. It had taken him a good half-day to unpack and stow the considerable provisions. There were two tents, not just one as he had originally thought, the second being for storage. Like everything else, it came with a little note of instructions. Someone had been to considerable length to put this package together – nothing seemed to have been forgotten, and he especially appreciated the small waterproof pack containing a box of sharpened pencils and a ream of A4 Bond. The woman must have second sight, he thought, for by the fourth day he had begun to write.

Like all writers, the process had been full of self-consciousness at the beginning. There is nothing more calculated to expunge the mind of any thought than a clean white sheet of paper. The pencil felt like a lead weight shackled to his fingers, quite defiant in its immobility. For what seemed like hours he chewed at it and used the pointed end to pick his teeth, staring out into the endless beyond. Somewhere far below a mountain leopard roared and the call of the ibis came hesitantly in upon the wind, a lonely, empty sound of total desolation that seemed to be the voice of the land itself as the lowering sun cast long shadows across the valley floor. It was possible to believe there was not another human soul for a thousand miles or more, and suddenly he just didn't care.

Suddenly the pencil had sprung from his mouth as if self-propelled and landed on the paper, moving across the sheet in the slanting style that drove his teachers mad. He let it run, no weight there now, his thoughts lucid and reflective in a quite extraordinary way.

All these years he had secretly harboured the thought that he would one day write something, but somehow had never found the time to start – and anyway his wife would have gone hysterical about it. Come to think about it, his wife got pretty hysterical about almost everything he did, and he wondered why he had let it stop him for so long.

Now he had the time and no excuses, no disturbance, no bills to pay, no way of paying them. The choice was not even his that he was there at all, and certainly not when he was to leave – for the moment he was a lost soul upon the face of planet Earth, and it must have been this that freed his mind, loosened his hand as, with amazement, he realised the picture before his eyes was no longer the one he was looking at.

No longer was he alone. There were people there with him now, grey at first upon the pages, shadowy figures, coming and going in and out of the fog of his subconscious. Then just as suddenly they began to have flesh colour, moving with a life of their own, talking to each other, and it was as much as he could do to keep up, his hand chronicling with desperate speed as he wore one pencil blunt, then the next, until eventually he had to stop and sharpen each in turn before he could continue.

At first he considered it might be a miracle, or was he hallucinating? He quickly dismissed both possibilities as non-sense – he had never felt more sober in his life. He knew what had happened. He had found a talent he could have barely guessed existed, only now and then half suspecting something might be there when flying kites of fancy alone in his room at night after the fifth bourbon had whittled his imagination brittle sharp. Yes, he thought, reading what he had written, it was good – not *that* good, but a good enough place to start.

He turned to the note still sellotaped to the radio, and stared at it with wry humour. *So Ephraim*, it read chattily, *if you do decide to do some writing (and I just think you might), make sure you tune into the Foreign Correspondent Services of the BBC and Voice of America, commencing Friday 18th October. If you are going to document the Tuesday Nemesis story, I only ask that you get the facts correct.* As usual there was no signature, but the writing was becoming familiar. In fact the face behind the mask of her photo in his pocket was the only thing he could not picture clearly in his mind, yet she seemed able to read his thoughts with the utmost clarity. Bitch, he muttered to himself, but with very little conviction now.

"Shit." Clive swore with vehemence as the phone jangled a long irritable peal. Still half asleep he picked it up, at the same time pressing a button on the bedside console which opened the curtains and let in the morning's light. "Yeah, what d'you want?" he spat. Anyone who called him on his private number before eight on a Saturday morning was in for a rough ride.

"Leonard Crisp of the US Federal Reserve Board here, Mr Feral. Sorry to bother you at the weekend, but I have to inform you that as of first thing Monday morning all clearing banks have been ordered to increase their liquidity reserves by five per cent."

"Five per cent!" Clive choked. "That's one hell of a hike. What's the panic?"

"No panic, sir, just a routine decision passed down by the Senate Finance Committee. It has received Presidential ratification."

Clive knew better than to argue the toss with Leonard Crisp. Crisp was a powerful man in his own right and could become very awkward when disposed to be so. "Okay, Mr Crisp," said Clive, forcing moderation into his voice. "I'll have it seen to at start of business on Monday."

"That'll be fine then, Mr Feral," said Crisp with the smooth laconic tone that Clive found so annoying. "Have a nice day."

Clive did not have a nice day – in fact he did not have a nice weekend. The Senate's decision was worrying, the more so for there appeared no logical reason for it. After a massive rescheduling of Third World loans any further defaults seemed unlikely, so what was it all about? Twice he tried to get through to Abel Satco and Victor Loeb but there was no answer from either.

It had been raining all evening, solid blinds of tropical rain that formed a curtain in front of the tent so Ephraim Krebs could not see the edge of the chasm a bare twenty feet away. The big fat drops hammered a constant tattoo on the canvas, masking the sound of the waterfall foaming into the lagoon at the back of the plateau, a pleasantly soporific sound that lulled the mind and dulled the senses.

The light was too faint for him to write any more, and he decided to turn in early and listen to the radio until he dropped off to sleep. Ridiculous though it was, he had never been more contented in his life, and he was about to drift into unconsciousness when something came over the airwaves that drew him instantly awake again: "Our correspondent in Washington reports persistent leaks that a new British device to be demonstrated at the Lincoln on Wednesday will have a profound effect on future energy research. A temporary news clamp has been ordered by the State Department until after Wednesday, and neither the inventor, Mr Paul Feral, nor the patent owners, the Tin Whistle Company, have been available for comment.

"Considerable activity has been reported in the banking world over the weekend but the Secretary of State for Finance has dismissed reports of imminent problems for the dollar as 'mere speculation'.

"Now over to Moscow where our correspondent in Bonn reports a new softening in East-West tensions—"

Krebs fought his way out of his sleeping bag, his mind suddenly as clear as lead crystal. In moments he was putting a match to the storm lantern, the flame at first spitting and spluttering before it became an unwavering feather of yellow light that made the tent glow out of the darkness like a tropical bug in search of a mate. He was set up and comfortable in the position he favoured and the pencil was running across the page once more.

"You sure you've heard nothing on the grapevine, Abe?" Clive asked mid-morning on Monday. He had called round the chiefs of the other banks and they all told him the same thing – that Leonard Crisp of the Federal Reserve wanted an extra five per cent kept on liquid hold. No one was able to offer a reason, and calling his broker had been a last resort.

"Nope. I ain't heard nothing more than you have," said Satco. "That kind of decision doesn't affect us too much."

"Just a long shot," Clive told him. "It just seems strange coming at this time."

"I'll grant you that," Satco shrugged. Sometimes he wished Clive Feral didn't use him as a confidant for all his woes.

Then just as suddenly the whole day turned round for Clive. As soon as he had cleared down from Satco the switchboard came through again. "Yeah, what is it?" he muttered.

"Got Victor Loeb on the line for you, sir. Says it's urgent."

"Okay, put him through," he brightened. "Vic – Clive here, I've been waiting to hear from you. How's things going?"

"Well, 29-29 is yours if you want it Clive. That's the good news. The bad news is that they're asking one and a quarter billion for it which is about twenty-five per cent up on its actual valuation allowing for property at a half billion and stock at roughly the same."

"Jeez! One and a quarter," Clive reeled back from the phone. "That's one hell of a lot of dough."

"That's what I thought," said Loeb. "We'll call the whole deal off if you want."

"No, no," Clive hurried. It would stretch his liquidity to its full extent and he would have to go to the market for the extra money. He could do it. He damn well *was* going to do it. He was not going to be prised from the pinnacle of his achievement by a mere quarter billion bucks.

"Go ahead and set it up, Vic," said Clive with full authority in his voice.

"If that's what you want, Clive," said Loeb, still some doubt in his tone. "As you know the signing is being set up in London for nine a.m. Wednesday, local time, and I have already instructed our associates in England to stand by to accept power of attorney on your behalf."

"Excellent, quite excellent," said Clive with enthusiasm now. He liked people who could think ahead, run ahead.

"Yes and allowing for the fact that London is zoned five hours before New York, by the time you arrive in your office at 9.00 a.m. our time, there will be a full inventory sitting on your fax machine. Our people over there will see to that."

"Yep. That'll be interesting. You certain this Tuesday Nemesis guy hasn't got wind of who's behind the buy-out?"

"I can't see how. There's no way I know they can do a full international company trace at that short notice, and we've tracked and retracked at least a dozen times to make it doubly difficult."

"Good," said Clive, feeling easier. "By the way, you can fire Ephraim Krebs. Write and tell him he can go stick his bill up his ass. He's not getting a red cent out of me."

"And what about his expenses?"

"He can stick those as well. I'm not paying for useless jollies half way round the world."

"If that's how you want it," Loeb closed off.

There was still a slight nag of doubt in Clive's mind but he could think of no real reason for it, and he rose and went down to the dealing floor. It was a good day and he could see the percentages rising on the master VDU as each fifteen-minute sector passed. For two hours he just sat and watched the activity, savouring the feeling of success and the delicious thought of Wednesday morning when the 29-29 Corporation would be his. The only blight on the operation was the extra two hundred and fifty million he had to find, and he needed to talk to Abe Satco about that. He keyed the numbers to his broker's private line.

"Abe, you okay for lunch?"

"Sure, Clive."

"Where?"

"Moulins on 23rd Street, if you're celebrating. Percy's Pizza if you're not," Satco joked.

"I'm celebrating," Clive told him confidently.

Two hours later Clive continued over a gin and Vermouth, "In the strictest confidence, Abe, you're not going to believe this but I'm on the verge of buying out the hottest trading outfit in the city."

"Oh, yeah! Which one?"

"There *is* only one. Apart from Price Whitney."

"You don't mean 29-29?"

"The very same."

"So you've done it at last!" Satco leaned forward in his chair, and gave Clive's hand a hearty shake. "You've done it at last, you critter. That's just terrific! And how did you pull that one off?"

"It's not quite pulled yet, Abe. The deal will not be squared until 9 a.m. on Wednesday morning, London time. That's why it still very much has the wraps on. It's a private treaty sale and I know damn well this guy Nemesis wouldn't let our nominee within sniffing distance if he knew I was behind the action."

200

"Yes, you do have something of a reputation," nodded Satco with a down-turned smile.

"Reputation be hanged. I'm successful, aren't I?" he growled.

"Without question you're the one they seek to emulate."

"There is one hiccough of a minor nature," Clive turned the subject round.

"Yeah?" Satco noted that there was now no humour in Clive's eyes.

"Yeah, Nemesis is asking about 250 million more than my original offer."

"Can't you raise it?"

"Sure I can raise it. I have fifty million of my own which I can move as a director's loan into the company. The property equity of Price Whitney is due for a revaluation and the additional funds can be leveraged against the new listings."

"So why are you telling me this?"

"Simply this. If there are any deals going which you know are going to take an immediate hike and I can get in and out in a day, it would shove up our kitty and make the revaluation borrowing less necessary. It has, of course, got to be one hundred per cent safe."

"That's the sort of margin to go for," grinned Satco. "How much were you thinking of?"

"My own fifty million, plus about 200 I can scrape out of our currency pool."

"Two hundred and fifty million," Satco sat thoughtful for several moments – just long enough for it to seem impressive. "You just have the damndest luck, Clive," he said at length. "This is utterly amazing."

"Yeah?" Clive queried, taken aback at the sudden intensity in Satco's stare.

"Yeah. It's almost as if you've got the devil's talisman in your pocket."

"Cut the riddles, Abe," said Clive eagerly. "What you got for me?"

"Just this. Just before I left the office to come here we received a buying order from Graff Spielberg for one million shares in Telstar Oils of Houston."

"Graff Spielberg? Isn't that the outfit that places the buying orders from 29-29."

"Exactly," confirmed Satco. "And how d'you reckon one million shares in Telstar Oil are worth?"

"About 700 million bucks – not a lot."

"No, not a lot. But it does happen to be roughly forty per cent of what some people are saying is a very undervalued company."

"I don't buy what other people say," scowled Clive.

"Other people, no. But 29-29, perhaps?"

"Okay. Maybe," conceded Clive. "What exactly are you suggesting?"

"That buying order won't have gone through yet. If you fancy a small stake yourself Clive of, say, 250 million bucks, I can legitimately hold Spielberg's buying order for one hour while you get your act together, and then run the two together. With that sudden level of buying there is certain to be a 100 per cent lift in price before trading ends today, and if you can hang in tomorrow the bulls will take it to the clouds. You can then either stay in and block 29-29's total acquisition, or take your profits and run. Problem solved."

Clive smiled. "Yes, you're right as usual, Abe," he said after a slight hesitation. "Count me in."

As trading drew to a close that day Clive stood behind his pit boss, Zadok Perret, as he sat at his terminal. "How's Price Whitney's stock looking today?" he asked.

"The bank's ordinary shares are still being strongly bought, sir," Perret said in respectful tones. "Risen steadily for the fourth consecutive day, some ten per cent in the past seven days."

This was good. It was probably mainly institutional investors, showing Wall Street's confidence in Price Whitney.

"Can you give me the latest quotes on Telstar?" Clive threw in casually.

"Telstar Oil?" Perret hid his surprise. That was a new one. "Sure thing, sir. Right away."

Clive watched him key his terminal. Then he frowned deeply. The price certainly had risen, but from seven dollars to only 8.22 dollars, not the fourteen dollars plus he had been expecting. "Shit," he swore aloud, making Perret jump nervously. "You sure that goddam thing is showing the correct information?"

"I'll check," Perret picked up his phone. "Could be a wrong entry, sir, but I doubt it. No, sir," he said after a moment. "8.22 dollars is right enough for Telstar Oil although it had jumped to twelve dollars earlier."

"Shit," said Clive again, but beneath his breath this time. "Shit, shit, shit." That unusual queasy feeling was nibbling at his guts again.

He didn't feel fully right until after he had phoned Martin late in the night. "Give me some good news," he said to his brother, with few preliminaries.

"Don't I always?" Martin's voice came back softly. "Something bothering you, Clive?"

"Nope. It's just that I'm committed to oil right now and I want to check that my Moroccan investment is as healthy as it should be."

"But of course it is, dear brother, of course it is. Despite losing Rory McDermid on the exploration side, production is way ahead of schedule. Should you want to sell out in a twelve-month, you'll treble your money."

"That's terrific, Martin, terrific," Clive said and rang off. He didn't mention there was a limit to their filial bond, that had he been able to sell at any profit tomorrow, he would have had his money back to the States before noon.

That night Clive Feral slept as well as his excitement would allow. He could not know that within two hours of dropping the receiver, Khaled Nadir, Minister for the Interior, had arrived unannounced in Martin's apartment overlooking the West AFrican Coast. He had barely time to shepherd the two naked boys out of sight before he was compelled to respond to the persistent ringing at the door.

"Yes, what d'you—?" he hissed in fury before the words dried in his throat. "Khalid Nadir!" he coughed, his lips cracking into a smile. "What a pleasant surprise. But do please come in."

"No, that won't be necessary, Mister Martin," said Nadir. "What I have to say needs few words. I'm afraid I have some very bad news for you." And Martin would never forget the perfectly evil smile that exposed the double row of gold-encrusted teeth.

CHAPTER 17

Karina arrived in Washington the day before the demonstration, and Paul found himself fighting forward at the airport barrier in a most un-English way. Perhaps it had been the two weeks of their separation which made him feel this way, but all he knew was she seemed more lovely each time they met, and he could barely believe this starlet figure bouncing along the aisle was searching equally hard for him.

"Paul!" she shouted as she moved out of the pedestrian run and draped herself over the barrier. "Oh, Paul."

"Karina!" he pulled her to him. "It's been so long. You must never stay away like that again."

"I won't. I promise I won't, my darling. Now take me to where we're staying. I just want to be alone with you."

They made love beneath the warm October sun slanting through the bedroom window, slept a little, then made love again with even more ardour than before, their bodies blending in a liquid union that drew its own blind to keep the whole world out. It was an exquisite harmony of minds that required no words of sustenance, no extra eloquence, and afterwards they drifted silently into sleep.

He awoke first, many hours later when it was still as warm but the sun was a crimson ball low in the Western sky. "Hey, look at the time," he kissed her closed eyelids one at a time. "It's nearly seven and I was going to take you out to dinner tonight."

She snuggled closer without opening them. "I don't want to go out to dinner. I want to stay in here and eat *you*."

"Silly. I'll tell you what, I'll try and get that jacuzzi fired up and we can take a bath together then decide."

"That sounds a lovely idea," she mumbled into his shoulder as he gently prised himself away. Her eyes were open when he returned for her, and her arms stretched up and clasped his neck as he picked her from the bed.

"Perhaps yours was the best idea," he said, dunking her in the suds and following her in. "After we've cleaned up, we'll get a bite in the motel."

"I don't care what I do as long as I do it with you," she sighed, picking up the sponge and soaping her breasts. "Why can't we just be silly and frivolous. Remember the words of that old song that goes something like 'let's go for a lark, take a walk in the park'? That's the way I feel right now. Tomorrow is going to be a never-ending day – business, business, and more business. I doubt if I'll get a look at you once the press take over."

"But you'll be there with me, won't you?" he frowned.

"There, yes, with you, no. I'll be out amongst the crowds. There's nothing I can contribute and I'd only be in the way. That's, of course, until later," she said, and winked wickedly at him.

He decided this was not the time to argue. Anyway, she was probably quite right.

The following morning, Wednesday October 23rd, a car arrived exactly at eight as arranged, and he kissed Karina gently on the lips without waking her, and made his way out.

"You might like to see the morning's papers, sir," the chauffeur said, passing a bundle to him in the back before they set off. "Seems like you're going to get quite a reception."

Paul scanned quickly through the assorted headlines and leaders, and his adrenaline began to pump as he saw how things had escalated since the Senate preview that Friday last.

He remembered the nudges and the smiles, the scepticism and raw humour, the ill-disguised jibes, all quickly melting into a baffled silence as the various experts they had brought with them probed the TEESER's inner workings and failed to find a flaw. "Well, if that ain't the damndest thing," one of the older members had thought aloud, scratching his head. "Who d'you say owns the patent?" he addressed himself to Paul.

"The Tin Whistle Company, sir," said Paul.

"The Tin Whistle Company!" the old man shook his head. "Sure as hell am going to grab myself a slice of that ass if there's any to be had."

Clive Feral had not slept well and woke up that Wednesday

205

morning more tired than when he went to bed. Whatever it was – anticipation, apprehension, or just plain fatigue – it was doing him no good at all, and he decided that as soon as he had integrated his purchase of 29-29 into Price Whitney Corporation he was going to take a break – go away for a few days' dog fighting. Dammit, I've earned it, haven't I? he said to himself.

He looked at the bedside clock, elbowing across the empty space on Karina's side to read it clearer. It was still only six in the morning, but the deal would have been completed in London two hours ago, although it would be another three hours before he could access Loeb's fax machine and check the fine print of the stock and equity holdings. He lay back again, coming as close to sleep as he had all night as he relished the coming bliss of walking into the Hartman building knowing it was all his and his alone.

He was almost gone when the bedside phone purred its soft call.

"Yeah? Who is it?" he dribbled with a start.

"Victor Loeb here, Clive. The breakdown of the 29-29 deal has just come through and I think you should come over here right away and take a look."

"Great," he rushed, fully awake now. "Everything okay, Vic, is it?"

"Not exactly," said Loeb, his voice oddly cool.

"Not exactly! What d'you mean 'not exactly'?" Clive's lungs exploded. "What's wrong?"

"That's for you to decide when you see the package. I don't feel we should discuss the matter on the phone."

"For heaven's sake, man, don't piss me about. What's the goddamn problem?"

"One that will be greatly exacerbated if this news leaks out – and from the evidence in front of me there appears a very good chance of that."

"What you trying to say?" Clive's eyes were narrow slits.

"It is not for me to say. It is for you to draw your own conclusions," said Loeb calmly. "I'll expect you in half an hour. What would you like with your hash browns this morning? Treacle or cranberry?"

Clive's habitual preoccupation with sartorial elegance was not in evidence today as he tore through the empty offices of Loeb's large practice. His shirt was open, his trousers beltless, and his hair had the hellish look of punk delapidation with none of the vestiges of style.

"Okay. Where is it?" he roared, throwing open the door so hard the handle smashed through a plate glass panel.

"There," Loeb pointed to the single sheet on the otherwise empty desk.

"Is that it?" he glowered incredulously into his attorney's grey, fleshless face. "There must be more than that."

"There will be, in the post today. Reams of confirming documentation. But that is, in essence, the horse you've bought."

Clive snatched it up and scanned the short document with one sweep of his eye. Every drop of colour drained from his face, his eyes glazed and the paper slipped through his fingers, fluttering to the floor like the seed of a sycamore tree. For several minutes not a single word was exchanged between the men.

Eventually it was Clive who whispered, "What went wrong, Vic?"

"Technically, nothing Clive," Loeb shrugged. "We've checked and double-checked. What you've bought is exactly one billion dollars' worth of goods at yesterday's close, exactly as the contract said. From a legal standpoint it is quite incidental that you've paid twenty-five per cent too much."

"You know that's not what I'm talking about." Clive's voice had a dangerous edge to it now, as the colour rushed back to his face. "All that portfolio consists of is fifty per cent miscellaneous oil bonds and a 500-million-dollar holding in the Price Whitney Bank. Goddamit Vic." His fist smashed down on Loeb's desk, "You've just let me buy half a billion dollar stake in my own goddam bank at twenty-five per cent over the going rate, which is high anyway because of 29-29's buying activity. Jees, are you some kind of nut?"

"We were acting exactly per your instructions," Loeb told him, his tone very cold now. "Do you want to listen to the tapes?" His hand went to an elaborate transcription unit on his desk.

"Tapes?" Clive sprang back.

"We tape all verbal instructions as a matter of course. Probably saves us a hundred million dollars a year in out-of-court settlements."

"But what about the property portfolio. The Hartman Building and the rest?" Clive ignored the slap.

"The contract specifically didn't guarantee any aspect in the content of the portfolio, only its proper valuation. One can only assume the real estate was sold off to provide liquidity to buy the stock in Price Whitney. They obviously felt that was the better bet."

Clive's eyes had become dangerously big like a toad's beading in on a fly, and his neck was cicatriced with throbbing veins as the pressure built within. Nothing showed on Loeb's face as he tried to recall the number of the nearest paramedic station should anything haemorrhage.

"And I don't suppose you've any clue who the buyer was of the real estate – the Hartman building and the rest?"

"As a matter of fact, yes. Our people queried this specific aspect, and the seller was surprisingly forthcoming. Apparently the best offer came from a little known concern called the Tin Whistle Company."

"Did it?" Clive's eyes narrowed. "And what about their currency trading unit which it was agreed would be part of the package. Or has that mysteriously been liquidated into Price Whitney stock as well?"

Loeb leaned back and drummed his fingers on the table. "Nope. That part of the deal still stands. As it happens, all their trading staff are on holiday for the next few days, but I have a guarantee you will be introduced to their key personnel next Tuesday, the 29th."

"But where the hell's their trading base if 29-29 comes clean out of property?"

"Now and then," said Loeb. "Someone asks me a question I don't know the answer to. That's one of 'em."

"Jees, Loeb." Clive spat with furious contempt. "Suddenly you seem the sort of guy who wouldn't stop me if I was about to jump under a train. You'd just make sure the goddam paperwork was okay after they cleaned up the mess."

"Think positively, Clive," Loeb smiled now. "Assuming those prices hold good, that twenty-five per cent loss is quickly recoverable on the scale you operate. You're just not used to taking any losses, and you're forgetting the asset their dealing talent will be to Price Whitney."

"The whole thing stinks," said Clive, "stinks to high heaven, and I intend finding out where the smell is coming from. Then someone's going to pay."

"You may possibly be right, Clive," Loeb twiddled his thumbs. "But before you start winding into the mood for some vendetta, you have one problem yet to fix."

"Oh yeah? What the hell's that?"

"It's a Federal Offence for any Company to own its own stock. You've just bought a whole bundle of yours and you need to think what you're going to do about it pretty goddam quick."

Clive didn't have lunch that day. Millions of bucks down the tubes was not a totally disastrous situation, but it needed to be contained. All morning he sat alone in the viewing gallery of the dealing room behind the one-way glass. Everything out there had a comforting air of normality about it, and right now it was normality he needed after the traumatic revelations in Loeb's office.

Somehow there just had to have been a leak. But by whom, to whom and for what purpose? And was Price Whitney the intended fall guy? Or could it have been anyone else? Also, if the whole thing was set up as a con, it was one hell of an elaborate one, and conmen didn't usually shoot for a mere twenty-five per cent on their own investment. But the real question in his mind was, who now owned the Hartman Building?

Nothing led in any particular direction, and if there were any lessons to be learned it was the oldest one in the book, *caveat emptor*. *Caveat emptor*, buyer beware, he smiled for the first time that day. Here was the great Clive Feral telling himself *caveat emptor*.

By two o'clock things were jelling in his mind, and he picked up the phone and called his broker.

"Abe, this is Clive. How you doing?"

"Pretty good. Hey, you sewn up the 29-29 deal yet?"

"Sure have, Abe," said Clive wishing he hadn't asked. Never before had he been coy about a business deal after the event.

"Good little number, eh?"

"Could be better, could be worse. I'll tell you more about it when we meet."

"Okay, buddy," Satco sounded surprised. "And what can I do for you?"

"I want to know the exact state of affairs in the oil market at the moment, Abe."

"In one word hectic," said Satco. "Like I said, it seems to be turning very bullish – very few sellers and quite a few big buyers around. We've just had a new account opened with us only this morning. They've ordered us to place 700 million bucks over ten selected oils at three o'clock this afternoon, with the hint they'll be back again in the morning to double the investment."

"Really?" nodded Clive, impressed. "And who are the latest Bigs?"

"You've probably never heard of them. I hadn't. They call themselves the Tin Whistle Company."

"The Tin Whistle Company," Clive glowered. This was the same outfit that now owned the Hartman Building. "So where d'you honestly reckon oil is going, Abe?" he said, pretending all was quite normal.

"Well it's only my professional opinion, Clive," said Satco, "but I feel oils could rise another ten per cent before the end of the account. After that I think there will be some consolidation and profit taking, and they'll then pull back a bit."

"Are you sure of that?"

"Can't be sure of anything in this business, Clive, as well you know. But have I given you a bum steer yet?"

"No, Abe. Not yet, you haven't."

Clive closed down and went straight across to the pit boss's rostrum. Zadok Perrett looked at first surprised, then the shark's teeth of fear appeared in his eyes as Clive whispered at length in his ear.

"But are you sure about this?" Perret questioned his master for the first time ever. "If you pull a billion out of the currency dealing purse for oil stock, we'll need to lay off half our dealers, not to mention that a portion of those funds are the liquid deposits of account holders."

"It is for twenty-four hours only, not a second longer," Clive hissed at him. "Are you questioning my judgement and instructions?"

"N-no, sir," Perret stumbled. "Of course not, sir. Right away, sir. I'll make the changes right away."

"Good," said Clive, walking away leaving Perret ashen like a stump of juniper tree stripped of its bark by lightning.

After he had gone, the silence at Perret's announcement to the floor was of the same awesome magnitude as greeted his recent proclamation that the rope had risen from 2,000 dollars to 3,000 dollars. No one quite believed it, yet all knew it to be true. Then one by one the screens went blank as the operators closed them down, their eyes blinking as if suddenly awakened from a deep trance. Then they began looking at each other with expressions akin to shock, their fingers limp appendages, oddly clumsy and awkward with nothing to do.

Perret shook his head. He hadn't known anything like this before. Unorthodoxy was the cornerstone of Price Whitney's success – but to divert half the liquid dealing pool into stock, for no matter how short a time! The words jumbled as his reasoning stalled, and he sat down, staring glassily out in front of him. The time was 3.15 p.m.

Clive went straight up to his apartment. He was suddenly very tired, and pressed the mute button on the phone and fell down on his bed in a dead sleep for the first time in several days.

At 3.30 p.m. the price of oil stock, which had risen steadily all day, jumped to record heights with the stimulus of the Price Whitney block order, and at 3.50 p.m. Abe Satco was set to leave his brokerage to join Loeb on the golf course, when his way was blocked by his secretary. "I have a call for you, sir," she said.

"Get someone else to take it, Margo. I'm off for the rest of the day."

"I think you should handle this yourself, sir," she pressed, concern etched in her face. "It's Tin Whistle back on the line, sir. They are instructing you to re-sell immediately that entire block of oil they bought earlier in the day."

Satco froze like a single frame from a Chaplin movie. Then with unusual slowness he returned to his desk. "Can I help you?" he picked up the receiver.

"Yes," the woman's voice said quietly. "This is the Tin Whistle Company. You are instructed to re-sell our earlier purchase of the day."

"The complete 700 million dollar lot in Telstar Oil?"

"To the last share, Mr Satco. This call is being recorded and is timed at 3.52 p.m. and if the block is shown not to have been offered to the market before 4.10 p.m., local time, our company will hold you personally liable for any difference in price between that quoted before 4.10 and that actually realised."

"Of course there will be no delay," Satco blurted furiously. "I take the strongest exception to any inference that we are dilatory in our handling of transactions." He didn't need these people's business if they were going to come up with this sort of shit.

"And I will issue you with a personal note of caution, Mr Satco," the woman continued as calmly as before. "If you leak the barest hint of this selling order to Clive Feral before the close of trading this afternoon – which is your intention even as I speak to you – I can guarantee that the brokerage firm of Abel Satco Incorporated will not exist one week from today. Now I do hope we understand each other, Mr Satco," her voice sung sweetly over the wires.

There was a long pause before he could relax his throat enough to croak, "Who am I talking to?"

"The time is now 3.54. You have exactly sixteen minutes to close the sale." She rang off.

CHAPTER 18

Paul could barely believe it, and neither could Professor Zachary Weinberger. Standing ovations within the hallowed portals of the Lincoln Institute were something of a rarity, but when the enthusiasm came from 500 hard-bitten cynics culled from the world's press, that was indeed nothing short of remarkable.

"Well, you sure wowed 'em today, Paul," shouted Zachary above the roar, shading his eyes from the TV lights and the Xenon flashes. "If I'd known it was going to be like this I'd have given you the main hall instead of the Arnot Gallery."

"If you'd offered me a tent on the back lawn I'd have been more than happy, Zach," Paul laughed. "It's only you and the people behind Tin Whistle who have given the scheme any support at all."

"Well, that has all changed now," the Professor beamed. "Look at 'em baying for you. I've seen nothing like it since the wind blew up Monroe's skirt."

"Well, I've finished my set piece, Zach. What now?"

"We'll never get rid of 'em 'till you answer some of their questions, Paul. How d'you feel about hanging in a little longer?"

"Fine. The way I feel today, I'll take on all comers," he grinned.

"Okay," said the Professor, handing him back the mike. "But watch out. They'll be looking for some personal stuff now to jazz up their copy with the human angle."

"That'll be all right," said Paul before keying the microphone and continuing. "Thank you, ladies and gentlemen, for my very warm welcome to your country, and even more for your reception to my little contraption, the TEESER energy machine." He paused a moment as the applause died and a ripple of laughter went through the audience. "Professor Zachery Weinberger, my host on behalf of the Lincoln Institute, says the gallery will remain open another five minutes if you have any questions. After that, the inaugural demonstrations will be officially closed and you are free to leave to file your copy. Now, who'll be first?"

A reporter stood up. "Are you now intending to reside in the States, sir?"

"Probably for some of the time, but I haven't decided yet."

"Do you regret having sold the patent to the Tin Whistle Company?" another reporter called out.

"The patent is not sold, only licensed for a finite number of years, and in any event I also own a small percentage of the Tin Whistle Company. So I am entirely happy with the arrangement. I am not a greedy man. Anyway," Paul told him amidst laughter, "it's difficult to have extravagant thoughts when you're used to living on 200 dollars a week."

Another man stood up. "Can you confirm the rumour, sir, that you are related to Clive Feral, the well known New York banker?"

"Yes, I am," Paul frowned for the first time. "He is my older brother."

There was a surprised murmur through the audience as the questioner went on, "Does Clive Feral or the Price Whitney Bank have any interest in your development?"

"None. Not in any way whatsoever," said Paul, his good feelings evaporating as the old furies began to boil again. "My brother was approached, but he declined for his own reasons. More than that I am not prepared to say."

"Price Whitney are reputed to be heavily into oil," the questioner put to him. "How d'you see Clive Feral viewing your sudden competition in the energy market?"

Paul turned to glare at the reporter, his face suddenly flushed and angry. "My brother has never considered me a threat, and I can think of no reason why his opinion should change now. Now can we have someone else please on a different topic?"

"Are you married, sir?" Another reporter jumped in.

"I am a widower. I have two young daughters back in England."

"Your invention must make you potentially one of the most wealthy men in the world. What will be your response when women start making you propositions?"

"Good question." Paul looked across to where Karina sat,

second row back, next to the outer aisle. She was smiling delightedly at the heated exchange – she had never known him raise his voice before and it thrilled her. He saw the mischief in her eyes and her grin as wide as a melon slice, nodding at him to say something in response, and his good humour suddenly rushed back again. "I think I'll just refer them to Miss Karina Darielle of the Tin Whistle Company. She knows how to look after all my interests very well," he told his audience, and watched as every head turned to follow his gaze. The grin fell from Karina's face and she shrunk lower in her chair.

Zach saw the drift and leaned over and took the microphone from him. "And there you have it, gentlemen. The inauguration is now complete. It only remains for me, on behalf of the Lincoln Institute, to thank Mr Paul Feral for demonstrating his remarkable discovery which I think you will all agree will change the shape of things to come. And not least I would like to thank you, the ladies and gentlemen of the press, for being here in such numbers and giving our little display such a warm reception. Thank you once more, and may I remind you that you will find telephone and telegraph facilities in the press offices on the floor below." And after the mike had gone dead he added, "And may the best man win."

"Just look at that," Paul pointed at the crush to get out the door. "They're like animals!"

The professor looked at his watch. "It's already a quarter past four, Paul. The TV and radio reporters are okay but those writing for the evening sheets have got about fifteen minutes to file before they're past their deadline."

"And when d'you think the first reports will be coming out?" Paul asked.

"A good question. I could be wrong, but I reckon the local radio stations will have something on the air by 4.30, and the TV will come on stream with their early evening news at 5.00. The first of the copy will be in the second edition of the evening papers to hit the streets about 7.00."

"And then what d'you reckon?" asked Paul.

"I reckon we should all duck 'cause there's going to be a whole load of shit coming out of some mighty big fans."

Abel Satco would not have cared to admit it, but he knew there was still a powerful volume of adrenaline pumping his veins twenty minutes after the woman had rung off. It was now 4.15 and the sell order had been entered and logged at 4.05

precisely so there could be no come-back from that quarter. But still an apprehension remained.

He sat watching the latest prices flicker monotonously on his VDU, hoping his pulse would calm down, but it didn't. For a complete stranger to know his relationship with Clive Feral held the potential for repercussions too horrendous to contemplate, and he stared, out of focus, at the screen as his mind jinked from one implausibility to the next.

This was doing no good, no good at all. He forced himself to look at the figures coming up on the screen. Oil was still drifting upwards despite the sell order he had just put through, but that would peg it, at least for the rest of the day, he considered, seeking consolation from the solid normality of the picture. But it did no good. He simply didn't believe it. His guts, which foretold the bad news just as well as the good, were churning into little knots of angry pain. Something somewhere was very badly wrong.

"Goddamn it to hell." He threw the switch to darken the display. "I've sure had it for today."

This time his secretary did not attempt to way-lay him as he strode through the door. Her face was caught in a frown as she wondered whether the remarkable Paul Feral the radio had been talking about for the last five minutes was any relation to Clive.

Clive awoke with a jerk that nearly threw his body off the bed. At first he thought it was morning, then just as quickly he realised he was still fully clothed. "Jeez, it's nearly nine o'clock," he muttered to himself, realising he had been asleep for over five hours, the roar of street noises now reduced to an evening murmur beneath a sky as black as a raven's plumage. He pressed the switches that drew the curtains and cued the lights, then made himself a coffee. On the stroke of nine he flopped in front of the TV, ready for the news.

"Good evening, ladies and gentlemen," the presenter was saying. "Tonight our headlines are from Washington. The world's press have been gathered this afternoon at the Lincoln Institute in response to rumoured developments in the energy business, and our reporter Dwight Carbonini is there now reporting to you live. Over to you, Dwight."

"Thank you, Raymond. Yes this is Dwight Carbonini reporting for RPKG 'News at Nine'. Today is one many of us reporters are unlikely to forget. Not for some visual act of war, violence, or apocalyptic piece of rhetoric from one of the world's leaders. No, today we have been in the modest and gentle hands of an unknown Englishman and his remarkable TEESER machine, a device that takes energy already existing in the air, concentrates and recycles it using the energy itself creates, and turns out the surplus in heat or electricity, whichever is required. In the words of its inventor, Mr Paul Feral, 'Today we are witnessing the planting of a tiny acorn. Brave is the man who will guess how big the tree will grow.' The truly remarkable thing about the TEESER machine," – the shot cut to Paul's address from the rostrum – "is that there is nothing truly remarkable about it at all. What we have here is the epitome of old tech – not an integrated circuit in sight, not a chip to be seen – you'll even get a blast of steam when she gets a bit hot. Can this be the way ahead? I think so. Your eminent physicists here at the Lincoln Institute and up from NASA seem to think so. Could we all be wrong? The answer is yes. But which way would you like to place your bets?"

The coffee cup did not touch Clive's lips. His hand had frozen an inch from his face, leaving his mouth parted in a silly pout as his eyeballs seemed to turn inside outside out. Paul was staring out at him from the screen. But was it Paul? This was a different person, his manner was relaxed and authoritative, his eyes bright and level, the hand holding the pointer steady with not a hint of a shake, and his voice carried in a way that seemed intended. It was the voice of command.

"That was Mr Paul Feral concluding at four o'clock this afternoon," Carbonini cut in. "Since then people have indeed been placing their bets. After a record rise in the oil index to a new peak of 1631 points earlier this afternoon, prices slipped back sharply from 4.30 onwards when the significance of today's events began to be assessed by Wall Street. Our financial correspondent says it is too early to draw many conclusions, but a period of profit taking and consolidation can reasonably be expected. At the close of trading prices were still falling swiftly and the oils index was dropping through 1557 – a loss of five per cent on the day's best."

"Five per cent!" Clive choked, his face deathly pale. That was fifty million dollars wiped off his stock purchase made only that afternoon. That plus the 250 million he had overpaid for 29-29, plus twenty-five million he would have lost on that part of the 29-29 portfolio in oils; put a total loss on the day's trading of 325 million dollars.

He immediately picked up the phone and called Satco's private number. "Hey, Abe, what the hell's happening?" he roared down the line. "I've just lost fifty million bucks on your advice. Why the hell didn't you call me earlier?"

"I tried to," Satco told him coldly, not mentioning it was only half an hour before, "but your phone was off the hook or something."

"Shit," cursed Clive seeing that the instrument was still set to mute. "Anyway, don't stall. Has everything gone completely goddamn mad? What d'you reckon I should do?"

"The answer to those two questions is, I don't know, and I don't know," said Satco, the chill remaining in his voice. "Just about anything could happen in this situation. Your guess is as good as mine. A lot of the smart money is already out of the market. That machine could prove quite devastating."

"What smart money?" Clive spat at him.

"The Tin Whistle Company are out clean, which is not surprising. You may have heard they own the patent on your brother's new invention which could kill a traditional sector of the oil market—" Satco paused, seeming to think, "No, I tell a lie," he went on. "There is something you can do. You can call Paul Feral and find out who owns Tin Whistle. If you can buy into the action there, you might be able to use it to manipulate the price of oil. But there is one thing I don't understand."

"What?"

"The reports are that for a long while your brother was hungry for funds to get his TEESER machine developed and patented. Why the hell didn't you get in then and take control? You could have either exploited it yourself, or stopped the damage this is going to do to oil."

"I phoned you for advice, not a goddam lecture," growled Clive and threw up the receiver. For the first time since his early adolescence he felt the tic beneath his left eye begin to twitch in embarrassing and uncontrollable spasms.

Satco was glad he had cleared the line. Clive Feral seemed to have changed. Suddenly he seemed to carry a subtle, quite unambiguous aura of calamity, like a new cadaver not quite yet begun to rot.

Clive now sat immobile in front of the telephone, his face very pale, his eyes wide and out of focus. Things were going wrong for him, very, very wrong, and he needed time to think.

Setbacks he could cope with. He had had them before, as he had disasters which had loomed and been cleverly averted. But this was something different. There was something ordered, structured almost, about what was happening here today. A stench of treachery was in the air, that sweet, pervasive stink of rotting carrion that goes with the whispers of betrayal. He could see things now, things he hadn't seen before. Suddenly coincidences were not coincidences at all. Before his eyes he saw a plan, a clever plan of masterful conception that was set to destroy him, once and for all, utterly and totally, everything laid out in neat progression as if pre-ordained. And he shuddered. He shuddered because he still could not see the face behind the mask.

It could be one of a hundred – two hundred – a thousand even. A small army of people had cause to hate him for one reason or another. There was also no doubt in his mind that there was someone in his camp passing information, and when he found out who it was, they would be as dead as the loser in a pit bull fight.

He was not altogether surprised when the phone rang and it was Martin.

"Hi, Martin," he said without enthusiasm. "What can I do for you?"

"I'm afraid I have some bad news Clive, very bad news," his brother answered.

"Go on," Clive told him, his voice very cold and very level.

"I'm afraid our total investment in the Western Sahara oil project has been completely wiped out."

"Go on."

"You don't sound surprised."

"I'm not. Go on."

"The region's in a state of war." Martin was spluttering now. "Insurrection and anarchy everywhere. I've lost everything I've ever owned, every damned cent," he wailed, and Clive knew he was crying. "The Polisario guerrillas have taken over all our wells, every one of them, and the government is doing nothing, not a damn thing, other than send half the nation's armed forces into the mountains to protect the new bismuth and tellurium mines owned by the Tin Whistle Company."

"Wasn't it Tin Whistle that poached your best man Rory McDermid?" Clive's eyes narrowed still further.

"Yes. Yes, it was. You remember?"

"Sure, I remember," said Clive and closed the call. His losses on the day had just gone up by another one billion dollars to 1.325 billion dollars. Someone was passing him the poison cup. That someone was Tuesday Nemesis – he was certain now.

CHAPTER 19

Across the Potomac River Route 29 traces a line through the swimmy bustle of mid-town Washington, past pristine buildings and finger-thin monuments, through the Arlington Cemetery where John F. Kennedy rests under a single flame that gutters quietly day and night at the head of an army of America's giants – men and women for ever silent beneath the grassy knolls of the land they chose to call their own and make great.

And then, as the traffic dwindles, Route 29 runs on out into the heartland of Northern Virginia. Here was a different place in time, untouched and unaltered for a hundred thousand years except for the thin arteries of roads an occasional village set in among the pine wood drifts.

"There it is!" Karina pointed eagerly. "Look, Paul. Clifton, just like it says on the map," she tapped the sheet on her knee. "I told you I was a good navigator."

"Have I ever doubted anything you ever told me?" He turned to her grinning, and her heart ached, but she knew she could not let it show, not yet.

"Soon be there," she told him. "And am I looking forward to that!"

Paul let the car run off down the narrow spline marked Clifton, and at once everything changed. They were in the woods now, the surface of the road paper-thin with frequent pots and crumbling at the edges, the tall pines dwarfing everything and making a dark curtain to hide all that lay behind. It was as it had always been, nature's random order undisturbed, protected now by wise zoning laws and local aquiescence and love of things past. But here and there a break would come, with open purlieus and corralled pastures and fine houses. They had arrived.

220

"Clifton", the rickety sign proclaimed, and immediately Karina sat up. "Oh! Isn't it quite delightful!" she murmured. "Just look at those old buildings. It's like something straight out of *Gone With The Wind*."

Paul stopped the car.

She was right. This was a place where all time stood still – a hamlet locked in the 1850s, untouched and untroubled, still modelling the grace and elegance of that time, a time of sophistication and refinement and great wealth for the lucky few who had gone on to build for themselves grand dwelling houses, mansions in the colonial mould, with their crenellated eaves, tall pillars and wide windows.

It was all still here, exactly as it was conceived over a century ago, but breathing tiredness and delapidation now. The old hotel was closed, boarded up as it had been for many years, and perhaps that would be the first to fall and rot away like its builder long before.

"What an amazing village," said Paul. "I can see why old Zach Weinberger has a place out here. It's so quiet, so peaceful."

"Yes, it is lovely," she nodded. "It was good of him to let us have it for a few days to escape the press. They're going absolutely crazy."

"I agree. I'm not cut out for this celebrity thing."

"But that's what you are now," Karina smiled at him.

Weinberger's retreat was on the outskirts of the village set high on a plateau overlooking the surrounding countryside. It was a mansion in the colonial mould like the others, but not in decline, the grounds immaculate, and the interior restored to its original splendour. Everything was in the period of a hundred years before, lovingly preserved not recently recreated, the elegant stuccoed ceiling intact with its grandeur undiminished, the air rich with the scent of eucalyptus leaves working their magic on the senses. "I'll give Zak one thing," Paul said. "The old boy certainly has got style."

It was not until the following morning, Friday 25th October, that the news began to filter through. A bundle of papers had arrived on the front porch, hurled there with great force and equal accuracy by a little boy on a bicycle. Paul went out and fetched them while Karina fixed the breakfast.

"This is incredible," he called through to the kitchen. "Just listen to what the papers have to say. 'Every home should have one,' that's one leader. 'British scientist offers world panacea for all future energy needs' – hey, that's a bit strong, and not even accurate. And try this, 'New TEESER machine spells end for wave power, wind power, hot rocks experimentation. Our science correspondent also suggests refined versions of the machine could eventually supplant nuclear and fossil fuel generating capacity.' And why not indeed?" agreed Paul.

"That's marvellous," said Karina, "What do the financial pages have to say?"

"Wall Street has really got the jitters," he went on. "Dow Jones is down a hundred points since Wednesday. But it's oils that have really taken the dive. Listen to this: 'From a peak of 1631 earlier this week, the oil index has plummeted from 1557 at Wednesday's close, down another 281 points on Thursday to finish the day at 1276. This represents a loss so far on the week of 18 per cent, and there is no sign that the bottom has yet been reached. Our financial editor says that some profit taking was due after the extended rise, but this semi-collapse seems entirely due to new energy technology demonstrated at the Lincoln Institute this week. Because of the likely knock-on effect, the government has already ordered the prime banks retain a further five per cent in total liquidity.' Incredible!" whistled Paul softly. "What have we done?"

"Nothing but good," said Karina soberly. "Nothing but good."

"That's not what the vested interests will be saying."

"To hell with the vested interests," said Karina with a sudden vehemence he had never heard before. "I hate the bully boys of big business," she went on. "The manipulators, the exploiters, the careless looters, vultures who pick over the pitiful remains of another man's dreams, those who corner a resource and hold the whole world to ransom. I hate them all – to the very last man!"

Paul stared at her astonished. "Hey, that's quite a little speech," he laughed, trying to soften her mood. "I don't think you'd like my brother, Clive. You've just summed him up exactly."

"No, I don't think I'd like your brother Clive." She laughed now, a thin and bitter sound that carried no humour.

She knew the time was close now – the moment when she would have to tell him everything, and she was dreading that moment like no other, for Paul Feral had come to mean more to her than she cared to admit. How he might take it was something she dared not contemplate. But there could be no turning back now.

222

"I'd like to go for a walk today," she announced suddenly. "Just you and me out there alone in the peace and quiet. I have to be back in New York on Monday afternoon, and I want to make the most of every second of every minute with you before I go."

"Monday? So soon?" he could barely disguise his disappointment. He then remembered they hadn't talked beyond the next few hours ahead. "I was hoping for at least a week with you. Just you and me together. I'm worried now the project is off the ground, Karina, you're going to disappear the same way you came – out of nowhere, into nowhere. Please don't do that," he almost pleaded.

Her heart ached also, but she knew before the day was out he might have changed his mind completely, and that would be worst of all, for she ached just as much for him.

"Shush," she touched his lips with a finger. "We'll talk some more later."

Dusk was coming in fast, but the air was still hot and fetid as if thunder was not far away. Already the fireflies had begun their nightly dance in the lengthening shadows, tracing weird alphabets that mingled and split and joined again against the black tapestry of trees. There was not a breath of wind, even the crickets had stopped their clack, the silence brooding as if awaiting something still to come.

Clifton was a place of destiny. It had been then, it was now. Out there on the silent plains two great armies had faced each other a century before, the thunder of cannon breaking the dawn and rending the air for a full twelve hours until silenced by the dusk on that awful day in 1861 when Johnson faced McDowell in the battle of Bull Run Creek. It was a terrible encounter, as murderous as any in the Civil War, leaving 3,000 Union soldiers and 2,000 Confederates dead and dying upon the soft green loam of North Virginia.

All was silent now a century on, no whistle of shot or scream of pain to disturb the soft dusk breeze, but the echoes were still there all the same.

Karina and Paul sat slightly apart. For a full hour she talked, as evening drifted into night, starting at the very beginning, explaining everything in the minutest detail. How it happened, why it happened, the madness of it all, knowing that she could not, must not, keep anything back from him now, for that time had long since gone. All the lies and deviations, all the subterfuge and deceits she laid bare, and not a word had he said as his face went pale. Then with an awful stiffness he stood up, and without looking back he walked slowly into the woods.

It was the longest, loneliest moment of her life waiting for his return. When he did his face hadn't changed, but his eyes were glistening brightly like diamonds from the bottom of a well. She tried to read his mind and failed.

"Well?" she asked, a quaver in her voice. "Tell me the worst, Paul. If you feel what I've done is unforgivable and you never want to be near me again, I'll understand. I just want you to know one thing. I love you very, very much. I think I always will." And she began to cry.

Paul didn't answer. He seemed to be looking through her, past her, his face still deathly pale in the light of the moon just peeping between the hills. Then he said in a very low voice, "I'd like to go back to the house now, Karina."

"I'm sorry it had to end this way, Paul," she said softly. "I truly am. I just hope one day you'll forgive me. Please say you will?"

"I'd like to go back to the house," he repeated, "and see if we can't find a bottle of champagne in old Zach's cellar. A toast is called for – to Tuesday Nemesis. Pity he won't be able to make it to the wedding."

Karina stood back from him and it was a moment before she spoke. "What are you saying, Paul?"

"I'm saying that I want to marry you, Karina. I have for quite a while now, and what you tell me changes nothing." Suddenly he smiled, and it was her old Paul there again. "Anyway," he went on, "I need someone to organise the funding of my next project, and I can't have you wandering off again, now can I!"

"Fool!" she rushed at him, and he caught her tightly in his arms. "You wonderful, silly, gorgeous, adorable man, my man. Make love to me now, my darling. Now, please now."

CHAPTER 20

"But the whole situation is crazy mad," Clive told them, a strange look in his eyes. "When's the rot going to stop? In just over a week the entire bottom has fallen out of the oil market, Dow Jones is crashing like it hasn't done in sixty years."

The three men sat in the observation room next to the dealing floor. The trading terminals were empty, the screens in darkness, a single security light throwing its feeble glow over the desolate scene as Satco and Loeb shifted uncomfortably in their seats.

"The market's charting unknown seas," said Satco. "No one could have predicted what's been happening out there over the last few days."

"I could barely get into my office this morning," said Loeb. "Wall Street is milling with sellers. Never thought I'd see anything like it in my lifetime. Apparently the same thing is happening in London and Tokyo. Panic-selling in the grand tradition of the old time bears like Jesse Livermore."

"To hell with Jesse Livermore. The situation is this," said Clive very quietly, his face deathly pale. "From the apex of its financial strength, the Price Whitney Bank is now worth a declining twenty per cent of its value this Tuesday of last week. I am expecting our accountants to show within the hour that we are technically insolvent. You both were wittingly, or unwittingly, complicit in the train of events that have led to this disastrous situation, a situation which could well mean the demise of the bank. I look to you both to come up with some answers on how the day can be saved."

"Excuse me, sir," his secretary interrupted over the paging intercom. "The *New York Times* is on the line sir. They want to know if it's true that Price Whitney are in trouble over oil investments. They also seem to think that the company has recently acquired some of its own stock. Can you speak to them, sir?"

"No, I can't," said Clive tersely. "Tell them I'm in conference. Tell them that any such rumours are quite fatuous and we'll sue if they go to print." Then to the men in the room, "There, gentlemen, you have all the evidence you need of a conspiracy to bring the bank to its knees. Someone with a deep knowledge of the bank's methods of working, and the relationship that exists between the three of us, has seen that I've been fed with bogus deals and bad information. That same person owned 29-29, and now owns the Tin Whistle Company which in turn owns the patent on the new energy machine responsible for the collapse of the market. I believe that person to be Tuesday Nemesis."

"Then the guy must be a genius," said Loeb. "And boy, he must hate your guts."

"You honestly believe this stuff?" questioned Satco. "I suppose it's just possible. But maybe he just got lucky at a time your luck ran out."

"No one gets *that* lucky. I've been betrayed, it's as simple as that," said Clive, his tone soft and dangerous.

"You needn't look at me," said Loeb, a trace of irritation in his voice. "Well, if there's nothing more I can contribute, I'll ask you to excuse me, gentlemen." He stood up.

"Me too," said Satco, looking at his watch. "With things as volatile as this I have to stay on top of my VDUs."

"Excuse me, sir." the paging intercom cut through again. "I have an urgent call for Mr Loeb. Is he still with you?"

"Yes," said Clive. "Put it through on the green phone."

Loeb took the call, not taking his eyes off Clive. Then he cleared down and said, "If your hunch is right, Clive, I think the end game is in play. That was Holt and Farthingale on the line. They say they have a client who is willing to buy Price Whitney from you at fifty cents a share."

"Fifty cents a share!" Clive exploded. "Price Whitney was at 200 dollars a share a week ago."

"That was a week ago. Today they started at forty. By your own admission the company is insolvent, and the shares are probably down at thirty by now, and with all the rumours flying, if they finish the day at fifteen you'll be very lucky. My guess is that if there's any more large scale selling, they'll be suspended by the Stock Exchange Bureau. In other words you could well be stuck with what you've got which could end

226

the day quite worthless. On the face of it, a complete buy-out at fifty cents a share could be a mite generous. What d'you reckon, Abe?"

"Put that way, it doesn't sound unreasonable."

"You're suggesting I knock Price Whitney out at fifty cents a share?" Clive thundered, disbelieving.

"We're not suggesting anything," said Loeb. "Just pointing out alternatives."

"Well you can point your goddam ass out of that door before I kick it out. Both of you!" Clive roared, towering over them, "Get out, goddamit, get out!"

For half an hour after they had gone Clive stood at the window, staring out over the unchanging New York skyline, seeing nothing as his brain travelled over the options with the speed of a running programme. Then he picked up the phone and spoke very softly. "Victor. You can tell Holt and Farthingale that I'll accept the offer on the conditions that the money is wired in full to my private account at the First National Panama Bank by no later than two o'clock this afternoon."

Clive then called Maynard and Goad Travel on 4th Street, and booked a flight to Panama for the early afternoon. And finally he called in Perret, the pit boss.

"Sir?"

"How much d'you make a year?"

"120,000 dollars last year, sir."

"And how would you like to go and live in Brazil."

"Not a lot, sir," said Perret puzzled.

"Ah, but supposing there was ten million bucks there waiting for you when you arrived."

"I'd love Brazil," said Perret.

"Then you are going to be very rich. And you are also going down in history as being part of the biggest banking fraud ever. You are immediately to arrange the liquidation of every negotiable asset the bank possesses, and that together with the entire funds on deposit with us are to be wired to these numbered accounts." He passed Perret a piece of paper with ten numbers on it.

"Okay sir, if you insist," said Perret, a strange expression on his face. Things were happening exactly the way she had said they would.

"I insist," said Clive. "Get to it." He rose and went to the lift. Now it was time to pack.

There was no hint that there was anything wrong as Clive

227

passed anonymously amongst the customers on the ground floor of the bank. He took the lift to the dealing floor, glancing in briefly upon the hectic scene, before continuing on up to his apartment.

He opened the door. At first he did not believe what he was seeing. The apartment had been systematically vandalised, the floor covered in thick black grease, oily hand and feet marks everywhere like a cowboy auto pit. Then he spotted a movement and saw the terrified young girl cowering in the corner, rocking backwards and forwards on her haunches, her hair matted with grease, her face so dirty it was hard to tell the colour of her skin. She was making a curious wailing sound as she sobbed desperately into her hands.

"Please don't do that," she wailed, suddenly lunging at him. "I love my daddy. Please don't give that gun to my mother. No, no, no," she screamed, hammering on his chest with her fists. "She'll kill him, I know she will."

"What the hell you on about?" Clive threw the girl off furiously after the initial shock had passed. "You vandalising little tramp! How the hell did you get in here?" His hand went for the phone to call the cops, but something made him pause. She seemed not to have heard. He stared at her hard, curious now. She had the stature of a teenager although she was dressed as a child.

"My mama loves my daddy," the girl wailed on with an awful banshee tremor. "She does, you know she really does. You know mama isn't well on Fridays. Why are you giving her the gun on a Friday? Please don't do it. Please don't do it. Please don't give her that gun!" Her voice went on and on, and up and up.

Clive suddenly felt an icy finger touch his spine. He knew this girl. He had heard those words before. It was many years ago but still they came through as clear as the day they were first uttered. The wretched child had come near to wrecking his plan then and here she was again like a flash of *déjà vu* in perfect action-replay, except now nearly twice as tall. He stared at her hard. Yes, it was little Katie Dando, old Dizzy Dando's daughter. She was always fooling around the greasing pits whenever he had called by, looking just like she did now, her hair matted, her face black with oil, her cheap cotton dress splattered with a hundred battery spills. At the time he had wondered what she really looked like. He never found out and it was a curiosity that didn't linger. It was only Dando's Cabs and the building he was after – and both of those he got.

And now she was here again over a decade later, and the heat of the room seemed to drop another few degrees as he stared hard at her.

She was smiling now. "Yes, you recognise little Katie Dando, don't you, Clive," she was saying. "Dirty little barefoot Katie whom you threw aside when she tried to stop you giving her mama that gun. You'll never forget that, will you, Clive? It was your first big swindle – the one that put you on your road to success."

"You're Katie Dando?" his mouth fell open.

"Yes," she smiled, going on. "I remember how well you did your research. How you came round to Dando's Cabs every day for a month to work out the routine. It didn't take you long, did it, Clive? My parents were simple folk. You knew Ma and Daddy got along just fine for six days out of seven, but you found out Fridays were always different. Friday was the day Mama went to her quack who filled her with uppers and downers and first she'd go quiet, then she'd go mad. And Friday was also the day Daddy got drunk, screwed his bar girl, and came home late – and they fought all night and made up in the morning. Yes, that was the way it was for the twenty years of their marriage. Twenty okay years until you gave Mama that gun. You killed my father, Clive, just as surely as if you pulled the trigger yourself. And you killed my mother, Clive, just as surely as you threw the switch on the electric chair."

Clive's head was churning as he listened. It wasn't the little girl talking any more it was a woman there now, and despite the Brooklyn ghetto brogue, the voice was chillingly familiar.

"Perhaps you know me better when I talk like this," she went on, her voice dropping to its normal mellow cadence as she swept her hair back with her hand. This time he was listening to the sound he knew so well, and the breath caught in his throat. "It's you Karina, isn't it?" he said, his voice ice cold. "And what exactly is the point of all this?"

"A matter of repaying a debt," she smiled at him, her teeth very white and quite evil in the mask of grime. "At first I was personally going to kill you for murdering my parents, but that would have been too kind and too quick for you, Clive, much too quick. You would have had no time to reflect on the misery you'd caused me, and many others like me. No, a bullet in the brain would have been far too good for you so I had to look for something else. I decided to take from you that one thing that really mattered to you more than anything else, that one thing without which you cannot function, or even think, that one thing that buys you the power to toy with other people's lives and enjoy your perversions. I decided to take from you your wealth Clive, every nickel, quarter and dime of it. Put you back in the gutter where scum like you belong. And I've done it, Clive. At this moment in time you're not worth a bean, not a red cent. Fifteen years of your life wiped away like it has never been."

"You're mad," said Clive, suddenly coming to terms with the situation. "You've been the spy in my camp all along. But you could never have put this act together all by yourself. Who's been pulling your strings?" He made a sudden lunge for her and caught her by the hair. "Tell me, you bitch! It's this Tuesday Nemesis guy, isn't it?" And he smacked her hard across the face. "I'll kill him. I'll kill you," he screamed, drawing his hand back for another swing. "Both of you'll wish you'd never been born."

The second blow never landed. Ephraim Krebs appeared from nowhere and his fist connected just below the bridge of Clive's nose.

Clive stared up from the carpet in blank amazement. "What the hell are you doing here, Krebs?" he choked, a trickle of blood beginning to soil his shirt. "I thought I fired you. Get the hell out of here," he screamed. "This is a private matter."

"Sure you fired me," Krebs drawled, blowing across his knuckles. "After I did a bundle of work for you and never got a dime in fees or expenses. Miss Darielle here kindly picked up your tab and I'm pleased to be working for her now. So watch your lip. I don't like my clients insulted."

"As I was saying," Karina continued, "there's nothing of you left but the clothes you stand up in."

"So you say," said Clive, and checked himself. Any information could be dangerous in this woman's hands. "Okay, you win. So how did you do it?" He suddenly smiled back at her, standing up and starting to brush down his suit.

"With surprising ease," she told him. "Originally I had no intention of becoming your mistress. I was going to wreck your business from the dealing-room floor. I had it all planned. It would have taken me five hours of bad trading to put Price Whitney into liquidation. One hour less than it would have taken Zadok Perret to discover anything was going wrong – and then it would have been too late."

"But you didn't do that?" said Clive, almost chattily now.

"No. I found out that you had a trading terminal in your

230

private apartment, and that caused me to change my strategy."

"Did it indeed?" Clive encouraged.

"Yes. I decided to become your mistress solely to access that terminal, and all day and every day when you weren't here I used it to deal in currency and futures. You've just bought my trading company for 1.25 billion dollars, a little over-priced, I think you'll agree. It's probably worth about seventeen per cent of that at this precise moment."

"The 29-29 Corporation. You've got to be kidding!" All colour went from Clive's face.

"Why should I tell you a lie? You can call my lawyers, Holt and Farthingale. I've authorised them to release full particulars upon request. But you can save yourself the bother by reading the morning's papers."

For a long moment Clive said nothing as the smile slowly came back on his face. "A very clever move indeed," he nodded at length.

"Yes, I thought so too," she agreed. "And you've probably heard of my other company, Tin Whistle?"

"I have."

"I thought you might. You've just sold your entire holding in Price Whitney to them at fifty cents a share – which is rather cheap in my opinion."

He said nothing, and she went on. "And you know Tin Whistle owns the patent on the new TEESER energy machine? Tin Whistle will be announcing later today that its developments cannot be expected to make significant inroads into traditional oil markets for at least five years. That should push the price of oil stock back up and stabilise the market. I expect to see Price Whitney back at 200 dollars a share by the end of the week. Price Whitney is my bank now, Clive, and you are technically trespassing."

"How extremely shrewd of you," Clive congratulated her with a grin that was almost generous now. "I seem to have been out-manoeuvred at every turn, Katie er, sorry, Karina." Then suddenly he added eagerly, "We could make a most amazing team if we worked together. How about you and me as partners? We'd be unstoppable."

"Unstoppable?" Her eyes rose. "But you are stopped, Clive, thank heavens. You are totally and utterly stationary. From hereonin you'll be about as welcome on the financial scene as a burnt-out currency dealer – which is, in essence, what you are."

He was tempted, very tempted to blow that fallacy, but

231

he contained the urge. Instead he said, "Your strategies fascinate me, Karina. Tell me more. You've won anyway. There's nothing I can do."

"You really want to know?" she smiled at him, the grease cracking into lines on her face. "That's indeed masochism on a grand scale."

"So, I'm a masochist."

"Well you'll find this good fodder then, Clive. And I must say you made things remarkably easy for me. Your paranoia in installing security cameras everywhere allowed me to monitor everything happening in the building – like your frequent meetings with Abel Satco and Victor Loeb. You relied far too heavily on their advice, Clive. You know that now. I could feed them anything with the total certainty they'd pass it on to you, which was extremely useful."

"I can imagine," smiled Clive. "I should have spotted your activities long before."

"Ah, indeed, the wisdom of hindsight," she consoled.

"Tell me about Tuesday Nemesis," he asked.

"Dear Tuesday Nemesis," she laughed now. "Such a good friend of mine, was Tuesday. How I wish he actually existed because I was growing quite fond of him."

"You mean there is no Tuesday Nemesis!" Clive's eyes narrowed.

"No – not as such. Tuesday Nemesis is a date set aside in your honour, Clive. Today is Tuesday, and today is your nemesis. I thought it would be nice to head up 29-29 with an appropriate fictional character to walk hand in hand with you to destruction."

"How very droll! A nice piece of poetic irony," Clive congratulated, the grin unflinching. "And your 29-29 Company – that was no doubt similarly contrived?"

"But of course, dear Clive, of course. I figured your financial execution should be a symbolic affair with full pageantry – all the bells and flutes and whistles – the whole works. The press releases have already gone out. But I figured any old day would not be good enough for you. It had to be a special day, like today, Tuesday 29th October – the anniversary of the great Wall Street Crash back in 1929 – the day the bubble burst. Today is the day your bubble bursts, Clive. The 29-29 Corporation was a ship destined for disaster from the moment its keel was laid. And you were to be the captain that took it to the rocks."

"A masterly piece of manipulation," Clive positively beamed

with sparkling eyes, the first hint of madness there. "And everything worked out exactly as you planned?"

"Exactly," said Karina.

"No, not quite exactly Karina," Clive moved very quickly. In a stride he was at the small desk by the window and in the same instant a Smith and Wesson -38 was in his hand. "Both of you stand quite still," he said very quietly with a madness in his eyes. "Don't try and follow me or you're dead. It will take half a day to get the lift fixed after I've finished with it," he laughed suddenly, a hysterical manic cackle. "And then you'll have the pleasure of unravelling a different scenario. And you'll find, dear Karina, that Clive Feral is not quite as dumb as you think, or as poor as you thought. In fact you're about 800 million dollars out." He fired two shots into the trading terminal and tore the telephone wires from the wall. Then he was gone.

Krebs turned to Karina, the admiration clear in his face. "You really are a most extraordinary woman, Miss Darielle," he told her. "But can I ask you one question?"

"Of course," she responded, turning on the coffee machine. "There are no secrets now." She had a towel in her hand and was beginning to wipe away the stage make-up that had served as grease.

"Why did you think I might make a writer, when I did not even know it myself?"

"I read your preliminary reports," she grinned at him. "They were really quite lyrical. I found I was almost enjoying reading about your strategy to ruin my plans."

"Oh," he said thoughtfully. "Well you were right, every which way."

"I usually am," she said.

The lift seemed to drop with interminable slowness, and as it fell he screwed a silencer on the gun. At the bottom he fired four rounds into the circuit panel and walked leisurely towards the street, smiling at his staff as he went. It would be the last time they saw him, and he couldn't give a damn. A new excitement was pulsing through his veins.

He stopped at Maybee's for a cigar. "Hey!" the cashier called after him. "You ain't paid. Put that back or I'll call a cop."

Clive spun round startled, the smile gone from his face. "You talking to me?"

"Sure I'm talking to you," the cashier said. "You're the only one thieving anything."

"I'll have you fired for this," he roared at her. "Goddam bitch."

"You ain't having nobody fired, buster," she said, her black eyes moist and glistening with unrestrained delight. "Clive Feral's lost his bank and lost his braces. It's all over town. You're a nobody like the rest of us now, you bastard. Now pay up or put it back."

Clive put it back, fury embedded in his face as he suddenly realised there was not a cent in the suit he was wearing.

Neither Satco or Loeb stood up when he found them talking earnestly in a corner of Jerym's Bar off 39th Street. "Good morning, gentlemen," he smiled, joining them at the table. "Can I have a few words with you."

"Not right now, Clive," Satco looked embarrassed and would not meet his eye.

Clive was still recoiling as Loeb said, "We're into some private business, Clive. It would be better if you called my secretary for an appointment. Anyway," he added, "I want to speak with you. You owe my firm £750,000 in fees for that 29-29 deal. I've just been on to Price Whitney about it and they tell me the new owner won't be picking up the tab."

The smile went from Clive's face like someone had sliced it with a razor. "Is that all either of you have to say?" he hissed, his face now a deathly white, the tic flickering beneath his eye like a nervous candle flame.

"There's not a lot else to say Clive, is there?" coughed Satco, his hand over his mouth. "Unless you want to buy some stock." He gave a low guffaw and as quickly stifled it.

"So I'll wait to hear from you," Loeb dismissed, turning back to Abel Satco. "Now as we were saying—"

Clive stood up and backed away from them, black hatred in his face. "One day I shall return," he murmured very softly, "and then you'll never laugh again."

On the way to the airport Clive's expression softened. In one hour he would be on his way to Panama and roughly 875 million dollars. He had checked with the travel agents and the tickets would be waiting for him to pick up from the departure desk.

There were no tickets.

The girl seemed to be expecting him and passed across a slender envelope. He tore it open, and that sudden awful chill froze his spine again.

234

DEAR CLIVE

JUST A BRIEF NOTE TO WISH YOU BON VOYAGE. NO, YOU WILL NOT BE GOING TO PANAMA. THE FBI HAVE OTHER PLANS FOR YOU NEARER HOME. THEY WANT TO KNOW WHY YOU WERE PLANNING TO DIVERT NEARLY A BILLION OF PRICE WHITNEY'S FUNDS TO YOUR OWN ACCOUNTS. I ADVISED MR PERRET OF THE PRUDENCE OF IGNORING YOUR REQUEST, AND NO DOUBT THE FBI WILL FIND HIS EVIDENCE OF GREAT VALUE AT YOUR TRIAL.

HAVE A NICE DAY.

KARINA DANDO DARIELLE

"Yes, Mr Feral, we would indeed like a word with you," said the face that had been standing close behind.

"Read all about it," the news seller called, as the first of the photographers spotted him and began to angle in, "Oil price jump after announcement by Tin Whistle. Price Whitney under new ownership as their shares hit record peak. Read all about it."